ACCUSED

Also by Mark Gimenez

The Colour of Law
The Abduction
The Perk
The Common Lawyer

ACCUSED

Mark Gimenez

SPHERE

First published in Great Britain in 2010 by Sphere
Reprinted 2010 (twice)

A CIP catalogue record for this book
is available from the British Library.

Hardback ISBN 978-1-84744-275-8
Trade Paperback ISBN 978-1-84744-276-5

Typeset in Bembo by Hewer Text UK Ltd, Edinburgh
Printed and bound in Great Britain by
Clays Ltd, St Ives plc

Papers used by Sphere are natural, renewable and
recyclable products sourced from well-managed forests and certified
in accordance with the rules of the Forest Stewardship Council.

Mixed Sources
Product group from well-managed
forests and other controlled sources
www.fsc.org Cert no. SGS-COC-004081
FSC © 1996 Forest Stewardship Council

Sphere
An imprint of
Little, Brown Book Group
100 Victoria Embankment
London EC4Y 0DY

An Hachette UK Company
www.hachette.co.uk

www.littlebrown.co.uk

The author – a BOI himself – dedicates this book to the residents of Galveston, Texas, who are working hard to rebuild their great Island after Hurricane Ike.

Acknowledgements

My sincere thanks to everyone at Sphere/Little, Brown UK, including David Shelley, Thalia Proctor, Sean Garrehy, Nathalie Morse, Andy Hine and Simon McArt, as well as everyone at Hachette Livre and Little, Brown in Australia and New Zealand and Penguin Books in South Africa. And a special thanks to all the readers around the world who have emailed me about my books. Your thoughts and comments are greatly appreciated. Also, thanks to Joel Tarver at T Squared Designs in Houston for my website and new release emails.

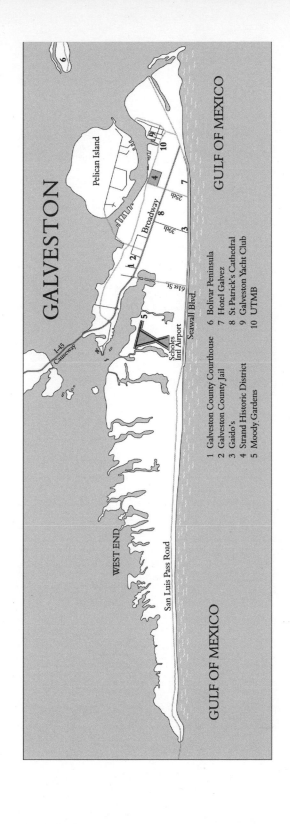

GALVESTON

Pelican Island

GULF OF MEXICO

I-45
Causeway

Broadway

25th

39th

61st St.

Seawall Blvd.

Scholes
Intl Airport

WEST END

San Luis Pass Road

GULF OF MEXICO

1 Galveston County Courthouse
2 Galveston County Jail
3 Gaido's
4 Strand Historic District
5 Moody Gardens

6 Bolivar Peninsula
7 Hotel Galvez
8 St Patrick's Cathedral
9 Galveston Yacht Club
10 UTMB

Innocence: The absence of guilt.
Black's Law Dictionary, Fifth Ed.

Prologue

When she opened her eyes, she did not know that her life would never be the same.

All she knew was that her body was shivering violently. She wrapped her arms around herself but felt even colder, almost wet from the sea breeze. The French doors leading to the deck outside stood propped open, and the breeze billowed the sheer curtains. In the vague light, they looked like whitecaps of waves rolling ashore. She glanced at the clock on the nightstand: 3:45 A.M.

She got out of bed – the tile floor felt damp beneath her feet, as if it had rained in – and went over to shut the doors, but the scent of the sea lured her outside. She parted the curtains and stepped out onto the deck. The house stood on tall stilts like an eight-legged white flamingo perched among the sand dunes; the second-story deck overlooked the secluded stretch of Galveston beach and the Gulf of Mexico beyond. She walked to the far railing where she could see the last ripples of high tide dying out just feet from the house. She inhaled the sea and tasted the salt in the air. She often woke and came out here in these quiet hours when the moon offered the only light, when all color was washed out by the night, when her world was painted only in shades of gray.

She lived her life in shades of gray.

She gazed out at the twinkling lights of the offshore drilling platforms dotting the distant horizon; she liked to think they were the lights of Cancún. She had often imagined taking the yacht straight across the Gulf the seven hundred fifty miles to Cancún – and never returning. Maybe one day she would.

Maybe. One day.

The breeze blew her short nightgown tight against her lean body; the silk seemed to stick to her skin. She clutched herself again. It was early June, and the night temperature had not dipped below eighty, but she had still caught a chill. A big wave splashed ashore, and the sea spray hit her. She licked the wet from her lips then reached up and wiped her face; she could not see the dark streaks down her cheeks that her hands had left in their wake, but her face now felt even wetter. She touched her cheeks again then looked down at her hands. Her palms were shiny with a wetness that was dark in the moonlight, dark and wet like . . .

She turned and ran back inside. She fought her way through the curtains then slapped her hands against the wall until she found the light switch – the stark white bedroom was suddenly ablaze with incandescent light. The shades of gray were gone. Her world was now painted bright red: red on the white bed sheets . . . red footprints on the white tile floor leading from the bed out to the deck where she had stepped . . . red handprints on the white wall where she had searched for the light switch . . . red on the white curtains where she had fought through them . . . red on her white nightgown . . . and red on her. Bright red. Blood red. His blood. She stood drenched in his blood. And he lay on the bed with a knife in his chest.

Rebecca Fenney screamed.

Chapter 1

Three hours later and three hundred miles to the north, Scott Fenney was drenched in sweat. The sun had just risen that Friday morning, only the fifth day of June, but the temperature was already pushing ninety. It was going to be a hot summer.

He was running the streets of Highland Park. He ran five miles every morning, before the town came alive, when the roads were still free of foreign automobiles and the air still free of exhaust fumes, when the only sounds were birds chirping in the tall oak trees that shaded the broad avenues and the only sights were other white men waging war against middle age in running shoes. Scott was only thirty-eight, so he could still avoid such a daily confrontation with his future. But he could not avoid a daily confrontation with his past.

He ran past the lot where the small rent house he had grown up in had once stood, home to mother and son, the poor kid on the block. He ran past the Highland Park football stadium where he had been a high school hero under the bright Friday night lights and the SMU stadium where he had become a college legend on a glorious Saturday afternoon in the fall of his twenty-first year. He ran past the law school where he had graduated first in his class then had struck out for downtown Dallas to find his

3

fortune in the law. He ran past the country club where lush green fairways bathed in a soft shower from low sprinklers, an exclusive golf course that would later that morning welcome the wealthiest white men in Dallas just as it had once welcomed him. He ran past the mansion he had once called home.

He was now the poor lawyer on the block.

It had been two years since that life had become his past. He had not mourned the loss of his partnership at the Ford Stevens law firm or the money that had come with being a successful lawyer or the things that money had bought – the home, the club, the car . . . okay, he did miss the car; it was a red Ferrari 360 Modena that could do zero to sixty in 4.5 seconds. But he had what money could not buy and what no one could fore-close, repossess, or otherwise take from him by legal process. He had his daughters. So while his morning run reminded him of the past, he did not long for the past. He had gotten over his past.

Except Rebecca.

She had not screamed or cursed or said goodbye. She had just left. She wanted nothing from him and took nothing – not her community property or her clothes or her child. After eleven years of marriage, she had just wanted out. So twenty-two months and eight days ago, she had walked out of their house and marriage and left town with the twenty-six-year-old assistant golf pro at the club. Scott blamed himself. If only he had been more attentive to her needs, more thoughtful toward her, more caring toward her, more . . . something. Whatever it was that a woman needed from a man. What she had needed from him. He had not given her what she had needed, so she had found it with another man. In another man's bed.

He now slept alone. When he slept. The other hours he lay awake and alone, thinking of her and wondering if he would ever again feel the love of a woman lying next to him, holding him, touching him, wanting him. He wanted to love again, to feel the heat of passion again, to experience that special connection – physical and mental – between a man and a woman, when he and she were one. Those moments were the best moments of a man's life. Those were the moments with Rebecca he recalled now.

He longed to share his life with another woman. But he couldn't, not until he understood why his wife had left him. Until he knew what she had needed and how he had failed her. So if he got a second chance at love, he wouldn't fail again. But for now Scott Fenney had no reason to stay in bed each morning.

So he ran.

Chapter 2

Scott entered the small cottage through the back door that led into the kitchen and was greeted by the smell of eggs, *chorizo*, and coffee. Consuela had already arrived and was cooking breakfast.

'Morning, Consuela.'

'*Buenos días*, Señor Fenney.'

Consuela was thirty, round, and Catholic. She wore three crucifixes and kept prayer candles lit on the windowsill. Her husband, Esteban Garcia, dropped her and the baby off each morning on the way to his construction job in Dallas. Little Maria sat in a high chair and smeared mushy food on her face. Scott leaned down to her.

'And how are you this morning, Señorita Maria de la Rosa-Garcia?'

She spit up something green.

'She no like *brécol*,' Consuela said.

'Don't believe I'd like broccoli for breakfast either.'

The fifteen-month-old child smiled at Scott as if she understood what he had said. He scrunched up his face and rubbed noses with her – she liked that – and said, 'You don't want that yucky broccoli, do you? Tell your *madre* you want *huevos rancheros* and *chorizo* so you can grow big and strong and get a *fútbol* scholarship.'

Her parents were Mexican nationals but she was an American citizen – born in the USA. She raised her arms to him.

'Oh, Uncle Scotty can't play now, honey. I've got to go to work.'

He gave the child a kiss on her forehead and a little hug and came away with slimy green broccoli on his cheek. It smelled awful – or maybe it was him. He swiped a sweaty sleeve across his cheek then grabbed a bottled water out of the refrigerator and walked down the hall to his daughters' bedroom. He knocked on the door.

'Come on, girls, I can't be late today. Closing arguments.'

The door opened, and his eleven-year-old daughters emerged from a small bedroom cluttered with posters of the Jonas Brothers and a smiling Michael Jordan on the walls, books stacked on shelves and scattered about the floor, clothes hanging over chairs as if one of them – guess who? – could not decide what to wear that day, and a small television with rabbit ears. They had pushed their twin beds together in one corner so they could read together at night. They shared clothes, they brushed each other's hair, they were like sisters – and now the law said they were.

Barbara Boo Fenney was wearing jean shorts, a black T-shirt with white print that read 'Obama Ba-Rocks My World', green retro sneakers without socks, and her red hair pulled back in a ponytail. She looked more like her mother every day, albeit less expensively dressed. Pajamae Jones-Fenney wore a color-coordinated short outfit, matching socks folded down neatly, and black-and-white saddle Oxfords. Her skin was tan and flawless, her hair brown and fluffy and cut in a bob. She too looked more like her mother every day. One girl was the product of his failed marriage, the other of his law practice. Two years before, he had defended Pajamae's mother against a murder charge and won, only to see her die of a heroin overdose two months later. Pajamae had no one except Boo and her mother's lawyer, so he had adopted her.

'Morning, girls.'

'Whereas, Mr Fenney,' Pajamae said.

7

'What's your pulse?' Boo said.

'I didn't check my pulse.'

'Do you feel faint or dizzy? Are you experiencing chest pain?'

'No, Boo. I feel fine.'

'A. Scott, I still think you should be on a statin.'

'I think you should change that T-shirt. The school won't like it.'

'I told her, Mr Fenney. I said, "Girl, you can't be wearing a T-shirt reminding these rich white folks there's a black man in the White House."'

The conservative Republicans in town – which is to say, the entire Town of Highland Park – had not gone for Obama. They had hoped that George W. would salve their electoral wounds by coming home to Highland Park, but he had retired to his old stomping grounds in North Dallas instead. Even Dick Cheney had forsaken his former home town for Jackson Hole, Wyoming. But Bush did give the Parkies a consolation prize: the $300 million George W. Bush Presidential Library would be located on the Southern Methodist University campus in Highland Park.

Boo shrugged. 'What are they gonna do, suspend me again, on the last day of school?'

She had been suspended earlier in the year for fighting. With a boy. He had called Pajamae 'Aunt Jemima' on the playground, so Boo had punched him in the mouth and made him cry. She had a heck of a right cross for a girl. Scott had threatened to take the school district to court – and more effectively, the story of a white boy bullying the only black student in school to the newspaper and local television – so the school had dropped the suspension after one day. Now, whenever the principal threatened Boo with disciplinary action for defending her sister against bullies, her standard response was, 'Call my lawyer.'

'Consuela has breakfast ready.'

The girls went one way down the hall and Scott the other. He entered the 'master suite' of the two-bedroom, fifteen-hundred-square-foot cottage. The master closet in his former residence dwarfed the small bedroom and adjoining bath. Scott undressed in the bathroom, stepped into the cramped shower, and stood under the hot water. The mansion and material possessions that had once given his life value were gone. His ambitious years, that period in a man's life when human nature and testosterone drive him to prove his net worth to the world – when the score is kept in dollars and cents – were over. For most men, the ambitious years extend well into the fifties, even the sixties, and come to an end only with a heart attack or a positive prostate exam, when a man confronts his mortality. But it wasn't the prospect of his own death that had brought his ambitious years to a premature end for A. Scott Fenney, at age thirty-six; it was the death of a US senator's son.

He got out of the shower, shaved, and dressed in a $2,000 custom-made suit; the suits and Consuela were all that remained of his past life. She was part of the family, and the suits still fit. And he was still a lawyer.

Scott returned to the kitchen where the girls were eating breakfast tacos and playing with Maria. 'Last day of school, girls.' Scott sat and ate his taco and studied his adopted daughter's face. 'Pajamae, are you wearing makeup?'

'Blush, Mr Fenney, like Beyoncé. You like it?'

'What's a Beyoncé? And please call me "Dad". It's been a year and a half.'

'Don't seem right, Mr Fenney.'

'Why not?'

''Cause you're Boo's daddy.'

'I'm your daddy, too, and don't you ever forget it.' He drank coffee and said, 'So what do you girls want to do this summer?'

'The other kids are going to Colorado, Hawaii, the south of France . . .'

'We can't afford that, Boo.'

'What can we afford?'

'Well, we could camp out in a state park.'

'That'd be fun. We could never go camping with Mother. She hated to sweat.'

9

'Boo, she's still your mother.'

'I don't have a mother.'

Her anger seeped out from time to time. Or was it a sense of shame? Everyone in Highland Park knew her mother had run off with the golf pro.

Scott turned back to Pajamae. She seemed glum, too.

'Pajamae, smile – you're about to graduate from fifth grade.'

'She doesn't smile because the other kids make fun of her,' Boo said.

'Because of her color?'

'Because of her teeth.'

'Her *teeth*?'

'My teeth are all crooked, Mr Fenney. It's embarrassing.'

She needed braces. Ten thousand dollars worth of dental work. Scott paid $30,000 in annual health insurance premiums for the three of them plus Consuela and Maria, but the plan did not include dental.

'Mr Fenney, when I'm playing pro basketball, how am I gonna do endorsements with crooked teeth? You see Michael Jordan's teeth? Look like a string of pearls.'

'Honey, I'll find a way to pay for braces, okay? Before next school year.'

'You promise, Mr Fenney?'

He nodded. 'I promise.'

She started to smile but caught herself.

Braces for Pajamae. Another financial promise he wasn't sure he could keep, like the mortgage and office overhead – unless he won the case that day and if the city didn't appeal the verdict and if . . .

Boo stood and tossed her napkin on the table.

'Let's get this fifth grade over with.'

Ten minutes later, Scott was driving the Volkswagen Jetta to the elementary school past the mansions of the most important people in Dallas – or at least the richest. The streets of Highland Park were no longer vacant. Mothers were taking their offspring

10

to school, and fathers were taking themselves downtown. From the back seat, he heard Pajamae's voice, sounding spooky.

'Boo . . . I see white people.'

They fell over each other laughing hysterically. They had seen *The Sixth Sense* – the edited version on network TV – and were always coming up with new variations on the 'I see dead people' line.

Of course, Pajamae did see white people. Only white people. Exactly one black family lived in Highland Park . . . and one black girl named Pajamae Jones-Fenney. The Town of Highland Park was a two-square-mile enclave entirely surrounded by the City of Dallas – the bright white hole in the middle of the multicolored Dallas donut. Few people of color could afford to live in Highland Park – the median home price was $1 million – and those who could, like the pro athletes who played football for the Cowboys, basketball for the Mavericks, and baseball for the Rangers, weren't keen on being protected by a police force whose standard operating procedure for traffic stops was 'If they're black or brown, they'd better have tools in the back'.

'A. Scott,' Boo said from the back seat, 'since we can't go to the south of France this summer, can we at least get cable?'

'No.'

'Can we have a cell phone? We can get a family plan.'

'No.'

'Can we have a Facebook account?'

'No.'

'Can we get our ears pierced?'

'No – and why would you want holes in your ears anyway?'

'I don't, Mr Fenney,' Pajamae said.

'A. Scott, we're the only kids we know without cable, iPhones, pierced ears, or who haven't seen *Juno*.'

'Because it's rated PG-thirteen and you're not thirteen.'

'It's PG-thirteen for mature thematic material and sexual content and language, but they only say the F-word once. We hear it more than that at recess.'

'Kids say the F-word?'

11

'Hel-*lo*. Come on, A. Scott, we're practically teenagers.'

'Two years, Boo. It'll come soon enough. Enjoy being eleven. When you're older, you'll miss it.'

'Do you miss being eleven?'

'I miss being nine.'

'Why nine?'

'I lost my dad when I was ten.'

'We lost our mothers when we were nine.'

So they had. The girls were quiet for a few blocks then Boo said, 'So can we at least have cable? Just for the summer. *Please.*'

'Boo—'

'A. Scott, it's hard on us – at school, living in Highland Park.'

'Because you don't have cable?'

'Because we don't fit in.'

'Why not?'

Pajamae joined the fray. 'Because I'm the only black kid in town.'

'And we're the only kids without a mother. Walking around the Village, everyone looks funny at us.'

'And cable will make life easier for you?'

'Yes.'

Scott had steadfastly refused their pleas for cable. But he now felt his resolve weakening: he couldn't give them a mother; he could at least give them cable TV. He was just on the verge of saying yes when he caught the girls grinning mischievously in the rearview. They were gaming him. Again.

'No.'

'But we can't watch *Sex and the City* reruns like the other kids.'

'Fifth-graders watch *Sex and the City*?'

'Oops. Forget *Sex and the City*. Think Discovery Channel.'

'No.'

She frowned as if pouting, but Boo Fenney wasn't the pouting type.

'Fudge.'

'Boo, don't say fudge. Everyone knows what you're really saying.'

12

'I like fudge,' Pajamae said. 'With pecans.'

They arrived at the elementary school. Scott felt like the class loser at a high school reunion when he steered the little Jetta into the drop-off lane behind a long line of late-model Mercedes-Benzes, BMWs, Lexuses, Range Rovers, and just in front, a Ferrari . . . a shiny red Ferrari . . . a 360 Modena just like the one he used to drive . . . he looked closely at the car . . . that *was* the one he used to drive. He caught the driver's face in the side mirror.

Sid Greenberg.

When he was a partner at Ford Stevens, Scott had hired Sid out of law school and taught him everything he knew about practicing law, but Sid now sat in Scott's sixty-second-floor corner office, represented Scott's rich real-estate client, and drove Scott's $200,000 Italian sports car. The ungrateful bastard. Scott could still smell the Connolly leather interior and feel the four-hundred-horsepower engine rumbling behind him. The Ferrari's passenger door swung open, and Sid's young son got out – *Hey, that's cheating, letting your kid out before the official drop-off point!* – so Sid could avoid waiting in line like everyone else. Scott shook his head. *Typical lawyer.* But when Sid turned his head to check for oncoming cars before pulling out, he had a big smile on his face, as if laughing at Scott driving a Jetta.

You laugh, Sid, but I'm saving a lot of money on gas.

Sid Greenberg had made the same choice Scott had made at his age. Two years ago, Sid had decided to check his conscience at the door each day and now he was driving a Ferrari. Two years ago, Scott had rediscovered his conscience and now he was driving a Jetta. Funny how that worked for lawyers.

'A. Scott, you need sex.'

He eyed Boo in the rearview. '*What?*'

'You look stressed. Just then, you were frowning. Sex relieves stress.'

'Where'd you hear that?'

'From Meredith.'

'Who's Meredith?'

13

'On the *Today Show*, this morning.'

'You girls need to watch PBS in the morning.'

'*Sesame Street?* I don't think so. Anyway, Meredith said stress is a leading cause of heart attacks in men. So if you have sex you won't have stress and thus you won't have a heart attack . . . like Sarah's dad.'

Bill Barnes, a lawyer Scott knew, had died of a sudden heart attack earlier in the school year. Little Sarah Barnes would grow up without a father. The girls had always fretted over their only parent's health – every blemish on Scott's face could be skin cancer, every headache a stroke, every memory lapse a sign of early onset Alzheimer's – their worries exacerbated by the relentless barrage of drug commercials on network television. Each new commercial brought a new medical worry for the girls. But since Sarah's dad, a heart attack had been their constant worry. They had recommended he take Lipitor to lower his bad cholesterol, Trilipix to raise his good cholesterol, Plavix to prevent his platelets from forming blood clots, and Crestor to prevent plaque from building up in his arteries. Sex, though, marked a new and more agreeable course of therapy. Unfortunately, it required more than a doctor's prescription.

'Don't worry, Boo, I'm not going to have a heart attack. I run every day, I still weigh one-eighty-five, my cholesterol's low—'

'Besides, it's embarrassing.'

'What is?'

'You're tall, blond, handsome, you don't have tattoos – you're the hunk of Highland Park and you don't have a girlfriend. The other kids think we have a loser for a father.'

'I don't think it's because I don't have a girlfriend.'

'Mr Fenney, you need a woman.'

'Like Ms Dawson,' Boo said.

Up ahead, Ms Dawson, the fourth-grade teacher, was working carpool. Her jet black hair glistened in the morning sun. She couldn't be older than twenty-eight, maybe twenty-nine. Scott had thought of asking her out, but it hadn't even been two full years since Rebecca had left him. Still, Ms Dawson was very attractive in her form-fitting blouse that accentuated her narrow waist and her snug slacks that—

'Ms Dawson would probably have sex with you.'

'You really think so?' He caught himself. 'I mean, *Boo*.'

The girls giggled. They knew all about sex now. Fifth-grade health class. Which was a blessing; Scott didn't have to have the talk with them. When he had turned thirteen, his mother had said to his father at dinner one night, 'Butch, it's time you had a father-son talk with Scotty. You know, about sex.' Butch Fenney had turned to his son and said, 'Don't have sex. Pass the potatoes.' But sex was more complicated these days and more dangerous. Sex can kill and eleven-year-old girls were having babies, so kids had to know the truth. Explaining the facts of life to girls was a mother's job; but they had no mother so the job had fallen to their father. Just when Scott had bucked himself up to do it – he had even bought a book – the girls had come home armed with all the facts. Thank God. A major single-father hurdle had been cleared.

'Ms Dawson has nice cheeks,' Boo said.

'Very nice.'

'The ones on her face.'

'Oh.'

'She's got a crush on you, A. Scott.'

'Really?'

'Big time, Mr Fenney. During lunch, she'll mosey on over and say, "Hi Boo, hi Pajamae", you know, like she's just visiting. Then she'll get around to asking, "So how's your father doing these days?" And I'll say, "Oh, 'bout the same as yesterday, Ms Dawson". Then she'll blush like white girls do and say, "Well, tell him hi". She's got the hots for you, Mr Fenney.'

'She does?'

'A. Scott, we're at that age – we need a mother. Ask her out. *Please*.'

'Oh, I don't know . . .'

Pajamae let out an exasperated sigh. 'Man up, Mr Fenney, and ask that woman out!'

15

Scott eased the Jetta up to the drop-off point. Ms Dawson opened the back door for the girls then leaned down. She said, 'Hi, Boo, hi, Pajamae,' but she looked at Scott. The girls leaned forward and kissed Scott on opposite cheeks and whispered in his ears –

'Ask her!'

'Now!'

– then climbed out of the car and ran up the walkway to the entrance. Before she shut the door, Ms Dawson stuck her head in and said, 'Scott, if I invited you over for dinner this summer, would you come?'

He wanted to say yes, but he said, 'No.'

Her face sank.

'Ms Dawson—'

'It's Kim, Scott. It's been Kim for two years.'

'Kim. I'm sorry. I've got to work through some things first . . . my ex-wife . . .'

'How long will she own you, Scott?'

'I don't know.'

She shut the door on him. Scott sighed and exited the school drive, cut over to Lovers Lane, and hit the Dallas North Tollway heading south toward downtown. He tried to put thoughts of Kim Dawson and Rebecca Fenney out of his mind and focus on a subject matter he knew more about than women: the law.

But he could not know that before the day was out his ex-wife would again assert ownership over his life.

Chapter 3

In a courtroom on the fifteenth floor of the Federal Building in downtown Dallas, A. Scott Fenney addressed a jury of twelve American citizens.

'Forty-six years ago, President John F. Kennedy was assassinated just a few blocks from where you now sit. The world's press descended on this city and exposed the ugly side of Dallas: a police force that ran roughshod over black citizens . . . a district attorney who won white votes in North Dallas by sending black men in South Dallas to prison . . . a city known as the "Southwest hate capital of Dixie" . . . a city run by rich white men who retired to East Texas on weekends to hunt and fish at the Koon Kreek Klub . . . a city President Kennedy himself described as "nut country". That was Dallas in nineteen sixty-three.'

Scott stood before the jury of nine whites, two Latinos, and one African-American. Dallas was now a minority-majority city, but money still ruled. Money makes the law and the law protects the money; and lawyers protect the people with money. But not this lawyer. Not any more. Scott was representing all residents of South Dallas in a class-action lawsuit against the City of Dallas. When he had left the Ford Stevens law firm – that is, when he had been fired two years before – Scott had gone to the other side, from representing corporations that pay to people who can't – not what most lawyers would call a shrewd career move; from representing those whom the laws protected to representing those whom the laws oppressed – the 'dissed' of Dallas. The dispossessed, the disenfranchised, the disrespected.

And so it was that day.

'That image of Dallas shocked the world – including the business world. And above all other things, Dallas was a city of business, by business, and for business. So the rich white businessmen who ran Dallas decided to polish up the city's image.

'Back then, seedy bars, strip clubs, and liquor stores lined the streets of downtown. Those businessmen wanted to close the liquor stores, but couldn't; the stores were protected by the zoning ordinance. So they struck a deal with the liquor industry: if they moved out of downtown, they could have free reign in South Dallas. Not in North Dallas where white people lived, but in South Dallas where black people lived.

'At the time, South Dallas was a thriving community of small businesses and families living in neat homes. Today, there are three hundred liquor stores in South Dallas – twenty-five stores per square mile – and South Dallas is a community of drunks, drug dealers, addicts, hookers, crack houses, and crime. And citizens are prisoners in their own homes, hiding behind burglar bars. There are no grocery stores, no shopping centers, no Starbucks in South Dallas. There is only liquor and hopelessness. That is the reality people in South Dallas live with every day. Those businessmen changed the image but not the reality of Dallas.

'But you can. You can change that reality today. You can get rid of the liquor and give the people of South Dallas hope. Right here and right now, you have the power to change Dallas.

'Those liquor stores are protected by the zoning ordinance, just as they were in downtown. The only way to get them out of South Dallas is to buy them out – at a cost of one hundred million dollars. The city leaders say they want to redevelop South Dallas, but they just can't afford that price tag. It's the economy, they say. Of course, the city can afford billions for a convention center hotel, for the basketball arena, for the Trinity River project, for everything North Dallas wants, but they can't afford to get rid of liquor stores in South Dallas.

'One million people live in Dallas. One hundred million dollars comes to one hundred dollars per person. That's all. One hundred dollars per person gets rid of every liquor store in South Dallas. One hundred dollars gets rid of the drunks and dealers and addicts and hookers and crack houses and crime. One hundred dollars frees the citizens of South Dallas from their prisons, allows them to remove the burglar bars from their homes and to rebuild their community. One hundred dollars rights this wrong. One hundred dollars, ladies and gentlemen. And you have the power to make it happen.'

Scott spread his arms out to the courtroom like a televangelist at his podium.

'This is where regular people like you have power. This is where people like you can change things. This is where real change in America happens, in courtrooms just like this all across the country, by juries just like you. Juries that stood up to the tobacco companies and the drug companies and Wall Street and even their own government. Juries that had the guts to do the right thing. Juries that changed America and made our lives better. Juries just like you.

'This is your chance to change Dallas.'

They didn't take the chance. An hour later – barely enough time for the jurors to go to the restroom, eat lunch, and take a single vote – the jury returned a nine-to-three verdict in favor of the City of Dallas. Nine whites versus three minorities. North Dallas versus South Dallas. Rich versus poor.

The story of Dallas.

Judge Buford dismissed the jury and motioned Scott back to his chambers then disappeared through a door behind the bench. Scott consoled the lead plaintiff, Mabel Johnson, a black woman who lived in South Dallas just east of the intersection of Martin Luther King Jr Boulevard and Malcolm X Boulevard. She was a

19

single mother. Her three young daughters walked to school past a half dozen liquor stores every morning and home every afternoon. She fought back tears.

'I'm sorry, Mr Fenney.'

'No, I'm sorry, Mabel. I'm sorry I couldn't make life better for you and your kids. For all the kids down there.'

'Down there', as if she lived in Mexico instead of just a mile south of where they now stood. She reached up and touched his cheek.

'You're still my hero, Mr Fenney.'

'I lost.'

'You tried.'

Mabel embraced him then walked out of the courtroom. Scott sat on the plaintiff's table and stared at his shoes. He no longer represented the trophy clients of Dallas, rich people who bestowed social status on their lawyers; the mere mention of his clients' identities at bar association meetings typically evoked perplexed head-shaking or muffled laughter from other lawyers. He no longer worked the margins of ethics and the law, that gray area where a lawyer's money is made; nor did he make much money. He no longer practiced law like he had played football. For one thing, he no longer viewed the law as sport; for another, he lost. A. Scott Fenney was not a man accustomed to defeat, either on the football field or in a courtroom. Two years before, in this very courtroom, he had experienced his greatest victory as a lawyer when the jury had returned a 'not guilty' verdict for Pajamae's mother. But the last two years had brought defeat into his life.

He had tried to make a difference. He had failed.

Another pair of shoes now entered his field of vision – brown wingtips – and Scott knew whose feet were in them before he heard the familiar voice.

'Hell of a closing argument, Scotty. Almost made me want to pay my hundred bucks. Almost.'

He raised his eyes to Dan Ford standing there. Dan was sixty-two, bald, and the senior partner at Ford Stevens, the two-hundred-fifty-lawyer Dallas firm that had previously employed A. Scott Fenney. Dan Ford was the man who had taught Scott everything he knew about practicing law, the man who had been Scott's father-figure for eleven years, the man who had single-handedly destroyed Scott's perfect life. He had come for closing arguments. A ten-lawyer team from Ford Stevens had represented the city. They had won. They would make millions. Which explained why Dan was smiling when he stuck his hand out to Scott. They shook, and Dan's expression turned to one of profound empathy.

'Scotty . . . you're trying to make the world a better place when you should be making money. You're wasting your talents, son. Come back to the firm. You can have your old office back.'

'I have an office.'

'Yeah, but your old office comes with a Ferrari, a Highland Park mansion, a country club membership, and a million-dollar paycheck.'

A million dollars. Funny, but Scott's first thought wasn't the Ferrari or the mansion and certainly not the country club where his wife had met the assistant golf pro. It was braces for Pajamae.

'Sid's driving my Ferrari and sitting in my office.'

'He won't be if you come back. Scotty, watching you today, it was like watching Secretariat in his prime pulling a tourist buggy. Made me sad, thinking of all the money you could be making. The hooker's case made you famous, you could be working the biggest cases in Texas. Instead, you're working for the little people, doing good instead of doing well. You take this case on a contingency?'

Lawyers his age at big firms like Ford Stevens billed $750 an hour − $12.50 every minute, almost twice the US minimum *hourly* wage − and they billed in minimum six-minute increments: thirty seconds reading a letter or a one-minute phone call would cost the client a minimum charge of $75. But not Scott's clients. He no longer billed by the hour. He now worked on a contingency fee: one-third of whatever he won, if he won. Big-firm lawyers billed by the hour and won even when their clients lost. Scott Fenney won or lost with his clients. Today, they had both lost.

'A third of nothing is nothing, Scotty. We're going home with millions, you're going home with a hug from your client. That make you happy?'

'Why do you want me back? I lost.'

Dan dismissed that concern with a wave of his hand.

'Jesus Christ couldn't have won this case, not in Dallas. But you should've won. Come back to the firm and be a winner again.'

'For corporations.'

'Who pay.'

'I'm doing okay.'

'That's not what I hear. You're behind on your office rent, can't pay your staff . . . you deserve better than that.'

He once had better than that. At Ford Stevens, Scott had made $750,000 a year, with benefits. Now he made $100,000 – in a good year. And this was not such a year. He had gone through every penny in his savings. He was broke.

'Look, Scotty, you can't take on these lost causes the rest of your life. How are you gonna take care of your girls, pay for their college, weddings . . .?'

Braces.

'You got life insurance?'

No.

'What if you die? Who's gonna raise those girls?'

He had named Bobby Herrin and Karen Douglas, his married law partners, as the girls' guardians in his will.

'Will they be able to afford two more kids?'

Hardly. They were soon to have their first child.

'You gonna send those two smart girls to UT? Don't you want to give them a good education? Harvard, Yale, Wellesley – think how proud you'd be dropping your daughters off at Wellesley for college. With that kind of education, their futures would be unlimited. But that'll cost a hundred thousand a year by the time they're eighteen. Times two. That's a lot of money, Scotty – you gonna ask Rebecca to pay for their college?'

22

'*Rebecca?*'

'You see that son of a bitch won another tournament? Trey?'

Trey Rawlins was the man Scott's wife had run off with. Dan was shaking his head.

'Two years ago, he's trying to cure my slice, now he's a star on tour and filthy rich. You could be too, Scotty − filthy rich. What'd you always tell our law student recruits? "You want odds, go to Vegas. You want a chance to get filthy rich by the time you're forty, hire on with Ford Stevens". You're only thirty-eight. There's still time to save your career. Except you won't be hiring on with Ford Stevens.'

'What do you mean?'

Dan Ford paused and took a deep breath, as if he were about to make a big announcement.

'Ford Fenney.'

'Ford Fenney?'

'Your name will be on the door, next to mine, where it belongs. Where it's always belonged. Scotty, you were always like a son to me.'

'Until you fired me. What was that, tough love?'

Scott had said no to his father-figure only once − and had gotten fired for it.

'That was a mistake. I'm man enough to admit it, I hope you're man enough to forgive me.' Dan shrugged. 'Besides, Mack's dead now, so there's no conflict.'

US Senator Mack McCall had died a year before of prostate cancer. He had been a Ford Stevens client. The conflict of interest had arisen when Scott had been appointed by Judge Buford to represent Pajamae's mother − a black prostitute named Shawanda Jones − who had been charged with murdering Clark McCall, the senator's son, after he had picked her up one Saturday night. Dan Ford had told Scott to throw the case to preserve McCall's presidential bid; Scott had said no. So Dan had fired him. And A. Scott Fenney's ambitious years had come to an abrupt end.

'Scotty, the firm's business is booming − I've added fifty lawyers since you left. Come share in it.'

23

'Booming? In this economy?'

'Bankruptcies. Business bankruptcies are at an all-time high, and lawyers get paid first, before the creditors.' Dan chuckled. 'You can't get rich without a lawyer and you can't go broke without a lawyer. Is this a great country or what?'

Dan's smile faded, and he put a father's hand on his son's shoulder.

'Come back to the firm. Do well for yourself . . . and your girls.'

'Dan—'

'Just think about it, Scotty, okay? Think about what's best for your girls.'

'Always.'

They shook hands again, and Dan walked off, his brown wing-tips clacking on the wood floor down the center aisle and out the double doors until the sound faded away. Scott sat alone in the vast courtroom, alone in his defeat. Alone with his thoughts.

One million dollars. A year. Every year. College. Weddings. Mortgage. Vacations. Cable TV. iPhones. Braces. Everything the girls needed or wanted. Except a mother. All he had to do was go back over to the dark side. Work for corporations who could pay $750 an hour to lawyers who sold their talents to the highest bidder.

And why shouldn't he?

If he had played pro football, he wouldn't have played for a poor, losing team just to make the games fair. He would have sold his talents to the highest bidder. No one faulted A-Rod for making $25 million a year playing baseball for the Yankees, the richest winning team in baseball. Why should A. Scott play for poor, losing teams? Why shouldn't he reap the rewards of his talents? Why shouldn't he provide for the girls? Why shouldn't he take them to the south of France for summer vacation – or at least to the north of America? Why shouldn't they go to Wellesley with the best girls in America? Why shouldn't Pajamae have teeth that look like pearls?

Why shouldn't he be filthy rich like the man his wife had run off with?

Chapter 4

United States District Judge Samuel Buford was seventy-eight years old now. The black reading glasses seemed too big for his gaunt face. His white hair was no longer thick; it was only wisps. From the chemo. Everyone had always said Sam Buford would die on the bench. They were right.

'You should've won,' the judge said when Scott entered his chambers.

Scott shrugged. 'Just another case lost.'

'Another lost cause.'

'Someone's got to lose those cases, Judge, or they wouldn't be lost causes.'

The judge gestured at a chair. Scott sat and gazed across the wide desk at the frail judge dwarfed by his leather chair and framed by tall bookcases filled with law books. Each time Scott saw the judge there seemed to be less to see; it was as if he were disappearing before Scott's eyes. And the judge now had the look of death about him, the same look as Scott's mother when the cancer had won out and she knew it. Judge Samuel Buford was a living legend in the law. But not for long.

'Scott, you can't make a difference if you can't pay your bills. It's okay to take on a few paying clients every now and then.'

'Making rich people richer . . . I can't seem to generate any enthusiasm for that line of work anymore.'

The judge gave him a knowing nod. 'Once you cross over, it's hard to go back.'

They regarded each other, two of a kind now.

'How are you holding up, Judge?'

'Doctors say six months.'

Sam Buford had been diagnosed with terminal brain cancer. But he was determined to clear his docket before he died.

'Why don't you retire, spend your time at home?'

'Doing what? Wife's been dead ten years now, the kids and grandkids live out of state, I don't play golf . . .' He paused and half-smiled, as if recalling a favorite moment. 'Scott, I ever tell you I almost retired two years ago, during that case?'

'The McCall murder case?'

The judge nodded.

'No, sir, you didn't.'

'Well, I would've, if you hadn't come back that day, said you were ready to be that girl's lawyer. You gave me hope.'

'Hope for what?'

'The law . . . lawyers . . . life. Glad you came back. Glad I didn't retire.' He tossed a thumb at the law books behind him. 'The law's been my life. Thirty-two years of judging, I made a difference.'

Sam Buford had wielded a gavel since Scott was in first grade. All the toughest cases in Dallas had come before him, but he would forever be remembered – and reviled by many – for ordering the desegregation of public schools so black children would receive the same education as white children.

'Yes, sir, you did. You're a fine federal judge.'

'You could be too.'

'I could be what?'

'A fine federal judge.'

'*Me?* A federal judge?'

'Scott, my bench will be vacant soon. I could put your name forward.'

26

'Judge, McCall's gone but both US senators from Texas are still Republicans. They're not going to put a lawyer who sues the same corporations that contribute to their campaigns on the federal bench. And the president won't nominate me unless they approve.'

Under Article Two of the US Constitution, the Senate must confirm every federal judge nominated by the president. For nominations to the Supreme Court, Senate confirmations become bloody battles between special interest groups pursuing single issues – abortion, gay marriage, affirmative action, the right to bear AK-47s – because they know that those nine justices – nine lawyers – will decide the most contentious issues of the day: a Supreme Court decision is the law of the land.

Appeals court nominations are only slightly less bloody, because those lawyers are justices-in-waiting. But district court judges – trial judges – must follow decisions of the appeals courts and the Supreme Court, so the special interest groups keep their powder dry on those nominations. Consequently, federal district judges are effectively nominated by the two senators from the state in which they will serve and confirmed by rubber stamp. It's called 'Senatorial courtesy': you don't object to my home-state judges, I won't object to yours.

The judge gave him a sly smile. 'Haven't you heard, Scott? I'm a living legend in the law.' He pointed a bony finger at his phone. 'I can call the president and he'll answer. He'd grant a dying legend his last wish. And our Republican senators need his signature on their pork-barrel legislation to get reelected – which is a hell of a lot more important to them than who sits on the federal bench here in Dallas.'

'But I'm not sure I'm up to it, being a federal judge.'

'You're up to it – because you possess the singular qualifica-tion for a federal judge.'

'And what is that?'

'You care.'

'But—'

'You'll be my age one day, Scott, facing death and looking back on your life, as I am now, judging the life you've lived, wondering if it was worthwhile, if the world will even know you were here. That's important to a man.'

The last two years, Scott had learned that a man sitting in judgment of his own life is a harsh judge indeed.

'If you don't take my bench, Scott, a politician will – a lawyer looking to move up in the world, a lawyer who won't make the tough decisions a judge must make for fear of the political impact on his career. An ambitious judge is a dangerous animal.'

'Judge, I—'

'Lifetime appointment, Scott, a lifetime of getting paid to help the . . . what did you call your clients?'

'The dissed.'

'Yes, the dissed. You could give the dissed a fair shake in that courtroom . . . you could make their lives a little fairer . . . a little less unjust . . . and you could make a good living – lifetime salary, pension, life and health insurance—'

'Dental?'

'Of course. You could be proud of your life, Scott, and still take care of your girls.'

The judge sat back and exhaled as if he were exhausted. Or dying. Scott felt as if he were losing a family member. If Dan Ford had been his father-figure, Samuel Buford had been his wise old grandfather-figure – not that the judge would claim any kinship with Scott's former senior partner.

'I saw Dan Ford in the courtroom. He trying to lure you back to Ford Stevens?'

Scott nodded. 'Ford Fenney. My name on the door and a million dollars.'

'That's a lot of money.' The judge coughed. 'Doing good or doing well – that's a daily decision for a lawyer, like other folks deciding between oatmeal or eggs for breakfast. You'll do well at Ford Fenney. You'll do good as Judge Fenney.'

'Is it a good life, Judge?'

'It is.'

United States District Judge Atticus Scott Fenney. His mother would be proud.

'Scott, I'd die a happy man knowing you'd be sitting at my bench. May I put your name forward?'

'Yes, sir. And thank you.'

Scott stood and shook Sam Buford's hand. He would never see the judge alive again.

For the first time in two years, A. Scott Fenney had options in life.

Option A, he could return to the downtown practice of law and a million-dollar salary – back to a professional life dedicated to making rich people richer and getting filthy rich himself in the process – and back to a personal life of Ferraris and Highland Park mansions and exclusive all-white country clubs. Maybe another trophy wife. The wife and life most lawyers dream of. Option A required only that he call Dan Ford and say yes to Ford Fenney.

Option B, he could embark on a new life as a federal judge and a $169,000 salary – a professional life of seeing justice done – and a personal life of financial security, life and health insurance – including dental – paid vacations, and a fully-funded pension. He could be proud of his life and provide for his daughters. It would be a good life. A perfect life for United States District Judge A. Scott Fenney. Option B, however, required the support of the two Republican US senators from Texas and Senate confirmation. Even with Judge Buford backing him, it was far from a sure thing.

Option C, he could continue his current life of losing lost causes and not making enough money to pay the mortgage, cover the office overhead, take the girls on vacation, save for college, or buy braces for Pajamae.

He crossed out Option C.

Scott had often driven around Dallas in the Ferrari whenever he needed to think things out. Funny, but he didn't seem to think as well in a Jetta. He parked and walked into the law offices of Fenney Herrin Douglas, an old two-story Victorian house located just south of Highland Park, and found the firm's entire staff gathered around the front desk. They looked like the cast

29

from *Lost*: Bobby Herrin, thirty-eight, the short, chubby character with thinning hair and a pockmarked face, always handy with a witty remark . . . Karen Douglas, Bobby's whip-smart and very pretty love-interest character (and now spouse), ten years his junior and seven months' pregnant with their first child . . . Carlos Hernandez, twenty-eight, the Latino character oozing *machismo* from every pore of his tattooed brown skin, six feet tall and two hundred pounds of muscle, dressed in black leather pants and a black T-shirt tight around his torso, studying to be a paralegal and the firm's Spanish translator . . . and Louis Wright, thirty years old, the gentle giant black character with the gold-toothed smile, the firm's driver and Fenney family bodyguard. Their expressions were somber, as if they had just been told they would never get off this island.

'Hey, guys, it's not the first case we lost.'

'We lost?'

Scott sighed. 'Yeah, Bobby, we lost.'

'Guess we don't get paid this month,' Carlos said.

Louis shot Carlos a sharp look.

'Don't worry, Carlos, I'll figure something out.'

No one said anything.

'*What?*'

The others glanced at Bobby as if he had drawn the black bean, then abruptly turned and headed to their respective offices. Before disappearing around the corner, Louis said, 'Mr Fenney, appreciate the new book.'

Pajamae would not call him Dad, and Louis would not call him Scott.

'That Fitzgerald dude,' Louis said. 'He's pretty good.' He stood tall and recited like a Shakespearean actor: ' "So we beat on, boats against the current, borne back ceaselessly into the past".'

F. Scott had been right: life seemed to beat A. Scott back into his past.

'Very good, Louis.'

Louis seemed proud as he walked out of the room.

'What's this month's book club selection?' Bobby said.

Louis's formal education had ended with ninth grade, but he yearned for knowledge. So Scott had introduced him to books. Louis had developed a real passion for reading. Each month, Scott gave him a new book. Last month it was *The Great Gatsby*. This month it was –

'*No Country for Old Men.*'

'Good book. Movie, too.'

Scott climbed the stairs to his office. Bobby followed, smacking the gum he had taken to chewing to quit smoking now that he was going to be a father.

'Billy,' he said.

Baby names. They were going to have a boy.

'Billy Herrin,' Scott said. 'Sounds like a shortstop.'

'Joe?'

'Maybe.'

'Sid?'

'No!'

Scott and Bobby had grown up together, two renters in Highland Park. Scott's football heroics had opened the door to success in Dallas for him, at least for a while. Bobby hadn't been a football star, so the door had been shut in his face. After SMU law school, Scott had gone on to a partnership at Ford Stevens, Bobby to a storefront in East Dallas. After eleven years on career paths heading in opposite directions, they had reconnected two years ago for the McCall murder case. They had practiced law together since. They now entered Scott's office.

'Uh, Scotty, on the news this morning—'

'Bobby, you're not going to believe what Buford wants to do.'

'What?'

'Put me up for federal judge, to replace him.'

'*No shit?* Wow, that's, uh, that's great, Scotty.'

Bobby had stopped smacking his gum. Scott saw the concern on his friend's face. Bobby was about to become a father and the 'Fenney' in 'Fenney Herrin Douglas' might leave the firm. They were barely making it now; without their lead lawyer, they wouldn't make it at all.

31

'Bobby, a federal judge gets to hire his own staff attorneys, like you and Karen. And a paralegal like Carlos and a . . . well, I'll have to figure out a position for Louis.'

'So we'd be federal employees?'

'With benefits.'

'Maternity?'

'I'm sure — it's the federal government.'

'I've never had a job with benefits. 'Course, I've never had a real job.'

'Well, you will now.'

'If you get confirmed.'

'A minor obstacle.'

'With two Republican senators? I won't count my benefits just yet. What about our clients?'

'Civil rights claims are federal cases tried before federal judges.'

Scott settled in behind his desk, leaned back in his chair, and kicked his feet up. Bobby sat across from him. They were quiet, both considering their legal futures. Scott gazed at the gleaming downtown skyline framed in the window like a portrait. Once again, downtown Dallas beckoned to A. Scott Fenney. But would he return to a corner office on the sixty-second floor or to a judge's chambers in the federal courthouse? To $1 million or $169,000? To Ford Fenney or as Judge Fenney? To money or justice? Two years before, he had faced the same choice; he had chosen justice. Which decision had cost him everything he had once held dear, including his wife. Everything except his daughter. But it had given him another daughter and another life, if not another wife. He would make the same choice again. And he would make the same choice now.

'You'll be a good judge, Scotty.'

'Thanks, Bobby. So what were you saying?'

'Oh . . . yeah.'

Bobby's jaws worked the gum hard again. He exhaled heavily.

'There was a murder down in Galveston and she's been arrested and charged—'

'She who?'

Bobby opened his mouth to answer, but Scott's phone rang. He held up a finger to Bobby then put the receiver to his ear and said, 'Scott Fenney.' He heard a heavy sigh, almost a cry, then a voice he hadn't heard in twenty-two months and eight days.

'Scott – it's Rebecca. I need you.'

Chapter 5

They would spend their summer vacation on Galveston Island.

It was the following Monday morning, and Scott wasn't thinking about Ford Fenney or Judge Fenney. He was thinking about Rebecca Fenney. His ex-wife was sitting in the Galveston County Jail, charged with the murder of Trey Rawlins. The man his wife had left him for was now dead.

Scott was driving the Jetta south on Interstate 45 through East Texas. Consuela was sitting in the passenger's seat and quietly saying the rosary – she was deathly afraid of Texas highways – and Boo and Pajamae were watching a *Hannah Montana* DVD on their portable player in the back seat while little Maria sucked on a pink pacifier and slept peacefully in her car seat between them. In the rearview Scott saw Bobby and Karen in their blue Prius, and behind them, Carlos and Louis in Louis's black Dodge Charger.

'Good God Almighty, Mr Fenney, what the heck is that?'

Pajamae was pointing out the left side of the car at a six-story-tall white statue overlooking the interstate like a giant toll booth attendant.

'Sam Houston. The father of Texas.'

'Mr Fenney, did you know that Sam Houston and a bunch of white boys just stole Texas from the Mexicans?'

Fifth grade had studied Sam Houston and sex.

'I heard something about that.'

'Our teacher said now the Mexicans are taking the place back, all of them moving here.'

'What's that?' Boo asked.

'Mexicans?'

'No – that.'

They were now in Huntsville, located seventy miles due north of Houston and notable for two structures: the Sam Houston statue and the state penitentiary. In the rearview, Scott saw Boo looking out the side window. He glanced that way and saw what she saw: bleak brick buildings behind tall chain-link fences topped with concertina wire and secured by armed guards in towers at each corner of the perimeter. The State of Texas incarcerated 155,000 inmates in those buildings behind those fences.

'A prison,' he said.

In the rearview, he saw Boo twist in her seat to stare at the prison until it was out of sight. She turned back. Her face was pale. Scott knew her thoughts had returned to her mother. The murder had made the network news Friday and Saturday evenings, and no doubt the cable coverage was nonstop; fortunately, the Fenney household did not have cable. He had told Boo about her mother, but he was able to shield her from the worst of the news.

'Mother's in a place like that?'

'No. That's a prison. She's in jail.'

'What's the difference?'

'I can get her out of jail.'

She had left him for another man, a younger man who had given her what she had needed because her husband had not. Scott Fenney had failed her. Now, two years later, she needed what only Scott Fenney could give her: a defense to a murder charge. This time, he wouldn't fail her.

'I didn't kill him,' she had pleaded on the phone. 'I swear to God, I'm innocent.'

Rebecca Fenney was not a murderer. Or his wife. But she was still the mother of his child. What does a man owe the mother of his child?

She said she had no money to hire a criminal defense lawyer. If Scott didn't defend her, a public defender would be appointed to represent her. Which was another way of saying, Rebecca Fenney would become Texas Inmate Number 155,001. She would spend the rest of her life in those bleak buildings behind those tall fences. Boo would visit her mother in prison.

She had left him, but she had not taken Boo from him. 'You need her more than she needs me,' she had said back then. That one act of kindness had saved Scott's life and had indebted him to her for life. He owed her.

A. Scott Fenney would defend the mother of his child.

Chapter 6

Galveston is a sand barrier island situated fifty miles south of Houston and two miles off the Texas coast, a narrow spit of sand thirty miles long and less than three miles wide. The city sits at the east end of the island, protected by a seventeen-foot-tall concrete seawall constructed after the Great Storm of 1900. West of the seawall the island lies at the mercy of the sea. So, naturally, that is exactly where developers – flush with cash during the great credit boom of the early twenty-first century – built hotels, high-rise condos, and luxury beach homes. The homes sat atop ten-foot-tall stilts, but they weren't tall enough to withstand a hurricane pushing a seventeen-foot storm surge. On September 13, 2008, Hurricane Ike washed away the West End of Galveston Island. Street after street was nothing but stilts, as if God had dropped a box of giant toothpicks that had fallen to earth and embedded in the sand. The few surviving houses held a lonely vigil on the desolate beach. In 1528, the Spanish explorer Cabeza de Vaca shipwrecked on Galveston Island and soon dubbed his new home the *Isla de Malhado* – the Island of Misfortune. The title still fit.

Scott had rented one of those survivors for $2,000 a month, half the going price before Ike. It was out past the condos and hotels and fishing piers off San Luis Pass Road, a two-story house on stilts with six bedrooms and four baths right on the beach. He parked the Jetta in the shade of the house. It was just after three.

'Look – the beach!' Boo said.

Galveston Beach was not white sand and blue water with sleek cigarette boats cutting through the waves like in Florida. The sand was tan, the water brown, and the boats oil and cargo tankers heading to the Ship Channel and the Port of Houston. But it was still a beach, something not found in Dallas.

The girls bailed out and ran to the sand.

Bobby parked the Prius behind the Jetta. He had followed Scott Fenney since ninth grade, like a young boy follows an older brother. Even during the eleven-year gap when Scotty had left him for Ford Stevens and a Highland Park mansion, Bobby had followed him in the society pages and business section of the newspaper. Now he had followed him to Galveston to defend his ex-wife charged with murdering the man she had run off with. He had tried to get Scotty to think it through, but he had said he had no choice: she needed him. He was going to Galveston. Bobby couldn't let him go alone. Bobby Herrin was either loyal to a fault or he had a serious worship thing going.

Scott shielded his eyes from the sun and watched the girls on the beach. He turned back when Bobby got out of the Prius and said, 'Forty-seven miles to the gallon, Scotty – doing seventy.'

A born-again hybrid driver. Bobby helped Karen out of the car. Her belly seemed bigger than when they had left Dallas. She had a funny expression on her face.

'Another accident?' Bobby said.

She nodded. Bobby turned to Scott.

'Every time she laughs or cries, she pees her pants. She wears adult diapers now.'

Karen was now the girls' de facto mother. They – and Scott – relied on her for the motherly touch, even though she was still two months away from being a mother.

'They're really not that bad,' she said. 'Although they do crawl up—'

The roar of a massive engine drowned out her voice and the image of her diaper crawling up from Scott's mind. The black Dodge Charger screeched to a stop, windows down and music blaring. Louis was singing along like a rock band's groupie, and Carlos was playing the drums with two pencils on the dashboard. Bobby shook his head.

'Five hours in a car without air-conditioning – the heat got to them.'

Scott checked again on the girls. They were splashing through the surf. He cupped his mouth and yelled, 'Stay where I can see you!'

The concert abruptly ended. Louis climbed out of the Charger and headed to the beach with a book in hand. Duty called.

'I got 'em,' he said.

Next to the house was a concrete basketball court, apparently the neighborhood playground when there was still a neighborhood. Under the house was an open garage. Scott counted four stilts in, then reached up and found the house key right where the rental service had said it would be. They climbed stairs to a deck overlooking the beach with chairs and a table with an umbrella. A digital thermometer mounted on the frame of a sliding glass door read '88' but the sea breeze made it seem cooler. Scott unlocked the door and entered the house. Inside was a spacious room with a kitchen at one end and a living area with a big-screen television at the other. Two bedrooms with private baths were on that floor, and four bedrooms that shared two baths were on the top floor. Karen and Consuela checked out the kitchen, Carlos the refrigerator, and Bobby the television. He pointed the remote at the TV like a gunman holding up a convenience store and commenced channel-surfing.

'CNN, CMT, TNT, MTV, HBO . . . We must have a hundred cable channels.'

The girls' wish had come true, at least for the summer.

'Consuela and I'll go get groceries,' Karen said. 'After Maria and I change our diapers.'

Bobby had not turned from the television. 'CNBC, MSNBC, Hallmark, Cartoon Channel, History Channel, Food Channel . . . Hey, pick up some beer, okay?'

'But not that light beer,' Carlos said. 'Man beer.'

Karen laughed. 'Man beer? Is that on the label? You want man beer, Carlos, you come with us. You can drive.'

'Yeah, okay. Mr Herrin, we get *Telemundo*?'

'I'm not there yet. Bravo, Disney, Discovery, SciFi . . . Yep, we got *Telemundo*.'

'Oh, good. I won't miss *Doña Bárbara*.'

'Carlos, do you drink man beer while watching soap operas?'

'No. Just baseball and *Dancing with the Stars*. That Julianne girl, she is hot.'

Scott felt as if he were starring in a reality show: *Survivor-Galveston Island*. *A lawyer defends his ex-wife accused of murdering the star pro golfer she left him for*. Who in Hollywood could dream that up? Who would dare? And the case would surely make the TV and tabloids. Scott Fenney might well end up the butt of jokes on Letterman – *The Top 10 Reasons a Lawyer Would Defend His Ex-Wife* – or at the annual state bar convention's gossip sessions. But if he didn't represent her, Rebecca Fenney would surely end up a prison inmate. He would blame himself, and one day, Boo would also blame him. He could not allow that day to come.

'Man,' Bobby said, 'we get all the sports channels – FSN, ESPN, Golf – '

Scott was standing at the open glass doors and staring out at a solitary seagull struggling against the wind when he realized the room behind him had fallen silent. He turned back. Everyone now stood frozen in place and focused on the TV. On the screen was the image of Trey Rawlins, shirtless and sweating – the man who had had sex with Scott's wife while she was still his wife – and who was now dead. He held up a glass of chocolate milk and in a smooth Texas drawl said, '*Golfers are athletes too, even if you do ride in an electric cart. So after your round, you need a recovery drink – and the best recovery drink is all-natural chocolate milk, just like your mama used to give you after school.*' He gulped down the milk in one continuous drink and emerged with a brown upper lip and a big smile. '*Got chocolate milk? Then get some.*'

The screen cut to the announcer: '*That was Trey's final commercial.*'

Behind the announcer was a view of a golf course; a byline read 'Houston Classic'. The pro golf tour was in Houston that week.

The announcer: '*Trey Rawlins was coming off a big win at the California Challenge the week before and was even odds to win the Open in New York next week. His murder has shocked the sports world and his fellow tour players.*'

'*I'm stunned,*' a tanned golfer in a golf visor said. '*Trey was like a brother to me.*'

'*I can't believe he's dead,*' another golfer said. '*I'm really gonna miss him.*'

'*I wish I had his swing,*' a third golfer said.

The Trey Rawlins golf swing now filled the screen in slow-motion. It was a long, fluid, powerful swing – a thing of beauty. They were both things of beauty, Trey and his swing. Even if you didn't follow golf, you knew of Trey Rawlins. His face was everywhere; he endorsed golf equipment, golf apparel, sports drinks, and chocolate milk. He was clean-cut and handsome, young and vital; his hair was blond, his face tan, and his eyes a brilliant blue. He had broad shoulders and a narrow waist.

'*He had it all,*' the announcer said. '*The swing, the putting stroke, the movie-star looks. Could he have been the next Tiger? Who knows? But in less than two years on tour, he had won four times, finished second seven times, and earned nine million dollars. His future was as bright as his smile. Trey Rawlins was the All-American boy.*'

Video played of Trey signing autographs for kids, teaching kids at junior golf clinics, visiting sick kids at a hospital, and announcing the establishment of the Trey Rawlins Foundation for Kids while surrounded by kids. He looked like Robert Redford in that scene from *The Natural*.

The announcer: '*Trey cared deeply about giving back to the community.*'

That was followed by more testimonials, first from Trey's sports agent: '*He wasn't just my client. He was my best friend.*'

And from his equipment sponsor: '*We were honored to have Trey endorse our golf products, which he honestly felt were the best on the market. I loved the guy.*'

And finally from a tour official: '*The fans have lost a great golfer and an even greater young man, and we have lost a brother, a member of the tour family.*'

The screen lingered on the image of Trey Rawlins with the sick kids.

Scott had never paid much attention to Trey when he had worked at the Highland Park Country Club. Trey Rawlins had been one of the young assistant pros who came and went with the seasons; A. Scott Fenney had been a member in good standing at the most exclusive country club in Dallas. They had not occupied the same social stratum. But then Rebecca Fenney had fled Dallas with the assistant pro who soon became a star on the pro golf tour; and A. Scott Fenney had soon lost his membership, his mansion, and his Ferrari – as well as his wife. But he had never blamed Trey. He had taken Scott's wife, but he couldn't take someone who wasn't there for the taking. So while Trey's death had brought Scott's wife back to him, it had brought him no solace.

When the broadcast resumed, the announcer said, '*Trey is survived by his twin sister, Terri Rawlins. Funeral services will be held Thursday at St Patrick's Cathedral in Galveston, where we now go live to Renée Ramirez for an update on the criminal investigation.*'

The picture cut to a beautiful young Latina reporter standing in front of the Galveston County Jail. '*Trey Rawlins, the fifth-ranked professional golfer in the world, was found brutally murdered in the bedroom of his multimillion-dollar Galveston beach house early Friday morning. He was only twenty-eight years old.*'

A video showed workers wearing white jumpsuits with 'Galveston County Medical Examiner' printed on the back removing a body from a white beach house.

Back to the reporter: '*Galveston County Police Detective Chuck*

Wilson gave a statement to the media Friday morning outside the murder scene.'

A clip from the interview played. The detective was middle-aged and tall and stood before a dozen microphones clumped together on a podium in front of the white house. He wore sunglasses and looked like Dirty Harry.

'At approximately three-fifty this morning police were called to the residence of Trey Rawlins, the professional golfer. Mr Rawlins was found in his bed, deceased. He had been stabbed. Police found Rebecca Fenney, age thirty-five, in the residence with his blood on her body and clothing. We questioned Ms Fenney, and at approximately eight this morning, we placed Ms Fenney under arrest for the murder of Trey Rawlins. She is currently being held at the county jail.'

An image of Rebecca and Trey in happier times appeared on the screen. The reporter said, *'Rebecca Fenney was Trey Rawlins' longtime companion on tour. She now stands accused of his murder. She's being held without bail pending her indictment by the grand jury, but she has denied killing Trey. I've learned that her ex-husband, a Dallas lawyer, has notified police that he is representing her. He is expected to arrive in town today, so I've been waiting here hoping to get a word with him. Back to you, Hal.'*

Hal, the announcer: *'Her ex-husband is defending her? For murdering the man she ran off with? Can he do that? Isn't that some kind of conflict of interest? Or at least a conflicted interest?'* Hal shook his head. *'Well, that proves he's a better man than me.'*

Back to the reporter: *'No, Hal, that proves he's a better lawyer than you. For enough money, a lawyer will represent anyone – even his wife who left him for the man she's now accused of murdering.'*

Scott sighed and said, 'Ex-wife.'

Chapter 7

The Galveston County Jail stands at 57th and Broadway, the main drag on the Island. The peach-colored, 1,171-bed structure is surrounded by palm trees and gives the impression of a retirement community. For some of the inmates, it might be.

When Scott steered the Jetta into the parking lot, Renée Ramirez and her cameraman were still camped out on the front sidewalk. But she was expecting a Dallas lawyer – a guy wearing a suit and driving a luxury automobile, not a guy wearing shorts and sneakers and driving a Volkswagen – so Scott walked right past her without attracting more than a coy smile and a whiff of her sweet perfume. He entered the lobby and went over to the bail window but turned at the sound of chains dragging across concrete: a line of tattooed men wearing white GALVESTON COUNTY INMATE jumpsuits and shackles shuffled past and through a secure door under the close supervision of two guards packing pump shotguns, but not before one inmate said something in Spanish to a female guard and grabbed his crotch, which earned him a rifle butt rammed into his ribs.

'Help you?'

Scott turned back to the window. A chubby young man who looked more like a mall cop than a certified Texas peace officer addressed him. He wore a khaki Galveston County Sheriff's Department uniform and sat at a desk on the other side of the window. Behind him, more uniformed officers sat at desks scattered about the room.

'I'm Scott Fenney from Dallas.' He handed his business card to the officer, who looked at it and frowned as if it were written in French. 'I'm representing Rebecca Fenney. I'm here to pick her up.'

The officer looked up from the card. 'Pick her up? What, like a prom date?' He shook his head. 'Sorry, buddy, you don't just *pick up* someone accused of murder. She's staying right there in that cell till the grand jury indicts her.'

'Oh. Okay. Then please give me a copy of the magistrate's written finding of probable cause.'

'Do what?'

'My client was arrested at eight Friday morning without a warrant and charged with a felony, to-wit, murder under section nineteen of the Texas Penal Code. Section seventeen of the Code of Criminal Procedure requires that she be released within seventy-two hours after her arrest unless a magistrate determines that probable cause exists to believe she committed the crime. That time period expired at eight this morning. So you must either show me the magistrate's determination of probable cause or release my client.'

The officer stared slack-jawed at Scott.

'To-*what*?' He held up a finger as if gauging the wind. 'Uhh . . . hold on a sec.' He swiveled around in his chair and called out. 'Sarge — we got a lawyer up here quoting the Penis Code. He's from *Dallas*.'

A weary-looking older cop eating a donut at a desk along the back wall glanced up from his newspaper. He finished off the donut, removed his reading glasses, and pushed himself out of his chair. He hitched up his uniform trousers then walked to the window. When he arrived, the officer manning the window held up Scott's business card. Sarge took it and held it at arm's length trying to find a focus point without his reading glasses. He finally gave up and instead gave Scott a once-over.

45

'You a lawyer?'

Scott nodded. 'Scott Fenney from Dallas. I represent Rebecca Fenney.'

Sarge jabbed his head at the officer manning the window.

'Junior here, he thinks he's some kind of comedian, been saying "Penis Code" since he hired on a year ago. Problem is, he's a one-joke comedian and it ain't even a funny joke.' Sarge sighed. 'But then, you don't get PhDs for jailers, do you, Junior?'

'Nope, sure don't, Sarge.'

Sarge eyed Junior a moment, then shook his head and turned back to Scott.

'So what can I do you for?'

'Release Rebecca Fenney.'

'And why would I do that?'

'Because the law requires you to.'

'The *law*?'

As if Scott had said 'the Pope'.

'My client was arrested without a warrant . . .' Scott repeated his recitation of the law for Sarge then added, 'And since my client has no assets, she must be released on her personal recognizance.'

'Is that so?'

'That is so, Sarge. So please give me either the magistrate's written determination of probable cause or my client.'

Sarge grunted and scratched himself then pivoted and went back to his desk. He put on his reading glasses, picked up his phone, and dialed. He didn't lower his voice.

'Yeah, Rex, we got a lawyer over here, says he represents the Fenney woman . . . No, he's from Dallas' – Sarge focused on Scott's card through his reading glasses – 'name's A. Scott Fenney . . . Hold on, I'll ask.' Sarge turned to Scott. 'You *the* A. Scott Fenney?'

'I'm the only one I know.'

Back to the phone. 'He don't know . . . What? . . . Hold on.' Back to Scott. 'You related to her?'

'She's my ex-wife.'

Sarge blinked hard. 'You're kidding?' Sarge returned to the

phone, a bit amused. 'Says she's his ex . . . Yeah, I'd let mine rot in jail, too, that no-good . . . Anywho, he says we gotta release her on PR 'cause she was arrested without a warrant and no one took her before a magistrate for a PC hearing and . . . Really? . . . I'll be damned . . . Okay, you're the boss.'

Sarge hung up and walked back to the window. To Junior he said, 'Cut her loose.' To Scott he said, 'The DA, he said you're absolutely right . . . and he said to come see him tomorrow morning.' Sarge nodded at the front door behind Scott. 'Down the street, in the courthouse.'

'I'll do that.'

Scott handed Junior the bag of clothes Karen had given him for Rebecca. Then he found a vacant chair among weary women and young children waiting for daddy to be bailed out of jail as if it were just part of their normal Monday routine and waited for his ex-wife to be processed out of jail.

He never had closure, as they say on TV. Never had a chance to say goodbye. Twenty-two months and eleven days ago she had left him. He hadn't spoken to her or seen her since, except once on television. One Sunday, a few months after she had left, Scott had watched the final round of a golf tournament Trey Rawlins had won; after he had putted out for the victory, the camera caught her jumping into his arms and kissing him – on national TV. Scott had never watched another golf tournament.

How should he greet her now? Should he shake hands with her? Should he kiss her on the cheek like Leno greeting a female guest? Should he hug her? How is a man supposed to greet his ex-wife who's accused of murdering the man she cheated with? How is a lawyer supposed to greet his new client who used to be his wife? What are the rules for this sort of thing?

He hadn't come up with any answers when the secure door opened, and she was suddenly standing there. She was dressed in a T-shirt, shorts, and sandals. She wore no makeup. Her red hair was ratty and cut shorter than before, but she seemed not to have aged a day in the two years. Her skin was still creamy with a hint of sunburn, and her body still remarkably lean and fit. Even

47

at thirty-five – even after spending three days in jail – Rebecca Fenney's beauty still stunned him.

Scott stood.

Her eyes darted around the crowded lobby like a lost child looking for her parents. She spotted him and almost ran to him. She was crying before she threw her arms around him.

'Oh, Scott. Thank God you came.'

She clutched him tightly for a long moment, then he felt her slim body sag in his arms. She sobbed into his chest. After all that time, she was back in his arms. She felt good even if she didn't smell so good. She finally wiped her face on his shirt and looked up at him.

'I'm sorry, I must smell awful after three days.'

'You didn't shower?'

'With those women? You wouldn't believe how many prostitutes are in Galveston. I was so afraid.'

He released her. 'Did they hurt you?'

'The women?'

'The police.'

'They brought me here in handcuffs, they took my clothes, hosed me down . . . Scott, they sprayed me for lice.'

'Why didn't you hire a lawyer to get you out of here?'

'I don't have any money.'

'On TV, they said Trey earned millions.'

'None of it's mine.'

'You could've put your house up to secure bond.'

'It's not mine either. Nothing is. The house, the cars, the yacht – everything belongs to . . . Why would someone kill Trey? This is all like a bad dream.'

'It's real. But I'm here now, Rebecca. I'll take care of you.'

She glanced around as if worried they had made a mistake and would throw her back in jail. 'Can we leave now?'

'Not out the front door. Reporter.'

Scott went back to the bail window, signed for her personal effects, and asked Sarge if Rebecca could leave out a back door. Sarge obliged. While he took her around back, Scott walked outside and past Renée Ramirez just as her cell phone rang. She answered and said, '*What?* He's here? I didn't see a lawyer go in.' She hung up and hurried inside, trailed by her cameraman. Scott got into the Jetta and drove around back where he found Sarge with Rebecca. He opened the door for her like a hotel doorman.

'Hope you enjoyed your stay, ma'am.'

Sarge shut the door and gave them a little salute. Scott drove around front just as Renée Ramirez and her cameraman came running back out.

'Duck down.'

Rebecca ducked her head until they had exited the parking lot. When she came back up, she said, 'What happened to the Ferrari?'

'Repoed. I lost everything. Sold the house to avoid fore-closure when the bank called the note.'

Scott stopped at a red light at Broadway. They sat in silence until the light turned green. He stepped on the gas pedal, and she spoke in a soft voice.

'Scott, they think I killed Trey. *Why?*'

'I don't know. But I'll find out.'

Scott parked on Seawall Boulevard, fronting the Gulf of Mexico.

'Let's walk.'

They got out. Rebecca lifted her face to the sun and closed her eyes, inhaling the fresh sea air like a lifer pardoned after thirty years behind bars.

'I'm free. Thank God. I thought I was going to die in there.'

Three days in county jail – she'd never make life in prison. They walked down the wide sidewalk. To their left were bars, restaurants, hotels, and condos across the boulevard; to their right was the beach, seventeen feet below. The air was warm and the blue sky free of clouds. The breeze blew strong and brought the smell of the sea to shore. Above them, white seagulls floated on the wind currents then suddenly dove down to the water and swooped back up with fish in their beaks. Down below on the beach, colorful umbrellas lined the narrow strip of sand.

Sunbathers lay on towels, surfers rode the low waves, and tourists tiptoed through the tide. Waves crashed against the jetties or died out in the sand. To anyone who observed them, they were just another couple strolling the seawall on a fine summer day, not a lawyer and his ex-wife who stood accused of murdering her lover. A police cruiser with lights flashing and siren wailing sped past. Rebecca froze until it was out of sight.

'Scott, I can't go back to that jail.'

'You won't.'

That assurance and the fresh air seemed to relax her. A block further down, she pointed at two rows of pilings extending into the Gulf.

'That's all that's left of the Balinese.'

From 1920 when the Eighteenth Amendment to the US Constitution prohibiting the manufacture, sale, transportation, and importation of intoxicating liquors in America took effect through 1957, sinners flocked to Galveston for booze, prostitution, and gambling. Galveston became known as 'Sin City'. And no venue on the Island offered more sin than the Balinese Room, a swanky South Sea-themed speakeasy situated at the end of a wooden pier extending six hundred feet into the Gulf of Mexico. Two Sicilian-immigrant barbers-turned-bootleggers named Salvatore and Rosario Macco brought sin and stars to Galveston. Frank Sinatra, Bob Hope, Jack Benny, and Groucho Marx played the Balinese, where a bartender concocted the first margarita. Proud locals dubbed their lawless island the 'Free State of Galveston' where sin reigned supreme until the Texas Rangers raided the Balinese Room and shut down vice on the Island. The Balinese's glory days came to an end, but the red building on the 21st Street pier had remained a Galveston landmark until Hurricane Ike washed it out to sea.

'Remember that spring break?' Rebecca asked.

He did. They had come to Galveston with a group from SMU, he the former football star and she the reigning Miss SMU. They had partied at the Balinese Room and had sex on the beach. Every night.

'I could never drive past the Balinese without thinking of that week,' she said.

'Why, Rebecca?'

'Those nights on the beach—'

'No. Why'd you leave me?'

Twenty-two months and eleven days he had waited to ask her that question.

'Scott, I . . .'

'I kept your letter. You said—'

'Don't, Scott. I'm not that person anymore.'

'Rebecca, what did you need from me that I didn't give you?'

'It wasn't you, Scott. It was me.'

'Was it because I lost everything?'

'It was because *I* was lost. I didn't know who I was. I was playing a role. All my life I had played a role. Little Miss Texas. Miss Dallas. Miss SMU. Miss Cheerleader. Mrs A. Scott Fenney of Highland Park. I felt like I was always onstage . . . or in a cage. Like an animal in the zoo, everyone staring at me. When the cage door opened, I ran.' She faced him. 'I'm sorry, Scott. I know I hurt you . . . both of you.'

They walked another block before Rebecca spoke again.

'Can I see her? Boo.'

Chapter 8

'And Scotty Junior was a girl named Boo,' Rebecca said.

Scott had parked in the shade of the beach house, but they had not gotten out. They sat and watched Boo on the beach. She had changed into a white swimsuit and was building a sand castle with a little shovel and bucket.

'Last time I saw her, she had her hair in cornrows.'

'That lasted a while, then she went to the ponytail.'

'She's so tall.'

'She's eleven now.'

'I sent her birthday presents.'

Boo had never opened them.

'How is she?'

'She's good. Makes straight As. They both do.'

'Both who?'

'She and her sister.'

'*Sister?* You remarried?'

'I adopted.'

He pointed at Pajamae, who came running down the beach to Boo. Louis soon followed and stood watch nearby, holding a book as if reading to the girls below or the gulls above.

'Shawanda's daughter.'

'That's her? The little black girl you brought home?'

Scott nodded. 'Her mother died. She's mine now.'

'She's living with you in Highland Park?'

'Yep.'

'How's that working?'

'It has its moments.'

'I read you got her mother off.'

'She was innocent.'

'So am I.'

They watched the girls a while longer, then Scott said, 'She might act mad at first, so be prepared.'

Rebecca took a deep breath and opened her door. They got out and walked to the beach. Pajamae spotted them and waved. Boo looked their way then shielded her eyes from the sun. Her hand dropped, and she stood frozen, as if trying to choose between her anger or her mother. After a long moment, she broke into a big smile and ran to her mother. Rebecca dropped to her knees and held her arms out; Boo dove into her arms, and they fell to the sand. Their heads of red hair became one. Scott left them alone and walked over to Pajamae and Louis.

'Boo's real happy to see her mama,' Pajamae said.

Louis looked up from his book. 'I expect she is.'

Pajamae stood motionless, watching Boo and her mother and wondering if she would lose her sister to that woman.

Scott arrived and said, 'Honey, let's find some seashells.'

'Soon as I finish this chapter, Mr Fenney,' Louis said.

'I meant Pajamae.'

'Oh. Say, I like this Cormac dude. Writes like real folks talk.' He snapped the book shut like a preacher who had just finished his sermon. 'Reckon I'll build us a fire ring. Mr Herrin, he says we gonna barbecue shrimp on the beach tonight.'

'Shrimp on the barbie and man beer on the beach,' Bobby said. 'Doesn't get any better than this.'

They were drinking bottled beer iced in a tin bucket stuck in the sand and eating char-broiled shrimp dipped in Louis's home-made Cajun-style barbecue sauce. Louis had constructed a fire ring from rocks that would have made a brick mason proud. Inside the ring, the fire spit flames up through a black grill that made the shrimp sizzle. They were sitting around the campfire like cowboys on a cattle drive. And there among his friends and his children and his wife – ex-wife, but still – Scott Fenney felt whole again.

The air had cooled enough for the girls to need sweatshirts. Boo's head lay in Rebecca's lap and Pajamae's in Boo's lap. They were fighting sleep, afraid they might miss something grownup and interesting. Consuela held Maria in her arms; the baby was wrapped in a blanket like a papoose. The moon and fire provided the only light. The burning wood crackled and popped and spit sparks that floated up into the dark night sky and filled the air with a sweet aroma. Rebecca's face glowed in the light of the fire. She had showered, and her red hair was now full and fluffy in the night breeze. She did not look like a murderer.

'You're in your eighth month?' she said to Karen.

Karen was eating ice cream. 'And enjoying every constipated moment of it.'

'Louis's barbecue sauce will take care of that,' Bobby said.

'Guaranteed cure for all that ails a body,' Louis said.

Rebecca held her plate out to Louis again. She was eating as if she'd been a political prisoner on a starvation fast in jail; but the food had improved her mood. She had spent the rest of the day walking the beach with Boo. When Boo had gone inside to clean up, Rebecca had stood alone on the beach, staring out to sea, as if the answer to her prayers lay out there, somewhere. Scott had gone to her and stood by her. She had seemed depressed, but that was to be expected. She was the prime suspect in a murder case. Rebecca now turned to Karen.

'Did you go to SMU?'

'Rice.'

'But you're pretty enough to have gotten into SMU.'

'I was smart enough to get into Rice.'

'Oh. So how'd you hook up with these guys?'

'I worked for Scott at Ford Stevens. Didn't care for that life, so I left to help them with Shawanda's case. Plus, I fell for a certain handsome lawyer.'

'But she married me,' Bobby said.

'Don't make me laugh, Bobby, I'll pee in my pants again.'

'Diaper.'

'You'll be a great father, Bobby,' Rebecca said. 'Seems like yesterday we were all at SMU . . . What happened to all that curly hair?'

'Too much testosterone. Makes you go bald.'

'Oh, that explains it,' Karen said. 'I've gained forty pounds and he still can't keep his hands off me.'

'I've only gained thirty,' Bobby said.

They talked and laughed and ate shrimp and drank beer, as if they were on a family vacation. Scott wished they were. But they were there because the man who had taken his wife was dead.

'We had a lot of good times back then,' Rebecca said.

'Last time we were down here, that spring break,' Bobby said, 'I almost got into a fight at the Balinese with some UT guys. Scotty saved me.'

'A. Scott got into a fight at the Village,' Boo said. She and Pajamae sat up. 'Mother, it was so exciting!'

'A fight?' Rebecca said. 'At a shopping center?'

'He beat up a car with his nine-iron,' Boo said.

'Why?'

'Because I didn't have a three-wood,' Scott said.

'Because the bad man followed me and Pajamae there,' Boo said, 'so I called A. Scott and he came and broke out the windows on the man's car with his golf club, then the man drove off. It was great.'

'What bad man?'

'McCall's goon,' Scott said.

'When was this?'

'The day you left,' Boo said.

55

'Oh.'

There was an awkward moment of silence. Everyone stared at the sand. Scott stood. 'Okay, time for bed.'

'Can Mother stay here? She can sleep with us.'

'She's going home.' To Rebecca: 'Where is your home?'

She pointed west into the darkness. 'About two miles down the beach. But I can't go home.'

'Why not?'

'The police told me not to go back when they released me from jail, said it was still a crime scene, said I can't even get my clothes.'

'They've got to finish processing the house soon. Then you can go back.'

'I don't think so. A lawyer for Trey's sister sent me a letter in jail, said I wouldn't be allowed back in, that she was the administrator of his estate and the sole beneficiary. Said she owns the house now, that I have no legal right to enter.'

'I need to see that letter.'

'Scott, I'll stay at a hotel . . . if you'll loan me the money.'

Scott had put the beach house on his credit card. Four thousand dollars for two months. Now a hotel room for Rebecca. Another expense he couldn't afford.

'Miz Fenney,' Louis said, 'you can have my room. Me and Carlos, we'll bunk in.'

Carlos finished off his beer then said, 'You snore?'

Louis shrugged. 'How would I know?'

Boo jumped up and tugged on her mother until she stood. 'Come on, we'll have a sleepover. The three of us.'

Rebecca looked to Scott. He nodded. Rebecca Fenney would stay that night and every night until the verdict was read.

Chapter 9

Scott was running the beach at first light.

Knowing that after almost two years Rebecca was again sleeping in the same house — in a bed just on the other side of two Sheetrock panels thin enough that he could hear her every movement — had kept him tossing and turning all night . . . and recalling memorable moments from their sex life. So when the sunlight hit the blinds of his room, he put on his shorts and running shoes and hit the sand.

He ran west, away from the rising sun. The wet sand glistened in the morning light and felt spongy beneath his shoes. The tide was out, and the beach sat wide, filled with a fresh assortment of seashells and sand crabs scurrying sideways and jellyfish stranded out of water. Seagulls picked over dead fish, and a pelican stood witness. The wind was down, the sea smooth, and the waves low swells instead of whitecaps. The air was fresh, and the beach was his.

He ran hard to burn up his desire for her. All that time without her, now they were suddenly living together again. He hadn't bargained for that. But then, he wasn't sure what he had bargained for when he agreed to defend her. It wasn't a lawyerly decision; it was a manly decision. He needed to know how he had failed her as a man.

Scott Fenney did not have to confront his past during that morning's run – because he was now living it.

Shortly after Rebecca had left him, a Dallas divorce lawyer who had suffered the same marital fate had shared with Scott his 'seven stages of wife desertion':

    (1) disbelief – you're numb with shock that your wife had actually left you for another man;

    (2) denial – you decide she must have a brain tumor, the only plausible explanation for such bizarre behavior;

    (3) anger – you lash out at her for betraying you;

    (4) remorse – you promise to change if she will only return so life can be the same again;

    (5) shame – you isolate yourself because you know that everywhere you go everyone knows;

    (6) blame – she left you and your child, but somehow you failed her. You blame yourself. It was your fault.

The first five stages, Scott had discovered, pass in due course. But the blame stage lasts . . . forever? And only when he had escaped from the sixth stage would he embark on the final stage: (7) recovery.

Would he ever recover from Rebecca Fenney?

He saw her in the distance, a lone figure dressed in white standing on the beach before a stark white house rising in sharp relief against the blue morning sky. The sun's rays highlighted her and the house and made them both glow. The sand rose up from the beach to a low manmade earthen dune, the developer's apparent attempt to tame the sea. The front portion of the house sat atop the dune, the back half atop tall stilts. But this was not a beach bungalow rented out to tourists and college kids on spring break. It was a four-story multimillion-dollar residence with a second-story deck extending out toward the sea; stairs led from the deck down to the beach. Yellow crime scene tape stretched between police barricades set up around the perimeter of the house. He stopped running and walked to her. She felt his presence and turned to him. Tears ran down her face.

'I dreamed last night that he was just at a tournament, and he came back. How can he be gone?'

She buried her face in his bare chest. Her tears felt cool on his hot skin, and she felt good in his arms. No matter what she had done to him, they still shared a child. When a man and a woman come together and create another human being, they forge a bond that is never broken. The marriage might break, but that bond does not. And so he now embraced that woman, the mother of his child, not the woman who had deserted him for another man. He held her and let her cry until she had cried out. Only then did he say, 'Rebecca, what happened that night?'

'I woke up and found him. Dead.'

'Before that.'

She wiped her face. 'We had dinner at Gaido's.'

'What time?'

'Seven.'

'Did you drink?'

'We both did.'

'Were you drunk?'

'We were celebrating.'

'What?'

She hesitated and turned away. 'Trey asked me to marry him.'

'After two years?'

She shrugged.

'What did you say?'

'I said yes.'

Two years and it still hurt.

'Who saw you there?'

'Other locals . . . Ricardo, our regular waiter.'

'Did you argue?'

'With Ricardo?'

'With Trey.'

'No. We were happy. It was a special night.'

'Did Ricardo hear Trey propose to you?'

'I don't think so. But we told him later.'

'Then what happened?'

'We came home.'

'Who drove?'

'Trey. He never let me drive the Bentley.'

'He had a Bentley?'

'Convertible. It's in the garage.'

'What time did you get home?'

'Ten.'

'Long dinner.'

'Like I said, it was a special night.'

'Then what?'

'We took a walk on the beach. Right here. Then we went to bed.'

'What time?'

'Eleven. Trey was going to get up early, practice for the Open.'

'Then you woke up?'

'I was cold.'

Her eyes fixed on the deck above them. Her voice was dispassionate, as if she had been a third-party observer of the events that night.

'The bedroom's right there, just off the deck. We slept with the French doors open, to hear the waves. I got up to close the doors, but I came out onto the deck. It's quiet out here, just the waves . . . the sea spray hit me, I wiped my face . . . but I still felt wet . . . I looked down at myself, saw something dark all over me . . . I ran back inside, turned the lights on . . . blood was everywhere . . . all over him . . . all over me. I slept in his blood.'

She started crying again. He put an arm around her shoulders.

'Rebecca—'

He waited until she turned to him. He needed to look into her eyes when he asked the next question – and when she answered.

'—did you kill him?'

She did not avert her eyes.

'No. I swear to God. Scott, I loved him.'

60

And Scott Fenney had loved her. Maybe he still did. He wasn't sure. But he was sure about one thing: after eleven years of marriage – eleven years sharing the same bed – he knew her. Rebecca Fenney was not a murderer.

They walked back to the beach house and found Consuela and Louis cooking breakfast, Karen feeding Maria – the baby wasn't taking to the broccoli any better that day – and Bobby, Carlos, and the girls watching TV. Boo jumped up and ran to him.

'A. Scott, we've got cable!'

'Just for the summer – and only the Disney Channel.'

She looked at him with an expression that said, *as if*, but she said, 'Did you check your pulse?'

'No.'

'Do you feel faint or dizzy? Are you experiencing chest pain?'

'Boo, I feel fine. Stop worrying.'

She frowned and turned to Rebecca. 'Mother, you were gone when we woke up.'

'I took a walk on the beach.'

'I would've gone with you.'

'Get dressed, Bobby,' Scott said. 'We're going to see the DA. And bring the camcorder. Karen, take Rebecca's statement.'

'Mr Fenney,' Louis said, 'how about some pancakes and sausage?'

'Maybe one. Or two. Of each.'

'Coming right up.'

'Louis, go over to Gaido's today . . . Carlos, you go with him, you might need to translate. Talk to a waiter named Ricardo. Find out what he knows, if he saw any strangers there Thursday night, someone who seemed interested in Trey.' Scott went into the kitchen and stepped close to Louis; he faced away from the room and said in a low voice, 'Ask him if he heard Trey propose to Rebecca.'

Louis nodded. Scott turned back to the room.

'Let's go, boys and girls, it's a work day.'

★   ★   ★

61

Scott ate breakfast then showered and dressed in what would be his standard Island attire: jeans, deck shoes, and a polo shirt. He only wore suits to court now, a benefit of not working in a large law firm, albeit one that did not quite offset the $750,000 salary. He went downstairs and out to the back deck where Karen was interviewing Rebecca. He paused and observed his ex-wife like a juror observing the defendant's demeanor. She was the accused and the only eyewitness. The jury would have to believe Rebecca Fenney.

'Rebecca,' Karen said, 'what'd you do after you came back inside and found Trey lying in bed with a knife in his chest?'

'I called nine-one-one.'

'From the bedroom?'

'Yes.'

'What'd you do after you made the call?'

'I stayed on the phone until the police arrived.'

'You didn't give him CPR?'

'No.'

'Why not?'

'There was so much blood . . . I knew . . .'

'Do you have a life insurance policy on Trey?'

'No.'

'Any joint bank accounts?'

'No. I don't even have a bank account.'

'How'd you pay your bills?'

'I didn't. Trey did. Or his accountant did.'

'What's his name, the accountant?'

'Tom Taylor. He has an office on the Strand.'

'How'd you buy things?'

'He gave me money. Trey.'

'How much did he give you, at any one time?'

'A thousand, sometimes more.'

'Cash?'

'Yes.'

'What'd you buy?'

'Stocks and bonds.' She shrugged. 'What else? Clothes and jewelry.'

'Did he give you money that day?'

She nodded. 'He was going to the club to practice all day, for the Open. He told me to go to Houston, buy something sexy. I guess because he was planning to propose that night.'

'What'd you buy that day?'

'The necessities – lingerie and shoes.'

'Where?'

'Victoria's Secret, Jimmy Choo…at the Galleria.'

'When did you return?'

'About six. Then we went to dinner.'

'Are you in his will?'

'I never asked.'

'Why not?'

'I wasn't his wife.' Rebecca held an envelope out to Scott. 'Here's that letter, from Terri's lawyer.'

Scott removed and read the letter. A Galveston lawyer named Melvyn Burke was representing the Estate of Trey Rawlins. Trey had died intestate – without a will – which made Terri Rawlins, his sister and only surviving relative, the sole beneficiary of his estate. Everything Trey owned would go to her. Rebecca would get nothing. Melvyn Burke instructed Rebecca not to enter the house or to remove any of the contents thereof. He also advised that she was not invited to Trey's funeral services and would not be allowed to enter the church.

'You ever meet this Melvyn Burke?'

Rebecca shook her head. 'I didn't know Trey had a lawyer on the Island.'

Karen continued her interview of Rebecca. 'So you didn't stand to gain financially from Trey's death?'

'*Gain?* I've got nothing now. No house, no car, no money, no clothes, no jewelry – nothing.'

'You have a child who still loves you.'

The two women regarded each other like fighters facing off before a boxing match. Rebecca finally broke away and glanced up at Scott, as if hoping he'd come to her defense. He couldn't. He could defend her against a murder charge, but not against deserting her child. She sighed and turned back to her pregnant interrogator.

'Karen, don't judge me as a mother until you've been one for a while.'

Karen's eyes dropped to her belly for a moment, then she looked back at Rebecca.

'That last night, did you and Trey have sex?'

'*Karen.*'

Rebecca again glanced up at Scott.

'Goes to motive.'

She sighed again. 'Yes.'

'Where?' Karen asked.

'On the beach. There's never anyone out here now, since Ike.'

'What were you wearing?'

'Lingerie I bought that day.'

'What exactly?'

She ducked her eyes. 'White silk babydoll and matching thong.'

'Did you change before you went to bed?'

'No. Why?'

'DNA. His. To prove up the sex.'

'They took my clothes, the police.'

Karen nodded. 'Evidence. Were any valuables missing from the house?'

'I don't know. They arrested me that morning, I haven't been back.'

'Were you and Trey here all week?'

'We flew in Sunday night, from California.'

'Why wasn't he playing last week?'

'He had just won the Challenge, he wanted to take a week off before the Open – the US Open – to rest and practice. It's a major.'

Scott had heard enough. For now.

'Karen,' he said, 'get a detailed timeline for that day, for Rebecca and Trey. We'll meet out here at the end of each day for status reports and strategy sessions.'

Scott turned to Bobby, who had been standing by the stairs and observing the interview.

'Let's go meet the enemy.'

Chapter 10

Galveston County Criminal District Attorney Rex Truitt focused through his black reading glasses and tied off a big blue squiggly lure. He seemed pleased.

'Relaxes me.'

'Tying lures?' Scott said.

'Fishing.'

'Good thing you live on an island.'

The DA looked like Ernest Hemingway with a law degree. He was sixty-three years old, burly, and BOI – born on the Island. His unruly hair and neat beard were white against ruddy skin that evidenced a long life lived on that sun-baked stretch of sand, except for seven years in Austin attending college and law school at the University of Texas. He had served as the DA for the last twenty-eight years and would retire in two. He wore a white short-sleeve shirt and a solid blue tie loosened at the neck; two thick cigars peeked out of his shirt pocket. The coat to his seersucker suit hung on a rack. He sat behind a wood desk in his wood-paneled office in the Galveston County Courthouse; on the desk were a dozen colorful lures and two thick black binders. Photos of the DA golfing and fishing hung on the side walls and mounted high on the wall behind him was an eight-foot-long blue sailfish. He presided over an office that employed thirty-nine assistant criminal DAs, four investigators, and twenty-five support staff, all working full-time prosecuting criminal defendants in Galveston County, Texas, population 285,000.

Scott and Bobby sat across the desk from him. Ensconced in a chair along the wall was a tanned young man wearing a slick suit, a silk tie, and shiny shoes. He had a full head of black hair and a sharp face, like a rat. Assistant Criminal District Attorney Theodore Newman had assumed the imperial pose of Michael Corleone in *The Godfather* after he had taken over the family business.

Scott had heard Rebecca's story. She swore she was innocent. But the DA thought she was guilty. Scott needed to know why.

'Mr Truitt—'

The DA eyed Scott over his reading glasses. 'Rex. This ain't Dallas.'

'Rex, my client sat in jail for three days – why wasn't she taken before a magistrate?'

'No probable cause to arrest her.'

'Then why did you?'

'I didn't. Cops did. I got no jurisdiction until they refer the case over for prosecution, which didn't happen until yesterday afternoon, when they got the prints off the murder weapon back. They're hers, by the way.'

Scott tried not to react, but the DA saw through it.

'She didn't tell you.'

'She didn't know.'

'I'm sure. But we have PC now.'

'Are you going to arrest her again?'

The DA shook his head. 'We'll wait for the grand jury to indict. I don't figure she's going anywhere' – another glance over his reading glasses – 'is she?'

'No.'

'I have your word?'

'You have my word.'

'She runs, we'll catch her and she'll sit in jail until that verdict is read.'

66

'She won't run. She's staying with us.'

'*Us?*'

'My family. I rented a beach house for the summer, out on the West End.'

'And your ex is bunking in? There a current Mrs Fenney?'

'No.'

'Kids?'

'Two girls. Eleven.'

'You brought your kids down for a murder trial?'

Scott shrugged. 'Single father.'

The DA grunted. 'Well, I apologize for the cops jumping the gun. Good ol' boys, they pick up on how to choke-hold a suspect pretty quick at the police academy, but legalities like probable cause, that's a harder grasp for them. But I figured she'd hire a big-time Houston defense lawyer, he'd get her out same day she was arrested.'

'She doesn't have any money. It's all Trey's.'

'Not anymore.'

The DA pushed one of the black binders across the desk.

'That's the murder book, everything we've got so far.'

'How do I know it contains everything yours does?'

The Assistant DA exploded out of his chair. 'Mr Fenney, are you accusing the district attorney of—'

The DA turned to his assistant and put his index finger to his mouth.

'Shh.'

He turned back to Scott but pointed a thumb at the Assistant DA.

'Ted wants my job in two years. Still wet behind the ears, but he'll get it 'cause his granddaddy was the DA before me – BOI, old Galveston family. So I've made it my personal duty to spend the next two years teaching Ted here about justice.'

'Rex,' Scott said, 'I didn't mean it personally.'

'I didn't take it personally. Hell, you'd be a damn fool to trust a DA these days, prosecutorial misconduct running rampant – that Duke DA hiding evidence, that DA up in Collin County having a secret affair with the judge during a capital murder trial – they still put the guy on death row – that Tulia DA convicting forty innocent black people on the lies of one undercover cop . . . How many innocent black men convicted up in Dallas have been cleared by DNA tests?'

'Twenty-five so far. Thirty-eight total in Texas.'

The DA shook his head. 'You imagine that? Spending ten, twenty years in prison when you're innocent? You think I want that on my gravestone, that I sent innocent people to prison? That's what keeps me up at night, wondering if I prosecuted the right people. If I obtained justice for the victim or perpetrated an injustice on the defendant. It's a solemn responsibility . . . *Ted*.'

The DA reached over and pulled the binder back to his side of the desk. He then pushed the other binder to Scott.

'Take mine. Scott, I don't hide evidence to obtain convictions. I enforce the law so I follow the law. And the law says you're entitled to every piece of evidence I've got, so you'll get it. If new evidence is discovered, you'll get it the same day I do.'

'I have your word?'

'You have my word.' He leaned back and crossed his thick arms. 'Scott, my job is to see justice done, and I intend to do exactly that. I think that means convicting your wife. But if it means setting her free and convicting someone else, so be it. If you find exculpatory evidence – or if I do – I'll dismiss the charges and apologize to her. Until then, I'm gonna prosecute your wife for the murder of Trey Rawlins.'

'Ex-wife.'

The DA grunted. 'The grand jury convenes Friday at nine A.M. You find anything that explains why her prints are on the murder weapon, I'll present it to the jury. Fair enough?'

Scott nodded. 'Okay if I attend the hearing?'

The Assistant DA again jumped out of his chair. 'Absolutely not! The grand jury is our domain!'

The DA sighed heavily and again turned to his assistant. 'Shh.' Then he turned back to Scott and scratched his beard. 'Not exactly a normal procedure, defense lawyer sitting in on the grand jury hearing. But seeing as how you're a guest on our fair island – and a Texas legend – why not? I'll have to ask the grand jury, but they usually do what I ask.'

'Legend? You mean football?'

'That, too.' The DA smiled. 'Been seventeen years and I still can't believe you ran for a hundred ninety-three yards against us.'

'We still lost.'

'You should've won.'

'I hear that a lot these days.'

'But I'm talking about that black prostitute's case, Senator McCall's son. Scott, you made me proud to be a lawyer that day.'

'The prosecution lost.'

'Justice won. An innocent person didn't go to prison. Always thought they should've made a movie about that case, get that McConaughey boy to star.'

'But he doesn't look anything like me,' Bobby said.

The DA chuckled. 'No, he don't.' To Scott: 'How's she doing, your prostitute?'

'She died two months after the verdict. Heroin overdose.'

'Damn. Sorry to hear that. What happened to her kid? Cute little gal, showed her on TV walking into the courthouse with you.'

'I adopted her.'

That amused the Assistant DA. 'You adopted a black kid? What, you trying to be a saint or something?'

Scott thought of Pajamae's teeth and shook his head. 'Just a father.'

'Ted,' the DA said, 'every time you open your mouth, you embarrass yourself. And me. So make out like that fish on the wall and shut the fuck up.' The DA exhaled and gathered himself. Then he talked to himself. 'Calm down, Rex, this is what they call a "teachable moment".'

He removed his reading glasses and swiveled in his chair to face his assistant.

'See, Ted, two summers back while you were trying to pass the bar exam for the second time, Mr Fenney was defending a poor black woman accused of murdering the son of a US senator, the most powerful man in Congress and the leading presidential candidate. Now most lawyers would've folded under the pressure, taken a dive to save their career. But he didn't. He defended her against the federal government and proved her innocent – and sacrificed his career and wife in the process. So you shouldn't be smirking at him, Ted, 'cause that makes you look stupid and it makes me look stupid 'cause I hired you. You should be learning from him . . . what it means to be a lawyer.'

He swiveled back to Scott.

'Young people today, they got no sense of respect. Don't know if I can teach Ted respect in just two years, but I'm damn sure gonna try.'

Scott snuck a glance at Ted. The DA's reprimand had had no visible effect on his assistant; it was clearly not the first, nor would it be the last. Theodore Newman was not yet thirty but he was already convinced of his place in the world, as A. Scott Fenney had once been. His thoughts were interrupted by the sound of Bobby smacking his gum.

'You're smacking again, Bobby.'

Bobby looked up. 'Oh. Sorry.' To the others: 'Trying to quit cigarettes.'

'Try cigars,' the DA said.

He pulled a cigar from his pocket and tossed it to Bobby.

'Cuban, but don't tell the FBI.'

'What's your proof, Rex?' Scott said.

'The guy I buy them from is from Cuba, he gets 'em from—'

'That Rebecca killed Trey.'

'Oh. Proof is, your wife was found in the bedroom with the victim, she was covered in his blood, and her fingerprints were on the murder weapon which was still conveniently stuck in his chest.'

'That's all?'

'That's usually enough.'

The DA removed a set of keys from a desk drawer and tossed them to his assistant, who got up and scurried out of sight like a cockroach under a dresser.

70

'Motive?' Scott said.

'I've pretty much ruled out suicide.'

'Rex, you've got to prove motive, means, and opportunity.'

'Hell, I got two out of three.' The DA smiled. 'But this kind of murder is usually committed because of love or hate or money.'

'She lost everything when he died.'

'Life insurance?'

'None. No joint bank accounts, and there's no will. Everything goes to his sister.'

'You talk to Melvyn?'

'He sent a letter to Rebecca, at the jail.'

The DA nodded. 'Melvyn's prompt like that. Maybe they had a fight, your wife and Trey.'

'Any evidence of a struggle?'

The DA shook his head. 'Maybe there was another woman.'

'He asked her to marry him . . . that night.'

'So she said.'

'She told you?'

'She gave a statement.'

'I told her not to talk to the cops.'

'She gave it before you called. Voluntarily. It's in the book.'

'Did she confess?'

'Nope.'

'She cooperated?'

'Yep.'

'Do killers cooperate?'

'Only the dumb ones.'

'She called nine-one-one. That seem unusual, for a killer to call the cops?'

'Somewhat.'

'Anything of value missing?'

'Not that we know of.'

'Did the cops give her a chance to check?'

'Nope.'

'So motive could've been robbery?'

'Except for her prints on the knife. Butcher. Eight-inch blade.'

'Did you trace ownership?'

The DA nodded. 'To their kitchen. Matched set. Which qualifies as "means".'

'*A kitchen knife?* She probably put her prints on it cutting a steak.'

The Assistant DA returned carrying a big clasp envelope. He handed it to the DA, then resumed his position along the wall. The DA put on his reading glasses, released the clasp, and removed a large plastic bag. Inside the bag was a long knife.

'Except her prints aren't aligned on the knife that way, like she was cutting something. They're aligned this way—'

The DA grasped the handle through the plastic with the blade pointing down.

'—like she was stabbing someone.'

The DA held the knife out to Scott. He hesitated a moment – he had held a murder weapon once before, the gun that had killed Clark McCall, but not the bullet that had actually cut a hole through his brain and ended his life – then took the knife. There was still blood on the blade. He tried to block out the image that flashed through his mind of Rebecca holding this knife as the DA had and driving the sharp blade into Trey Rawlins' chest. He raised his eyes to the DA and knew that his mind was displaying the same image. There was a moment of silence as they regarded each other, the DA assessing Scott's reaction to the murder weapon bearing his ex-wife's fingerprints, Scott trying to hide his thoughts of a jury returning a 'guilty' verdict in *The State of Texas vs. Rebecca Fenney*. He placed on the desk the knife that had cut a hole in Trey Rawlins' chest and ended his life.

'Did you know him?'

The DA nodded. 'Since the day he was born. I grew up with his dad. His folks were killed six years ago, drunk driver crossed over, hit them on the highway. Devastated the boy, he was real close to his folks, especially his dad . . . golf pro out at the club, taught Trey how to play. Took the boy a few years to pull himself together, but he did. I was real proud of him.'

Scott turned to the Assistant DA. 'You're about Trey's age. Did you know him?'

The Assistant DA shook his head. 'He was a year older than me. We didn't run in the same circles. He was a star athlete. I wasn't.'

The DA aimed a thumb at his assistant. 'Drama club.'

'Did Trey use drugs?'

'She say he did dope?'

'No. I'm just asking. He was of that age.'

'Oh. Well, he drank pretty hard after his folks died, but he got that under control when he started golfing again. But dope? No way. Nothing was found at the home, and if Trey was a doper, I would've known it. We know every dealer on the Island and we watch them. It's a small island.'

The DA exhaled and ran his hand through his hair.

'Trey was a real good boy. Started that foundation for kids, donated a million bucks for Ike recovery, hung out at the club when he wasn't on tour, taught kids, played with the members . . . hell, he even tried to fix my golf swing – 'course, that would've required surgery.' The DA paused. 'Scott, don't tear him down.'

'What do you mean?'

'I mean, standard defense tactic these days is to put the victim on trial, drag his life through the mud, make the jury think he deserved to die – like the killer did society a favor.'

'I don't do that.'

'Good. 'Cause he was our hero.'

A. Scott Fenney knew something about being a hero. He knew people wanted their heroes, but their heroes were just people – with all the faults of other people. And when those faults are revealed – as they always are – the people come down hard on their heroes.

'Was sand recovered from the bed or his body?'

The DA seemed surprised by that question. 'Matter of fact. Why?'

'They had sex on the beach that night.'

The DA shrugged. 'One of the advantages of living on the Island.'

'Maybe, but why would she kill him right after having sex?'

The Assistant DA chuckled and said, 'Maybe she didn't have an orgasm.'

The DA grimaced then pointed a finger at the sailfish on the wall.

'Be the fish, Ted.' To Scott: 'You gonna introduce that at trial, the sex on the beach? Your wife and another man?'

'Goes to motive, like you said.'

The DA removed his reading glasses. 'You know, thirty-eight years of practicing law, I figured I'd pretty much seen it all. But a lawyer defending his ex charged with murdering the man she left him for? Scott, that ain't normal. Lawyers don't do that. Hell, *men* don't do that. Why are you doing that? Why are you defending your wife?'

'I don't want my daughter to visit her mother in prison.'

'You might be the best lawyer in Texas, Scott, but you're not the only lawyer in Texas.'

'I'm the best she can afford.'

'There's always the public defender.'

'Like I said, I don't want my daughter visiting her mother in prison.'

'But have you thought this through? The downside for you? What this case could do to your reputation? After what you did in the McCall case, I'd hate to see you become a . . .'

'Punch line?'

An empathetic nod from the DA.

'Better I end up a punch line than she end up a prison inmate.'

'Well, you're a better man than me.'

'Or crazier.'

'Or that. Don't believe I could defend my ex, not after what she did to me.'

His eyes showed that his thoughts had gone to another place and time. Scott tried to snap him back to the moment.

'She said the cops asked her to take a polygraph.'

'What?' The DA was back in the present. 'Oh, yeah, but you called, told the cops to lay off. But the invitation's still open.'

'Will you drop the charges if she passes?'

74

'Will she plead guilty if she fails?'

They both knew that polygraphs were inadmissible in a court of law. And the DA knew Scott wasn't about to submit his client to a polygraph because it would only hurt her; the DA would never dismiss charges on a polygraph, not with her prints on the murder weapon. And a failed test would be made public, taint the jury pool. There was no upside to Rebecca's taking a polygraph test: it might be ninety-five percent reliable, but that other five percent could get her life in prison.

'Motive, Rex – why would she do it?'

'I don't know. But it'll come out. Always does. There's always a reason for one human being to kill another. Might be a stupid reason, but there's a reason.'

'You really think she stabbed him then slept in his blood?'

'You really think she slept through his murder? Someone came into that room and stabbed him while she was sleeping right next to him, and she didn't wake up?'

'She said they were drinking pretty hard at Gaido's.'

'Which means she could have killed him then passed out next to him. Or maybe she lay in his blood to raise just such a question.'

'That seem reasonable to you?'

'Scott, we had a murder case down here where the wife caught her husband with his mistress in a hotel parking lot so she hit him with her car then circled the lot and ran over him three more times. Big Mercedes-Benz sedan with the V-8. And we had those three astronauts in that love-triangle case – female astronaut drove from Houston to Florida to kill another female astronaut, wore a diaper so she could drive straight through. When it comes to love, nothing's reasonable. Or unreasonable.'

'My wife wears a diaper now,' Bobby said as if to himself. After a moment of the silence that followed, he looked up and saw everyone looking at him. He shrugged. 'She's pregnant. Bladder issues.'

The DA grunted.

'You got anything, Bobby?' Scott said. 'Other than the diaper update?'

'Autopsy report?'

The DA pointed at the binder. 'In the book. Preliminary report, anyway. Cause of death was sharp force injury. Knife severed his aorta. He bled out.'

'Toxicology?'

'Pending.'

'DNA?'

'Also pending.'

'Can we see the crime scene?'

'When?'

'Now.'

'I'll have my investigator open the house for you.' The DA put his reading glasses on, picked up his phone, and dialed. He spoke into the phone. 'Hank? Rex. Meet Scott Fenney and Bobby Herrin at the Rawlins house . . . Yeah, they're representing the Fenney woman . . . His ex . . . That's what I said . . . Give him full access . . . Now.' He hung up. 'You'll like Hank. Ex-FBI, worked the Drug Task Force down on the border. Retired here, for the fishing. I talked him into working for me.'

'Why can't Rebecca get back into her house?' Scott asked.

'It's not her house.'

'She lived there.'

The DA turned his palms up. 'Take it up with Melvyn and the sister.'

'Who's the judge on this case?'

'Shelby Morgan. Forty, attractive, single.'

'Attractive?'

'Shelby's a gal . . . and ambitious – never a good trait in a judge, male or female. But she's BOI, from an old-line family, like Ted here, so she's our judge. She wants to move up, been waiting for a case like this for years, something with potential.'

'For what?'

'Publicity. This case could be her stepping stone.'

'Great.'

The DA chuckled. 'You'll like her . . . about as much as hemorrhoids. Speaking of which, I need to warn you.'

'What about?'

'Renée Ramirez. Houston TV reporter, she covers the Galveston beat. Good-looking gal, but annoying as hell. She's an IBC – Islander by choice. BOIs don't trust IBCs.'

'I dodged her at the jail yesterday.'

The DA nodded. 'She's a looker, ain't she? Got the body of a Playmate and the bite of a pit bull. And she's got her teeth into this case, been calling every day. I don't try my cases in the press, Scott, so she won't get anything from this office. But she's been pining for a network job, might see this case as her ticket, so watch out for her.'

'The American way, everyone using a murder case to move up in the world.' Scott shook his head. 'What about her clothes?'

'Oh, Renée dresses real nice – tight pants, short skirts – she's got great legs and—'

'Not *her* clothes. Rebecca's.'

'Oh.'

'Can we take them?'

The DA nodded. 'Just let Hank watch what you take.'

'What about her makeup?'

'Isn't there a law says a woman's entitled to makeup?'

'Jewelry?'

'Talk to Melvyn.'

'Thanks, Rex.'

The DA nodded then said, 'Scott, you ever been to a murder scene?'

'No.'

'Well . . . it ain't like on TV.'

Scott picked up the murder book and stood. He and Bobby walked to the door, but Scott turned back and said, 'There'll be a good explanation.'

'For what?'

'Her prints on the knife.'

'I'd like to hear that explanation . . . when you figure it out.'

'She's the only suspect?'

The DA gestured at the bloody butcher knife on the desk. 'Only her prints on the murder weapon.'

'She didn't have a motive to murder. You know anyone who did?'

'Who'd want to kill Trey?'

'Rex – that's what I intend to find out.'

Chapter 11

'Trey Rawlins was the Island's favorite son – he's dead and you're defending your ex-wife who killed him, but you want the senator to make you a federal judge?'

'She didn't kill him.'

'They arrested her.'

'She's innocent until proven guilty.'

'If you say so.'

'I don't, Ken – the Constitution does.'

When Mack McCall had died, the governor appointed a state legislator from Galveston to serve out his term. US Senator George Armstrong would decide if Scott would become US District Judge A. Scott Fenney. The senator's aide, Ken Ingram, had called Scott on their way out of the courthouse. Judge Buford had not wasted any time; he had already put Scott's name in the hat for his federal bench. So Bobby was driving the Jetta to the crime scene while Scott talked to Ken on his cell phone.

'Won't help your cause, Scott, you and your ex in the tabloids and on TV every night. That won't play well in the Senate chamber.'

'I'm defending my wife – how many senators are cheating on theirs?'

Ken chuckled. 'Young women are a perk of higher office,

Scott, like limos and better health care. And that's the difference – they're already in office. You're not.'

'She's entitled to competent counsel. That's also in the Constitution.'

'Voters don't read the Constitution, Scott. They read the newspapers. Well, some still do, but the others watch TV. And this case sounds like a goddamned soap opera. Renée's gonna have a fucking field day.'

'It's not my job to worry about the press, Ken.'

'Well, it is my job, Scott.' He breathed heavily into the phone. 'The senator's gonna be in town next weekend, wants to meet you for dinner Saturday night. I'll call you with the details.'

Ken disconnected without saying goodbye.

'I guess there's no sense in reading the federal government's employee benefits manual yet,' Bobby said.

'Might want to hold off for now.'

'You gonna be okay with that? If she costs you the judgeship?'

'I have options.'

'Ford Fenney?'

'Name partner, I could hire you and Karen and Carlos. I'd have to figure out something for Louis.'

'We don't want that life, and neither do you.'

'I failed her before, Bobby. I can't fail her again.'

'First thing, Scotty, you didn't fail her – she left you and Boo. And second thing, don't let a guilt trip ruin your life.'

'She'd never make it in prison, Bobby. She'd give up and die.' Scott stared out the window at the sea. 'We're her only hope.'

They drove the rest of the way in silence.

Two miles past their beach house they turned into a subdivision – 'Lafitte's Beach – The Treasure of the West End' – situated atop the earthen dune Scott had seen from the beach that morning. It had once been a high-end neighborhood, but most of the homes had been reduced to stilts. The developer's attempt to tame the sea had failed. Ike's surge had crested the dune and taken the houses out to sea.

But not Trey Rawlins' house. It fronted the beach but appeared undamaged. Scott had seen the beach side of the stark white house that morning; now he saw the street side. Two palms trees stood out front; the driveway led to four garage doors. Stairs on both sides led to a veranda and the front entrance on the second floor, above which was another story with a pilothouse at the top. Bobby parked at the curb and cut the engine. They stared at the house where Trey Rawlins' life had ended.

'Scotty, her prints on the murder weapon – that ain't good.'

'I've been blindsided before, but Rex, he's a sly dog, tying off a lure then dropping that bombshell like he's asking if we wanted coffee, see how we'd react.'

'Well, I damn near shit my pants.'

'He'll never prove motive.'

'He won't have to, not with her prints on the knife. Jury'll look past motive real fast. If we're gonna win this case, Scotty, we gotta do two things: explain how her prints got on that knife and put someone else on trial.'

'Whoever stuck that knife in Trey Rawlins.'

'If she didn't.'

'She didn't.'

'Scotty, don't forget the first rule when representing a corporate executive or a criminal defendant.'

'Assume they're lying?'

'Exactly.'

'She's not.' He hoped. 'You ready?'

'Are you?'

'No, but I've got to go in. You don't.'

Bobby blew out a big breath. 'What does Pajamae always say? Man up?'

They manned up and got out. A police cruiser and an unmarked car were also parked out front. A tall, lanky man emerged from the unmarked car and walked over. He was wearing a Hawaiian print shirt, jeans, and a cap that read 'Galveston County DA's Office'. He looked like Jimmy Buffett with a gun.

'Hank Kowalski. I'm the DA's investigator.'

They made introductions, then Hank waved a hand at what was left of the neighborhood. 'Used to be million-dollar places. Now you can buy this sand for a song. Before Ike, *New York Times* likened the Island to the Hamptons. No one's calling it the Hamptons now.'

'They're not going to rebuild?'

'Most were second homes owned by out-of-towners. They just said to hell with it, took their insurance money somewhere it don't flood.'

Five homes had once stood on that stretch of the beach; now two did, Trey's and another house under repair just a hundred yards down the street where the sound of hammers hitting nails reverberated like guns at a firing range.

'Judge Morgan's place,' Hank said. 'She's staying in town until it's fixed up.'

Brown-skinned workers scrambled over the high roof of the judge's home with no apparent worries about falling forty feet to the sand below. With the three houses in between washed away, the workers would have had an unobstructed line of sight to the Rawlins house. They would have seen Trey and Rebecca coming and going.

'They didn't see anything,' Hank said.

'But did they *do* anything?' Scott said.

'We asked, they denied . . . in Spanish.'

'Illegals?'

'You know any American citizens who'll roof homes in this heat?'

'Did Trey's house sustain any damage?'

'Nope.' Hank pointed toward the beach. 'Those piers, they're twenty-five feet above the sand. Water never got up to the house. Heard he spent four million on this place, one million just on hurricane-proofing, but it worked. Ike packed a hundred-ten-miles-per-hour wind, didn't blow a shingle off this place. Come on, I'll give you a tour.'

'Okay if we videotape?'

'Rex said whatever you wanted.' Hank reached to his back

82

pocket then held out latex gloves. 'Wear these – but don't touch nothing.'

They all put gloves on. Bobby retrieved the camcorder and the murder book from the car. He handed the book to Scott. Bobby filmed the exterior of the house, then they ducked under the yellow crime scene tape and followed Hank into the garage through a side door. Hank hit a switch; fluorescent light flooded the vast space where a dune buggy, a BMW racing motorcycle, a black Hummer, a red Corvette convertible, and a black Bentley were parked.

'Trey motored around the Island on the bike or in the Bentley. Two hundred grand. Your wife drove the Corvette.'

Scott could see Rebecca Fenney driving that Corvette with the top down and a smile on her face.

'She mentioned a yacht.'

Hank nodded. 'Down at the marina. We searched it. Nothing. Come on, let's go up. Everything's the same as that night, except for the crime scene processing.'

'Nothing's been removed?'

'The body, a three-fifty-seven Magnum revolver, a nine-millimeter Beretta—'

'He had guns?'

'This is Texas, Scott – everyone has guns.' Hank chuckled. 'Magnum was found under his pillow. Loaded. Not sure how he could sleep with that thing under his head.'

'If she wanted to kill him, why didn't she just shoot him?'

Hank shrugged. 'Ask her.'

'Anything else removed from the house?'

'His wallet, cell phone, cash, jewelry, and laptop. We're checking calls, emails, websites he frequented, fan mail to his website. I'll get you copies of everything.'

They climbed stairs from the garage floor to the second story. Hank unlocked a door, and Scott entered the house where his wife had lived with another man. He tamped down his rising emotions and scolded himself: *think like a lawyer, not like a man.*

'Maid came twice a week,' Hank said. 'Mondays and Thursdays. She was here that day.'

They followed Hank into a kitchen with a stained concrete floor and stainless steel appliances, cabinets, and countertops. Scott put on his glasses – he used to wear them just to appear smart to his rich clients; now, after sixteen years of reading the law, he actually needed them – and opened the murder book. He found the photos and evidence collection report for the kitchen.

'No blood was found in the kitchen?'

'Nope. But we got prints – his, hers, the maid's, and one unidentified set. Right there.' Hank pointed to a spot on the island counter where black fingerprint dust marred the shiny steel finish. 'Full hand prints. We figure male, and a big man from the size. He must've been leaning onto the counter.'

'You run them?'

Hank nodded. 'No match. He's not in the system.'

Hank pulled a drawer open. Inside were seven steel knives in a tray with molded spaces for eight knives. The biggest space was empty.

'Murder weapon,' Hank said. 'Butcher knife. Her prints are on it.'

'So Rex said. Would you open all the drawers and cabinets?'

Hank did, and Bobby filmed everything. 'Nice liquor cabinet. Trey liked the good stuff.'

'And the refrigerator, Hank.'

It was a double-wide with a freezer drawer below. Hank held the door open while Bobby squatted and filmed the contents and narrated.

'Beer . . . a bottle of wine . . . protein bars . . . lots of chocolate milk . . . and the biggest watermelon I've ever seen.'

Scott put his hands on his knees and peered into the refrigerator. The watermelon occupied one entire shelf. It had been split in half, lengthwise. The red pulp lay exposed like brain matter.

'Just the way we found it,' Hank said. 'Nothing's been touched.'

The kitchen opened onto a living room with leather furniture, a fireplace, a flat-screen television on the wall, and a bank of windows that offered a stunning view of the beach and sea.

Scott's mind conjured up scenes from Rebecca's life here, the same scenes he had played over and over the last two years, like reruns of his favorite show. Now he had the actual setting for those scenes. His emotions rose again, so he consciously forced himself to focus on his job as her lawyer instead of his regrets as her husband.

Think like a lawyer, not like a man.

'No evidence was collected from the living room,' Hank said. 'Let's go upstairs first, then we'll come back down to the crime scene. You might need some fresh air after that.'

They climbed a set of stairs to the third floor which had two guest bedrooms and baths and a home theater. No evidence had been discovered or collected from any of the third-floor rooms, so Hank led them up another set of stairs to the pilothouse.

'Trey's office.'

Wood-framed windows surrounded the space. The street was visible out the front, the beach and sea out the back. The room was wood and leather with a wet bar. Golf trophies crowded shelves, and photos of Trey with other famous golfers and framed golf magazines with Trey on the covers hung on the walls. In one corner three putters stood against the wall and balls waited below on a putting mat that ran the length of the room, as if Trey had practiced his putting that morning. In another corner sat a massive white golf bag with *Trey Rawlins* in black script down the side.

'You go through the bag?' Scott asked.

'Nothing except golf balls and condoms.'

'*Condoms?*'

Hank shrugged. 'For the rain delays, I guess.'

'I'd hate to drag that bag up those stairs,' Bobby said.

'He didn't have to.' Hank went over to the wood wall and opened a closet – except it wasn't a closet. It was a dumb waiter big enough for a pro golf bag – or a human being. Hank pushed a button inside the door; the elevator slowly descended.

'Opens down in the garage,' Hank said. 'No prints, no blood.'

'The killer could have entered the house that way.'

85

'She didn't have to, Scott. She lived here.'

Scott stepped over to the desk. A phone, a pad, and a pen sat at the ready. There was a vacant space front and center.

'Laptop was right there.' Hank pulled the desk drawers open for Bobby to film. He opened a lower drawer and said, 'Trey kept this one locked.'

'Why?'

'See for yourself.'

Bobby aimed the camera down and whistled. 'Chocolate milk wasn't the only thing Trey had a taste for.'

Scott came around the desk. Inside the drawer were dozens of DVDs with naked girls on the covers and titles like *Fleshcapades* and *Virgin Territory*. Scott's eyes met Bobby's, and he knew they were thinking the same thought: All-American boys don't watch pornography. Bobby couldn't restrain a smile.

'Got porn?'

They weren't shocked; porn was part of the culture now. They were excited – not by the porn – but by the crack in the 'good Trey' they had seen on TV. Was Trey Rawlins another star athlete whose perfect public image belied a dark private life? Nothing excites a criminal defense lawyer more than a victim's dark side revealed – it takes the jury's focus off the defendant and puts it on the victim. A savvy defense lawyer puts the victim on trial. Would Scott put Trey on trial to save Rebecca's life?

'Aw, hell,' Hank said, 'you can rent this stuff at the family video store. Stay at the best hotels and you can get room service and hardcore. Myself, I'd rather watch football – less violent.'

'Maybe so, but porn doesn't exactly fit his golden boy image.'

'Everyone's got their secrets,' Hank said.

'Question is,' Bobby said, 'did Trey Rawlins have any other secrets?'

They pondered that possibility for a moment, then Hank said, 'Let's do it.'

They followed Hank downstairs and to the door leading into the master bedroom. Hank stopped and reached to his back pocket then handed a small plastic trash bag to each of them.

'What's this for?' Scott asked.

'So you don't contaminate the crime scene.'

Hank opened the door, and Scott stepped inside a dark space that smelled like his mother's bedroom the day she had died. Death had its own smell.

'Brace yourself, boys.'

Hank hit a switch, and bright lights illuminated the room like an OR.

'Jesus.'

The blood took Scott's breath away.

The bedroom was stark white – white bed, white walls, white tile floor, white furniture, white curtains. The blood offered the only color. It was everywhere. It didn't seem possible that one human body contained that much blood.

'Didn't take luminol to find the blood at this crime scene,' Hank said. 'Knife cut his aorta, heart pumped till it gave out.'

Scott stared at the bloody bed where his wife had had sex with another man . . . and where that man had died. He thought he had long ago come to terms with the fact that his wife had lain with another man. He was wrong. He was just now coming to terms with that fact – with that image – of Rebecca and another man – in that bed – having sex . . . and then someone stabbing that butcher knife into his chest while he slept. Had Rebecca been that someone? His face flashed hot. He couldn't seem to get a breath in the stale air.

'Scotty, you don't look so good.'

'Use the bag!' Hank said.

Hank opened the French doors. The sea breeze blew in and freshened the air. After a few minutes, Scott could breathe again. He tried to block the image of his wife and Trey from his mind. But he couldn't help thinking, *what the hell am I doing here?*

'Bad time to quit smoking,' Bobby said.

'Okay,' Hank said, 'here's the lay of the land.' He walked over to the bed, stepping carefully to avoid the blood on the floor. 'Trey was found lying on the far side of the bed, away from the deck doors.'

Scott turned the pages of the murder book until he found the photos of the victim: Trey Rawlins lying naked in that bed, the butcher knife embedded in his chest, his body soaked in blood. Scott looked up from the photo to the bed. Nothing had changed, except the blood seemed a darker shade and Trey's body was gone.

'Your wife slept on this side, near the doors. Said she woke at three-forty-five Friday morning with a chill, said the doors leading to the deck were open. She got up to close the doors but went out onto the deck.'

'Any blood on the doors or the door handles?'

'Nope.'

'So the doors were open?'

'Yep.'

'Prints?'

'His and hers.' Hank motioned to them. 'Come on . . . watch out for the bloody footprints. Hers.'

They followed Hank out the doors and onto the white wood deck, stepping around more bloody footprints, and over to the far railing. Scott inhaled the sea air. Seagulls circled above the surf in search of fish. A shrimp boat headed into port with that day's catch, and an oil tanker headed out to sea. From the judge's house down the street came the sounds of Spanish and hammers. A lone jogger ran past on the beach below. It was all as if Trey Rawlins had not died in this house just five days before.

'Said she stood here at the railing,' Hank said, 'looking out to sea. Spray hit her, she wiped her face, felt wet, looked at her hands. Saw something dark, ran inside and turned the lights on.' Hank turned to Scott. 'You ready?'

'For what?'

'To go back in.'

He wasn't. He did not want to confront the blood again. But he took a few more deep breaths and followed Hank back inside. Hank pointed at blood on the white curtains and the wall around the light switch.

'That's when she saw Trey. She called nine-one-one.'

He pointed at the white phone. More blood.

'Cops came up the back stairs to the deck and through these doors, found her standing right here, holding the phone.'

'She talked to the dispatcher the entire time?'

'Yep. Nine-one-one call's in the book. On a CD.'

'She didn't do anything after she called?'

'Nope. Just before.'

Scott viewed the photos of his ex-wife from that night, standing there in a short white nightgown soaked in blood and looking like a frightened child.

'Detectives came out, questioned her, arrested her, took her to jail. They collected a blood sample and her clothes. It's all in the book.'

'All the bloody prints – on the floor, the wall, the phone,' Scott said, 'they're hers?'

'Yep.'

'No other prints in the entire room?'

'Not in blood. But we lifted the maid's prints and two other sets, both unidentified. Not in the system.'

'Where?'

Hank pointed. 'One set on the headboard, about middle of the bed—'

'Film this, Bobby.'

'—like someone was holding on.'

Bobby raised an eyebrow to Scott.

'No other prints?'

'Nope. And we dusted damn near every inch of this room.'

'What about the other set?'

'In the closet.'

Hank led them into the master bathroom. The center room featured a glassed-in shower and a Jacuzzi tub. Scott imagined Rebecca reclining in a bubble bath with a glass of wine after a hard day at Neiman Marcus, as she often had in their bathroom. Leading off each side were separate his and her vanities and dressing rooms.

'This one was Trey's,' Hank said.

They followed Hank into a spacious dressing room with wood shelves and drawers, a leather sofa and chair, a full-length mirror, and a flat-screen TV on the wall. The racks were filled with men's clothes, mostly golf apparel and golf shoes.

'Right there,' Hank said, 'two full palm prints on the mirror. Probably female, from the size.'

Hank was pointing at the mirror about six feet up. The prints were aligned in a way that suggested the person was leaning into the mirror with her hands spread out above, as if being frisked by a cop or . . .

Another raised eyebrow from Bobby.

'These unidentified prints,' Scott said, 'the ones on the kitchen counter, the bed headboard, and this mirror – they're all from different persons?'

'Yep.'

'And no matches?'

'Nope. They're not in the FBI database. You get fingerprinted once, you're in the database forever.'

'So we know at least three different people other than Trey and Rebecca and the maid were in this house at some time and none of them has ever been arrested?'

'Or worked in child care or as a school bus driver or a federal employee.'

'What do you mean?'

'You want to work for the federal government or do anything with kids, you gotta get printed and pass a criminal background check first.'

'Really?'

'Yep. When I started with the Bureau, I did background checks for federal agents, attorneys, judges . . . Pretty damn boring, so I transferred to the Drug Task Force, over in El Paso.'

'When did you say the maid came?'

'Mondays and Thursdays.'

'So she was here that same day?'

'Yep.'

'Did she clean the surfaces where the prints were found?'

Hank frowned. 'Good question.'

'If she wiped those surfaces Thursday, then the prints would have been made between the time she left and when the cops arrived and sealed off the house as a crime scene Friday morning.'

'Cops' prints are in the system, and everyone who entered the house wore gloves.'

'Hank, those prints might belong to the murderer.'

'Except only your wife's prints are on the murder weapon.'

'You got the maid's number?'

'In the book.'

Hank took the murder book from Scott and turned to the witnesses section. He pulled out his cell phone and dialed. After a moment, he said, 'Rosie Gonzales? . . . Hank Kowalski, with the district attorney's office . . . That's right, we spoke Friday. Rosie, when you cleaned the Rawlins house last Thursday, did you wipe the island counter in the kitchen? . . . With soap and Clorox and Pine Sol? . . . Okay, what about the headboard in the master bedroom? . . . Unh-huh . . . And what about the mirror in Mr Rawlins' closet? . . . Was anyone else in the house that day? . . . When did you leave? . . . Okay. Thanks.'

Hank ended the call and turned to Scott.

'She cleaned the kitchen counters Thursday, finished at noon, so those prints were put there sometime after she left and before the murder.'

'What about the other prints?'

'She didn't clean the headboard or the mirror that day. Does that once a month.'

'So those prints could have been put there in the last month?'

'Yep.'

They returned to Trey's bathroom. Hank opened the cabinets, and Bobby filmed the contents, the usual male paraphernalia and several bottles of prescription pills.

'What was he taking?' Scott asked.

Hank held up one prescription bottle. 'Viagra.'

'Porn and Viagra,' Bobby said with a smile. 'Trey Rawlins endorsed more than just golf clubs and chocolate milk.'

91

'CIA's bribing Afghan warlords with these blue pills,' Hank said. 'Most of the agents I worked with at the Bureau took them. Hell, most men I know take 'em.'

'We don't. Do we, Bobby?'

'Well, uh . . .'

Scott turned to Bobby. 'You take Viagra?'

Bobby shrugged. 'I'm married to a woman ten years younger than me. There's a lot of pressure.'

'What about all that "I'm bald because I'm loaded with testos-terone" stuff?'

'Hey, my first two wives left me. I'm not taking any chances with Karen.'

Scott turned back to Hank. 'What about the other pills?'

'One's a beta–blocker, blood pressure medicine. The other's Prozac.'

'Isn't that for depression?'

Hank nodded. 'My wife takes it. Says being married to me is depressing.'

They followed Hank into Rebecca's dressing room, every square inch of which was packed with dresses, shirts, slacks, shorts, coats, sweaters, scarves, hats, and shoes – a lot of shoes.

'She sure likes shoes,' Hank said.

'You should've seen her closet when we were married.'

'A woman is an expensive habit.'

'Why would she kill Trey and give all this up?'

'Maybe he was giving her up.'

'He proposed to her that night.'

'So she said.'

'Rex said we could take her clothes.'

Hank nodded. 'I gotta watch what you take.'

Scott stepped to a dresser and opened several long flat drawers. All contained lingerie. The sexy stuff. As if this were a Victoria's Secret showroom instead of a closet. In the top drawer were complete sets with the price tags still attached, apparently from her shopping trip that Thursday. He held one set up: black lace bustier . . . matching garter belt . . . black sheer hose with a seam

92

up the back . . . and a matching black thong. Scott stared at the undergarment, imagining Rebecca wearing this outfit for Trey. He wasn't sure how long he had been staring before he snapped to the fact that he wasn't alone. He turned and saw Hank and Bobby staring at the tiny thong he was holding up. He felt his face flush. He dropped the thong into the drawer.

'Bobby, call Rebecca and see what she wants, okay?'

'Yeah, Scotty, I'll do this.'

Scott walked out of the closet.

Thirty minutes later, Scott was outside leaning against the Jetta when Bobby and Hank appeared; each carried two oversized trash bags. Scott opened the back door. They tossed the bags inside the car.

'What'd she want?' Scott asked.

'Everything. We bagged up the entire closet.'

They made two more trips into the house for her clothes. Then Scott and Bobby shook hands with Hank and climbed into the Jetta. Scott started the engine and turned the air conditioner on high. They sat in silence until Bobby said, 'Scotty, what are we doing here?'

Scott did not answer. Because he did not have an answer.

'Jesus, that bedroom looked like a Tarantino movie,' Bobby said.

'You thinking what I'm thinking, about those prints on the headboard and mirror?'

'Yep. They're from women. One was holding onto the head-board, the other leaning into the mirror.' Bobby turned to Scott. 'Our All-American boy took Viagra, watched porn, and had sex with two other women in that house in the last month.'

Chapter 12

Miss SMU had worn a black bikini for the swimsuit competi-
tion – and she wore it again that day on the beach. They had
found a secluded spot. He waded into the water and watched her
perform a striptease on the sand. Then they had sex in the surf.

It seemed like yesterday instead of thirteen years ago.

An hour after leaving the crime scene, Scott sat on the back
deck drinking a man beer. He needed one after learning that his
ex-wife's fingerprints were on the knife that killed Trey Rawlins
and seeing the bloody bed where he had died. His eyes were now
alternating between the murder book in his lap and Rebecca
and Boo on the beach down below – between Rebecca in the
bloody nightgown and Rebecca in the black bikini she was now
wearing. She was still a remarkably beautiful woman, and he still
felt drawn to her.

But what was he doing here? Was he on a guilt trip, like Bobby
said? And what if she were guilty? Defending his ex-wife who was
found innocent would not hurt his chances for a federal judgeship. Defending his ex-wife who was found guilty of murdering
the man she had left him for would kill any chance. He would
have only one option in life. And when it came to Rebecca
Fenney, could he ever think like a lawyer and not like a man?

He looked down at them again. Boo waved to him, and he waved back.

'I hated you.'

'I know.'

'Do you know how embarrassing it is for a girl my age?'

'What?'

'Mother, it was in the paper – everyone knows you ran off with the golf pro!'

'I'm so sorry, Boo.'

'Pajamae and me, we thought maybe A. Scott could marry her mother—'

'Her *mother*? But she was—'

'Only twenty-four. Way too young for him. But she died.' She paused. 'Sometimes I wished you had died, too, so the other girls wouldn't tease me.'

Boo had been really happy to see her mother again after almost two years, but a day later the anger had returned. She just couldn't keep it inside her. All the bad memories had come rushing back into her thoughts – the other kids teasing her, saying her mother was just a 'ho' – now she wanted to hurt her mother like her mother had hurt her. So she tried to think of things to say that would hurt her mother the most.

'We sold all your clothes.'

'Even my Jimmy Choos?'

'Every pair. And your Luca Luca dresses.'

'I loved those clothes.'

'Didn't you love me?'

'Of course.'

'Then why'd you leave me? Was it my fault?'

'No, Boo, it wasn't your fault. The walls closed in on me.'

'*Walls?* What walls?'

'Boo, you're too young to understand. When you're a woman, you will.'

'I understand you're not supposed to leave your family.'

'No. You're not.'

95

'We don't have a mother to go on our field trips. A. Scott's the only father.'

'He goes on your field trips?'

'Of course. The mothers are really happy when he comes.'

'I bet they are.'

'We cried a lot back then.'

'You and Scott?'

Boo nodded. 'We saw you on TV one time, at a golf tournament. I started screaming, "There's Mother! There's Mother!" Then your boyfriend hugged and kissed you because he won and A. Scott turned the TV off and went outside and sat alone for a long time. I think he was crying.'

Mother didn't say anything.

'That day you left, you said I'd be better off without you.'

'And were you?'

Boo lied. 'Yes.'

Boo looked up and saw tears running down her mother's face, and she thought, *Good. It's your turn to cry.* She had wanted to hurt her mother, and she had, but now she felt bad for having done it. She took her mother's hand.

Louis's sudden presence startled Scott. How could a three-hundred-thirty-pound man walk so softly? Scott had been focused on Rebecca and Boo down on the beach.

'I had a woman once,' Louis said. 'Loved her till it hurt. And that's all I got from her. A big case of hurt.'

Man's need for love transcended race, color, creed, socio-economic status, and size.

'What'd you find out at Gaido's?'

'They got good fried oysters.'

'From Ricardo.'

'Said Mr Rawlins and Miz Fenney, they came there a couple times a week, when they was in town. Said he didn't see no strangers that night, just the locals. Said they was drinking and acting real happy that night, said they was pretty drunk time they left, which wasn't unusual. He never heard 'em fussing. Ever. Except—'

'Except what?'

'He said Mr Rawlins had a fat lip that night, like someone hit him in the mouth.'

'Did Ricardo hear Trey propose to her?'

'No, sir, said he didn't hear that. Said they got up to leave, so he went to the front door with them, then Mr Rawlins, he went to the men's room. Ricardo said goodnight to Miz Fenney, went back to work before Mr Rawlins come back.'

'But he knew Trey had asked her to marry him?'

'Yes, sir. He knew.'

'So when did they tell him?'

'Not *they*, Mr Fenney. Her. She told Ricardo.'

'We, me, us – why does it matter?'

'It matters, Rebecca, because we don't have a witness who heard Trey propose to you. It's just the word of an accused murderer.'

'Scott, he asked me to marry him.'

Scott had gone down to the beach and sent the girls inside to clean up for dinner. He and Rebecca were now sitting in low chairs under an umbrella on the beach facing the sea. She still wore the black bikini, but he saw the black lingerie.

'I believe you. But the grand jury's going to indict you Friday.'

'But I didn't kill him! Just because I was sleeping next to him in his blood, that's not proof I killed him! Scott, why do they think I killed him?'

'Because your fingerprints are on the murder weapon.'

She turned to him with an incredulous expression. '*What? How?*'

'That's what I need you to tell me.'

'I don't know.'

'The knife was from your kitchen.'

'*Our* kitchen?'

Scott nodded. 'The matched set in the drawer. The police didn't tell you?'

'No.'

'It was the butcher knife. Where'd you buy that set?'

'I didn't. Trey got it at a corporate outing, a year or so ago. They always get free stuff like that.'

'Did you use that knife?'

'Of course. My prints must've been on it from before, when I cut something.'

Scott decided not to mention that her prints were aligned on the knife in a stabbing grip rather than a cutting grip. He didn't want her to make up a reason; the DA and jury would see through a lie. Nor did he mention the unidentified prints on the headboard and the mirror in Trey's closet. He didn't want to go there just yet.

'Why did Trey have a fat lip that night? Did you hit him?'

'No. He said he slipped in the shower at the club, hit the wall, bloodied his lip.'

'Did you notice the construction crew down the road?'

She nodded. 'They whistled and yelled in Spanish whenever I drove by.'

'They ever come around the house?'

'Not that I know of. You think they might've . . .'

'Anyone might have, Rebecca. We've got to find the person who did.'

He let her absorb that information, then he said, 'Tell me about the pornography.'

He expected a reaction, but she only shrugged.

'That's what men his age do these days. It passes for romance.'

'Like taking Viagra?'

Another shrug. 'He said a lot of guys on tour take it.'

'We also found prescriptions for a beta-blocker and Prozac. Did he have high blood pressure or suffer from depression?'

'No.'

'He didn't have any medical problems?'

'He was twenty-eight years old, in perfect health.'

'The police found an unidentified set of prints on the island counter in the kitchen. Any idea who they might belong to?'

'Rosie?'

He shook his head. 'Not hers. Those prints were placed there sometime after noon on Thursday, when Rosie finished cleaning, and before the murder.'

'But no one else was in the house that day except me and Trey and Rosie.'

'Someone else was.'

'Who?'

'The killer.'

'"The Guilty Groupie"?'

Bobby nodded. 'Network morning shows ran updates on the case, while you were out running. That Detective Wilson, he gave an interview, said there are no other suspects. Said she did it.'

'How is she supposed to get a fair trial when they put that on national TV? Why do they do that?'

'Ratings. Gruesome murder cases attract viewers. The "Craigslist Killer"' – a Boston University med student who stalked prostitutes through craigslist and killed them – 'and the "Model Murder"' – a former dating show participant who murdered his ex-wife/model then stuffed her body in a suitcase and fled to Canada where he hung himself in a hotel room – 'and the "Gym Gunman"' – a lonely man often rejected by women who walked into a gym and gunned down twelve women – 'they're yesterday's news. She's today's news. Media tagged her the Guilty Groupie.'

'She wasn't a groupie, and she's not guilty. Did Boo see it?'

'No. I changed the channel.'

'Thanks.'

After dinner, Rebecca had taken the girls down to the beach to scour the sand for seashells. Consuela and Louis were on kitchen duty – he was teaching her Cajun cooking and she was teaching him Spanish – and Scott was holding Maria at the table on the back deck. She had her mother's sweet smile. The first day's investigation had dealt the defense team a few surprises, so they had gathered for their initial strategy session. Karen wore a maternity sundress and manned her laptop. Carlos wore a tight muscle shirt that exposed his biceps and tattoos. Bobby puffed on the DA's big Cuban cigar like Fidel Castro.

'It's still tobacco,' Karen said.

'I'm not inhaling.'

'Famous last words.'

'Carlos,' Scott said, 'I know you're studying with Karen to be a paralegal, but I need you to do another job for a while.'

'Sure, boss.'

'You ever roof a house?'

Carlos chuckled. 'My folks came up from Mexico. I grew up roofing houses in East Dallas with my dad. I can roof a house in my sleep.'

'Good. There's a construction crew working at a house down the street from the crime scene. Mexican immigrants. Go over there tomorrow morning and see if you can hire on, get to know the men, find out if they know anything. Or did anything.'

'You mean, if they killed him?'

'Or know who did. Or saw anything. And take some baggies – if you can get their prints on something, bag it. But don't get caught.'

'All right . . . undercover work.'

'And Carlos – don't wear leather.'

Carlos grinned. 'Okay, boss.'

Scott turned to Karen. 'Karen, you get a timeline for Trey and Rebecca?'

'Right here.' She tapped on her laptop. 'Trey left for the country club at nine, practiced all day . . . Rebecca left about ten, spent the day shopping at the Galleria in Houston, got back at six . . . they went to Gaido's at seven. You know the rest.'

'Rosie cleaned the house that morning, left at noon. So the house was empty all afternoon. Maybe one of those workers came in, got the layout, robbed the place, took the knife, came back later and killed Trey.'

'You think those prints on the kitchen counter belong to one of those construction workers?' Bobby said.

'They'd have big hands. And they had a direct line of sight to the house, they would've seen everyone coming and going. They'd know Trey had fancy cars, money . . . and that they were out of town a lot.'

'But if he left his prints in the kitchen, why not somewhere else in the house? And on the knife? And as far as we know, nothing was taken. Why would he come back just to stab Trey?'

Scott shook his head. 'I don't know. But those construction workers are our only suspects.'

'Rebecca's prints are on the murder weapon,' Bobby said.

'She's innocent.'

'Shawanda's fingerprints were on the murder weapon, the gun that killed Clark McCall – you thought she was guilty.'

'I was wrong. I'm not going to make the same mistake again.'

'What if this time it's not a mistake?'

'Bobby, you know her. You think she could've done that?'

'Scotty, I knew her thirteen years ago, when we were in law school. I don't know her now. All I know is her prints are on the knife that killed Trey Rawlins. That alone will get her life in prison.' Bobby exhaled a cloud of smoke, which Karen waved away. 'Look, Scotty, I know criminal defense lawyers represent guilty people all the time – but we don't.'

Scott turned back to Karen. 'You never met Rebecca until yesterday. You interviewed her this morning. What's your evaluation?'

'She seemed credible. She shops all day, comes home, they go to dinner, Trey proposes, they get drunk, have sex on the beach – DNA will prove up that – and they go to bed at eleven. Preliminary autopsy report puts time of death between midnight and three. So an hour or two after they go to bed, she suddenly decides to stab him with a butcher knife? I don't buy it. And I think she'd make a good witness. She was very poised.'

'Too poised,' Bobby said. 'If you'd been murdered five days ago, I wouldn't be speaking in complete sentences yet.'

Karen smiled at him. 'That's sweet.'

'She's still in shock,' Scott said. 'This morning on the beach, she broke down. But I'm not sure we can put her on the stand.'

101

'Scotty, if she doesn't want to spend the rest of her life in prison, she's got to take the stand and tell the jury she didn't do it,' Bobby said. 'And if she didn't, we've got to tell the jury who did. She had the means – the knife was in the kitchen – and the opportunity – Trey was sleeping in bed next to her – so it comes down to motive. Why would she do it? No will, no life insurance, no joint assets . . . and now she's homeless. She stood to lose everything and did.'

'I'm running asset searches,' Karen said. 'And guys, I think we need to dig into Trey Rawlins big time. Boy hides his porn, might be something else he's hiding.'

'Guns, porn, Viagra – not exactly the All-American boy in those commercials.'

'Actually, Scotty,' Bobby said, 'that is All-American stuff today. But it doesn't fit his public image, drinking chocolate milk and cheering up sick kids, which gives us something to work with – juries hate two-faced defendants . . . and victims. Except you told the DA you wouldn't put Trey on trial.'

'I know.' Scott turned to Karen. 'You're right. The "good Trey" we saw on TV might not be the real Trey. Bobby, you go over to his country club tomorrow, find out what they know. Karen, you do your searches, dig up everything you can on Trey . . . and while you're at it, find out what you can about the judge. Looks like she's going to be on the prosecution team. Carlos, you hang out with those construction workers, see what they know. I'm going to see Trey's accountant. Anything else?'

Karen glanced at Bobby who glanced at Carlos who glanced at Scott.

'Spit it out.'

'We've been thinking,' Bobby said. 'Maybe she should take a polygraph. We could find a private guy, keep it confidential. If she fails, we bury it. If she passes, we take it to the DA. And at least we'd know what we're dealing with.'

'And if she refuses?'

'That tells us what we need to know, too.'

Scott considered the idea for a moment then sighed. 'Find someone, Karen.'

Maria grimaced and grunted, and a foul smell suddenly filled the air. Scott stood and handed the baby to Bobby.

'Here. You need the practice.'

Bobby held the baby up and peeked inside her diaper. He made a face.

'Shit – that ain't guacamole.'

Scott stepped to the railing and stared out to sea. Red buoys bobbed offshore. The sun was orange at the horizon and shot yellow streaks across the water, the waves broke into whitecaps and rolled lazily ashore, the heat of the day had eased and the evening promised to be pleasant. Any other summer, this would be the perfect vacation. But not this summer.

'Bobby, maybe I am here on a guilt trip. I don't know. But I'm doing this because I don't think she's a murderer and because I don't want Boo to visit her mother in prison . . . and because I'm responsible for her.'

'She's not your wife anymore.'

'She's the mother of my child. I'll always be responsible for her. You'll understand, when that baby is born.'

Scott watched Rebecca with the girls on the beach. If he didn't defend her, if he didn't at least try to save her life, and she spent the rest of her life in prison, he – and Boo – would serve out the sentence with her. He could do the time – he had already served two years – but he couldn't do that to Boo.

'Bobby, I've got to do this. You and Karen don't. It's okay with me if you want to go back to Dallas.'

'Like that's gonna happen.'

He stuck a fist out to Scott. They bumped knuckles, a male-bonding ritual.

'We're brothers, Scotty.'

'Thanks. Now let's find the guy who put those prints on the kitchen counter. He's the killer.'

Chapter 13

On the morning of September 8, 1900, thirty-seven thousand people lived on the Island, Galveston was the financial and shipping center of the southwestern United States, and the Strand in downtown was known as the Wall Street of the Southwest.

By the morning of September 9, 1900, six thousand people were dead, the Strand sat under fifteen feet of water, and Galveston lay in ruins. The 'Great Storm' – a Category 4 hurricane packing one-hundred-forty-miles-per-hour winds – had come ashore during the night. A hundred years later, that storm still ranked as the deadliest natural disaster in US history, and Galveston still had not recovered its former glory.

'I'm still in shock,' the accountant said.

At nine the next morning, Scott sat in Tom Taylor's office located above an art gallery in a renovated Victorian building on Postoffice Street in the Strand historical district. Tom had been Trey's CPA.

'I can't believe he's dead.'

Tom Taylor looked more like the lead singer for the Beach Boys than a certified public accountant. He wore jeans, a wild shirt, and a white puka shell necklace. His skin was tanned and his hair long and gray and held back by blue reading glasses pushed up over his forehead. His face was grim, and his hands were small.

'You really gonna do that? Defend your ex?'

'Apparently.'

'Well, I called Rex to make sure it was okay for me to talk to you, then Melvyn, since he's representing the estate. He said there's no accountant-client privilege, said you could subpoena me and the records anyway. So what do you want to know?'

'Who killed Trey?'

'That detective, on the morning show, he said your wife did.'

'Ex-wife. She didn't.'

'So, what, you're searching for the real killer, like Harrison Ford in that *Fugitive* movie? How does that involve me?'

'You handled Trey's money. People kill for money.'

'And love.'

'I'm betting on money.'

'I suppose you would.'

'How long had you known Trey?'

'Since he was born. I grew up with his dad, Jim Rawlins. Rex and Jim and me, we went to Kirwin High School together, played golf. Jim was the club pro.'

'Rex said his parents died in a car accident.'

Tom gave a somber nod. 'Six years ago. They were driving home from Austin, Trey's college graduation. He was all set to turn pro, but their deaths hit him hard. The boy was lost without his dad to coach him. Came home and started drinking, didn't stop for two years. I'd drive the seawall, see him sitting out on a pier, drinking alone.'

'How'd he get it back together?'

'One day he just showed up at the club and started practicing again. Took him two years to get his game back. He worked up at that Dallas country club—' Tom grimaced. 'Sorry. Anyway, the rest is history.'

'Did Trey have problems with anyone?'

'What kind of problems?'

'Lawsuits, enemies . . .'

105

'You'll have to ask Melvyn about lawsuits, but we don't do enemies here on the Island, Scott. We're Sin City, live and let live – hell, you gotta be laid-back to live on a big sandbar waiting for the next hurricane to wash it away. Or half-crazy. We got our share of crazies but not enemies. You want enemies, you live in Houston. Galveston, it's more a state of mind than a place on a map. Think Key West with Catholics.'

'Did he still drink a lot?'

Tom shrugged. 'This is Galveston. Define "a lot".'

'Did he ever get arrested for DUI?'

'Not that I know of.'

'Did he owe anyone?'

'No, and I'd know if he did. I paid all his bills. Tried to get him to put money away for after the tour, but I wasn't too successful with that.'

'He spent a lot of money?'

'He burned through cash, damn near every dime he made. Paid four million for the beach house, half a million for the cars, two million for the boat, a million for the Malibu condo, about that much for the ski lodge in Beaver Creek . . .'

'You ever go inside the beach house?'

'Once. He had a party when they moved in.'

'Did he pay his taxes?'

'Every penny he owed. I did his returns. His tour earnings were wired directly to his bank account. His endorsement money was paid quarterly, went to SSI, they deducted their commissions, wired the rest to his account. I got all the statements.'

'Were you a signatory on the account?'

Tom nodded. 'Like I said, I paid his bills.' He looked Scott in the eye. 'I didn't steal his money. It's all documented.'

'You do the books for his foundation?'

A slight smile. 'Well, the Trey Rawlins Foundation for Kids, that was just a bank account. More of a PR deal.'

'Did you handle any money for Rebecca?'

'What money? As far as I know, only money she's got is what Trey gave her.'

'Did you do her tax returns?'

'No income to report.'

'Did he say anything to you about marrying her?'

'No. But you might ask Melvyn.'

'I will. What's SSI?'

'Sports Score International. Big sports agency. They represent hundreds of pro athletes.'

'Who's his agent?'

'Nick Madden. He's in their Houston office.'

Chapter 14

An hour later, a sleek young receptionist wearing tight black Capris, high heels, and an intoxicating perfume escorted Scott down corridors adorned with images of famous athletes sporting product logos. She stopped at an open door and motioned Scott into an expansive corner office. At the far end, a young man stood facing the floor-to-ceiling window with an earpiece and microphone fixed to his skull.

'Give me a fucking break, Stu. Half a million a year to endorse your clubs? That's an insult. I won't take any deal to Pete for less than two million.'

'That's Nick,' the receptionist said. Then she left.

'Yes, Stu, I know Pete hasn't won since Reagan was in the White House . . . Yes, I know he's forty-nine and heading to the senior tour next year . . . Yes, I know he's not ranked in the top hundred . . . or five hundred . . .'

Nick Madden could have been Jerry Maguire's little brother. His black hair was slicked back and looked wet, he was wearing a blue golf shirt and khaki pants, and he was gesturing at a laptop perched on a table against the window; on the screensaver was a formula: WM^2.

'WM squared, Stu, that's the only ranking that matters when

it comes to endorsement money, and you know it. And our last poll numbers put Pete's WM squared ranking at eighty-eight percent. That's off the freakin' charts, Stu.'

Sports Score International's offices were located on the fortieth floor of a skyscraper in downtown Houston. The windows offered big views of the city and the walls big blow-ups of more famous athletes in action: Kobe Bryant dunking a basketball, A-Rod batting a baseball, David Beckham kicking a soccer ball, Tom Brady throwing a football, Roger Federer hitting a tennis ball, Trey Rawlins swinging a golf club. One corner of the office looked like a golf pro shop with clubs propped against the wall and boxes of balls and shoes stacked on the floor. The rest of the office resembled a sports bar with air hockey and table football, a pinball machine, and a bar with a flat-screen television on the wall above. The TV was broadcasting a golf tournament; the sound was muted but the byline read 'Houston Classic'.

'A million?' Nick sighed loudly. 'Tell you what, Stu – I'll take a million less for Pete if you pay a million more for Paul. He's younger and ranked higher than Pete and he might actually win a tournament this year . . . What? . . . Of course I get twenty percent of his, too. Hell, Stu, I'd charge God twenty percent.' He laughed. 'That's right, we are robbing Pete to pay Paul.' Another hearty laugh. 'All right, one million for Pete, three million for Paul. Email the contracts, we'll set up a press conference.'

Nick disconnected then pumped a fist at the world outside the window.

'Yes! Eight hundred grand in commissions and it's not even noon!'

He had a big grin on his face when he turned and saw Scott standing there. Scott recognized him from the golf broadcast Monday.

'Nick, I'm Scott Fenney.'

The grin dropped off Nick's face; his expression turned somber.

'Rebecca's husband.'

'Her lawyer.'

He came around the desk, and they shook. Nick Madden did not have big hands.

'I can't believe Trey's dead.' He sat on the edge of his desk. 'A butcher knife . . . Jesus. Terrible way to go.' Nick shook his head, as if he were still in shock. 'How can life be so fragile? One day he's here and everything's perfect, and the next' – he snapped his fingers – 'gone like that. A hundred million dollars.'

'A hundred million dollars?'

Nick nodded. 'In lost commissions.'

Nick Madden wasn't mourning his dearly departed client but his dearly departed commissions.

'It's been six days since he died, Nick – don't take it so hard.'

Nick took offense.

'Hey, I got him deals for clubs, balls, apparel, a sports drink, and chocolate milk. And I had deals in the works for credit cards, candy bars, cell phones, and cars . . . Japanese, the Americans are owned by the government now. Over his career, I was looking at maybe five hundred million dollars in endorsements – twenty percent of which would've been mine. So excuse me for being a little upset.'

'On TV, you said he was your best friend.'

Nick offered a lame shrug. 'More like I was his best friend . . . and brother, father, mother, and minister. Athletes are high-maintenance clients, Scott. But bottom line, this is big business' – he pointed out the window; in the distance, dark smoke spewing from the refineries lining the Houston Ship Channel was visible against the blue sky – 'just like the oil business. And I just hit a dry hole.'

Scott gestured at the phone. 'You have other clients – Pete and Paul.'

'They're fillers. Trey was gonna be my Tiger.'

Nick stood and walked over to the bar.

'You want something to drink? Beer, bourbon' – Nick held up a bottle – 'Gatorade?'

Scott shook his head.

'Tiger signed with Gatorade for a hundred million bucks,'

Nick said. 'If Trey had won the Open, I could've gotten ten, maybe twenty million for his next sports drink deal. You win a major, it's a gold mine – the endorsements.'

The look on his face was that of a man recalling the great love that got away. He exhaled heavily.

'So what do you want from me?'

'Information. I need to know about Trey's life on tour.'

'Why?'

'Because I'm trying to find his killer.'

'I thought Rebecca killed him? The Guilty Groupie.'

'She's innocent.'

'Is the grand jury gonna indict her? You think they've got probable cause?'

'You sound like a lawyer.'

'Agent for pro athletes these days, you learn a lot about criminal law.'

'Friday. Unless I find the killer first.'

'Two days? Good luck with that.'

Nick stepped over to the pro shop in the corner and shuffled through boxes.

'You want some golf shoes? What size do you wear?'

'No thanks.'

'Balls, putter, a driver . . . ?' He picked up a club. 'Longest driver on tour.'

Scott shook his head. 'How long were you Trey's agent?'

Nick practiced his swing and posed as if watching the flight of his ball. 'Since he got on tour, two years ago. I rep our golfers. I played in high school, couldn't get a scholarship, so I majored in business. Hooked up with SSI straight out of college, been here eight years now.'

'Tell me about SSI.'

'Our motto is, "We score for our clients". We represent three hundred athletes worldwide, closed over six hundred million dollars in endorsement deals last fiscal year.'

'Offices like this don't come cheap.'

'You like it?' Nick put the club down, walked over to the

games, and played a pin ball. 'Athletes have the attention span of kindergartners, so I got these to keep them occupied while I deal with their lawyers and wives. Especially the football players.' He shook his head and smiled like an old aunt pinching her nephew's cheek. 'They're just big kids . . . really big kids.'

'You represent football players, too?'

'No choice. They're pain-in-the-ass prima donnas and functional illiterates, but this *is* Texas.' He chuckled. 'Still, no better place to be a sports agent. Up in the Northeast, out in California, they spend their education money on math and science. We spend our education money on football. Which is why Texas produces the best football players in the country.'

'And California and Massachusetts get stuck with all the mathematicians and scientists.'

'Exactly.'

Nick apparently wasn't trying for irony.

'Nick, you ever been to Trey's beach house in Galveston?'

'Sure. Nice place.'

'When was the last time?'

'Right before Doral. Couple months ago.'

That ruled Nick out for the unidentified prints on the kitchen counter – and Scott was pretty sure Nick wouldn't have been in Trey's bed or closet.

'Scott, I was gonna make a lot of money off Trey. I didn't kill him.'

' "Show me the money" – is that the deal with sports agents?'

'What? Oh, from that movie. Yeah, Scott, that is the deal – for agents and athletes. You gotta understand something about Trey – about most pro athletes today. Everyone who was part of his life – me, Rebecca, his sponsors – we lived in Trey's world. He didn't live in ours.'

Like a lawyer and his richest client.

'He really would've made five hundred million over his career?'

'Tiger's made a billion, and he's only thirty-three. He made a hundred million last year from endorsements. Trey was on track to make twenty million this year.'

'I need copies of all his endorsement contracts.'

Nick frowned.

'I can subpoena them.'

Nick nodded. 'I know. Every time one of my athletes gets divorced, the wife's lawyer subpoenas all contracts, correspondence, emails, earning statements . . . I'll have to clear it with legal, but I'm sure I can get you copies without a subpoena.'

'What can you tell me about Trey?'

Nick shrugged. 'Like what?'

'Did he have any health problems?'

'*Trey?*'

Nick picked up a remote control, pointed it at the TV screen, and clicked through a menu. The screen abruptly flashed on to the image of Trey Rawlins.

'His marketing video.'

The video featured clips of Trey's long drives and winning putts, his life off the course – running the beach without a shirt on, piloting a sleek boat without a shirt on, driving the BMW bike without a shirt on –

'Healthy as a horse,' Nick said. 'Look at that body. Six foot, one-eighty, ripped. Check out those abs. Those other fat boys on tour take their shirts off, you'd fucking throw up. Trey's numbers among women eighteen to thirty-five were off the charts.' He froze the video on Trey's bare chest. 'He waxed his chest.'

'Why?'

'Manscaping. All the movie stars do it. Shows off the pecs and abs better. Women love that.'

'Oh.'

– giving interviews – 'Yes, sir' . . . 'No, ma'am' . . . 'I'm blessed' . . . 'I love my country' . . .

'Market research tells us which words and phrases resonate with the buying public. Trey was a natural – programmed without sounding programmed. And he smiled. Most of the guys, they get face time on TV – which is why sponsors pay players to put their logos on their caps and shirts – but they put their game faces on, look like they're passing a goddamned kidney stone instead

113

of playing golf for millions. Trey, he flashed that smile, win or lose. Fans loved that – and that's money in the bank, brother.'

The video froze on Trey Rawlins' golden smile.

'That's all the public knows of a pro athlete. They're never gonna meet him in person, so an athlete's public image is derived entirely from a thirty-second commercial. We can craft any image we want, and the public will buy into it – just like they bought into Tiger. See, Scott, ninety percent of a star athlete's income is from endorsements, so his public image is critical. And let me tell you, creating a positive image for some of these self-centered prima donnas, that takes a magician. Or kids. Guy can be the biggest asshole in the world, but surround him with a bunch of smiling kids, the buying public thinks he's a goddamn saint.' Nick stared at Trey's image on the screen. 'Trey Rawlins was the golden boy.'

'We found prescription drugs at his home, for high blood pressure.'

Nick smiled. 'He took a beta-blocker.'

'You knew?'

'I figured. Hard to make a three-foot putt for a million bucks when your heart's pounding out of your chest. Beta-blockers control the stress hormones, which slows the heart, steadies the nerves. Anti-anxiety drugs work, too.'

'He had Prozac.'

Nick shrugged. 'Covered all his bases.'

'He took drugs to putt better?'

'The miracles of science.' Nick chuckled. 'Hey, baseball and football players take steroids to play better. At least beta-blockers and Prozac are legal.'

Porn, Viagra, using kids for PR and prescription drugs to putt better. What else would Scott learn about Trey Rawlins?

'Anyone on tour who might've wanted Trey dead?'

Nick laughed. 'You mean other than Goose?'

'Who's Goose?'

'Trey's ex-caddie.' Nick held his hands up in mock surrender. 'Hey, Goose might've wanted him dead, but he didn't kill Trey . . . I don't think.'

114

'Tell me about him. Goose.'

Nick put a DVD in the player then clicked the remote. The screen now showed a still frame from behind of Trey Rawlins standing in the fairway of a golf course. Next to him stood the massive white golf bag Scott had seen at Trey's house. And next to the bag stood a short, stocky man with a gray goatee and ponytail wearing shorts and a tunic that read 'Rawlins' in block letters and above that in script 'The Mexican Open'. He had a big cigar clamped between his teeth.

'Clyde "Goose" Dalton,' Nick said. 'A lifer on tour, real popular with the fans, they're always yelling "Goose! Goose!" when he walks down the fairway.'

'Why Goose?'

'All the caddies have nicknames – Fluffy, Doc, Bones . . .'

'But why's his nickname Goose?'

'Oh. 'Cause he waddles like a duck.'

'Why not Duck?'

'You want people yelling "Duck! Duck!" on a golf course?'

'Good point.'

Nick gestured at the screen. 'This was down in Acapulco, back in April. Tour's trying to expand into Latin America. Nice weather and great beaches, but it's a little unnerving to see Federales with AK-47s walking down the fairways. They got into a shootout with some cartel gunmen at the resort down the beach while we were there.' He chuckled. 'Vacationing in Mexico these days is like starring in a fucking Schwarzenegger movie.'

Nick started the DVD. The scene went into motion. Goose tossed some grass into the air then consulted a little notebook like a preacher reading the Bible.

Goose: '*Two-twelve to the hole, two-oh-two to clear the front bunker. Uphill into a breeze.*' Goose pulled a club out of the bag and held it out to Trey. '*Five-iron.*'

Trey: '*Give me the six.*'

Goose: '*Big lip on the front bunker. Come up short, it's a bogie. Hit the five.*'

Trey: '*Six.*'

Goose: '*Five.*'

Trey: '*Give me the goddamned six.*'

Goose shook his head and swapped clubs then yanked the golf bag out of view. Trey made a smooth swing then posed on his follow-through. The camera cut to the ball in midair, rising high above the course then arching majestically – and diving down into the front sand trap. The camera cut back to Trey and Goose in the fairway.

Goose: '*Bunker. Probably buried.*'

Trey: '*Damnit!*'

Goose took a thoughtful puff on his cigar then blew out a cloud of smoke. '*Good decision, Trey, to go with the six.*'

Trey flung the iron at Goose, who ducked under it. He gave Trey a long hard look, then stared down at the club as if trying to decide whether to pick it up. After another long puff on the cigar, he leaned over and retrieved the club. He put the club in the bag then grabbed the strap and hefted the golf bag onto his shoulder. Trey and Goose walked side by side up the fairway. Goose did in fact waddle like a duck. The cameraman followed close behind like the cameras on that reality dating show Scott had caught the girls watching one night.

Trey: '*You gave me the wrong yardage.*'

Goose: '*You hit the wrong club.*'

Trey: '*I got the wrong caddie.*'

Goose: '*When in doubt, blame the caddie.*'

Trey: '*No – fire the caddie.*'

Goose: '*What?*'

Trey: '*You're fired.*'

Goose dropped the golf bag. '*You're firing me?*'

Trey stopped and faced Goose. '*You can't count . . . Are you deaf, too?*'

Goose: '*Who's gonna carry your bag the last four holes?*'

Trey pointed off-camera: '*I'll get a Mexican. They can't be any worse than you.*'

Goose glared at Trey then abruptly pushed him hard in the chest. Trey stumbled back then jumped at Goose. The two men grabbed each other like pro wrestlers, went down to the ground, and rolled around on the lush green fairway. Nick was laughing so hard he was crying.

'A pro golfer and his caddie fighting in the middle of a round – you can't make that shit up.'

Back on the screen, other players and caddies were trying to separate Trey and Goose. Trey brushed himself off and walked over to the rope that lined the fairway and kept the fans away from the players. The cameraman followed. Trey pointed at a beautiful Mexican girl and said, '*You want to caddie for me?*'

Someone interpreted for her. She broke into a big smile. '*Sí.*' She ducked under the rope and walked with Trey over to his bag. She was voluptuous and billowing out of her tight shirt. Trey stuck his hand out to Goose.

'*Give me the yardage book.*'

'*Go to hell. It's mine.*'

Trey grabbed at the book. They struggled a moment then Goose pulled away with the book. Trey puffed up.

'*Fine. Keep it.*' To the Mexican girl: '*Pick up the bag.*'

She struggled to lift the golf bag, then she and Trey walked off. She turned back and waved to her friends outside the ropes, as if she had just won *The Bachelor*. Goose stood alone on the wide fairway with the camera in his face; his expression was that of a fired auto worker. He put the big cigar in his mouth, sucked hard, then blew out another smoke cloud. He then turned slowly to the camera and made a quick movement; the picture was suddenly of the blue sky.

'What happened?'

'Goose decked the cameraman.'

'No. To Goose and Trey.'

'Oh. Tour fined them both, but it only aired on a few cable outlets, got out on YouTube, but golf sponsors aren't exactly the YouTube demographics. So no big PR problem.'

'What's Goose doing now?'

'He's a good caddie, got picked up by another player. Pete Puckett.'

'What'd Trey do without Goose? Who caddied for him?'

'He tried to bring that Mexican gal up, but she couldn't get a visa. Fucking Homeland Security. He only played three tournaments after Mexico, so he picked up local caddies. I was trying to get one lined up before the Open next week.'

'So if Goose hired on with another player, why was he mad at Trey?'

'Because Trey won that tournament and a million bucks. He never paid Goose his ten percent.'

'Caddies get ten percent?'

'For a win. Seven percent for a top ten finish, five below that. Tiger's caddie makes a million a year.'

'That's a lot of money. Might be a motive for murder.'

'I don't think he'd kill Tiger.'

'For Goose to kill Trey. The hundred thousand.'

'Oh. Well, Goose sure as hell wanted to strangle Trey that day.'

'Where can I find him? Goose.'

Nick clicked off the TV. 'Let's go.'

'Where?'

'To the tournament.'

Chapter 15

Nick Madden drove a BMW convertible, and he drove it fast. They were on a highway heading north out of downtown in the fourth-largest city in America. Only two hundred fifty miles apart, Dallas and Houston couldn't be more different. Dallas was plains land, Houston swamp land. Dallas was white collar, Houston blue collar. Dallas was the Cowboys, Highland Park, and Neiman Marcus; Houston was *Urban Cowboy*, Enron, and a rocket ship to the moon. The only thing the two Texas cities had in common was that each claimed an ex-president named Bush as a resident.

Nick yelled over the wind noise. 'You were a star football player in college?'

Scott nodded.

'Why didn't you go pro?'

'Wasn't big enough.'

'You never heard of steroids?' Nick laughed. 'Tour started testing golfers for steroids, like those pudgy bastards wearing stretch-waist Dockers are juiced. Hell, they should be testing them for cholesterol, number of Big Macs they put away. 'Course, steroids wouldn't help those fat boys anyway – they hate to work out. More wives in the fitness trailer than players. Like your wife.'

Nick veered off the highway without slowing and screeched to a stop at a red light. Scott turned to Nick.

'Were they happy together, Rebecca and Trey?'

Nick shrugged. 'Traveling first-class around the world, staying in five-star hotels, buying everything they saw – what's not to be happy about?'

'Did Trey love her?'

'That's a hard question when it comes to pro athletes. Their one true love is the guy in the mirror. But, yeah, I think he did.' He gave Scott a sympathetic glance. 'Gotta be tough to hear that.'

'I'm a big boy. Was he going to marry her?'

'Never mentioned it to me.' Nick cut a glance at Scott. 'Seems odd, you defending her when she dumped you for Trey.'

'It's called loyalty.'

Nick snorted. 'You wouldn't last long as a sports agent. You learn pretty quick that athletes got the loyalty of a pit bull. They cheat on their agents, their wives, and their taxes. So you take care of number one.'

'Agents have a fiduciary duty, Nick. The law says you've got to put your clients' best interests ahead of your commissions.'

Nick laughed. 'The law never represented a pro athlete.'

Nick steered the Beemer into a high-end suburban community. They drove down wide streets of magnificent homes and then through the open gates of a country club with a big banner that read 'Houston Classic'. Nick stopped at a barricade manned by two cops. He flashed his credentials like an FBI agent, and he got the same respect; the cops scrambled to remove the barricade. Nick accelerated across the parking lot and turned into a vacant space. The lot looked like a Cadillac showroom.

'Courtesy cars,' Nick said. 'Players fly into town on private jets, get a free Caddy for the week, free hotel, free food, free everything. Nice life, long as you can stay on tour. But there's always a younger hotshot wanting to take your place in the Caddy.'

Or Ferrari.

They got out and walked toward the entrance gate.

'Back in the days of Arnie and Jack,' Nick said, 'celebrities sponsored pro golf tournaments. You had the Bob Hope, the Bing Crosby, the Frank Sinatra, the Andy Williams . . . then the tour went corporate. Now you've got the Mercedes-Benz, the Sony, the BMW, the Barclays, the Deutsche Bank, the Stanford St Jude . . .'

He chuckled.

'Tour had to drop Stanford from the tournament name when the Feds indicted him for running a seven-billion-dollar Ponzi scheme. Allen Stanford, he lives here in Houston – actually, he's living in jail until his trial – he bought himself a knighthood on some Caribbean island, calls himself "Sir Allen". Guy went to college in Waco, now he thinks he's a fucking Knight of the Round Table. Can't you see him in federal prison, demanding the other inmates call him Sir Allen? Those bad boys gonna show him *To Sir with Love*. That was an old movie I saw on cable.'

He flashed his credentials, and they entered the tournament grounds. The world might be mired in the worst recession since the Great Depression and Texas in the worst drought in half a century – lakes were drying up, water was rationed and cost more than gasoline, the land was so parched and brittle that one errant cigarette could torch the entire state – but the recession had apparently exempted pro golf and the drought this golf course. It looked like an oasis in the Texas desert with lush green fairways lined with tall pine trees and a blue lake sparkling in the distance. A stately clubhouse stood off to one side and massive white tents to the other. A red blimp hovered overhead in the blue sky, colorful neon signs adorned the tents, loud cheers erupted every few minutes, and the air smelled of popcorn and cotton candy, all of which gave the place a circus-like atmosphere. Nick abruptly stopped and spread his arms, his face that of a kid who had just spotted the clowns.

'What do you see, Scott?'

Scott glanced around. 'Golfers, caddies, fans . . .'

Nick was shaking his head. 'You see WM squared.'

'WM squared? What's that?'

121

'W-M-W-M. *White men with money.* Affluent middle-aged white men, thirty-five to sixty-five, the target demographic for sports advertising. That's where your sports dollars are today, Scott, and that means pro golf. No other sport can offer advertisers WM squared. I made that up myself.'

Scott now noticed that all of the fans were in fact white and most were middle-aged men. There were no people of color in sight. It looked like Highland Park Day at the tournament.

'What about football, basketball, baseball? Those are popular with white men.'

Nick snorted. 'Working-class white men. WM squared are lawyers, doctors, CEOs – white men with incomes in excess of two hundred fifty thousand – the white guys Obama's raising taxes on.' He chuckled. 'This place could pass for the fucking Republican National Convention, especially the players. They hate paying taxes more than making a double-bogie.' He shook his head. 'You ain't gonna find anyone out here who voted for Obama, except maybe the guy shining shoes down in the locker room.'

They walked past the white tents – 'Merchandise tent . . . margarita tent . . . media tent' – the first tee and the ninth green, and white, well-dressed, and well-behaved fans. This was not the raucous atmosphere of a pro football or basketball game with loud drunken fans painted in team colors and taunting the opposing players with profanities. These fans waited patiently for their favorite golfers' autographs and politely fell silent when a player teed off or putted. Genteel applause greeted putts that dropped and empathetic groans putts that did not. The scene seemed from another sports era, perhaps not quite like the old newsreels of Yankee games with white fans dressed in their Sunday best, but the fans were still –

'White and polite,' Nick said. 'That's the way WM squared want their sports, Scott. And that means golf. Go to a major league baseball game today, it's like you're at a fucking bull-fight in Juarez. All the players are named Rodriguez and speaking Spanish. WM squared don't speak Spanish, Scott.'

Nick waved to a young golfer strutting past followed by his entourage.

'And football and basketball players, they're all homeboys from the 'hood, foul-mouthed, chest-pounding, crotch-grabbing, gun-packing, tattooed-and-taunting homies who brought the 'hood culture to the pros.' Nick shook his head. 'WM squared don't like homies, Scott.'

Nick acknowledged another golfer trailed by kids seeking autographs.

' 'Course, what do you expect? You give a twenty-year-old black kid from the ghetto ten million in cash 'cause he can dunk a basketball or catch a football, what do you think he's gonna do? Invest in a retirement account with Schwab? Hell, no. He's gonna bling himself out with a chrome-plated Hummer and gold jewelry and high-powered guns, then go back to the 'hood and show off to his homies. He ain't suddenly gonna start wearing Tommy Hilfiger.'

Nick was amused by his own words.

'Which leaves pro golf to provide the white-and-polite, English-speaking, non-violent, suburban sports experience for WM squared.'

'Tiger's black.'

Nick dismissed that comment as if he were annoyed by a gnat.

'Tiger transcends race. He's the best there ever was and he's a marketing machine because he's programmed like a fucking computer – at least until he drove his life into a tree.' Nick shook his head. 'I preach to my athletes all the time: never text your mistresses. Do they listen? No, they don't.' He sighed. 'But Tiger, he'll be back. WM squared will forgive him because he ain't a homie – no trash talking, no tattoos, no guns. He always acted polite, and he endorsed white man products – Nike, Tag Heuer, Gillette, Buick, American Express.' Nick grinned. 'Homies wouldn't be caught dead behind the wheel of a Buick and they don't carry American Express when they go shopping – they carry Smith & Wesson.'

He thought that was funny.

'White and polite – that's the key to success in golf marketing, Scott. Boy scouts, not homeboys.' Nick's attention was suddenly diverted. He called out to a player. 'Yo, Jake! My man! You seen Goose?'

The player's cap and clothes sported logos for a dozen different sponsors. He yelled, 'Practice tee!' Nick waved a thanks to the player.

'Jake's one of my guys, looks like a goddamned NASCAR driver. Because advertisers are chasing WM squared onto the golf course. Nike started off selling sneakers, now they sell golf clubs, balls, shoes, and clothes. Under Armour, they made their name making sports underwear endorsed by pumped-up black football players. Now they make golf clothes for fat white guys. Hell, even Clint Eastwood's got his own golf apparel company, Tehama. Good stuff.'

Nick Madden, sports agent, paused and took in his world.

'This is the whitest place in America – a pro golf tournament. We're not at a muny course down in the ghetto, Scott. We're in the suburbs, baby – because that's where WM squared lives. White men with money.'

His expression changed, as if he had had an epiphany, and he turned to Scott.

'Can I trademark that? WM squared?'

'Probably.'

Nick smiled. 'Might be some money in that.'

'Let's find Goose.'

They found Goose on the practice range, drinking beer from a can, jotting in a little notebook, and sitting on a red golf bag with *Pete Puckett* stenciled down one side.

'Hey, Goose,' Nick said.

Goose didn't look up at Nick or smile at Nick. Clyde "Goose" Dalton was a squat man with muscular legs protruding from baggy shorts and thick arms from a white T-shirt with 'Who's Your Caddie Now?' printed across the front. His cap was pushed back on his head, revealing a sunburned forehead beaded with sweat. His hair was gray and pulled into a ponytail, and his matching goatee needed trimming. He had the complexion of a construction worker –

'The fuck you want, Nick?'

– and the vocabulary.

'Jesus, you're still pissed off? Give it up, Goose – he's dead.' Nick turned to Scott. 'I got him caddied up with Trey, now he blames me because Trey stiffed him.' Back to Goose: 'Where's Pete?'

'Eating lunch.' He held up the beer can. 'I'm on a strict liquid diet.' He nodded at Scott. 'Who's the spectator?'

'That the infamous yardage book?' Scott said.

'Got one for every course on tour. Make 'em myself, walk off the exact yardage from every tree and sprinkler head to every pin position on every green.' He glanced up at Scott. 'Who are you and what the fuck does infamous mean?'

'It means notorious, and I'm Scott Fenney.'

'Rebecca's husband.'

'Lawyer.'

Now Goose smiled. He stuck a hand out, and they shook. Goose had big hands.

'I'll contribute to her defense fund,' Goose said.

'Better save it for your own lawyer.'

Goose pulled his hand back and frowned. 'The hell's that supposed to mean?'

'Where were you last Thursday?'

'Caddying for Pete, at the Atlantic Open.'

'Where's that?'

'Orlando,' Nick said. 'Pete played Thursday and Friday, didn't make the cut. Means he didn't play the weekend.'

'Well, actually,' Goose said, 'Pete didn't play Friday either. He DQ'd Thursday.'

'*DQ'd?*'

'Yeah, he seemed real out of sorts at the pro-am and right from the git-go on Thursday. Opened with a four-putt snowman' –

Nick, to Scott: 'An eight . . . number eight looks like a little snowman.'

– 'then threw his putter all the way to the second tee. I knew we were in for a long day.'

'Why'd he DQ?' Nick asked.

'Wrote down the wrong scores for two holes, signed the card.'

Nick, to Scott: 'Automatic disqualification.' Back to Goose: 'Why didn't I hear about that?'

'Maybe because Pete's a grown man and don't figure he's gotta report in to his snot-nosed agent every fuckin' day.' Goose shrugged. 'That, or he forgot.'

Goose's attention was diverted by a flashy girl in a short skirt and a halter top slinking by on high-heeled wedges. Goose leaned over as if trying to look up her skirt.

'She's gonna make a golfer happy tonight,' he said.

'Now that's a sweet two-piece,' Nick said.

'Two-piece?' Scott said.

'She's wearing exactly two pieces of clothing: the halter top and miniskirt. Nothing else touching that body.'

'I think the time is right for Viagra,' Goose said.

'I may need to seek immediate medical attention,' Nick said, ''cause this might last more than four hours.'

Nick and Goose laughed and fist-punched. They had bonded over a two-piece. She wasn't alone. There were many young, beautiful women wearing only two pieces of clothing in attendance – not as many as at a college football game, but more than Scott would have expected at a pro golf tournament.

'Groupies for golfers,' Goose said.

'Bald, pudgy, out-of-shape bastards,' Nick said. 'But they got gorgeous gals hanging on their arms because they're rich. You know why they don't wear underwear?'

'The players?'

'The two-pieces.'

'I hate to even guess.'

Nick grinned like a teenage boy with a girlie magazine. 'They sit right behind the green, wait for the players to walk up, then flash 'em a crotch shot.'

Goose chuckled. 'Shit, every time me and Trey walked onto a green, there was a chorus line of crotches. Camera guys had to be careful not to broadcast that across America on a Sunday afternoon.'

Scott tried to refocus the conversation on his murder investigation.

'Goose, did you stay in Orlando Thursday night?'

Goose reluctantly pulled his eyes off the two-piece. 'Nope. Flew back to Austin.'

'What time did you get in?'

'About five.'

'It's only a four-hour drive from Austin to Galveston. You could've been there by nine at the latest. Time of death was after midnight.'

'I didn't kill him.'

'You ever been to his beach house?'

'I ain't never been to Galveston.'

'You didn't travel with Trey?'

Goose snorted. 'Don't work that way. Players, they travel in private jets. Caddies fly commercial. We pay our own way. Players stay in five-star hotels. We double up in cheap motels by the highway.'

'Will you take a polygraph?'

'To prove I stayed in cheap motels?'

'To prove you didn't kill Trey.'

'No one said I did.'

'You stayed in Austin Thursday night?'

'I live there.'

'Any witnesses?'

'That I live there?'

'That you stayed in Austin that night.'

Goose finished off the beer, belched, and dropped the can by the golf bag.

'I got drunk that night.'

'Where?' Scott said.

'Broken Spoke.'

'Anyone who'd remember you being there Thursday night?'

'The other regulars won't remember they were there.'

'What about the bartender?'

'It ain't that kind of place. It's a dance hall.'

'So you got drunk in a dance hall but no one can vouch for you. Pretty vague alibi, Goose.'

'Didn't know I needed one.'

'Six days since he died – you don't seem too upset.'

'He treated me like shit.'

'And he fired you.'

'You think I killed him 'cause he fired me?' He spit. 'Hell, if caddies killed their pros for firing them, tour wouldn't have enough players to field a foursome.'

'Trey owed you a hundred thousand.'

Goose's eyes flashed dark. 'Damn right he did. I was gonna sue the bastard. I can't now . . . Can I?'

'And he humiliated you on TV, replaced you with a Mexican girl.'

'He banged her after the round.'

'What?'

'Yeah, Rebecca got the runs, drinking the water. While she's stuck in the bathroom, Trey's humping the Mexican gal in a pool cabaña.'

Scott glanced at Nick; he gave Scott a 'heck if I know' shrug. Scott turned back to Goose. 'A hundred-thousand-dollar debt – that's a pretty good motive.'

'So is screwing my wife.'

'You don't have a wife,' Nick said.

Goose gestured at Scott. 'I meant him . . . and Brett.'

'*Brett?*' Nick said.

'Who's he?' Scott said.

'Brett McBride. Tour player, ranked two-eighty-seven in the world.'

Scott turned to Goose: 'Trey was—?'

Goose nodded. 'Screwing his wife.'

Nick's mouth dropped open. 'Trey was screwing Tess?'

Goose chuckled. 'Who wasn't?'

'When?' Scott asked.

'Whenever he could.'

'How long do you think he was?'

Goose shrugged. 'I don't know. I never saw him naked.'

'No. How long do you think he was screwing Tess?'

'Oh. They hooked up at the Hope back in January.'

Scott turned to Nick. 'You didn't know?'

Nick shook his head. 'I tell my athletes, if I don't get twenty percent, I don't want to know about it.'

'You know her? This Tess?'

Nick nodded. 'Everyone knows Tess, if you know what I mean. Brett was a judge in the Miss Hooters pageant in Vegas last year. She was runner-up; they got married five months later, at the Reno tournament.'

'And you represent him, too?'

Nick nodded again. Scott turned back to Goose.

'A jealous husband . . . Did Brett know?'

'They're still married.'

'Did Rebecca know?'

'I don't think so.' He pulled a cigar out of the golf bag, bit off the tip, and spit it across the practice tee. 'Trey was an idiot, taking a chance on losing her over Tess. I mean, Tess is hot, sure, but Rebecca's world-class gorgeous. She had options out here, could've switched bags anytime she wanted.'

'Trey ever mention to you that he was going to marry her? Rebecca.'

'Nope.'

Goose dug around in his shirt pocket, pulled out a wooden match, and struck it on the bottom of the golf bag until it ignited. He put the flame to the cigar and puffed until the cigar caught fire. He took a long drag and exhaled smoke then gave Scott a thoughtful look.

'Lawyering for your ex — what's that all about? She must be paying you a boatload of Trey's money.'

'She doesn't have any money. All of Trey's money goes to his sister.'

Goose grunted. 'He stiffed her, too, huh? Figures.' He sucked on the cigar and blew out smoke. 'You know, I've always wondered something, about Rebecca?'

129

'What's that?'

'Is she a natural redhead?'

'Goose, as a general rule, I don't punch caddies, but I'm willing to make an exception with you.'

Goose grinned. 'Still touchy about the ex, huh? Wait'll you got three of them.' He stood and said, 'I gotta pee.'

Goose hefted the big bag. He ducked under the rope that kept the fans off the range and walked off. He didn't pick up his beer can.

'Are they here? Brett and Tess?'

Nick shook his head. 'Brett played this morning – today's the pro-am – then had a corporate gig this afternoon. Tess goes with him, makes him seem more attractive, if you know what I mean.'

'They'll be here through Sunday?'

'If his play this year holds true, Brett'll miss the cut, fly home Friday night. You want to talk to them, you'd better come out tomorrow or Friday. I'll be here.'

Scott pulled a pen from his pocket. He squatted and inserted the pen into the top opening of Goose's beer can.

'I'll buy you a beer, Scott.'

'I don't want the beer. I want Goose's fingerprints.'

'Why?'

Scott looked up at Nick. 'Because Goose might've stuck that butcher knife in Trey Rawlins' chest.'

Chapter 16

'Galveston nine-one-one. What's your emergency?'
  'There's a knife in his chest!'
  'Whose chest?'
  'There's blood everywhere!'
  'Whose blood?'
  'I think he's dead!'
  'Who's dead?'
  'Someone killed him!'
  'Who?'
  'Trey! Trey Rawlins!'
  'The golfer?'
  'Yes!'
  'Ma'am, I'm dispatching police to your location.'
  'Thank God! Hurry!'
  'Who killed him?'
  'I don't know.'
  'Is anyone else in the house?'
  'I . . . I don't know. I hope not.'
  'Where are you?'
  'In our bedroom.'
  'Stay there. Stay on the phone until the police arrive.'

'*I hear the sirens. Tell them to come up the back stairs. The doors are open. I'm right inside.*'

'*What's your name?*'

'*Rebecca Fenney.*'

'*Stay with me, Rebecca.*'

A few minutes passed. The dispatcher's voice could be heard in the background and Rebecca's intermittent '*Oh, God*' and '*Trey*' and '*so much blood*'.

Then the dispatcher's voice came back on. '*You still with me, Rebecca?*'

Her voice sounded weak: '*Yes.*'

'*Rebecca, the police are there.*'

In the background: '*Police! We're coming in!*'

'*I'm in here! Thank God you're here!*'

'*Ma'am, are you okay?*'

'*Yes.*'

'*Don't move until we clear the house.*'

In the background: '*House is clear. Ma'am, hang up the phone, I've got dispatch on my radio . . . Dispatch, it's a murder scene. Send out homicide, ME, crime scene . . . Shit, send everyone.*' A pause. '*The poor bastard.*'

The tape ended, and they sat without speaking. It was the next morning, and Scott and Bobby were sitting in the Jetta outside St Patrick's Cathedral listening to the 911 call on the CD player and looking at the crime scene photos of Rebecca with Trey Rawlins' blood streaked down her face like war paint. Parked across the street was a satellite TV truck; loitering nearby was Renée Ramirez in a tight short skirt.

'The DA was right,' Bobby said.

'About what?'

'Renée. She does have great legs.'

Inside the church, the funeral mass for Trey Rawlins was taking place.

'You think the caddie killed him?' Bobby asked.

'Goose has big hands and a good motive – a hundred thousand dollars.'

132

'A bus token will get you killed in some parts of Dallas. You gonna take his prints to the DA?'

'Tomorrow, at the grand jury. We wouldn't get them back in time anyway, and Rex wouldn't stop the indictment even if Goose's prints match those on the kitchen counter, not with Rebecca's prints on the murder weapon. After the hearing, I'm going back out to the tournament, talk to Brett and Tess McBride, get their prints. Trey and Tess, that's a good motive for a jealous husband. You were right, Trey cheated on Rebecca.'

'She cheated on you, he cheated on her. Funny how that works.'

'Yeah. Funny.'

'Least we've got more suspects.' Bobby ticked them off on his fingers. 'The three unidentified sets of prints at the house, the construction workers—'

'Is Carlos on that?'

'He hired on yesterday.' Back to his fingers. 'Goose, Brett, and . . .'

'Rebecca.' Bobby nodded. 'She didn't sound like a killer on that 911 call.'

'No, she didn't. But her prints were on that knife stuck in Trey's chest.'

'The others had motives, Bobby. She didn't.'

'Unless she knew about Trey and Tess.'

'Yeah. Unless.' Scott considered that possibility. 'Only if Trey were leaving her for Tess. What else?'

'Karen's reviewing Trey's endorsement contracts—'

SSI's legal department had released copies without a subpoena.

'—and running assets searches on Trey and Rebecca. I've been through the murder book, read all the witness statements and police reports. I'm waiting for the final autopsy report, toxicology, and DNA.'

'Grand jury will indict tomorrow, we'll fast-track the trial, so you and Karen prep for that.'

'Yep. Oh, I went out to Trey's country club, talked to the

133

assistant pro. He said Trey came out that morning, Thursday, but he left just after noon, didn't come back.'

'Rebecca said he practiced all day, while she shopped in Houston.'

'He lied.'

'About a lot of things.'

Bobby gestured at the church. 'They're coming out.'

He grabbed the camcorder and filmed the funeral guests exiting the church.

'That's Trey's sister,' Rebecca said. 'Terri hates me.'

The image on the screen was of a young woman in a black dress. Scott, Bobby, Karen, and Rebecca were inside watching the funeral tape. The girls were outside with Consuela and the baby. Louis was watching them. Carlos was roofing.

'Why?'

'She thought I was too old for him, didn't want him to marry me. At least that's what he said.' She shook her head. 'I should've gone to the funeral.'

'Media was there,' Scott said. 'Wouldn't have been good.' He pointed at the screen. 'There's the DA and his wife, Tom Taylor and his.' An older man in a suit and a woman walked next to them. 'Who's that?'

'I don't know.'

On the screen, Renée Ramirez stuck a microphone in the DA's face, but he waved her off. She wasn't happy.

'Rebecca, you should stay here at the house.'

'Why?'

'That reporter—'

'Renée.'

'You know her?'

'Everyone on the Island knows Renée. She did a profile of Trey.'

'If she finds out you're here, she'll set up camp out front.'

She gestured at the screen. 'Where's Nick? Didn't he come?'

'No.'

'That's odd. I don't see any of the tour players. First round of the tournament in Houston is today, but still . . . you'd think some of the players would've come.'

'Freeze that frame, Bobby.' On the screen was the image of a very pretty and very young blonde woman. She looked like a high school girl. 'Is that Tess McBride?'

'No, that's Billie Jean Puckett. Pete's daughter. I don't see Pete.'

'What does he look like?'

'Like Rambo with a two-iron.'

'She looks like a kid.'

'She's only seventeen. She used to caddie for Pete, until he picked up Goose.'

'After Trey fired him.'

'Down in Mexico.' She frowned. 'You don't think Goose killed Trey?'

'Trey didn't pay Goose the hundred thousand he owed him. Goose wasn't happy about it. Bobby, fast forward to the cemetery.'

The tape sped up then slowed to normal speed. The scene showed a crowd gathered around the gravesite as the casket was lowered into the ground at the Galveston City Cemetery. After the burial, the crowd lingered a while then drifted away. Except for Billie Jean Puckett.

'Why'd she stay after everyone else left?' Rebecca said. 'Why'd she come?'

They watched the image on the tape. The girl sat next to the grave and seemed to be sobbing. Rebecca stared silently at the screen. Finally, she turned to Scott.

'Why'd you think she was Tess?'

'Rebecca . . . Goose said Trey was having an affair with Tess.'

She shook her head. 'No. Tess played around, a lot, but not with Trey. We were friends, she wouldn't do that to me. Neither would Trey.'

'You did it to me.'

'I'm sorry, Scott.'

'No. I mean, it happens. Even when you think it'd never happen.'

'I would've known.'

'I didn't.'

'Will you take a polygraph?'

'To prove I didn't know about Tess?'

'To prove you didn't kill Trey. If you pass, the DA might drop the charges.'

'And if I don't pass?'

Scott didn't say anything.

'Don't worry, Scott, I'll pass. I'm not the Guilty Groupie.'

'So you'll do it?'

'Sure. And I don't believe Trey had an affair with Tess.'

That she agreed to take a polygraph told Scott all he needed to know about his client. But there was more he needed to know about his ex-wife.

'Why didn't you tell me the truth back then? How you really felt?'

They were walking the beach at sunset. With ten people living in the house, the beach offered the only privacy available for a confidential conversation between an attorney and his client – or a man and his ex-wife.

'Scott, we learn when we're girls to lie to men.'

'Why?'

'To survive. So we don't hurt our man's fragile psyche and lose him and our place in life. "Yes, honey, of course, you're the first". "Of course, you're the best". "Of course, I came".'

'Did you lie to me about that?'

'No.'

'Are you lying now?'

'No.'

'How do I know?'

'You don't. Men never know when we're lying to them. Men don't want to know. Men can't handle the truth.'

'Do all women lie?'

'All women live in a man's world, so all women lie. They have to. At least all women who depend on a man for their survival. Everything we need comes from a man – our homes, our cars, our jewelry, our shoes – because it's a man's world. You see on TV these women writing books about dating and marriage, they're all titled "How to Marry a Rich Man". And the advice is to lie. Lie about your past, lie about your future, lie about your needs and wants and desires, lie about who you really are so he'll marry you. We lie to get married and we lie to stay married. We can't tell the truth and risk having our existence taken from us.'

'Men don't have a clue about women, do we?'

'Not a clue.'

They walked through the sand in silence.

'Scott, why do you think women buy millions of romance novels every year?'

'I don't know.'

'Because in romance novels the women aren't dependent on men, not sexually or financially. They're in control of their bodies and their bank accounts, they have the power, they have the money. Not being financially dependent on a man, that's a woman's true romantic fantasy.'

'I guess we should make women take polygraphs before marriage.'

'We'd find a way to beat it. Truth or lie, right or wrong, black or white – that's a man's life. Women live in shades of gray.'

Scott stared down the sand to the girls playing in front of the house with little Maria and Consuela in a Mexican peasant dress. Louis stood nearby reading his book.

'Will Boo and Pajamae lie to men?'

'Yes, they will.'

'I don't want them to.'

'Then go back to Ford Stevens and make millions so they'll be financially independent. So they can be honest with the men in their lives. So they don't have to hide who they really are. So they won't have to compete for their men every day of their lives.'

'Compete for their men?'

'Scott, a woman always has to compete for her man.'

'Why?'

'Because in every woman's life, there's always another woman.'

Rebecca spoke as if reading a verse from the Bible.

'The players competed on the course, we competed for the players off the course. More tour women working out in the fitness trailer than tour players.'

'That's what Nick said.'

She patted her flat abs. 'Two hundred sit-ups a day, an hour on the StairMaster, another hour on the Bowflex. I could compete.'

She was in very good shape. Which was evident in the skimpy yellow bikini. The sea breeze brought her scent to him. He breathed her in.

'And it's worse for a beautiful woman.'

'Why is it worse to be beautiful?'

'Because a beautiful girl is supposed to be a sex object, not a person. She's supposed to sell her beauty to the highest bidder – that's a beautiful woman's career path. That's how my mother raised me, to be a thing of beauty, to be admired and purchased by a man. And men expect to buy you, just like they buy a sports car. A beautiful woman is a possession a man shows off to other men, and when that possession gets a little dinged up, he trades it in for a new model. You saw the women out there on tour – you see any ugly women with those rich golfers?'

'No. So you knew about Trey and Tess?'

'No. But I'm not stupid. On tour, there are always women making themselves available to the players. Christ, Tess McBride was a Hooters girl.'

'She placed second in the Miss Hooters pageant.'

'I placed first in the Miss SMU pageant, and there's not a Hooters girl in the world who can compete with an SMU coed.'

She was right.

'I'm going to talk to her. Tess.'

'When?'

'Tomorrow, at the tournament.'

'Why?'

'Because I think someone on the pro golf tour killed Trey.'

138

Chapter 17

Four fail-safes exist to protect the accused in the American criminal justice system: the district attorney, the grand jury, the judge, and the trial jury.

In Texas, politics quickly overcomes the district attorney and the judge – they're lawyers, they're ambitious, and they're elected. And emotion and prejudice overcome trial juries before they are even seated. By the first day of trial, the publicity surrounding the case – especially a high-profile murder case – has overwhelmed the jurors' impartiality. Judgments have already been made, if not rendered. Every lawyer knows that there is no such thing as an impartial jury. Everyone is partial. Which leaves the grand jury as an innocent person's only hope for justice.

In Texas, one shouldn't hold out much hope.

Grand juries in Texas are selected pursuant to the 'key man' system: the presiding judge picks three grand jury commissioners – that is, three friends – who in turn pick twelve grand jurors – their friends – who then sit as the grand jury. A few judges have recognized the bias inherent in the key man system and have opted for random selection of grand jurors from voter registration records – but only a few, because to buck the system is to ensure that you will never move up to higher judicial office.

Judge Shelby Morgan wanted to move up.

Scott sat on the front row and observed the twelve friends – the Galveston County Grand Jury – gathered that morning in the courtroom. Non-lawyers would expect a grand jury to be just that: grand. Special. Noble. It wasn't. It was painfully normal. The jurors were all white men, which did not present a constitutional issue since Rebecca Fenney was white. Only one juror wore a tie; the others wore shirts and slacks or jeans. One owned an Italian restaurant, another a furniture store, a third an insurance agency. One was a dentist, another the plant manager at a refinery. All were BOI – born on the Island. It seemed more like a meeting of the local rotary club than a grand jury about to decide whether an American citizen should stand trial for murder.

They did not appear mean-spirited. In fact, they appeared like the men you might meet on the street, men who smiled and said 'hidi' and held doors open for ladies, men who readily stopped and fixed a stranded woman's flat tire, men who attended church. They were just regular folks who cared about their community.

And like regular folks, they feared crime.

They saw on television and read in newspapers about brutal, stupid, senseless violent crimes committed every day in America, and they were afraid. They couldn't keep criminals off the Island, so they did the only thing they knew to keep their Island safe: they indicted every person the district attorney brought before them. And why shouldn't they? They had voted for the DA. They trusted him. If he said someone should stand trial, who were they to question his judgment? They weren't lawyers. He was. They didn't know the law. He did. And he had promised to keep them safe from crime.

No lawyer in America holds more power than a county prosecutor.

At exactly nine o'clock, Galveston County Assistant Criminal District Attorney Theodore Newman, his face aglow with a

140

prosecutor's power, stood and told the grand jurors that Rebecca Fenney murdered Trey Rawlins by stabbing an eight-inch butcher knife from her own kitchen into his chest while he slept in their bed. He called one witness, Detective Chuck Wilson, who testified that Rebecca Fenney's fingerprints were found on the murder weapon.

None of the grand jurors asked a single question.

By law, no one – not even the district attorney – is allowed inside the room while the grand jurors deliberate and vote to either 'true bill' – indict – or 'no bill' – decline to indict – the accused. So at nine-fifteen that morning, Scott was sitting outside on a bench in the corridor. The fact that a grand jury was voting at that very moment to indict his ex-wife for murder – and knowing he was powerless to stop it – made his face flush hot. He would have to tell the mother of his child that she would stand trial for murder and that if convicted, she could be sentenced to life in prison.

But not to death.

The death penalty may be assessed only for 'capital murders': serial murders; murders of children, cops, firefighters, judges, and prison guards; murders committed in the course of a rape, kidnapping, robbery, or arson; and murders for hire. Simply shooting, stabbing, or beating another human being to death with a baseball bat will get you five years to life in prison.

If the district attorney had his way, Rebecca Fenney would spend the rest of her life inside those bleak brick buildings behind the tall fence with concertina wire. Her ex-husband was her only hope.

Scott's face still felt hot when the world around him suddenly turned a bright searing white. He thought the girls' fear had come true – he really was having a heart attack or perhaps a stroke – until he heard a female voice: 'Mr Fenney, do you think the grand jury will indict your wife?'

Scott shielded his eyes from the light and saw a woman holding a microphone in his face. Renée Ramirez.

'Ex-wife.'

Scott stood and walked down the hall to the men's room.

★ ★ ★

141

By nine-thirty, the grand jury had voted to indict Rebecca Fenney for murder.

Indictment starts the clock ticking in the American criminal justice system. Both the US and Texas Constitutions guarantee the right to a speedy trial. Under federal law, the defendant must be tried within seventy days of indictment; the general rule under Texas law is one hundred eighty days, unless the defendant agrees to a continuance. Most do. Rebecca Fenney would not. She could not afford to live in doubt for more than six months, and her lawyer could not afford to live in Galveston for more than sixty days.

The clock was now ticking on Rebecca Fenney's freedom.

Renée Ramirez had retreated to the first-floor lobby, and Scott was again sitting on the bench outside the grand jury room when the DA sat down next to him. Rex Truitt's face was not aglow with power; it was weary with the responsibility of putting American citizens in prison for the last twenty-eight years.

'You really gonna do it? Defend her?'

Scott nodded. 'I have to.'

'Bring her in Monday. I'll hold the warrant till then. We'll book her and arraign her. Nine A.M.'

'Thanks, Rex. That wouldn't happen in Dallas.'

'This ain't Dallas.' The DA loosened his tie. 'Might want to leave out the back way. Renée's out front. She's a goddamn pit bull with makeup.' The DA leaned back. 'Twenty years, Scott.'

'What?'

'Plea bargain. Twenty years for her guilty plea. Life expectancy of a white female in the US is seventy-eight. She'll be eligible for parole in ten. We'll agree not to oppose it. She'll be forty-five, have thirty-three good years left. But if we go to trial, Scott, we're asking for life without parole. She did it, and the jury will convict her.'

'She didn't do it, Rex.'

'You find any evidence of that?'

'I found someone with a motive to murder Trey.'

'Who?'

'His ex-caddie. Clyde Dalton, goes by "Goose".'

'I've seen him on TV. What's his story?'

'Trey fired him down in Mexico a few months ago—'

'I remember something about that.'

'Then refused to pay Goose the hundred thousand he owed him.'

'A hundred grand? That's what caddies make?'

'Ten percent for a win.'

'Shit, I should've been a caddie.'

'Goose wasn't happy about it. He was caddying in Florida last Thursday for another player, but he flew back to Austin that same day, got in at five, which means—'

'He could've driven down here in time to kill Trey.'

Scott nodded.

'Except his prints aren't on the murder weapon.'

Scott reached into his briefcase and removed the baggie holding Goose's beer can. 'His prints are on this can. I can get a private lab to run them, but you could have the state lab run them, see if they match the unidentified prints at the crime scene. See if he was in Trey's house that day.'

'You trust me not to hide the results?'

Scott looked the DA in the eye. 'I do.'

The DA took the baggie. 'Okay, I'll run 'em. What else?'

'We learned some things about Trey.'

'Such as?'

'Porn and Viagra.'

'You're gonna put him on trial, aren't you?'

'No. I'm going to find his killer.'

'Just look across the dinner table tonight.' He ran his hand through his white hair. 'Scott, I take Viagra. Hell, every guy over forty out at the club swears by that blue pill. It's the elixir of youth, and it's legal. So is porn. Stay in a five-star hotel and you can watch it for free. Not my cup of tea, but what a man does is his business, as long as he doesn't do it with children or in public.'

'But porn and Viagra – that doesn't exactly fit his All-American

143

chocolate-milk public image, does it? Maybe there's another side to Trey Rawlins.'

'Scott, some pro athletes are exactly what they seem to be. Some don't have a dark side.'

'Rex, you ever heard of denial?'

'Have you?'

'Trey never executed a will.'

He was the older man in the suit at the funeral. And Melvyn Burke wore a suit that hot and humid Friday morning. He had practiced law on the Island for forty-two years. Wills and estates mostly, some contracts and real estate. He was representing the Estate of Trey Rawlins and he appeared to be carrying the weight of the world on his slumped shoulders. Thirty minutes after leaving the courthouse, Scott sat on the other side of Melvyn Burke's desk.

'So under the intestacy laws,' Melvyn said, 'his entire estate goes to his only surviving relative, Terri Rawlins, his sister. Rebecca's entitled to nothing.'

'You represented Trey on all his legal matters?'

Melvyn nodded. 'Except his endorsement contracts. His agent handled those. I handled his personal matters – the house, cars, boat. Rex let you take Rebecca's clothes from the house?'

'And makeup. Can she have her jewelry? They were gifts from Trey.'

'I'll talk to Terri.' He exhaled heavily. 'She's really got the red ass for Rebecca.'

'Why?'

'Because she thinks Rebecca killed her twin brother.'

'What do you think?'

'I think you should hire another lawyer to represent your wife.'

'Melvyn, I couldn't afford to hire myself. Why?'

'Because a lawyer can only defend his client. He can't love her, too. You lose, Scott, it'll ruin your career. And your life.'

'Would you stand by and watch an innocent person be sent to prison?'

Melvyn's eyes dropped, and Scott knew there was more to learn from Melvyn Burke. Behind his eyes resided a lifetime of clients' secrets – and the burden that comes with keeping them secret. For a moment, Scott thought Melvyn would not speak again. But he finally looked up and said, 'The car is hers.'

'What car?'

'The red Corvette. Trey had me put the title in her name.'

Melvyn opened a clasp folder and removed a set of car keys. He slid them across the desk to Scott.

'Car's not part of the probate estate. You can take it.'

'What are you going to do with the rest of Trey's property?'

'Estate sale. Terri doesn't want the house where her brother was killed or the Bentley he drove. And she lives in Austin, so she's got no use for the yacht. With the economy, it's not exactly the best time to sell a two-million-dollar boat. Broker says we'll be lucky to get five hundred thousand.'

'Was Trey involved in any lawsuits?'

'No.'

'Melvyn, you got any idea who might've killed him?'

'Rex says your wife did.'

'She didn't. I'm trying to find the real killer.'

'So what do you want from me?'

'Information. About Trey. Did he say anything to you? About anything going on in his life? Anything that might tell us who killed him? Was he going to marry Rebecca?'

'Attorney-client privilege, Scott.'

'Your client's dead.'

'The privilege lives on, you know that.'

'His sister is his personal representative. She can waive it.'

'She won't.'

Scott held out his card. 'That's my cell phone. If you think of anything, Melvyn, please call me. I don't want an innocent person to go to prison.'

'Grand jury indict her?'

'This morning.'

Chapter 18

Murder is about motive. A reason to kill. The district attorney was right: there's always a reason for one human being to kill another. But Rebecca Fenney had no reason to kill Trey Rawlins. She had no motive to murder.

But Goose did. Men kill for money. Trey had refused to pay the one hundred thousand dollars he owed Goose. Bobby was also right: in some parts of America a few bucks will get you killed. A hundred thousand was a whole lot of motive.

And Brett McBride had a motive: Trey was having sex with his wife. Men kill in fits of rage and passion. History is replete and prisons are crowded with men who caught their wives having sex with another man and who then murdered that man – although until recently such an act had been deemed justifiable homicide in Texas.

Rebecca Fenney had no motive to murder Trey Rawlins, but she still stood indicted for his murder. She would stand trial and, if convicted, be sentenced to prison for life. Unless Scott found the real killer. Someone who had a motive to murder.

He was betting on a jilted caddie or a jealous husband.

★   ★   ★

Scott walked through the entrance gate to the Houston Classic just after one that same day. The circus atmosphere and WM squared and two-pieces had returned for the second round. He went into the merchandise tent and purchased an official tournament tote bag then found Nick Madden outside a hospitality tent drinking a beer and talking on his cell phone.

'Shit, is that a felony? . . . How old was she? . . . Sixteen? . . . He could just deny it, say she's lying 'cause he's a big star . . . Oh, they got DNA evidence? . . . Dumbass never heard of safe sex? . . . What's he looking at? . . . Five to ten? . . . Jesus, that's gonna kill his endorsements.'

He noticed Scott and held up a finger. He soon disconnected.

'Football player. His idea of a good time is getting stoned and screwing a high school girl. Sophomore. How am I supposed to make money off guys like that?' He sighed and shook his head. 'We create the perfect public image for our athletes – teach them how to say a complete sentence without using the F-word, dress them up, get their teeth whitened, surround them with kids . . . then they have a fucking profanity-filled meltdown on national TV or they get caught with drugs or dog-fighting or carrying a loaded gun into a New York nightclub or screwing an under-aged girl and their perfect image is blown to kingdom come . . . and their endorsements with it. WM squared don't like that kind of shit, Scott.'

He took a swig of his beer then pointed a thumb at the tent behind him that bore the name of a national bank.

'Bank's broke, using their bailout money for a beer bash.' He held up his bottle. 'Beer's free – you want one?'

'No thanks.'

'So, did the grand jury indict her?'

'This morning.'

'Goose still a suspect?'

'The prime suspect.'

'But Rebecca's going to trial?'

'Unless I find the killer.'

'What if you already have?'

147

'Why didn't you go to the funeral?'

'I was working a deal for another client, corporate sponsorship—'

'That's more important than Trey's funeral?'

'It was for that client – I got him two million, just to put a company logo on his bag and cap.' He drank his beer. 'Look, Scott, athletes are high-risk clients. Some are gonna self-destruct, with alcohol or drugs or girls' – he held up his cell phone – 'like this guy. He's making ten million this year, next year he's gonna be making license plates. That's just the way it is with pro athletes.'

'Did Trey self-destruct?'

Nick averted his eyes just as a loud cheer went up from the eighteenth green.

'Someone made a putt.'

'No tour player showed up.'

Nick turned his palms up. 'Can't have a funeral on Thursday – first round of the tournament.' He chuckled. 'Some guys out here had their kids' births induced so they wouldn't interfere with their tournament schedules. No way a funeral gets priority.'

'Where can I find Brett and Tess McBride?'

'Brett's on the course, which means Tess is in the margarita tent.'

Nick led the way toward another white tent.

'Tell me about him.'

'Not much to tell. Brett's only claim to fame is that he's a dead ringer for that guy in *Sling Blade*. Could be why Tess cheats on him. Anyway, Brett's thirty-seven and on the downside of his career, not that he ever really had an upside. Fifteen years on tour, he's never come close to winning.'

'How can he make a living out here if he never wins?'

'Because everyone on tour makes at least a million. See, Scott, maybe twenty players got a real chance of winning out here, the rest of the guys are just fillers – they fill out the field. But it beats working for a living as a country club pro, giving lessons to old ladies and selling shoes. Brett played every tournament last year, never finished higher than thirtieth, still made over a million.

Two years ago, he finished in the top ten at Tahoe – you'd think he'd won the fucking Super Bowl.'

'What's Tess's story?'

Nick just grinned.

'Every time I see her, I want to order chicken wings and a beer.'

Tess McBride was lean, blonde, and dressed like a Hooter's girl. She wore red short-shorts and a white T-shirt tight across her ample bosom. They were admiring Tess from across the tent where waitresses in miniskirts and cowboy boots served cold beer to WM squared and margaritas to hot two-pieces. A big screen TV broadcasting the tournament hung on one wall of the tent, a beer booth with neon signs occupied another, and a margarita bar with a tiki hut decor the third. Tess stood near the margarita machine and held a big plastic goblet filled with a slushy green concoction. Two young men who looked like college athletes bookended her.

'She's twenty-four,' Nick said as they weaved their way around tables toward her. 'Thirteen years younger and a helluva lot better looking than Brett. The money improves his looks, but still . . .'

When they arrived, Nick interrupted her conversation with the young men like a father breaking up a teenage groping session on the den couch.

'Excuse us, boys, but we need to talk with *Missus* McBride.'

The men recoiled as if Tess had suddenly revealed a nasty rash.

'You're *married*?' one of the men said.

Tess answered with a lame shrug. The college boys retreated to the beer booth.

'Thanks a lot, Nick.'

'You *are* married, Tess.'

'I was just having a little fun.'

'You're always just having a little fun.'

'You sound like my mother when I was in high school.'

'Well, Tess, corporate sponsors don't like their athletes' wives acting like horny high school girls. You keep this up, they'll dump Brett and you'll be back waiting tables at Hooters.'

149

She smiled at Scott. 'I finished second in the Miss Hooters Pageant last year.'

Nick rolled his eyes. 'So you've told everyone on tour.'

'Which got me a spread in *Playboy*.'

'And you sure as hell spread 'em.'

Tess looked Scott up and down. He had stopped off at the house and changed into jeans, sneakers, and a polo shirt. She leaned into him, close enough for him to smell the tequila on her breath.

'And who are you, cowboy?'

'Scott Fenney.'

Her eyes lingered on him for the long moment that it took for his name to register in her cloudy mind. She frowned and leaned away.

'You're Rebecca's . . .'

'Ex,' Nick said.

'Lawyer,' Scott said. 'I need to ask you about Trey.'

'I gotta go.'

'I can subpoena you.'

'I can lie.'

'In a court of law that's called perjury.'

'And that means what to me?'

She took a step.

'I can also subpoena Brett.'

She stopped. 'You're a bastard.'

'I'm a lawyer.'

'That's what I said.' She inhaled the margarita then exhaled. 'What do you want to know?'

'Were you having an affair with Trey?'

'My sex life is private.'

Nick laughed. 'Since when?'

She flashed him a dirty look.

'Tess,' Scott said, 'I can talk to Brett if you'd prefer.'

'He'll divorce me if he finds out . . . maybe.'

'So you and Trey were having an affair?'

She shrugged a yes.

'How long?'

She held her hands apart.

'No. How long did your affair last?'

'Oh.' She giggled. 'Two months. Until the Riviera.'

'You traveled to the Riviera together?'

'I wish. The Riviera tournament in LA. Back in February.'

'The affair ended four months prior to his death?'

She counted on her fingers. 'February, March, April, May . . . Yes.'

'But you did have an affair with Trey?'

'We had a little fling. Started at the Hope, ended at Riviera.' She smiled. 'Our California swing.'

She drank her margarita and asked the bartender for another.

'Why?' Scott said.

She shrugged. 'Why not? We were just having a little fun. Which I don't have with Brett. Before we got married, we partied every night. Now all he wants to do is sit in the hotel room and watch CNN. Nancy Grace.'

Nancy Grace – 'Justice Served Nightly' – was a popular legal affairs talk show.

'Matter of fact, Nancy had a segment about Trey's case last night.' She frowned at Scott. 'Are you a famous lawyer?'

'Maybe in this part of the world.'

'Are you a rich lawyer in this part of the world?'

'No.'

A knowing nod. 'That's why she left you for Trey.'

Scott started to think like a man, so he forced himself to think like a lawyer.

'So Brett doesn't know about you and Trey?'

'No. And I'd like to keep it that way.'

'Did Rebecca know?'

'Nobody knew. We were discreet.'

Nick laughed again. '"Tess McBride" and "discreet" in the same sentence? I don't think so.'

She made a face and stuck her tongue out at Nick. Scott felt like a recess monitor at the elementary school. Tess drank her margarita and stared at Scott.

151

'You're her ex – but why are you her lawyer?'

'It's called loyalty,' Nick said.

'It's called lunacy,' Tess said.

Nick chuckled. '*Lunacy?* That's a big word for you, Tess.'

She nodded. 'One of Nancy's guests said it last night. They were all laughing about him and one said, "We know the old saying that a lawyer who represents himself has a fool for a client, but what's a lawyer who has an ex-wife for a client?" Another guest said, "Nuts". They all laughed, and the first one said it's lunacy for a lawyer to defend his ex, said she had no idea why you'd do that. I like Nancy.'

'She's the mother of my child,' Scott said.

Tess's eyes got wide. '*Nancy Grace is the mother of your child?*'

Nick laughed. 'Tess's bra size is also her IQ.'

'Rebecca,' Scott said. 'Rebecca is the mother of my child. That's why I'm defending her.'

'Oh, yeah . . . Boo.' Tess smiled. 'Rebecca showed me her picture. Cute kid.' The smile left her face. 'My mom and dad got divorced when I was ten. It was never the same.' She drank her margarita and said, 'I miss him.'

'Your dad?'

'Trey.'

'Did you love him?'

'My dad?'

'Trey.'

'No. I miss the sex. Best sport sex I ever had.'

'Sport sex?'

'You know, athletic sex . . . wild sex . . . crazy sex.' Tess McBride's eyes glazed over, and she licked her red lips. 'Better-than-a-workout, full-body-sweat, hot-steaming-panting-and-grunting-like-wild-animals sex.'

Scott and Nick blinked hard in unison.

'Wow,' Nick said. 'I didn't even need Viagra.'

'Don't you have sport sex?' Tess said to Scott.

'Not anymore.'

She gave him a coy smile. 'I could help you with that.'

'Did you practice safe sex?'

Rebecca would need to know.

'I'm not stupid.'

'Just loose,' Nick said.

She shot him another dirty look.

'Where was Brett last Thursday night?' Scott said.

'Where else? In a hotel room watching Nancy Grace.'

'He played Friday morning,' Nick said. 'In Orlando.'

'At eight,' Tess said. 'They don't fire up the margarita machine until noon, so I slept in.'

It seemed improbable that Brett could have killed Trey between midnight and three A.M. in Galveston and gotten back to Florida for an eight A.M. tee time. But a defense lawyer never discounted someone with a motive to murder.

'Have you ever been to Trey's beach house in Galveston?'

'No.'

'Has Brett?'

'No. Look, Brett doesn't have the balls to make a five-foot putt to win, much less murder someone . . . or satisfy me.' She shook her head. 'I should've been a Mormon.'

'A *Mormon*?' Nick said.

'Yeah. Then I could have four husbands – one to support me, three to satisfy me.' She smiled. 'And they'd have built-in beer buddies. A win–win deal.'

Nick stared at her in apparent disbelief at what he had just heard.

'Tess, Mormon women don't get four husbands. Mormon men get four wives.'

'*Really?* Well, that sucks.'

Tess downed her margarita. She placed the goblet on the bar and waved to the bartender. Scott opened the tote bag and pulled out one of the freezer-sized Ziploc plastic baggies he had brought with him that day. He reached past Tess, took the goblet by the stem between his fingers, and dropped it into the baggie. He then put the baggie into the tote bag. Tess had observed Scott's actions with a wry smile.

'I didn't kill him.'

'Who did?'

'Maybe Rebecca. She's the Guilty Groupie.'

'Was she?'

'Guilty?'

'A groupie?'

'No. I'm a groupie. I love having sex. She loves having things.'

'So why would she kill Trey and lose everything?'

'She wouldn't.'

'Did he say anything about marrying her?'

'When? While we were having sex?'

'Anytime.'

'That was the only time I saw him. And no, he didn't.'

She sipped the fresh margarita the bartender had delivered.

'You ever see them fighting?'

'No. Never. They were happy.'

'Did they drink?'

'Everyone on tour drinks. There's a lot of free time.'

'Why didn't they get married?'

A shrug. 'She didn't want to push him, risk losing everything.'

'Why'd you end the affair?'

'I didn't. He did.'

'Why?'

 ''Cause he started up with Lacy.'

'*Lacy Parker?*' Nick said.

Tess nodded. 'I told him we could do a threesome, but Trey was kind of small-town, you know. He would only cheat with one woman at a time.'

Scott turned to Nick. 'Who's Lacy?'

'Donnie Parker's wife. Hot little number, used to do porn movies. They met during the first round of the Vegas tournament, got married right after the last round.' He shook his head. 'Something about Vegas.'

Scott turned back to Tess. 'Did Rebecca know about Lacy?'

'She never said anything to me. We were friends.'

'*Friends?* And you had an affair with Trey?'

154

She shrugged. 'I was better friends with him.'

'What about Donnie?'

She laughed. 'No way. Shortest driver on tour.'

Scott turned to Nick. 'What's his story?'

'His story is, I can't buy an endorsement for a player married to a former porn queen. One day he was bitching because of all the endorsements I got for Trey, I told him, "Donnie, patrons of porn don't get paid to endorse chocolate milk!"'

'Were they at the Orlando tournament? Lacy and Donnie?'

'No,' Nick said. 'They were home in San Diego. Donnie's been rehabbing a bum rotator cuff the last two weeks, with his therapist out west.'

'But if Trey was having an affair with Lacy at the time of his death—'

'He wasn't,' Tess said.

'How do you know?'

'Because he left her for Riley.'

'*Riley Hager?*' Nick said. He threw his hands up. 'Jesus, is there any woman on tour Trey didn't screw?'

Tess's eyebrows crunched slightly, as if she were thinking.

'Maybe the older wives.'

Nick faced Scott. 'Riley is Vic Hager's wife. He's ranked fifteenth in the world. He made the cut in Orlando, finished eleventh.'

'And you're his agent, too?'

Nick shrugged. 'Riley used to be an underwear model in LA. She was voted second hottest WAG on tour.'

'What's a WAG?'

'Wives and girlfriends. There's an online rating system for athletes' WAGs, for each sport. It's a big deal, all the girls want the title.'

'I was third,' Tess said with pride.

'Who was first?'

Nick and Tess exchanged a glance.

'Rebecca,' Scott said.

Nick nodded.

'She's eleven years older than me,' Tess said, 'and her body is still perfect. And abs like that after a baby? Amazing.'

Scott turned to Nick. 'You didn't know about this?'

'Yeah, her abs are amazing.'

'No. About Trey's affairs?'

'I was his agent, Scott, not his pimp.'

'What's the deal out here, all this *Desperate Housewives* stuff?'

'You got four groups of players on tour.' Nick ticked them off on his fingers. 'You got your single guys, they screw everything with tits. You got your guys with girlfriends, they party hard every night. You got your married without children – some stray, some don't. Most of the guys are real sticklers about the Rules of Golf, not so much the vows of marriage. And you got your married with children, they bring the wives and kids on tour during the summer, it's like being in fucking McDonald's every day. Trey – I guess he found those wives looking for a little fun. Like Tess.'

'My middle name,' she said with a smile.

'No wonder we found Viagra in Trey's bathroom.'

'Hell, looks like he was servicing half the women on tour. Can't keep that up on protein shakes alone.' Nick smiled. 'They pop those blue pills like M&Ms out here.'

Scott turned back to Tess. 'Why?'

'Why what?'

'Why did all these wives have affairs with Trey? Why did you?'

She smiled. 'You saw him – he was gorgeous. Our husbands aren't. Jesus, Brett looks like that guy in *Sling Blade*.'

'But you married him,' Nick said.

''Cause he's rich. Sort of. And I was really drunk that night.'

'Ah, true love.'

'Did Rebecca know about Riley?' Scott said.

'She didn't act like it,' Tess said.

'So at the time of his death, Trey was having an affair with Riley Hager?'

'No.'

'But you just said—'

156

'I said he left me for Lacy and Lacy for Riley. But he left Riley, too.'

'For whom?'

'Billie Jean.'

'*Billie Jean Puckett?*' Nick said.

She nodded. 'He started up with her a few weeks before he . . . died.'

Nick, to Scott: 'Pete's daughter. She's seventeen.'

'Hard to compete with a teenager who doesn't even know how to spell cellulite,' Tess said. 'Even for Riley.'

They left Tess to the margarita machine and walked outside. Scott needed a breath of fresh air, even if the air were ninety-five degrees.

'Five WAGs plus the Mexican gal, all before the US Open,' Nick said. 'That's a whole season for most guys.'

'Is every WAG out here a Hooter's girl, a porn queen, or an underwear model?'

'No, of course not, Scott. Some are former *Playboy* Playmates and *Penthouse* Pets. For gorgeous gals like Tess and Lacy and Riley, those gigs are straight shots to the altar with a rich athlete.'

'Why?'

''Cause that's where pro athletes shop for wives. *Playboy* and *Penthouse*, that's like the social register for them. Guy wins the World Series, he marries a Playmate. Guy wins the NBA championship, he marries a Pet. Guy wins the Super Bowl, he marries a supermodel.'

'Why?'

'Because he can. See, Scott, football and basketball stars, they've had gorgeous gals all through high school and college, they ain't suddenly gonna settle for the nice girl next door. Did you? And golfers, they've been dreaming of having a gal like Tess or Lacy or Riley since they were thirteen with acne and whacking off in the shower. They were the guys who had to wear husky pants, who didn't have a date to the prom, who weren't good enough athletes to play football or basketball. So their dads took them out to the golf course. Ten years later, they're on tour and filthy rich.

157

Now they can have those girls they dreamed about. This is their adolescence – with money.'

Tess McBride had walked up.

'The margarita machine break down?' Nick said with a smile. But Tess wasn't smiling.

'There's something else you should know,' she said.

'What?'

'Pete knew . . . about Trey and Billie Jean.'

'How do you know?'

'Pete confronted Trey in the locker room at the Challenge, slammed him up against the lockers. Brett was there and . . .'

'And what?'

'Pete threatened to kill Trey, if he didn't stay away from Billie Jean.'

Scott walked away fast; Nick caught up.

'Pete's temper is legendary on tour,' Nick said. 'If you haven't been cussed out by Pete Puckett, you either haven't been on tour very long or your name is Tiger.'

'Tell me about him,' Scott said.

'Pete's ranked five-seventy-eight in the world, which means there are high school juniors ranked higher than him. Won the British Open twenty-four years ago, a few minor tournaments along the way. He's forty-nine now, been running on fumes the last decade, hoping to make it to the senior tour next year, kind of like a pension fund for old golfers.'

'Where does he live?'

'Ranch outside Austin.'

'Where Goose lives.'

Nick nodded.

'Rebecca said he looks like Rambo.'

Nick snorted. 'Shit, he'd kick Rambo's ass. Pete ain't one of these fat boys out here. He's big, got arms like tree trunks, from chopping cedar on his place. And he's an ornery old cuss. Old-style, smokes big cigars, eats red meat, drinks hard liquor, ain't afraid to say what he thinks – more like an Arnold Palmer than a Tiger Woods, but without Arnie's ability. Or charisma. Pete's a prick.'

158

'Anything else I need to know?'

'Yeah – don't piss him off.'

'He threatened to kill Trey a week before he was murdered. Then he DQ'd last Thursday. So if he flew home from Florida with Goose and got into Austin at five, he could've driven to Galveston before midnight. He could've killed Trey.' Scott looked at Nick. 'Or *they* could've killed Trey. Both had motives, the golfer and his caddie. Is that just a coincidence? We've got to find Pete Puckett.'

They found Billie Jean Puckett instead.

They were jogging up the eighteenth fairway when Nick spotted her sitting alone under a tree on the far side of the fairway. Between them and her lay forty yards of green grass roped off on both sides. Allowed inside the ropes were the players, caddies, scorekeepers, officials, on-course reporters and cameramen, marshals, and security for the big-name players. Kept outside the ropes were players' wives, girlfriends, groupies, and children, vendors, sponsors, and agents, and a lawyer trying to defend his ex-wife against a murder charge.

They couldn't cut across the fairway. So they jogged all the way around the green and down the far side. When they got to Billie Jean, she didn't look up. She was leaning back against the tree with her knees pulled up and her arms wrapped around her legs. Her face was buried in her arms. She wore shorts and sneakers and a T-shirt. Her blonde hair was pulled back in a ponytail. Nick spoke softly to her.

'Billie Jean.'

No response. Nick squatted next to her and touched her shoulder.

'Billie Jean.'

She slowly looked up. She was a cute kid. She didn't look like a Hooters girl or an adult movie star or an underwear model. She looked like a high school cheerleader. And she had tears in her eyes.

'Hi, Nick.'

Her voice was small.

'You okay, kiddo?'

She wiped her face. 'Just sad.'

'About Trey?'

She frowned a bit. 'What do you mean?'

'I know . . . about you and Trey.'

'You were at his funeral,' Scott said.

She glanced up at Scott then said to Nick, 'Who's he?'

Nick stood. 'Rebecca's ex-husband . . . and lawyer.'

She held her hand up to Nick. He took her hand and pulled her up.

'Thanks.'

Without another word, she ducked under the rope and ran across the fairway, dodging the players and caddies and marshals and cameramen.

'Shit.'

Scott and Nick looked at each other then shrugged and ducked under the rope and chased her.

'Hey, get off the fairway!' one of the players yelled.

'Nick!' another player shouted. 'What the hell are you doing?'

Nick glanced back and yelled without breaking stride, 'Hey, Paul, I got you three million on your club deal!'

'*Three million?* Wow! Thanks, Nick!'

Paul gave his caddie an enthusiastic chest bump.

They reached the other side, ducked under that rope, and ran on. Billie Jean had a head start, and they weren't gaining on her.

'She's fast for a girl!' Nick yelled.

'She's fast for a human!'

'She's cutting through the margarita tent!'

They ran into the margarita tent. They didn't find Billie Jean, but they found Tess McBride flirting with another Joe College. She pointed to the back exit without being asked or breaking eye contact with her new beau. They ran out back and spotted Billie Jean heading into the merchandise tent. They followed and cut through displays offering golf apparel and equipment and – *shit!* – Scott knocked over a pyramid of golf balls and sent hundreds

160

of balls bouncing off the concrete floor like pin balls. They lost her. They stopped outside the tent and scanned the crowd. Nick jumped up onto an official's golf cart. He pointed like a hunting dog.

'She's heading to the clubhouse!'

They arrived at the clubhouse just in time to see Billie Jean duck inside the door to the ladies' locker room.

'Damn.'

They stood there and caught their breath.

'This is fun,' Nick said.

'Why's she on tour? Shouldn't she be in school?'

'Pete's wife died five years ago, breast cancer. Pete brought Billie Jean out here with him, raised her on tour. Instead of home schooled, she's been tour schooled. She's a real spunky kid, always pulling pranks on the network guys.' He smiled. 'One time she mooned—'

The smile suddenly left Nick's face. He was now staring past Scott. Scott turned and found himself face to face with a large, angry man holding a long iron over his right shoulder like an ax.

'You chasing my girl?'

'Scott,' Nick said, 'meet Pete Puckett.'

Pete Puckett was a tall, thick-bodied man with a hard face and a cigar clamped between his teeth. He looked as solid as a brick outhouse, and from his expression, he possessed a similar personality. His shirt sported dark sweat stains under both arms; his gray hair was matted below his white cap. His thick mustache was gray. His skin was leathery and sun-reddened. He was a golf pro, but he had the hands of a roughneck. Pete Puckett had very big hands – and his left hand was now clenching Scott's shirt.

'Oh, Pete,' Nick said – he was obviously trying to defuse the situation – 'I got you a million, for your club deal.'

Without removing his eyes from Scott, Pete said, 'Thought you said not a penny less than two.'

Nick gave him a lame shrug. 'It's the economy, Pete.'

Pete addressed Scott. 'What do you want with my girl?'

Scott did not feel physically threatened by Pete Puckett – Pete was bigger, but Scott was younger – although that club would certainly leave a mark. And he wanted Pete pissed-off – a pissed-off witness doesn't think before testifying. So, at the risk of a pro golfer swinging a long iron at him, Scott decided to ramp up Pete's anger.

'Did you kill Trey because he was having sex with Billie Jean?'

Pete put his red face close to Scott's; his breath smelled of whiskey and cigars.

'You leave her out of this.'

'She's in it, and so are you, Pete. You threatened to kill Trey. There's a witness.'

Pete released Scott's shirt. 'Who are you?'

'Scott Fenney. I'm Rebecca's lawyer.'

'He's her ex,' Nick said.

'Maybe you killed Trey,' Pete said. 'For taking your wife.'

'I have an alibi – do you? I didn't have a motive. You did.'

'She's only seventeen, goddamnit! But that don't mean I killed him.'

'Did you?'

'No. Your wife beat me to it.'

'How do I know you didn't kill Trey?'

Pete snorted. 'That should be obvious.'

'Why?'

''Cause I wouldn't have stabbed the little bastard. I would've beaten him to death with this fucking one-iron.' Pete pointed a gnarly finger in Scott's face. 'You leave Billie Jean alone or I swear to God I'll take this one-iron to you.'

Pete Puckett pivoted and stormed off. After a long moment, Nick shook his head and chuckled.

'He is such an old-timer. No one carries a one-iron anymore.'

162

Chapter 19

'Mother, did you kill your boyfriend?'

'No, honey, I didn't.'

'So you won't have to live in that prison?'

'What prison?'

'The one we drove past coming down here, in Huntsville.'

'No, I won't have to live there.'

'Good.' She hesitated then said, 'I had to ask.'

'I know.'

'Sometimes I beat up boys at school.'

'You beat up boys?'

Boo nodded. 'When they bully Pajamae. They're big jerks.'

'It's normal to feel that way about boys at your age.'

'But when I'm older I'll like boys?'

'Yes. You will.'

'Are they better then?'

'A little.'

'But you liked boys, right?'

'Oh, yes, I liked boys.'

Boo's anger at her mother had abated over the last few days. She didn't know what abated meant, but A. Scott said it was natural for her to be really angry at Mother at first and then not

163

so much after spending time with her again. These walks on the beach abated her anger, he had said. All Boo knew was that she didn't like to feel so angry. Especially at her mother.

'Boo, it's okay to like boys, but don't ever depend on a man.'

'Except A. Scott. I can depend on him, right?'

'Yes. You can always depend on him.'

From down the street, Scott saw Louis and Pajamae shooting hoops on the basketball court next to the beach house. Boo was a tomboy, but Pajamae was an athlete. She was long and lean and faster than anyone in fifth grade, girls or boys. She played point guard on her 11–12U rec team in Highland Park. The rich little white girls couldn't stay on the court with Pajamae Jones-Fenney. Her dream was to get a college scholarship and then play women's pro basketball – after she got braces.

She would have teeth that looked like pearls.

Driving back from Houston, he had made a decision: even though this case would likely cost him the federal judgeship, he would defend Rebecca, he would prove her innocent, and then he would return to Dallas and provide for his girls – even if it meant returning to a corner office on the sixty-second floor, even if it meant representing rich clients who could pay $750 an hour, even if it meant becoming a name partner in Ford Fenney and making a million dollars every year. He would do what he had to do, and he would do it for his girls. His daughters would not be WAGs or groupies or porn stars or seventeen and having affairs with older men. His daughters would go to Wellesley College so they could be strong, educated, independent women who did not have to lie to survive in a man's world. His daughters would have a chance at a good life, even if their father had to give up his chance and be a rich lawyer again.

A man takes care of his children.

Scott got out of the red Corvette. He had returned from the tournament and picked up Bobby on the way over to Trey's house. The guard had given them entry to the garage. Bobby pulled up in the Jetta and got out with the tote bag containing

164

the fingerprint evidence Scott had collected that day from Tess McBride, Lacy Parker, Riley Hager, and their husbands. He had met Trey's women, all of whom had loved sex with Trey but hadn't loved him and none of whom had heard Trey mention marriage to Rebecca, and their husbands, all of whom seemed completely clueless. They were still suspects, but Pete Puckett was the prime suspect. He wasn't clueless; he knew about Trey and Billie Jean.

'Nice wheels, Mr Fenney,' Louis said.

He and Pajamae had come over to check out the Corvette. Now Rebecca and Boo walked up. Scott turned to Rebecca. She was wearing a confused expression and a green bikini and looking every inch the hottest WAG on tour. He held the keys out to her.

'The car is yours.'

'How?'

'Melvyn Burke – Trey's lawyer – he said title's in your name.'

'Trey never told me.'

'That's not all he didn't tell you.'

'Like what?'

'Let's take a walk.'

They went to the beach and walked to the water's edge and stared out to sea.

'Boo was asking me about boys,' Rebecca said.

'She's at that age – a girl needs a mother.'

Rebecca sighed. 'Tell me.'

'Tess McBride, Lacy Parker, Riley Hager, Billie Jean Puckett . . . Trey had affairs with all of them.'

Her expression told Scott that she did not know.

'No. He was faithful to me.'

'I talked to all of them. They admitted it. Except Billie Jean. She ran.'

She looked away, but Scott saw her tears.

'That's why she came to the funeral,' Rebecca said. 'Billie Jean.'

'Pete threatened me with a one-iron today at the tournament.'

'That's Pete.'

'He also threatened to kill Trey if he didn't stay away from Billie Jean. Brett McBride witnessed it. Happened in the locker room at the Challenge, one week before Trey was murdered.'

She faced him.

'My God – you think Pete killed Trey?'

'He had a motive. But the grand jury indicted you.'

'I don't think they killed him, boss.'

Carlos wore work clothes and work boots, but looked no worse for the wear after a week on the roofing job when he climbed the back stairs to the deck where Scott was sitting. Rebecca had wanted some time alone on the beach. Carlos plopped down in a chair.

'Why not?'

'They're illegals, up here for the work. But a couple of 'em, they got gang tatts. Bad dudes. They'd slice you up for smokes. And they saw the rich dude and the red-haired woman coming and going.'

'So why don't you think they did it?'

''Cause after killing him, they would've raped her and then killed her and stolen everything in the place and probably torched the house then made a run for the border. These are not criminal masterminds, boss.'

He held up a big plastic bag with five beer bottles inside.

'Still, I got their prints.'

'Give those to Bobby. Good work, Carlos. And thanks, I know that wasn't fun.'

Carlos held up several green bills. 'Hey, I made twenty-five bucks.'

'An hour?'

'A day.'

Carlos stood and started to the door but turned back.

'Oh, boss, those workers, they saw another woman down there, at the house.'

'When?'

'Same day he was killed. A blonde girl. And a man – a big man.'

166

Chapter 20

Billie Jean was blonde, and Pete was big.

If Scott could obtain their fingerprints and prove they were in the Rawlins house the day Trey was murdered, he could establish (a) motive – Trey was having sex with Pete's seventeen-year-old daughter, (b) means – the knife was in the kitchen drawer, and (c) opportunity – if those were Pete's prints on the counter, that would confirm his presence in the kitchen that day. He could have taken the butcher knife from the drawer and stabbed Trey Rawlins. With that evidence, the DA might dismiss the indictment against Rebecca Fenney and ask the grand jury to indict Pete Puckett. So Scott had returned to the tournament the next afternoon to find Pete and Billie Jean Puckett, but he had found Nick Madden instead.

'Look, Legend,' Nick was saying into his cell phone, 'you gotta play one year at UT then you can go pro, okay? "One and done", that's the NBA rule. Hell, you don't even have to go to classes. The tutors will get you through the first semester, then once the season starts, you just play basketball. When the season ends in March, you can bail, wait for the draft . . . And that big check. Until then, Hook 'em Horns, baby.'

He disconnected and shook his head at Scott.

'High school player.'

'He already thinks he's a legend?'

'No, that's his name. Legend. Kid's six-ten, top basketball prospect in the state, but he doesn't want to play even one year of college ball. Wants to go straight to the pros. He asked me, Mr Madden, what am I gonna major in? Like he's gonna major in pre-med. I said, pre-NBA. Kid can't balance a checkbook, but he'll be worth fifty million time he's twenty.'

Nick was standing by the putting green drinking a beer. It was Saturday, the third round of the tournament.

'Where's Pete?' Scott said.

'Austin. Withdrew, drove home with Billie Jean yesterday.'

'He's running scared.'

'I guess he's the prime suspect now?'

'He threatened to kill Trey in front of a witness a week before he was murdered. That'd make him the prime suspect.'

'They're flying up to New York on Monday, for the Open next week. Don't know why he's wasting his money, he doesn't have a snowball's chance in hell of even making the cut. They'll be in San Antonio the week after that.'

'I could drive up to his house in Austin tomorrow.'

Nick shook his head. 'Don't even think about it, Scott.'

'Why not?'

'Because Pete's a big hunter.' He chuckled. 'They did one of those "Getting to Know the Player" segments on a network broadcast last year with him. Now the other guys, they introduce mama and the kids, give the viewing audience a tour of their mansion and trophy room, that sort of thing. Not Pete. He takes the reporter and cameraman deer hunting on his place, blows Bambi's head clean off, then field dresses the fucking deer on national TV. Takes his big ol' knife and guts that animal like he's slicing a Thanksgiving turkey. Got blood all over him, made me want to throw up.'

'Pete's good with a knife, huh?'

Nick's expression turned thoughtful. 'Yeah. Real good. Guns, too. You go on his land without an invite, Scott, he's liable to

168

shoot, shovel, and shut up. Safer to wait till San Antonio, at least as safe as it's ever gonna be with Pete.'

'You finished with that beer?'

Nick turned the bottle up then said, 'I am now.'

Scott held a baggie open. Nick looked from his beer bottle to the baggie to Scott. 'You think I killed Trey?'

'No.'

'Why do you want my prints?'

'So I can cross you off the suspect list.'

Nick dropped the bottle into the baggie. 'You do that.'

'Have you ever been arrested, indicted or convicted of a felony?'

'No, Senator, I haven't.'

US Senator George Armstrong had greeted Scott with a handshake and a criminal background check. They were having dinner at Gaido's, a Galveston landmark because of a blue crab the size of a small car perched atop the roof as if waiting to snag an unsuspecting diner with its huge claws. A sign read 'Caught in Galveston Bay'.

'Good. Last year I nominated a guy to head up the Drug Enforcement Agency. FBI fingerprinted him, ran a background check, turns out he had been arrested six times back in college, for drugs. Pretty goddamn embarrassing. Like Obama's Treasury Secretary – guy runs the IRS but forgot to pay thirty-four thousand in taxes. Blamed it on a software program that's moron-proof.'

Scott followed the maitre d' and the senator – who glad-handed every person of voting age in the place – into the main dining room and over to a table by the window with a nice view of the beach across the seawall. Gaido's was an elegant place featuring wood accents, real tablecloths, waiters in white waist-coats, and the aroma of fried seafood. Ken Ingram, the senator's aide, had called Scott just as he was leaving the golf tournament and asked him to join the senator for dinner – 'And if you want to be a federal judge, you'd better be there.' So Scott had braved the big blue crab and entered the restaurant.

169

'Boy, we took a big hit with Ike,' the senator said. 'Seventy-five percent of all homes flooded, three billion in damages here on the Island, twenty-nine billion total . . . but like we say, "It's an ill wind that blows no good".'

'What was the good of Hurricane Ike?'

'Destroyed all the public housing on the Island. Our poor folks are gone.'

'You're not going to rebuild the public housing?'

'If you build it, they will come . . . back. If you don't, they won't.'

'Where will they live?'

'Somewhere else. Austin, maybe. Bunch of goddamned bleeding heart liberals, I'd like to ship every poor person in Texas to Austin, see how much they care then. See, Scott, the public housing crowd, they were holding the Island back – welfare, drugs, crime, test scores dragging down our school system – just like South Dallas is holding Dallas back. Imagine if one day Dallas woke up and South Dallas was gone. Well, that's what Ike did for us. All those folks, they're gone. Now we can transform the Island into another Hamptons like we always wanted. A nice place for rich white folks.'

'Maybe you could put up a gate on this side of the causeway, make the entire Island a gated community.'

The senator frowned. 'You know, that's not a bad idea.'

'I was joking.'

'Oh. Still . . .'

The senator was rich and white. His hair was gray and perfect. He was in his late fifties and wore slacks and a short-sleeve island shirt. Scott had seen him numerous times on the Sunday morning political talk shows. Senator George Armstrong was handsome, articulate, and a leading voice of the Republican Party. He ordered a gin and tonic, folded his hands on the table, and said, 'You know, Scott, when Ken told me you were representing your ex-wife who's charged with murdering the man she ran off with, I said exactly the same thing I said when I first heard that McCain picked Palin for his VP.'

'What's that?'

' "What the hell was he thinking?" ' The senator chuckled. 'Men just don't think straight when it comes to women, do we?'

'She's innocent.'

'No doubt. But Palin cost McCain the White House. You want your wife to cost you the federal bench? You lose this case in my hometown, Scott, I won't be able to back you even if Sam Buford does think you're the best thing to come along in the law since Clarence Darrow. Called me up himself, Buford did, said I'd be dumber than a stump if I didn't appoint you to his bench when he died.'

The waiter dropped off his drink. The senator drank half.

'He's my hero,' Scott said.

'You're a hero to a lot of people, too.'

'SMU fans.'

'Not football, Scott. That murder case, McCall's son.'

'You know about that?'

The senator laughed. 'You went on national TV and accused the senior US senator from Texas of obstructing justice . . . yeah, I know about that.'

'Oh. Look, I . . .'

'Impressed the hell out of me.'

'It did?'

'And a lot of other conservatives, all across the country.'

'Conservatives?'

'Sure. We hate the federal government. You stood up for an American citizen against the United States government. Shit, Scott, they should make a movie about that case. And you should make a fine federal judge.'

Scott couldn't fight a smile. He saw himself entering a court-room as Judge A. Scott Fenney. He could have a good life and still be able to provide for his daughters.

'Why, thank you, Senator.'

The senator downed his drink and gestured to the waiter for another.

'So, Scott, as long as you win this case and pass the FBI's criminal background check, you're number two on the list.'

Scott felt the smile leave him. 'Number *two*?'

'Behind Shelby Morgan.'

'The judge on my ex-wife's murder case?'

The senator nodded.

'Does she know I'm number two?'

'Yep.'

'Well, that should make for a fun trial.'

The senator smiled. 'Like being in bed with a pit bull.'

Scott now saw himself entering the Ford Fenney law firm.

'Sorry, Scott, but I owe her.' The waiter delivered another cocktail. 'That's politics.'

'A federal judgeship isn't about politics, Senator.'

'Since when? Now don't go naïve on me, Scott. You and I both know, *everything* is politics. The Supreme Court decided – actually, six lawyers decided – that there's a constitutional right to an abortion – where's that in the Constitution? They made it up, to suit their politics. Then five lawyers on the Court said "public use" in the Fifth Amendment actually means "public benefit" – like James Madison didn't know the difference between "use" and "benefit" – and the government can condemn your home for a fucking football stadium if it'll generate more taxes. That's not law, Scott, that's politics.'

The senator shook his head.

'Constitutional law is the greatest hoax ever perpetrated on the American people. But both parties love it because a Supreme Court decision trumps democracy. You don't have to convince a majority of the people you're right, just five lawyers. Five fucking lawyers and you win your political victory.' He sipped his drink and shook his head again. 'Everything is politics. Why do Democrats want to grant citizenship to twelve million illegal Mexican immigrants? Because they care about those poor people? No. Because they want twelve million more Democratic voters. Politics. Why do Democrats want a government-run health care system? Because their voters are gonna get free health care, our voters are gonna pay for it. Politics. How much we pay for corn, milk, beef, steel . . . politics. How many miles to the gallon

172

our cars get . . . politics. How much pollution we breathe . . . politics. Who sits on the federal bench . . . also politics.'

Scott felt like the moderator on one of those political talk shows.

'The deal works like this, Scott: Texas senators pick our federal judges, New York senators pick theirs. Someone tries to go around us, we "blue-slip" the nominee, he never gets a committee vote much less a floor vote.'

'What's a blue-slip?'

'Veto, same as being black-balled at a country club. Means the home-state senators can block any judicial nominee for their state. Without blue-slips, the Senate would descend into chaos. Blue-slips keep things orderly.'

'If not democratic.'

'Democracy happens every six years in the Senate, Scott. Rest of the time, politics rules. Which is good for you.'

'Why?'

'Because I voted for Roberts' assault weapons bill.'

Ron Roberts was the senior US senator from Texas.

'He wants to ensure that every American citizen has the unfettered opportunity to buy an assault weapon at a gun show – how stupid is that? He's pro-guns and pro-life and doesn't see the irony. But now he owes me, said I can pick our next federal judge. You're my first choice, but I owe Shelby.'

He didn't specify the debt.

The senator finished off his drink. 'We'll hold off on the background checks until Buford dies. That would look unseemly, I think.'

He ordered another drink.

'I don't like it anymore than you, Scott, having to put Shelby up for federal judge.' He exhaled heavily. 'I guess we can both hope she did something stupid when she was young and fails her criminal background check.'

Chapter 21

Scott arrived back at the beach house just as Bobby was leaving in the Prius.

'How'd it go with the senator?' Bobby asked through his open window.

'I'm number two for the job . . . behind Judge Morgan.'

'You're shitting me? Can this case get any weirder?'

'I have a feeling it can. Another ice cream craving?'

'Mint chocolate-chip. I'm running a tab at the 7-Eleven.' Bobby's ice cream runs had become a nightly occurrence. 'Between diapers and ice cream, I didn't know how expensive a pregnant woman could be.'

'Use a condom,' Boo said.

'*What?*'

'If you have sex with Mother.'

'I won't.'

'Use a condom?'

'Have sex with your mother.'

Scott had climbed the back stairs and gone directly up to the girls' bedroom to tuck them in. He found them huddled together reading a novel about vampires in love. They no longer required his reading services at bedtime. He missed it. They were growing up too fast, and sex ed had only accelerated the aging process. So he had made a deal with them when they had become a single-father family: they could talk to him about anything, ask him any questions they wanted, and he would always tell them the truth and never get mad. They took him up on the deal on a regular basis. Fifth grade had brought a lot of questions about sex. He had learned not to overreact.

'She had sex with that dead man, Mr Fenney. And he had sex with those other women— '

'Were you two eavesdropping?'

'Unh-huh, we sure were, Mr Fenney.'

'If you have sex with Mother, it's just like you're having sex with all the women the dead man had sex with, Ms Nelson said so in health class.'

'AIDS, Mr Fenney.'

'Why were you eavesdropping?'

'I need to know,' Boo said.

'Know what?'

'If Mother killed her boyfriend.'

'She didn't.'

'That's what she said, but she lied to us before.'

'She's not lying about this, Boo. And I'm not going to have sex with her.'

'You used to.'

'When we were married.'

'Do you want to again?'

'Get married?'

'Have sex with her? It would relieve your stress.'

'So you don't have a heart attack, Mr Fenney.'

'A. Scott, are you healthy enough for sexual activity?'

'Boo, you sound like a commercial.'

'Well?'

'Yes. I think. Look, I'm not going to have a heart attack, and I'm not going to have sex with your mother.'

'She might try to seed you,' Pajamae said.

175

'*Seed* me?'

'Sedate you,' Boo said.

'*Sedate?* You mean seduce?'

'That's it. To tempt or lead astray, Ms Nelson said. Boys usually do it to girls, but Ms Nelson said it can go both ways. And Mother's got a lot of sexy clothes, more than she used to have. We looked at her stuff while she was gone.'

Pajamae nodded a confession.

'You shouldn't snoop around her stuff.'

'I used to go into her closet all the time. She's still my mother, you said so yourself.'

'Yes, but – what do you mean, while she was gone?'

'Mother put on her wig and went somewhere in her car today.'

'What wig?'

'A black wig. She said she didn't want anyone to recognize her.'

Scott nodded. 'Reporters. Where'd she go?'

'I don't know. But she was really happy when she got back.'

What would make a woman really happy in the middle of the day? As Scott saw it, there were three possibilities: shopping, chocolate, or sex. She didn't have any money for shopping and chocolate was too fattening for the hottest WAG on tour. That left sex. Was she cheating on Trey? On Scott again?

Scott returned downstairs to the living room where he found Carlos and Louis slouched at opposite ends of the couch and Rebecca and Karen sitting in chairs and staring at the TV. It was a commercial.

'What's a five-letter word for "bank job"?' Louis asked.

'Why?' Carlos said.

'That's three letters.'

'No, why do you want to know?'

'For this here crossword puzzle.'

'Why are you doing crossword puzzles?'

'To improve his vocabulary,' Karen said.

176

'Oh. Thief.'

'Is that a job?'

'It is for the thief.'

'Where's Bobby with my ice cream?' Karen said.

'You'd better sit down, Scott,' Rebecca said.

Scott sat. The commercial ended and returned to the local evening news from Houston. The anchor introduced the next story.

'Now for our first installment of "Murder on the Beach", we go live to Renée Ramirez in Galveston.'

The picture cut to the reporter holding a microphone on the front steps of the courthouse. Carlos sat up.

'*Estoy enamorado.*'

'You're in love with every beautiful woman you see,' Karen said.

'What's your point?'

'*Trey Rawlins,*' the reporter said, '*was murdered nine days ago. He was buried Thursday at Galveston City Cemetery, and yesterday the grand jury indicted his longtime lover for allegedly stabbing him to death with a butcher knife from their own kitchen. The national media has dubbed Rebecca Fenney the "Guilty Groupie", and with good reason. I've learned that her fingerprints were on the murder weapon—*'

Scott jumped up. 'How'd she get that?'

'The DA had to leak it to her,' Karen said. 'Or that detective.'

'*—and that there's no evidence that anyone other than Rebecca Fenney entered the bedroom the night Trey was found dead in his bed. Prosecutors are convinced that Ms Fenney did in fact kill Trey, a conclusion bolstered by the fact that she has refused to take a polygraph exam.*'

'Damnit – that taints the jury pool! Rex said he didn't try his cases in the press.'

Back on the TV: '*But while convinced she killed Trey, prosecutors are confounded by the apparent lack of a motive. Why would Rebecca Fenney kill the man who gave her everything from the clothes she wore to the Corvette she drove? She claims Trey proposed to her that same night. Surely that will all come out at trial, which promises to be another O.J. circus-like spectacle, particularly with the news that guns, porn, and*

177

Viagra were found in the residence and with the confirmation that Ms Fenney is being represented by her ex-husband, A. Scott Fenney from Dallas. Scott Fenney was a star football player at SMU back in the early nineties—'

On the screen now was a clip of Scott running the football against Texas.

'—and became a legend when he rushed for one hundred ninety-three yards against UT. But he became a legal legend two years ago when he defended Shawanda Jones, a black Dallas prostitute charged with the murder of Clark McCall, the thirty-year-old son of the late US Senator Mack McCall.'

The screen showed Scott, Shawanda, and the girls on the courthouse steps after the verdict.

'She's gorgeous,' Rebecca said.

'She was.'

Renée Ramirez appeared on-screen. *'Ms Jones was acquitted by a federal jury in Dallas, but died of a heroin overdose two months later. Scott Fenney adopted her daughter. Rebecca Fenney began an extra-marital affair with Trey Rawlins while he was an assistant golf pro at the Highland Park Country Club where the Fenneys were members. She left Scott Fenney for Trey, and now he's representing her. Now that's a man who really meant "until death do us part". Of course, that could happen. At Trey's funeral service this past Thursday, I spoke with his twin sister, Terri Rawlins.'*

The picture cut to the front of the church and the young woman Rebecca had identified as Terri on the funeral tape. She looked like Trey.

'I hope they give her the death penalty.'

Scott turned to Rebecca just as she turned to him. Her face was pale.

'The death penalty?'

'It's not a capital murder case, Rebecca. They can't give you the death penalty.'

'But this is Texas.'

Back to Renée Ramirez: *'While I certainly believe in "inno-cent until proven guilty", I must ask why Rebecca Fenney, an indicted*

178

murderer, is not in jail at this hour? Why was she released on her personal recognizance? Is the DA extending professional courtesy to Mr Fenney because he's a Texas legend and thereby endangering the good citizens of Galveston? Is Mr Fenney receiving preferential treatment because of his political connections — he was seen dining with our own US Senator George Armstrong tonight at Gaido's. Rumor has it that Mr Fenney is up for a federal judgeship. It is all quite interesting. Perhaps Judge Shelby Morgan will have something to say about all of this when Ms Fenney is arraigned next week. Finally, Rebecca Fenney is reportedly residing until trial with Mr Fenney and his family in a rented house here on the Island. Hopefully there are no sharp knives in the kitchen. Reporting live from Galveston Island, this is Renée Ramirez.'

They went to commercial break.

'The DA was right,' Scott said.

Karen looked up. 'About what?'

'Her. She is annoying as hell.'

'Bitch,' Louis said.

'That, too.'

'No, that's a five-letter word for "female dog".'

Chapter 22

They were dressed for church the next morning when Rebecca came downstairs looking like she hadn't slept all night. Scott caught Karen giving Bobby a quick glance.

'Where are y'all going?'

'To church,' Scott said.

'You go to church now?'

'Pajamae got us going.'

'You want to go with us, Mother?'

'Maybe next week, honey. I couldn't sleep. Anyone make coffee?'

'I liked that preacher,' Pajamae said. 'He was interesting.'

They were driving back from church down Broadway when Scott spotted the red Corvette parked on 40th Street adjacent to the Galveston City Cemetery. He pulled over and parked.

'I'll be right back.'

Consuela was up front, and Maria was sleeping in her car seat between the girls in the back. Scott got out and stepped over the low rock wall surrounding the cemetery. A woman stood alone among the graves; she had black hair, but he knew it was Rebecca. He walked over the graves to her. She was wearing sunglasses and a black wig. She was standing over Trey Rawlins' grave, and she was crying.

'I guess you never really know someone,' she said.

'Were you happy with him?'

She nodded. 'I loved him. I thought he loved me. But I didn't know the truth.'

Scott thought of the Trey Rawlins he was getting to know. What else would he learn about the man lying in that grave?

'I'm sorry,' she said.

'For what?'

'Because now I know how much I hurt you.'

'Rebecca, you need to stay at the house. I don't want Renée Ramirez to know where you're at.'

'That's why I wore the wig.'

'The wig works, but not the car. Everyone on the Island knows you drive that red Corvette.'

'Oh.'

'Where'd you get the wig?'

'From my closet. I told Bobby to bring everything.'

They played tourist that day. Scott tried to forget that he was in Galveston for a murder trial and to just be a father for the day. The top tourist attraction on the Island is Moody Gardens, a 'public, non-profit educational destination utilizing nature in the advancement of rehabilitation, conservation, recreation and research'. The Gardens' three glass pyramids rise tall above the Island: the Aquarium Pyramid, where the girls shrieked at the sharks and posed with the penguins; the Discovery Pyramid, where they worked the interactive science and space exhibits; and the Rainforest Pyramid, where they touched the turtles and chased the birds and butterflies flying about the one-acre-under-glass living rainforest that housed plants, birds, and fish from Asian, African, and South American rainforests. They watched and even smelled the dinosaurs in the 4D film *Walking with Dinosaurs*, took a ride on the Colonel Paddlewheel Boat, and finished the day swimming and playing on the white sand at the Palm Beach pool. Rebecca looked stunning in her black wig and white bikini.

She had recovered from her morning melancholy. She acted upbeat and energetic. She laughed and played with the girls. It was as if the knowledge of Trey's affairs had released her from his hold. As if she were free of Trey Rawlins. Over him. She was a different woman. When they walked out to the cars, Boo stopped Scott and said, 'Mother's changed. She smiles . . . she's sweet . . . she sweats. I like her again.'

Late that afternoon they played a game of touch football on the beach. Consuela, Maria, and Karen sat under a big beach umbrella and cheered. It was supposed to be two-hand touch, but Rebecca put a full-body tackle on Scott; he didn't complain. Afterwards, he walked up to the house to check on the final round of the Houston Classic, but stopped on the deck and looked back at Rebecca. She and Boo were walking hand in hand far down the beach. They were growing close again. He wondered what an eleven-year-old girl talked to her mother about.

'Would you mind having sex with A. Scott?'
    '*Boo.*'
Mother had a shocked expression.
    'What?'
    'You know about sex?'
Boo nodded. 'Health class.'
    'I should've been there, to talk with you about it.'
    'A. Scott tried to, but he was pretty lame. He gave us a book, with drawings.'
    'So why are you asking?'
    'A. Scott needs sex.'
    'He's not dating anyone?'
    'Nunh-unh. Ms Dawson – she's the fourth-grade teacher – she's got a big crush on him, but he won't ask her out.'
    'Why not?'
    ''Cause of you.'
    'Is she pretty?'
    'Very.'

'Prettier than me?'

'No.'

Mother smiled a little.

'Do you want him to date someone?'

'He has us, but he needs someone his own age. And he needs sex. I told him Ms Dawson would probably have sex with him.'

'Why?'

''Cause she's got the hots for him.'

'No. Why does he need sex?'

'So he doesn't have a heart attack.'

'*A heart attack?*'

'Unh-huh. From the stress.'

'Is he under a lot of stress?'

Boo nodded. 'He's not making much money, because he represents poor people who can't pay. I think we're broke.'

'I didn't know.'

'He tries not to let on, but he's worried. And he won't take any of the medicine he's supposed to take, so sex is the only hope for him. So we were thinking – me and Pajamae – that maybe you could have sex with A. Scott again so he doesn't die on us?'

'Well, I guess I could try. For his health.'

Donnie Parker won the Houston Classic. He didn't look like a killer.

Pete Puckett did. He was good with guns and better with knives. He killed and gutted animals. He had his hands in blood. He threatened to kill Trey if he didn't stay away from Billie Jean, and Trey didn't. Had Pete carried through on his threat? Did he have his hands in Trey's blood? Did he stab that butcher knife into Trey Rawlins' chest? Scott needed Pete's fingerprints to prove Pete Puckett guilty and Rebecca Fenney innocent, but Pete would be in New York all week for the US Open. He wasn't fleeing the country, so Pete Puckett's prints would have to wait until the tour returned to Texas. Rebecca Fenney's fate would have to wait another week.

★　★　★

They cooked hamburgers and drank beer on the beach that night. At ten, Scott tucked the girls in bed then went out on the back deck where he found Rebecca standing alone at the far railing. She was still wearing that white bikini. The sea breeze blew her hair and brought her scent to Scott.

'Boo says you're stressed because you're broke.'

'She's a thirty-year-old woman trapped in an eleven-year-old body.'

'She also said you need sex. She's worried you'll have a heart attack, said you refuse to take your medications.'

'My medications?' Scott laughed. 'They want me to take every heart drug advertised on TV.'

'So you're not having heart problems?'

'No. The girls just worry. Bill Barnes – you remember him? – he died of a heart attack.'

'Oh, my God.'

'Ever since, the girls have worried I'll have a heart attack, too.'

'Is it true?'

'That I need sex?'

'That you're broke?'

'Yep, I'm broke. But I have options.'

'Such as?'

'Ford Fenney. Dan Ford offered to change the firm's name, pay me a million a year to come back.'

'Are you going to?'

'Not if Option B comes through.'

'What's Option B?'

'Judge Fenney.'

'You're going to run for judge?'

'Appointed. Federal bench. Sam Buford's dying of cancer, wants me to replace him. But that requires the US senators from Texas to back me.'

'Oh.'

'Yeah. Oh.'

'And I'm not helping, am I? My case? What if Option B doesn't come through? Do you want to go back to the firm?'

'No. But I will. For the girls. So they don't have to lie to survive.'

'But what about your life? Your happiness?'

'Theirs comes first.'

'So you'll never have the life you always wanted?'

'I made too many mistakes to have the life I wanted.'

'Me. I was your mistake.'

'It wasn't your fault, Rebecca.'

'I had the affair.'

'But I had the career. I didn't give you the attention you needed.'

'And I had the Highland Park lifestyle, shopping and society balls, wearing five-thousand-dollar dresses.'

'You paid five thousand dollars for a dress?'

'You paid two hundred thousand for the Ferrari.'

He smiled. 'I did.' He shook his head. 'That car was so . . .'

'Sweet?'

'I was going to say arrogant. But it was a sweet car. Sid's driving it now.'

'*Sid Greenberg?* In your Ferrari? Now that's just wrong.' She laughed. 'It's a nice night, let's take a walk.'

They went down the stairs and onto the beach.

'You always wear bikinis?'

She shrugged. 'I live on a beach. You don't like it?'

'No, I like it.'

'Good.'

'Secluded out here.'

'Since Ike. This last week, Scott, it's been like the old times.'

'Except for a pending murder trial.'

'Except for that. When do I take the polygraph?'

'Karen's setting it up. You're not worried?'

'I have nothing to worry about. I'm innocent.'

'Prisons are full of innocent people.'

'Okay, now I'm worried.'

'Sorry.'

She laughed. 'I'm not worried because you're my lawyer.' She paused then said, 'Scott, why are you my lawyer? Why are you doing this? Because you still love me?'

'Because you're still Boo's mother.'

'She's lucky.'

'That you're her mother?'

'That you're her father.' She took his hand. 'But you do still love me, don't you?'

The night air had a hint of cool. She put her arm through his and leaned into him as they strolled. He felt her skin against his, and he thought of all the times their bodies had been skin to skin. He missed those times. She abruptly stopped, turned to him, and kissed him. She pressed her body against his, and he felt the old desire for this beautiful woman rise in him again. Like the old times.

When he was at Ford Stevens, the male lawyers had often gathered after-hours and drank and talked about women and marriage, about how the heat of passion they had initially enjoyed had subsided after a year or two of marriage and it was only then that they had gotten to know their wives as people rather than objects of desire. For some of the lawyers, that had not been a good thing; they soon divorced and rediscovered the passion with a younger woman. The others had settled into a marriage in which children replaced passion. They had accepted the tradeoff – little league baseball in place of passionate sex – as an inevitable fact of life. Of course, Dan Ford's take on the matter was more succinct: 'Hell, Scott,' he had said, 'marriage isn't about love; it's about survival.' But then, Dan had always been a romantic bastard.

Scott had listened to the other lawyers complain about their sex lives, and he had felt lucky. Because his wife and his marriage were different. He had it better than those other lawyers. He had Rebecca. From the moment their eyes had first met and their hands had touched and their desire for each other had risen inside them, and for the next eleven years of marriage, sex had been as much a part of their life as breathing. It was as if sex were their reason for breathing. They had had sex anywhere and everywhere, anytime and all the time. Their heat for each other had never subsided . . . until she had taken up with Trey. Her passion had found another man but his had never found another woman. He had always wanted her, physically and desperately. He still wanted her. And she wanted him again.

'Are you healthy enough for sexual activity?' she said.

Breaking through the heat was Boo's admonition to use a condom.

'Rebecca . . .'

She released him and skipped down the sand, her arms spread and turning in circles. Then she stopped and faced him. She untied her top and tossed it aside. She pushed the bikini bottom down and kicked it away. Then she ran into the surf.

'Come on – for your health.'

He went to her.

He embraced her and lifted her and kissed her, hard this time, and he wanted her as desperately as the first time. And it felt like the first time as the heat consumed them, and they touched each other. He had missed the heat of passion. He had missed being one with a woman. And he would miss it now. He had failed again.

'Sorry, it's been a while.'

She smiled. 'Don't worry – there'll be more opportunities.'

She dove into an oncoming wave then surfaced and brushed her hair back with her fingers. The moonlight captured her face.

'God, I love the water,' she said. 'Being in it, on it.'

They sat in the gentle surf. She pointed out to sea. The lights of the offshore drilling rigs twinkled in the night sky.

'Cancún is seven hundred fifty miles that way.'

They sat in silence for a time then she said, 'Scott, if I'm not . . . well, you know . . . we could try again. I'm not the woman who left you. I know a lot more now. I know you're the best man I'll ever know. And I know who I am now. I'm not the beauty queen or the society belle anymore, and I don't want to be. I know I don't deserve her or you, but I want to be her mother again. I want to be your wife again. If you both can

187

forgive me.' She turned to him. 'Scott, maybe we can both have the life we always wanted.'

'Missy Dupree made chair of the Cattle Barons' ball.'

'*Missy Dupree?* Oh, God! She's so . . . me two years ago . . . except she's enhanced.' Rebecca smiled. 'Remember what I wore to the last ball? Powder blue fringed suede miniskirt and silk halter top, matching cowboy boots, and a pink suede cowboy hat. I spent days putting that outfit together.'

'You looked good. How much did it cost?'

She laughed now. 'You don't want to know. What'd you do with it?'

'Sold it. We had a yard sale.'

'In Highland Park?'

'Yeah, it was quite the event.'

'I can only imagine.' She shook her head. 'Society balls, social climbing, gossiping about other women at lunch . . .'

'What'd you call it?'

'Scandal soufflé. I'm sure they had a field day with me back then . . . and now. Rebecca Fenney on trial for murder and defended by her ex-husband – that'll keep them busy all summer.' She turned to him. 'When is the trial?'

'We'll find out in the morning.'

The sea offered the only sounds for a time, until Rebecca spoke.

'Did you miss me?'

'Every day.'

Scott stared out to sea. She was right: he did still love her. But should a lawyer love his client? Could he think like a lawyer if he loved her like a man? Was Melvyn Burke right, that a lawyer can only defend his client, not love her, too? That this case would destroy his career and his life? And what secrets was Melvyn Burke hiding behind the attorney–client privilege?

Chapter 23

Scott held Rebecca's hand as they entered the Galveston County Jail for her formal booking at nine on Monday morning. Junior again manned the lobby window, and Sarge stood next to Junior, hands clasped behind him, as if awaiting a dignitary's arrival.

'I guess you didn't dress up for me,' Sarge said.

Scott was wearing a $2,000 suit that day.

'I'm surrendering Rebecca Fenney for arrest and booking.'

Sarge held up a document. 'Rex brought over the arrest warrant himself this morning, said you'd be bringing her in, said I was to – what was it, Junior? – "extend all courtesies to Mr Fenney and his client", whatever the hell that means.'

'It means, be nice.'

'Hey, I got no dog in this fight, Mr Fenney. We'll book her, then transport her down the street to the courthouse for the arraignment. Judge'll set bail, we'll bring her back over, you can bond her out right here. And Detective Wilson's a jackass.'

'What?'

'Going on TV, saying she's guilty. Cops ain't supposed to do that.'

Scott turned to Rebecca. Her face belonged to a frightened child. She hadn't slept again the previous night.

'Scott, I can't go back in there. Those women, they'll hurt me.'

'No, they won't. It'll be okay, I promise. I'll see you at the courthouse.'

He squeezed her hand, then tried to release her, but she clung to him.

'Scott, I can't!'

He wiped a tear from her face. 'They have to book you.'

She abruptly turned and bent over. She couldn't sleep, but she could throw up. Scott pulled out his handkerchief and wiped her mouth. She was crying.

'Junior!' Sarge yelled. 'Get out there and clean that mess up!'

When Sarge opened the secure door, Scott led Rebecca over to him. The cop façade dropped from Sarge's face at the sight of her. He sighed.

'I'll book her myself.'

Sarge put an arm under hers as if he were escorting Rebecca Fenney into the high school prom instead of the county jail. The secure door swung shut behind them.

The new Galveston County Courthouse's modern architecture seemed out of place on the Victorian-style Island. Construction costs for the courthouse and adjacent jail totaled $92 million. Justice didn't come cheap in America.

Scott found the 147th District Courtroom on the second floor. The plaque on the double doors read 'Honorable Shelby Morgan, Presiding Judge'. He entered the courtroom and walked up the center aisle past spectator pews occupied by exactly two people: Terri Rawlins, and her attorney, Melvyn Burke. Under the ethics rules, a lawyer may not speak to another lawyer's client unless the lawyer is present. Melvyn was present, so Scott stopped.

'Melvyn.'

'Scott.' To his client: 'Terri, this is Scott Fenney, Rebecca's lawyer.'

'I'm sorry for your loss,' Scott said.

Terri Rawlins gave him a hard look. 'You should be. Your wife killed my brother.'

190

'Terri, do you think I'd be representing my ex-wife who left me for Trey if I thought she killed him?'

'Lawyers will do anything for money.'

'Not this lawyer. And she has nothing now. She's not paying me.'

'Is that why you want her jewelry?'

'No, Terri. Keep the jewelry.'

'I don't want it.' She reached down and came up with a brown bag. She held it out to Scott. 'Take it.'

He took it.

'Trey asked Rebecca to marry him that night.'

'No! He didn't! She's lying! He wasn't going to marry her.'

'Did he tell you that?'

She didn't answer.

'Terri, let Melvyn tell me what he knows about Trey's life. Waive the attorney–client privilege. Please.' Scott looked directly at Melvyn when he said, 'So an innocent person doesn't go to prison.'

'No – and she's guilty.'

'What are you hiding, Terri?'

'That's enough, Scott,' Melvyn said.

Scott gave Melvyn a long look then continued up the aisle and through the gate in the bar. Bobby, Karen, and Carlos had already arrived and were sitting at the defendant's table. Scott placed the bag on the table.

'What's in the bag?' Bobby asked.

'Her jewelry.'

A side door opened and a deputy sheriff escorted Rebecca into the courtroom and over to the defendant's table. She now wore a white jumpsuit that dwarfed her slender body. GALVESTON COUNTY INMATE was printed across the back.

'You okay?'

She nodded, but her eyes took in the courtroom where she would be tried and either acquitted and set free or convicted and sent to prison for the rest of her life. The air of confidence she had exhibited just the day before was gone. The American

191

criminal justice system had finally gotten to Rebecca Fenney. She was scared to death.

The DA and the Assistant DA entered through the back door. Ted Newman walked over to the prosecution table and Rex Truitt to Scott. They shook hands, and Scott introduced Rebecca to the DA.

'Sarge treat you okay during booking? I've been working on his manners.'

Rebecca nodded at the DA but stared past him at the vacant jury box. The DA reached into his briefcase.

'Here's a copy of the indictment.'

Scott handed the document to Karen then turned back to the DA.

'Did you see Renée Ramirez's report Saturday night?'

The DA nodded. 'I told you she was annoying as hell.'

'You also told me you don't try your cases in the press.'

A common prosecutorial tactic was to try a criminal case first in the press prior to trial – leaking evidence and having detectives give interviews and offer personal views about the defendant's guilt – and then in a courtroom at trial. Evidence that is not admissible in court gets admitted in the press. By the time the jury is seated, every juror is convinced of the defendant's guilt. Which, of course, is the point: it's much easier to convict when you've stacked the jury.

'I don't.'

'Then why was that detective on the network morning shows, calling her the Guilty Groupie?'

The DA sighed. ''Cause Wilson's a prick, wants to be famous.'

'That's unethical.'

'Wanting to be famous?'

'Going on TV before trial, declaring the defendant guilty.'

'He's a cop. That's what cops do.'

'You think Wilson told Renée about the fingerprints? And the polygraph?'

'Renée's real friendly with the cops.'

'I figured she'd be here.'

192

The DA smiled. 'I didn't release the arraignment date.'

Just then the double doors behind them flew open and reporters and cameramen surged forward, led by Renée Ramirez. The DA's smile faded.

'But I guess the judge did. Don't let her rattle you.'

'I've been here before.'

'And now you're here again.'

'Find your leak, Rex. And plug it.'

The DA went to the prosecution table but did not sit because the bailiff called out, 'All rise!' The door to the judge's chambers opened and Judge Shelby Morgan appeared. She stepped up to the bench and gazed upon her courtroom like a queen upon her subjects – or like a model posing for the cameras. Rex hadn't exaggerated: she was the most attractive judge Scott had ever encountered. She had blonde hair and lean facial features that made Scott suspect the black robe concealed a fit body. The bailiff called the case: 'State of Texas versus Rebecca Fenney. Arraignment.'

'Please make your appearances,' the judge said.

'Galveston County Criminal District Attorney Rex Truitt and Assistant Criminal District Attorney Theodore Newman for the state.'

'A. Scott Fenney, Robert Herrin, and Karen Douglas of Fenney Herrin Douglas, Dallas, Texas, for the defendant.'

'Mr Truitt, would you please read the indictment?'

'Ted will.'

The Assistant DA read: 'In the name and by authority of the State of Texas . . .'

Ted Newman spoke in a monotone through the procedural parts of the indictment but put his drama club experience to use in the charging statement.

'. . . Rebecca Garrett Fenney, did then and there intentionally and knowingly cause the death of an individual, Trey Rawlins, by stabbing him with a knife, which act constitutes murder under section nineteen–point–zero–two of the Texas Penal Code. Against the peace and dignity of the State.'

'Will the accused please rise?' the judge said.

The 'accused'. His ex-wife. The mother of his child. Accused of murder. Scott helped Rebecca to her feet. Her body trembled.

'You are the Rebecca Garrett Fenney named in the indictment?'

'Yes.'

Her voice was almost a whisper.

'Ms Fenney, how do you plead to the charge contained in the indictment?'

Thirteen years before, when this woman had stood next to him in a white wedding dress in a church and said, 'I do', Scott would never have imagined that one day she would stand next to him in a white jail jumpsuit in a courtroom and say, 'Not guilty'.

'A plea of not guilty has been entered in the docket. Mr Fenney, does your client demand a jury trial?'

'Yes, Your Honor. And the earliest available trial setting.'

The judge flipped through her docket. 'I have a setting available on July twentieth. Thirty-five days, Mr Fenney – you sure you want that speedy of a trial?'

Thirty-five days. The clock was ticking on Rebecca Fenney's freedom.

'We'll take it.'

Like booking a hotel at a popular resort.

'Will that work for the state, Mr Truitt?'

'That'll work, Judge.'

'Pretrial conference on July thirteenth, jury selection on July seventeenth, bail is denied. The defendant will be remanded to the custody of the Galveston County Sheriff pending trial.'

'*What?*'

Rebecca clutched Scott. 'No! I can't go back!'

The judge had fixed a glare on Scott. 'Is that an objection, Mr Fenney?'

'Yes, Your Honor, defense objects. The defendant presents no flight risk and no risk to herself or to the community. Judge, you can't deny bail.'

'That federal judge in Houston did.'

'What federal judge?'

'It was in the paper this morning, he denied bail to Sir Allen pending his trial.'

'Who the hell's Sir Allen?'

'Allen Stanford, he's charged with running a seven-billion-dollar Ponzi scheme.'

Scott remembered now. Nick Madden had mentioned him.

'What's that got to do with this case?'

'You said I can't deny bail. If he can, I can.'

'Your Honor,' the DA said, 'Stanford had private jets at his disposal, he had homes and cash offshore, he had resided outside the US most of the last decade, and he had dual US and Antiguan citizenship. He was a true flight risk. I must agree with Mr Fenney – there is no flight risk here. She's not going anywhere.'

Judge Morgan was not pleased. Her face flushed red and her jaws clenched tight, but the cameras prevented an injudicious outburst. She glared at the DA, but he seemed unfazed.

'Fine,' the judge said. 'Bail is set at one million dollars.'

'Your Honor,' Scott said, 'Ms Fenney has no assets and cannot satisfy such an onerous bail. We ask that the defendant be released on her personal recognizance.'

'PR on a murder charge? I don't think so, Mr Fenney.'

Without breaking eye contact with the judge, Scott reached out to Karen. She slapped a stack of documents in his hand. Scott gave a copy to the DA then walked over and handed a copy to the judge. Karen addressed the court from a sitting position.

'Your Honor, this is our brief on bail. The US Supreme Court ruled in *Stack v. Boyle* in 1951 that bail is excessive in violation of the Bail Clause of the Eighth Amendment if set in an amount exceeding that necessary to ensure the defendant will show up for trial. The Court also ruled that—'

'Your Honor,' the Assistant DA said, 'the defendant is charged with a bloody brutal murder that shocked our community—'

The DA was reading the brief. Without looking up, he held up an open hand to his assistant. 'Easy, Ted. This is about the law, not those cameras.'

'Your Honor,' Karen said, 'the defendant has resided in

Galveston County for almost two years and will continue to reside in the county.'

'Not in that house, she won't. So where will she reside?'

'In a vacation house here on the Island. We'll give Mr Truitt the address.'

'If she has no assets, how is she affording that?'

'Your Honor,' Scott said, 'Ms Fenney is residing with us. I am also her ex-husband. I rented a house for the summer to try this case. We're all living there, including Ms Fenney's daughter. She's not going anywhere.'

'And she agrees to wear a GPS-tracking ankle bracelet at all times and not to leave the Island,' Karen said. 'She will surrender her passport to the district attorney.'

'Your Honor,' the DA said, 'Mr Fenney has personally assured me that the defendant will present herself for trial. With the GPS monitor and the passport surrender, the state does not object to release on PR.'

'I do. Two hundred fifty thousand. If you object to that bail, Mr Fenney, you can file your brief with the federal court in Houston. My clerk will give you directions. I think we're done here. I want to see counsel in chambers.'

She stormed off the bench and through the door to her chambers. She wasn't happy, but neither was Scott. The DA stepped over to him.

'You like her already, don't you?' To Karen: 'Great brief. You should be a law professor . . . or better yet, move down here to the Island. I'll fire Ted and hire you.'

The deputy sheriff stepped over and took Rebecca by her arm. Her eyes were wide with fear. She grabbed Scott's arm. The deputy tugged gently, but she did not release her grip.

'Scott, please don't let them take me! I can't stay in that jail!'

'You won't have to. I'll bond you out.'

'How? Two hundred fifty thousand dollars? You're broke.'

'I'll figure something out.'

'Scott, please . . . those women.'

The DA stepped over to the deputy. 'Tell Sarge to put her in a separate cell.'

The deputy nodded then pulled Rebecca through the side door. Scott felt the anger rising inside him. An ambitious judge was a dangerous animal.

'Stay calm, Scott,' the DA said. 'So I'm not bailing you out of jail.'

The judge was removing her robe when they entered her chambers. She was lean and wore tight black slacks, black high-heels, and a fitted white blouse. She appeared younger than forty. She hung the robe on a coat rack then sat behind her desk.

'Rex, did you see Renée's report?'

'Yep.'

They took seats in front of the desk. The judge stared at the DA but pointed at Scott. 'Did you let her out on PR because of him?'

'No, Shelby. Because that's the law.'

'Maybe so, but you made us look like fools.'

'The law will do that sometimes.'

'Are we off the record, Judge?' Scott asked.

'Yes.'

'Then what the hell's going on?'

'Careful, Mr Fenney.'

'Denying bail, then a million dollars, now two-fifty. The DA doesn't object to her release on PR – why are you insisting on bail?'

'She's charged with murder.'

'She's not a flight risk or a danger to the community. She's agreed to remain on the Island pending trial—'

'Where? Where on the Island?'

'On the West End, at an undisclosed location. For her safety.'

'She'd be safer in jail. Hell, you'd be safer with her in jail.'

'You can't set bail to punish the defendant, force her to stay incarcerated through the trial.'

'I can't go any lower than that – Renée would have a field day.'

'That's grounds for recusal, Judge. Karen, prepare a motion.'

The judge's face flashed red again and this time she lost it.

'Don't you fucking dare!'

'Judge, I don't live here. It won't affect my law career, having a judge pissed off at me. My only concern is that the defendant get a fair trial. If you can't give her that because of your concern about the press coverage . . . or for other personal reasons . . . then I'll file that motion. And I will take that to the federal court.'

'Mr Fenney, I can hold you in contempt!' She pointed a manicured finger at Scott. 'You're not a legend in my courtroom! You're just another goddamned lawyer!'

'Judge, my client—'

'Your wife.'

'My client is entitled to a fair trial and I'm gonna make damn sure she gets one. If you can't give her a fair trial, then recuse yourself and let another judge do it.'

Judge Shelby Morgan glared at Scott.

'She'll get a fair trial, Mr Fenney.'

When they exited the judge's chambers, the DA whistled and said, 'Damn, Scott, you really know how to make a good first impression.'

'I try. I figured we might as well clear the air now, before we go to trial.'

'Oh, I think you cleared the air all right. But what's the personal reason?'

'The judge and I are both up for a federal judgeship in Dallas.'

'Buford's bench?'

Scott nodded. 'He's dying.'

'Heard he was sick.'

'Senator Armstrong said he owes Judge Morgan.'

'I expect he does.' He didn't elaborate. 'So Shelby might be leaving the Island, huh?' The DA smiled. 'Hell, not all bad news then.'

They opened the courtroom doors and a dozen cameras and reporters shoving microphones into their faces and shouting questions surged toward them like a wave in the Gulf that had started off Mexico. Renée Ramirez was the leader of this pack.

'Mr Fenney, why are you defending your ex-wife when she's charged with murdering the man she left you for?'

Scott maintained his lawyerly expression. 'Because she's innocent.'

They pushed forward to the elevators.

'Why won't she take a polygraph?'

'Because polygraphs are not reliable indicators of guilt or innocence, which is why they're not admissible in any court of law in America.'

'Why were her fingerprints on the murder weapon?'

'Are your fingerprints on your kitchen knives?'

Scott saw Renée's obvious frustration with his answers and figured she'd give up. She didn't. She had one more question.

'Mr Fenney – do you still love your wife?'

Scott knew his expression had let him down, and so did Renée. She had a 'gotcha' grin on her face.

'Ex-wife.'

Carlos had jogged ahead and gotten an elevator; he held it open for the others. Once they were aboard, he let the doors close, shutting out the cameras. The DA turned to Scott. 'You okay? That last one was a cheap shot. But that's Renée.'

'I'm a big boy.'

Bobby held up the official Houston Classic tournament tote bag.

'Rex, we've got some evidence for you.'

'And I've got some evidence for you.'

Chapter 24

The DA sat behind his desk under the sailfish, and Ted Newman and Hank Kowalski sat against the wall. The defense team faced the DA from across his desk. Karen opened her laptop like a gunner setting up field artillery. Bobby opened the tote bag and removed the baggies containing the fingerprint evidence Scott had collected at the golf tournament. He placed them on the desk.

'Ah, more fingerprints,' the DA said. 'Well, Hank ran Goose's prints. Didn't match the unidentified prints at the crime scene. Who are these from?'

'Suspects.'

Hank stepped over and examined the baggies one by one; each was identified with initials. 'Glass marked "TM" . . . soda can marked "LP" . . . plastic container marked "RH" . . . Houston Classic golf programs marked "BM" and "DP" and "VH" . . . Budweiser beer bottle marked "NM" . . . five Corona beer bottles marked "CW".'

The DA turned to Scott. 'You don't want to tell me who they belong to?'

'Not yet.'

The DA nodded. 'Run 'em, Hank.' To Scott: 'That it?'

'For now.'

200

'Okay. My turn.' The DA pushed a thick stack of papers across the desk. Scott handed them to Bobby. 'Item one: log and copies of all emails to and from Trey over the last six months, including to his website. My tech man got them off his laptop.'

Bobby scanned the log and said, 'None to or from the other women.'

The DA: 'What other women?'

'We've learned that Trey was promiscuous,' Scott said.

'Promiscuous? Last time I checked the Penal Code, that ain't illegal in Texas, thank God, or we'd never clear the docket.' The DA chuckled. 'Hell, Scott, if I looked like him and was rich like him, I'd damn sure be promiscuous.'

'With married women?'

The DA shrugged. 'Maybe not with our gun laws. What married women?'

'Other golfers' wives. On tour.'

'You know this for a fact?'

'They admitted it.'

'You're gonna put Trey on trial, aren't you?'

'No, Rex, I'm going to find his killer.'

'She's over at the jail. Look, Scott, Trey was young and rich and famous – didn't you have some fun when you were young?'

'Not with married women.'

The Assistant DA snorted. 'Well, at least you know Trey wasn't picking on you, taking your wife.'

An awkward silence captured the room. The DA grimaced, a common expression when the Assistant DA was present. Scott waited for the DA to reprimand his assistant, but instead the DA bent over, opened a lower desk drawer, and came back up with a box of dog biscuits. He stuck his hand inside the box and pulled out a little brown biscuit. He flipped it over to his assistant.

'Down, boy.'

The others choked back laughter, but the Assistant DA's face flushed a bright red. 'Rex, are you trying to humiliate me?'

'No, Ted, you're doing a damn fine job of that on your own. I'm trying to teach you humility. There's a difference.' The DA turned to Karen: 'Sure you don't want to move to the Island? You could be the first female DA in the history of Galveston.' The DA gestured at the baggies. 'These their prints, the women's?'

'And their husbands'.'

'You figure a jealous husband for the killer?'

'Could be.'

'Could be your wife was the jealous party.'

'Trey proposed to her that night.'

'So she said.' The DA pushed another document across the desk. 'Item two: list of websites Trey visited over the last six months. Common theme seems to be porn.'

Scott passed it on to Bobby. Karen leaned toward Bobby to read the list.

'Did he go onto Facebook?' she said.

'Every day the last couple of weeks,' Bobby said.

'What's your point?' the DA said.

'Trey could have communicated with someone through their Facebook account, online but outside his email accounts.'

'Like who?'

Karen tapped on the laptop keyboard then turned the screen toward the DA. On the screen was a Facebook profile.

'Like her.'

'Who's Billie Jean Puckett?'

'Pete Puckett's seventeen-year-old daughter.'

'The golf pro?'

Scott nodded. 'Trey was having an affair with Billie Jean. Pete threatened to kill him if he didn't stay away from her. Happened at the Challenge tournament in California, one week before Trey was killed. There was a witness, another golfer.'

'I take it he didn't? Stay away from her?'

'No. He didn't.'

The DA again gestured at the baggies. 'You got Pete's prints?'

'Not yet. But he seems capable of violence. He threatened me after his round on Friday, with a one-iron.'

'A one-iron?' The DA grunted. 'Most pros carry the hybrids now, you can hit the ball higher—'

'The prints on the kitchen counter are from a big man. The construction workers down the street, they told Carlos they saw a big man at Trey's house the day he was killed. And a blonde girl.'

Hank snorted. 'They told us they didn't see nothing.'

'You're a cop,' Carlos said.

'True.'

'I've seen Pete on TV,' the DA said. 'He's a big man. And Billie Jean's blonde?' He glanced at the Facebook profile again.

'She is,' Scott said. 'And Pete's a hunter, good with guns and knives. And he was in Trey's house that day.'

'Can you prove it?'

'Not yet.'

'Let me know when you can.'

'Rex, I think Pete Puckett killed Trey.'

'Thought the caddie killed him?'

'You just said his prints didn't match.'

'Scott,' Karen said, 'we should subpoena Facebook, get all of Billie Jean's messages. Maybe she said something to Trey about Pete's threats.'

The DA turned his palms up at Scott. 'Facebook, MySpace, Twitter, sexting – you ever feel like you're living in a parallel universe?'

'All the time,' Scott said, 'with two eleven-year-old daughters.' To Karen: 'Where's their headquarters? Facebook's.'

Karen typed. 'California. Their only presence in Galveston County is online. No way they comply with a state court subpoena.'

'They might if I sign the subpoena,' the DA said.

'You'd do that?'

'Sure. Like I said, Scott, I think your wife killed Trey. But if she didn't, I want to find out who did.' To Karen: 'Write the subpoena, Professor.'

'I usually write the subpoenas,' the Assistant DA said.

'I know.' To Scott: 'Even if Pete was in Trey's house, his prints weren't on the knife. Your wife's were. You got that good explanation yet?'

203

'Not yet.'

'Let me know when you do.' The DA handed over another document. 'Item three: phone logs, landline and cell. His landline bills were at the house, so we ran all those numbers. The logs list all calls, the parties, dates, times, and duration of the calls.'

Scott scanned the logs. 'Lots of calls to Terri and Rebecca. None to the other women.'

'What about his cell?' Bobby said.

'We got the log off the phone,' the DA said.

'He might've deleted some calls. But every call – even the deleted ones – shows up on the phone bills. We need to subpoena Trey's cell phone records.'

'Okay. Write that one up, too.'

'Trey's last calls that Thursday were to and from Rebecca, Tom Taylor, and a Benito Estrada at six-eighteen P.M.' Scott said. 'Who's he?'

The DA leaned back in his chair and cut a glance at Hank. 'Well, that brings me to item four: the toxicology report.' He picked up a document and read. 'Trey Rawlins' blood alcohol level at the time of his death was point-two-six, three times the legal limit. He also had cocaine in his system. Six hundred nanograms per milliliter.'

'How much is that?'

'A lot.'

'Enough to cause an overdose?'

'I asked the ME that same question. Can't have a murder case if the victim died before he was stabbed.'

'We could still charge her with abuse of a corpse,' the Assistant DA said.

The DA ignored his assistant. 'ME said he was alive when he was stabbed because his heart pumped out so much blood.'

'Was cocaine found in the house?'

'Nope.' The DA rubbed his face. 'Good thing his dad's dead 'cause this would've killed him.' He looked up at Scott. 'I'm no longer in denial about Trey.'

'Good.'

'Now it's your turn, Scott.'

'My turn for what?'

'To end your denial. About your wife.'

The room turned quiet, and Scott became aware of his own breathing.

The DA stared at the report. 'We took a blood sample from her, too. Her blood alcohol level was point-two-two.'

'She said they'd been drinking at Gaido's.'

'And we can probably suppress that at trial,' Karen said. 'No PC to draw her blood and—'

'Incident to her arrest,' the Assistant DA said.

'She wasn't arrested for DUI.'

'No. For murder.'

'But the law requires—'

Scott held up his hand to Karen. The DA had not looked up from the report. There was more.

'What is it, Rex?'

The DA looked up now. 'Scott, your wife had cocaine in her system, too. Four hundred nanograms. She was drunk and stoned. Could be why she slept in Trey's blood.'

During a football game at SMU, Scott Fenney, number 22, had been knocked unconscious. When he came to, he felt dazed and confused, as if his mind couldn't put two words together. So he felt now. So Bobby subbed for him.

'Could be why she didn't wake up when the killer came into the bedroom and stabbed Trey.'

'Look, Scott,' the DA said, 'I know y'all have a daughter, so I'm not going to release this report. But it'll come out at trial.'

Scott tried to grasp the thought that Rebecca had used cocaine. He couldn't.

'You're sure? About the cocaine?'

'You can run your own tests, we took extra blood from her.'

The DA slid the report across the desk. Scott did not pick it up.

'So what's all this got to do with Benito Estrada?'

'He's a known drug dealer on the Island. Him and Trey, they were cell phone buddies. Means Trey was a regular customer. And a special one.'

'Tell me about him. Benito.'

'Twenty-eight, Harvard-educated, BOI. Runs the Gulf Coast operation for the Guadalajara cartel. Considers himself a businessman, even acts like one – supports the community, gave half a million for Ike relief, something of an icon among his folks. But he runs his operation like a business, so we haven't had the turf wars and gun battles in the streets like the border towns.'

'In Mexico?'

'In Texas.'

'The Zetas brought the drug war across the river,' Hank said.

'Who are the Zetas?'

'Enforcers for the cartels. Ex-commandos in the Mexican Army – we trained them, then they hired out to the cartels. All that stuff you've seen on TV about the drug war in Mexico – kidnappings, eight thousand murders last year, headless bodies hanging from overpasses and dumped into the Rio Grande – that's the Zetas' handiwork. Those guys make the Mafia look like middle-school bullies. And they control the country. We've put Mexico on the verge of collapse as a nation.'

'How?'

'Drug money. Mexicans send the drugs north, Americans send weapons and twenty billion in cash south to the cartels – every year. Imagine if the Saudis sent twenty billion a year to Islamic extremists in the US and they used that money to kill eight thousand Americans last year – we'd want to bomb Saudi Arabia back into the Stone Age. But we tell the Mexicans to keep the dope south of the river 'cause we know Americans won't stop using. Easier to blame it on the Mexicans than to accept responsibility for all those people getting killed.'

'And these Zetas are in Texas?'

'They're everywhere now. Five local dealers in Atlanta, they owed the cartels two hundred thousand dollars, didn't pay, so they sent the Zetas in. They beheaded the guys, put it on

206

YouTube. You cross the cartels, you're a dead man. Usually after being tortured and sliced up like a side of beef. The Zetas don't just kill people – they send messages.'

'Where can I find Benito? I need to talk to him.'

'Benito's not going to talk to you.'

'Never know till you try.'

'Except trying might get you a bullet in your head.' Hank snorted. 'Look, Scott, I don't know how you do things in Dallas, but you don't just drive over to Market Street and talk to Benito Estrada. You either wear a badge or you go in shooting. Preferably both. Scott, Benito's got thugs bigger than buses.'

'I've got Louis.'

Chapter 25

'Just like in the book, Mr Fenney,' Louis said. 'Ain't no country for old men.'

Benito Estrada maintained offices in a three-story historical structure abutting a yoga studio on Market Street in the trendy part of downtown Galveston. It had the appearance of a real-estate office, except for the two thick-bodied Latino thugs standing guard out front under a red awning. Their loose Mexican wedding shirts bulged at the waist; they were armed and dangerous and perfectly within the law in Texas. As long as their guns were concealed, they were legal.

'Working for the cartel,' Carlos said, 'you ain't gonna grow old.'

Scott had sent Bobby and Karen back to the beach house. They were soon to be parents, and they were the girls' guardians under A. Scott Fenney's Last Will and Testament. They didn't need to be in the line of fire. Scott had driven past the building then stopped a half block down the street to plot out a strategy. No strategy had occurred to him when Carlos said, 'I'll handle this, boss. These are my people.'

Carlos stepped smartly down the sidewalk, clad in black leather from head to foot, past a silver Maserati parked along the curb and over to the thugs. He gave them a hearty smile, stuck his hand out, and said, 'Buenos días, amigos.'

'Fuck off,' the taller thug said.

Carlos recoiled and withdrew his hand. 'Nice attitude.'

He retreated to Scott and Louis, who patted him on the shoulder.

'Must not know they're your people.'

Carlos exhaled and shook his head as if faced with an imponderable mystery. 'Folks these days, they just can't be friendly. Why is that?'

'We live in a conflicted time,' Louis said. 'Folks struggling to find meaning in their lives. When they don't, their frustrations manifest in hostility toward their fellow man.'

'You really think that's it, with those guys?'

Louis stared at the thugs. 'I think those guys are assholes need to be stuffed down a concrete culvert.'

Louis said it as if he knew how to do it and might. Scott was about to take his chances with the thugs when a car pulled up to the curb next to them. Hank Kowalski got out. His big gun was prominently displayed on his hip.

'Rex thought maybe I should drop by.'

'Thanks, Hank. But let me take a shot at these guys first. So to speak.'

Scott walked over to the thugs and held his business card out in front of him like a white flag of surrender – but he was relieved to hear the others' footsteps behind him.

'I'm Scott Fenney. Is Mr Estrada available?'

'No, he ain't available,' the shorter thug said.

'Would you mind checking? It's about Trey Rawlins. I'm a lawyer representing Rebecca Fenney.'

The thugs glanced at each other then at Hank; the taller one said, 'Wait here.' He took Scott's card and went inside. The other thug maintained his position in front of the door. A few minutes later, the taller one returned and gestured at Scott.

'Benito will see you.'

They all took a step toward the door.

'Only the lawyer.'

Scott turned to the others. 'I'll be okay. Wait here.'

'Mr Fenney,' Louis said, 'if you want, I could break both their necks.'

The thugs' eyes got wide. Hank chuckled.

'No, Louis, just be cool.'

Scott followed the thug inside and to the elevators.

'Hands up.'

Scott put his hands in the air. The thug patted him down then said, 'Third floor.'

Scott stepped inside the elevator and punched the button for the third floor. The elevator made a smooth journey up two levels then the doors opened on a young, handsome, meticulously groomed Latino man dressed in a pink polo shirt that hung like silk, white creased shorts, and *huaraches*. His black hair was smoothed back, and his goatee was expertly trimmed. His cologne smelled expensive. He offered a bright smile and an open hand to Scott. He was unarmed.

'Mr Fenney, I am Benito Estrada. It is an honor to meet you.'

Scott shook Benito's hand. 'Why?'

'The hooker's case, up in Dallas. Took *cojones* to go on national TV and call a US senator a criminal . . . just like it took *cojones* to walk up to *mis amigos* downstairs and say you want to see Benito Estrada. I like that.'

'Then you'll really like this: did you kill Trey Rawlins?'

Benito chuckled. 'Perhaps you would like something to drink, Mr Fenney? Spring water, herbal tea, espresso – I have Starbucks?'

'No, thanks. And call me Scott.'

'And I am Benito. Please, come in.'

The elevator was at one end of an office that occupied the entire third floor of the building. A large desk stood along one wall and above the desk was a bank of closed-circuit TVs showing the street scene around the building. On one screen were Hank, Carlos, and Louis – mostly Louis.

'Now that is a bodyguard,' Benito said.

A sitting area with a leather couch and chairs stretched along

210

one wall of windows and a wet bar along the third wall with a flat-screen TV mounted above. It reminded Scott of Nick Madden's office, absent the game tables. And Nick and Benito had a mutual client.

'Why have you come to me?' Benito asked.

'Trey's last phone conversation was with you.'

'Ah.'

'Why'd you agree to see me?'

Benito smiled. 'Never know when I might need a good defense lawyer.'

'I don't represent drug dealers. I have kids.'

'I do not sell to kids. I am a businessman, selling the people what they want.'

'They may want it, but they don't need it.'

'No different than the State of Texas selling lottery tickets to poor people.'

'The lottery is legal. Your business isn't.'

'Just because the state made theirs legal. And give it a few years, people are sick of funding the war on drugs. They want to spend those billions on health care. They do not care if someone snorts coke or shoots heroin or if their drug habit kills thousands of Mexicans each year. Eighteen metric tons of heroin cross the border each year, five hundred tons of cocaine, fifteen thousand tons of marijuana, God knows how much meth – *gringos* want their drugs and they are going to get them, from someone. Might as well be me. And no, I did not kill Trey.'

'Will you take a polygraph?'

'They indicted your wife for his murder, not me.'

'Did Trey buy cocaine from you?'

'Let us sit.'

Benito escorted Scott to the sitting area. He sat on the couch facing the window; Benito sat in a chair facing Scott and crossed his legs. He gestured at the window behind him.

'Across the street, the Feds have cameras on my front door twenty-four/seven. I feel like a Hollywood movie star, and they are my paparazzi.'

'How long did you know Trey?'

'We grew up together. He lived in the nice part of town, the south side near the beach. I lived in the housing projects on the north side, near the docks. I now live on the beach, and the projects, they are gone, washed away by Ike. As are the Latinos and the blacks. They all moved to the mainland, no place to live here. The Anglos, like your friend Senator Armstrong, they hope the Latinos and blacks will stay gone from the Island. They think it will be good for business, if the rich tourists do not see us. BOIs have always treated us like IBCs, like we do not belong on the Island, even if we too were born here. But Trey, he did not treat me that way. He treated me like a human being. He came to my apartment, and he dated my sister, took her to the prom, gave her the corsage of white carnations as if she were the Anglo prom queen. We were like brothers.'

'How'd you get into this business?' Scott said.

'Went to Harvard, minority scholarship. No jobs on Wall Street, credit crunch and all, so I came back to the Island. But the only jobs for a minority – even with a Harvard degree – are waiting tables for tourists. When this position came open a couple years ago—'

'How?'

Benito sighed. 'My predecessor, he cooked the books.'

'What happened to him?'

'I did not ask.'

'But you sold to Trey?'

'Yes.'

'A lot?'

'On a regular basis.'

'Did he come here?'

'No. He knew about the surveillance, they would spot that black Bentley or that BMW bike, know it was him. He was high-profile here on the Island. It would not do his career any good to be seen on TV entering my office, so he required a more discreet arrangement. I made deliveries personally, to his house.'

'You do that for a lot of your customers?'

212

'Only two. Now only one.'

'So you've been in his house?'

'Of course.'

'Have you ever been arrested?'

'Twice. Charges were dismissed.'

'But you were fingerprinted?'

'Yes.'

Benito's prints were in the system, which meant his prints did not match the unidentified prints at the crime scene.

'You seem to operate without much interference from the law.'

Benito smiled. 'Let us just say that no one wants me on the witness stand, telling the world who my customers are.'

'Let's stick with one customer. How'd you make the deliveries to Trey's house?'

'He gave me a key to the garage door. I put the product in the dumb waiter, pushed the UP button for the fourth floor. His office.'

'How often did you make deliveries?'

'Weekly.'

'When?'

Benito shrugged. 'Whenever.'

'During the day?'

'Yes.'

'And how did he pay you?'

'When I returned, the money would be waiting for me.'

'In the dumb waiter?'

'In the Hummer.'

'So you had no problems with Trey?'

'I did not say that.'

'What was the problem?'

'Trey owed me five hundred thousand dollars.'

'That's a lot of cocaine.'

'It is very high quality. He wanted only the best. And I assumed he shared with your wife.'

'So why didn't he pay? He was rich.'

213

'He did not inform me when he went on tour, so I made my weekly deliveries. He would be gone two, three, sometimes four weeks at a time. I would put each week's delivery in the dumb waiter, with the prior deliveries. He would collect the deliveries when he returned, and he always paid me in full. This past April, he went on tour again – I know, because I saw him on TV, he missed a very short putt and lost – but this time the dumb waiter was empty every week. And there was no money in the Hummer. So I assumed he had someone collect it for him, send it to him on tour.'

Benito exhaled heavily.

'I trusted Trey. Like a brother. So one day he called me, said he had been out of town for six weeks, said he needed a delivery. I said he must first pay what he owed, five hundred thousand. He said he did not receive the deliveries. I explained how I had made the deliveries, how the dumb waiter was empty each week . . .'

Benito shook his head; he seemed genuinely upset.

'He accused me of cheating him.'

'Did you?'

'No. I made the deliveries.'

'So what happened to the cocaine?'

'I do not know. But he should have stopped delivery while he was gone, like you do with your newspaper. Risk of loss passes to the buyer upon delivery. That is the law.'

'What, you were going to sue him?'

'We do not file lawsuits.'

'You kill.'

'I don't.'

'The Zetas do. Did they know Trey owed you?'

Benito nodded. 'I am a distributor. They handle collections.'

'Benito, why are you telling me all this?'

He stroked his goatee and sighed. 'Because I am afraid that I failed my brother. The last few months, Trey was not the same person I knew. At first, I thought it must be the cocaine, he was using more and more. But now I think not. I think there was more going on.'

'What?'

'I do not know. But he seemed very stressed. And afraid. He bought guns.'

'Maybe to protect himself from the Zetas.'

'Maybe. Maybe someone else. Scott, I do not want your wife to go to prison for a crime she did not commit.'

'You think she's innocent?'

'Yes.'

'Why?'

'You are defending her – why do you think she is innocent?' Benito sat back. 'A black hooker accused of murdering a senator's son and now your ex-wife accused of murdering a pro golfer – why do you take on such causes? For the money?'

'What money?'

'For the fame?'

'I don't want fame.'

'Then why do you do it?'

Scott sighed. 'I'm not sure.'

'And do you think you will be able to prove that she is innocent? Your wife?'

'She's innocent until proven guilty.'

'Scott, I am Latino. I know the reality of the law.'

'You spoke to Trey on the phone the night he was killed?'

'Yes.'

'Did you talk about his debt?'

'Yes. I was trying to save his life.'

'How?'

'To get him to pay what he owed, so the cartel did not send the Zetas after him. He was my friend, Scott. I did not want to see him harmed.'

'Did they send in the Zetas?'

'Perhaps. But I do not think so.'

'Why not?'

'Because she is still alive. Your wife.'

215

Chapter 26

'God, that jail is awful.'

Thirty minutes after Scott had bailed Rebecca out, she was still trembling.

'At least I don't have to wear that ankle bracelet.'

'Don't jump bail, Rebecca, or I'll lose the house.'

Scott had pledged his house to secure her bond and release from custody.

They had driven from the jail to the beach and were now walking along the seawall. Joggers ran past, kids zipped by on skateboards, and parents pushed strollers with young children aboard. The Island street scene was nice, and it was decidedly not Dallas. There were no Neiman Marcus mothers, no Armani dads, no Jacadi Paris girls, and no Hugo Boss boys. There were tie-dyed T-shirts and cargo shorts and neon flip-flops. Galveston was a Wal-Mart town, the poor man's Riviera. But not for long, if the senator had his way.

'Scott, you know how you said prisons are full of innocent people?'

He nodded.

'If I'm convicted, what happens?'

'I'll appeal, try to get the conviction overturned.'

'How long does that take?'

'Two or three years.'

'Do I get to live out here? While you appeal?'

'No. You go to prison.'

'But what if they realize I'm innocent? What happens then?'

'They release you and say, "Sorry. Have a nice life".'

But Scott was not worried about that happening because Rebecca Fenney would not survive two or three years in prison. She might be a survivor in society, but not when taken out of society. She would die in prison. They came to a bench and sat.

'The toxicology reports came back.'

Her shoulders slumped, and she stared out to sea.

'Jesus, Rebecca . . . *cocaine*? Why?'

'I only did it a few times.'

Two years before, her affair with the assistant golf pro at the club had stunned Scott like a blow to the head – he still had a hard time believing she had had sex with Trey during the day then had come home to her family that night – but the thought of his wife using cocaine seemed inconceivable. Shopping till she dropped, he knew that Rebecca Fenney. But snorting cocaine through a straw? That was not the Rebecca he knew. How could she do it? How could anyone do it? How many of the people strolling the seawall that fine day did it? If Benito's figures were correct – he said the cartels sent five hundred metric tons of cocaine into the US annually – a lot of these people did it. But none of them were standing trial for murder in thirty-five days.

'You know Benito Estrada?'

'No.'

'I do. I just met him, before I bailed you out. He sold cocaine to Trey. A lot.'

She nodded. 'I was really worried about it. He started about six months ago, at least that's when I found out about it. At first he said it was to celebrate a great round, then to get over a bad round, then after every round. He said he had it under control, but the last few months, it was every day.'

'He owed Benito five hundred thousand dollars.'

217

'For cocaine?'

Scott nodded. 'Benito called him that night, tried to convince him to pay, said he didn't want Trey to get hurt, by the Zetas.'

'Who are they?'

'The cartel's killers.'

'Why didn't Trey pay him? He had the money.'

'He thought Benito had cheated him.'

'You think they killed Trey? Those Zetas?'

'I don't know. Was he stressed out, before his death?'

'No. He won the Challenge the week before.'

'Why'd he buy guns?'

She shrugged. 'Crime on the Island. So he started carrying a gun in the car.'

'Why didn't you tell me, Rebecca?'

'That he carried a gun?'

'That you used cocaine.'

'I didn't want Boo to know.'

'It'll come out at trial . . . and it won't be good when it does.'

They stood and walked again, but Scott did not hold her hand this time.

Louis walked over to where Carlos was working on two surf-boards laid out on the sand. 'What's a six-letter word for "entertain at bedtime"?'

'Hooker.'

Louis grunted. 'Fits.' He filled in the blanks on the crossword puzzle then said, 'What are you doing?'

'Cleaning these boards. Found them under the house, pulled them out for us.'

'What do you mean "us"?'

'Me and you, man – we're gonna learn to surf this summer. Boo wants to learn, but the boss said no.'

'Why?'

'Guess he figures she might drown.'

'No, why do you think I want to learn to surf?'

' 'Cause we're at the beach.'

218

'I saw that *Jaws* movie. I figure there's sharks out in that water.'

'None big enough to eat you.'

'That *Jaws* shark ate a boat. Reckon they'd be big enough to take a bite out of me.' Louis looked out to sea for a time. 'One thing I've learned, Carlos, there's always someone bigger and meaner.'

Carlos chuckled. 'Benito's men?'

'That could've turned ugly.'

'Testosterone will do that.'

'Mean will do it, too.'

'Zetas are mean. Think they killed that white boy?'

'They killed a black boy, down in the projects. Figured he was safe down there, that Mexicans wouldn't come into South Dallas. But they did. Armed like the infantry, a dozen of 'em. They found him, chased him down, shot him to pieces. Like in a movie. You know how much he owed? Ten thousand.'

'Trey Rawlins owed them five hundred thousand.'

'Not no more he don't.'

'The cocaine,' Karen said. 'Scott, that's bad evidence. How can we put Rebecca on the stand now?'

'We can't.'

'Which makes conviction more likely,' Bobby said.

'What'll happen to Boo then?' Karen said.

They were on the back deck. Rebecca and Boo were on the beach.

'Scott, I'm not one to butt into your personal affairs—'

Bobby laughed. 'Since when?'

'I'm sorry,' Karen said. 'Never mind.'

'Karen,' Scott said, 'you've been the girls' mother for the last two years. We wouldn't have made it without you, okay? You've earned the right to butt in. What's on your mind?'

She gestured down at Boo and Rebecca. 'They seem to be getting close again.'

'She's her mother.'

'Biological only. Scott, I've been carrying this baby for almost eight months now. There's no way I'll ever leave this child. How could she?'

'Karen, failure is not an option in Highland Park. It can be a tough place—'

'Life is tough. Scott, defending her is one thing, but don't make excuses for her. She abandoned her child. There's no excuse for that. Would you ever leave Boo or Pajamae?'

'No.'

'Okay. She shouldn't have left Boo.'

'Agreed.'

'They were apart for two years, now they're back together for what, two months when the trial's over. What if she's convicted and they're apart again − for five to life? That would devastate Boo.'

'I couldn't just leave her in Dallas. She wouldn't have stood for that.'

'No, she wouldn't. But it's going to hurt her badly − if Rebecca's convicted.'

Scott stared out to sea then nodded.

'Then we can't let that happen.'

Renée Ramirez presented another 'Murder on the Beach' report on the ten o'clock news that night. She opened with footage from the arraignment, Rebecca in her jail jumpsuit pleading 'not guilty' and Renée peppering Scott with questions in the corridor outside the courtroom ending with 'Do you still love your wife?' and Scott's stunned expression. Then Renée went live from Galveston.

'*Judge Shelby Morgan set the trial date for July twentieth and bail at two hundred and fifty thousand dollars. I interviewed Terri Rawlins after the hearing.*'

Terri appeared on the screen and said, '*Now she can sit in jail where she belongs.*'

Back to Renée: '*But Rebecca Fenney is not in jail tonight. Her ex-husband and lawyer, A. Scott Fenney, bonded her out by pledging his Highland Park house. She is now staying with him and his family*' *in a rented beach house until the trial. I've heard about carrying a torch for an old love, but this guy is taking it a bit far.'* Renée smiled and shook her head. *'Confidential sources at the courthouse have confirmed that the toxicology results showed significant levels of cocaine in Trey Rawlins' blood at the time of his death, and also in Rebecca Fenney's blood that same night.'*

'Damnit!' Scott pointed at the TV. 'Who's leaking this stuff?'

'That detective,' Bobby said.

Back on the screen: *'Earlier today I interviewed Louise, a prostitute who spent three nights in the same cell with Rebecca Fenney.'*

A hard-looking female face filled the screen. Louise was not a high-priced hooker. She worked the street corners of Galveston. She said, *'Oh, she bad. I seen it in her eyes. She killed that white boy. She guilty as sin.'*

Chapter 27

'Pick and roll, Mr Fenney,' Pajamae whispered.

They were playing basketball on the court next to the house. Three on three: Pajamae, Boo, and Scott versus Bobby, Carlos, and Louis. Sitting in lawn chairs in the shade of the house were the fans: Rebecca, Karen, Consuela, and Maria. Pajamae was dribbling in place, and Bobby was guarding her. Scott circled the court then came up from behind and took a position right next to Bobby – the 'pick' – blocking his path to Pajamae; she darted past Bobby, and Scott pivoted off his pick – the 'roll' – and went hard to the basket looking back for Pajamae's bounce pass and –

'Unnnhh.'

– collapsed to the concrete. He had rolled right into Louis with a good head of steam; running into a brick wall would have been a more pleasant experience. He first heard Rebecca's voice – 'You okay, Scott?' – and then Karen's laughter and her voice – 'I peed in my diaper. Maria, you need a clean diaper, too?'

It was the following Sunday, Father's Day, and this father was now stretched out flat on his back on the warm surface staring up at Louis's broad face and the blue sky and white seagulls beyond. Boo's frantic face appeared above him and she cried out, 'Oh, my God – is he breathing?'

She dropped to her knees next to him and gently slapped his face.

'A. Scott, speak to me!'

She put her ear to his chest then came up with her arms spread to the heavens.

'He's alive!'

'I'm fine, Boo.'

'Oh.'

More faces came into view – the amused faces of Bobby and Carlos and finally the frowning face of Pajamae Jones-Fenney. She punched her hips with her fists.

'Damn, Mr Fenney, can't you run a pick and roll?'

'No. I can't. Not against Louis. And don't cuss.'

'Well, you wanna be my daddy, you gonna have to man up on a B-ball court. You ever see homies playin' hoops in the 'hood? You playin' street ball now, mista.'

'Pajamae, it's not the NBA finals.'

But she had already returned to the game. 'Yo, my man.' She shot the ball over to Carlos. 'Your ball out, bro. We two down.' Scott heard her muttering to herself. 'Black girl got a white man for a daddy, how she gonna learn basketball good enough to get a college scholarship, tell me that?'

Louis extended a big hand to Scott. He took it, and Louis lifted him to his feet like he was air. 'You okay, Mr Fenney?'

Scott nodded, but he wasn't sure.

'Boss,' Carlos said, 'we'll trade Mr Herrin for Pajamae.'

'Thanks a lot, Carlos,' Bobby said.

'No offense, Mr Herrin, but you ain't got no shot.'

'I got you out of jail six times.'

'That's true. Never mind.'

Carlos passed the ball to Bobby, who air-balled a ten-footer, which evoked a 'see what I mean' expression from Carlos. Scott grabbed the rebound and passed it over to Pajamae. She faced off Carlos. He spread his legs wide and got down low.

'Come on, girlie, show me what you got?'

Pajamae smiled, made a quick fake right, then passed the ball

223

through Carlos's open legs, picked up the ball behind him, and nailed a banker over Louis.

'That's what I got, homeboy.'

'*Homeboy?* I'm Mexican.'

'Pajamae,' Scott said, 'your mother insisted you use correct English, and you do, except when you're on a basketball court. Then you street talk. What's up with that?'

'Oh. I'm being authentic.'

'Authentic?'

'Unh-huh. See, black folks street talk when they play hoops, it's part of the culture. So if I'm gonna be a black basketball star when I grow up, I've got to sound authentic, like I came from the streets. Shoe sponsors love that kind of life story.'

It actually sounded reasonable.

'And I'll have to get tattoos.'

'Why?'

'You ever see an NBA player without tattoos?'

Boo joined them. 'If she gets a tattoo, I'm getting my ears pierced.'

'She's not getting a tattoo and you're not getting holes in your ears.'

'Shit.'

'Don't cuss.'

Being a father wasn't easy, on or off a basketball court. Texting, sexting, sex, drugs, cable, profanity, porn, tattoos – there were just too many bad influences in kids' lives these days. But a good parent fought the fight every day. As Scott Fenney had and would. He would get these two girls through middle school, high school, and college, hopefully without any permanent damage or tattoos. He would be there for them when they were tempted or taunted or teased. He would answer their questions about sex honestly. And he would never use drugs. He would be their father.

'Happy Father's Day, Scott.'

Two hours later, Rebecca brought him a bowl of ice cream out on the deck. She sat and watched the waves wash ashore.

'When was the best time of your life?' she asked.

'Now. With the girls.'

'But you're broke and you don't have anyone.'

'I have them.'

'Do you have fun? The kind of fun a man needs.'

'I have father fun.'

'Is that enough?'

'It may have to be.'

'It doesn't have to be, Scott. You can have fun with me again.'

The girls needed a mother, and he needed a woman. Could Rebecca be a mother to Boo again . . . and to Pajamae? Could she be his wife again? Could they all go back to the way they were, as if the last two years had never happened? As if she had not run off with the golf pro, as if he were not now dead, as if she had not been accused of his murder, as if she had not used cocaine? How could she be a good mother if she were a bad influence? Would that work? Could it ever be the same? Could they have fun again?

And when they went to bed, would Trey lie down with them?

'Pete still winning?' Scott asked.

'He's up by one, on the fourteenth hole.'

'Unbelievable. Better eat this inside, see if he can finish it off.'

They went inside and found everyone lounging on the couch and chairs and eating cake and ice cream and the girls rolling on the floor laughing hysterically.

'What's so funny?' Scott asked.

'Cialis commercial,' Karen said. 'They mentioned the possible side effects, you know, "seek immediate medical help for an erection lasting more than four hours". That tickled the girls.'

'That'd damn sure tickle me,' Carlos said. 'But I wouldn't call no doctor. I'd throw a party.' He gestured at the TV. 'What I don't get is, that Cialis commercial always shows the man and woman in separate bathtubs. How can you do it like that?'

'Oh,' Bobby said, 'what you do is—'

'Bobby!' Karen said. 'The girls.'

'Oh.' To Carlos: 'Later.'

'When those commercials come on,' Scott said, 'change the channel.'

'They're on every channel,' Karen said.

'What's a four-letter word for "Turkey neighbor"?' Louis said.

'Peas,' Carlos said.

'Iran,' Bobby said.

'I ain't never had no turkey and iran for Thanksgiving.'

'They're countries – Turkey and Iran.'

'Oh.'

Scott plopped onto the sofa and watched the US Open, which featured narrow fairways, fast greens, glamour shots of WAGs in the gallery, and commercials targeting WM squared: fast cars, long drivers, and drugs for prostates that have enlarged and penises that won't. Pete Puckett resorted to his trusty one-iron and hit every fairway and green the final round. On the eighteenth hole, he tapped in a short putt to win.

Pete Puckett had won the US Open.

It was his first win in over twenty years, and the sports shocker of the year. Pete high-fived Goose then walked off the green and wrapped his arms around his young daughter. The TV crew stuck cameras in their faces as they cried together and the microphones caught Pete saying, 'I wish your mama was here.' Nick Madden stood next to them. When Pete released Billie Jean, Nick hugged him like a boy hugging his grandpa. Pete accepted a check for $1.35 million and the silver trophy then stepped to a microphone set up on the green.

'I dreamed of this day for twenty-six years out here on tour. And now, for that dream to come true . . . I just wish my wife could be here.' He hefted the trophy high and gazed into the sky. 'Dottie Lynn, this is for you.'

He put his arm around his daughter. Tears streamed down Billie Jean's face, but Scott couldn't help wondering if some of her tears were for Trey Rawlins.

Holding the US Open trophy aloft, Pete Puckett didn't look like a killer – but a father would kill to protect his child. A twenty-eight-year-old man had seduced his seventeen-year-old daughter. Pete had learned of the affair and had threatened to kill Trey if he didn't stay away from Billie Jean. He had done what any father would do. He had tried to protect his daughter.

Had he killed for his daughter?

The law allowed network TV to show commercials for erectile dysfunction cures and seventeen-year-old children to have sex, but fathers didn't. What would Scott do to a man who lured Boo or Pajamae into sex at seventeen? It frightened him to think what he might do . . . what he could do. What any man could do. What a father would do. That dark side of a man resided in every father. We suppress it and control it and deny it – but it's always there. Waiting. For when it was needed. When a father needed to be a man . . . in the worst way a man could be.

Had Trey Rawlins brought out the worst in Pete Puckett?

'Louis, if Mr Fenney marries Miz Fenney again, Boo'll have her family back together. They won't want a little black girl in the way.'

'Mr Fenney, he adopted you. You ain't no little black girl. You're his girl.'

'You think it's okay for a white man to be my daddy? Even if he can't play basketball?'

'I think you're blessed to have any man love you as much as Mr Fenney does and want to be your daddy. Ain't no color to love.'

'But my mama's dead.'

'Your mama was gonna die sooner than later, that's just the way it was for her. But you could've ended up with no one instead of Boo and Mr Fenney.'

'I'd still have you.'

'That's a fact, but Mr Fenney, he knows how to be a daddy. I don't.'

'But I already had a daddy, so how can Mr Fenney be my daddy?'

'You already had a daddy?'

'Unh-huh.'

'So what'd he look like?'

'I don't know.'

'He ever play with you?'

'No.'

'Live with you?'

'No.'

'Take care of you?'

'No.'

'Love you?'

'No.'

'Then you ain't never had no daddy, girl. Till Mr Fenney.'

'But he's Boo's daddy. Don't seem right, me taking some of his love from her.'

'It don't work that way. A man's love expands to meet the demands.'

'Huh?'

'You ain't taking love from Boo, you adding love to Mr Fenney. His heart is like a tree – it grew bigger for you.'

'Huh?'

'He's got twice as much love now that you're in his life.'

'Oh.'

'Pajamae!'

She looked over to Mr Fenney and Miss Fenney and Boo playing in the surf. Mr Fenney was waving her over. Louis nudged her.

'Go on over to your father, girl.'

What was he doing here?

Had he made a mistake when he agreed to represent Rebecca? He had no doubt there was a good explanation for her fingerprints being on the murder weapon, but there was no explanation for her using cocaine. How would he explain that to the jury? Juries don't like that kind of evidence in a murder case. They like a clean and sober defendant – and no direct evidence tying the defendant to the crime – in order to acquit. They have to believe beyond all reasonable doubt that the defendant is innocent. An

American jury's greatest fear is not convicting an innocent person but acquitting a guilty person. Being ridiculed in the press for abdicating their responsibility – their duty – to put people in prison. Why would the police have arrested her and the DA have charged her and the grand jury have indicted her if she weren't guilty? A presumption of guilt burdens every juror's mind when he or she takes a seat in the jury box on the first day of trial – which was now only twenty-nine days away. Would he be able to overcome that presumption and prove his ex-wife innocent? Would he be able to prove that Pete Puckett – or perhaps the Zetas – had killed Trey Rawlins? Or had A. Scott Fenney taken on the biggest lost cause of his career? And sacrificed his career? Again.

He realized he was staring at Rebecca and Boo was standing next to him. He looked down at her. Her eyes went from him to Rebecca and back to him. She smiled.

'Are you having a Cialis moment?'

Two hours later, the sun was low, the girls were inside, Miss Fenney was doing her yoga on the beach, and Carlos had talked Louis into going out on the surfboards.

'Miss Fenney, she's a fine-looking woman. And flexible.'

'Don't go there, Carlos.'

They had paddled out – way out. Louis and Carlos were bobbing on surfboards in the Gulf of Mexico, Carlos looking like he should be the lifeguard at a maximum security prison pool with his black hair slicked back, his dark sunglasses, his tattoos on his muscular arms – and Louis feeling scared. He gazed around at the sea of brown water that surrounded him. It was vast and it was deep and it was filled with creatures who belonged in the water – unlike him. He was a three-hundred-thirty-pound black man who belonged on dry land.

'Louis, you think you ever gonna be a daddy?'

'I hope so. You?'

'Hell, I might already be one. We got *machismo*, we don't need no Cialis.'

229

'Figure you'll get married and have a normal family, like Mr Fenney?'

Carlos laughed. 'Normal?' He waved a hand at the beach. 'Ain't nothing normal going on over there, the boss defending his ex-wife. That's *abnormal*. And no, I don't figure either one of us is ever gonna get married.'

'You're handsome.'

'Why, thank you, Louis, you're kind of cute yourself . . . in a big way.'

'Why not? We're good men – a few priors maybe, but no violent crimes.'

'No *convictions*.'

'I stand corrected.'

''Cause women, Louis, they don't want good men, they want rich men. And I don't figure on ever being rich. Hence, I ain't never gonna have a wife.'

'*Hence?*'

'I heard the boss say it. Sounds good.'

Louis nodded. 'It does. So you're saying we're gonna be alone all our lives?'

''Fraid so, bro.'

'Damn.'

'But think of the bright side.'

'What's that?'

'You ever get a chance to cheat with a woman like Miss Fenney, you can cheat without getting caught.'

'But it ain't cheating if you don't have a wife.'

'Exactly my point.'

'Your point don't make no sense.'

'My point is, you'll always be a free man.'

'And alone.'

'That, too.'

'You done with your point?'

'Yep.'

'Okay. Now that you got me out here, what the hell am I supposed to do?'

'Wait for a good wave, then lie down and paddle like the devil himself is after your ass. Once we get going, we just stand up on the board and ride that mother all the way to shore.'

'Just like that?'

'Yep.'

'What if we fall off? Figure that could kill us?'

Carlos laughed. 'Hell, Louis, it ain't falling off that's gonna kill you – it's the sharks eating you.'

'*Sharks?* You see a shark?'

Three hundred yards due north, Scott, Karen, and Bobby were on the back deck. Bobby said, 'Tell me they're not really going to try that.'

They did. A big wave – for Galveston Beach – rose behind Carlos and Louis. They lay down on the boards and started paddling. When the wave was almost upon them, they squatted on the boards then . . . stood.

'I'll be damned. They're surfing.'

They waved their arms wildly trying to maintain their balance on the boards, and they did – for about five seconds. Then the wave overcame them and sent them and their boards flying. They went under . . . and stayed under. Scott stood. Just when he was about to run down to the beach and play life-guard, their boards surfaced, then Carlos popped up, followed by Louis. The waves rolled them ashore. They coughed sea water then struggled to their feet and looked at each other; then they smiled and high-fived. 'Now that's what I'm talkin' about!' Carlos shouted.

'They're nuts,' Karen said.

'Hank Herrin,' Bobby said.

Karen stared at him with an incredulous expression. 'And you are too if you think I'm naming our son Hank.'

'I'm seeing a home run hitter.'

'I'm seeing a guy with tattoos wearing a wife-beater T-shirt and spitting tobacco juice out the window of his pickup truck.'

Bobby shrugged then turned to Scott. 'I checked in with the

answering service. The network morning shows called. They all want an interview with you and the Guilty Groupie.'

'That's not gonna happen.' Scott sat back down. 'Okay, guys, we're on the clock. Four weeks till trial. Where do we stand?'

'Our strategy,' Bobby said, 'is to, (a) explain why her prints are on the murder weapon, and (b) find out who killed Trey. Anything on (a)?'

'No. What about (b)?'

'The suspect list keeps getting longer,' Karen said. She tapped on her laptop. 'So far we have the construction workers, Goose, Brett McBride, Donnie Parker, Vic Hager, Pete Puckett, and Benito Estrada and the Zetas.'

'Brett, Donnie, and Vic have alibis for that night, but anyone with a motive stays on the list. And I don't rate the construction workers very high, but I asked Carlos to go back to work there, see if he can get some information about the cocaine . . . if they stole it. Which would explain why Trey thought Benito cheated him.'

'So that leaves Goose, Pete, and Benito and the Zetas.'

'Goose's prints didn't match the ones on the kitchen counter.'

'We need Pete's prints.'

'I'm going to the San Antonio Open on Wednesday, to get them.'

'So the prime suspects are the pro golfer who just won the US Open, a Mexican drug cartel, and your ex-wife.' Bobby unwrapped a piece of gum and popped it into his mouth. 'Should've waited until after this case to quit smoking.'

'I completed the asset searches on Trey and Rebecca,' Karen said. 'No surprises. Rebecca's got nothing except the Corvette. I got the subpoenas to Hank, he served them on Facebook and the cell phone carrier.'

'Anything on the sister?' Bobby asked.

'No,' Scott said. 'But her lawyer, Melvyn Burke, he knows something.'

'What?'

'I don't know. Terri won't waive the attorney-client privilege.' To Karen: 'What about the judge?'

'UT undergrad, dean's list, cheerleader. UT law school, graduated with honors. Private practice for ten years, then elected judge five years ago. No big cases.'

'Until now. Pretrial motions?'

'I'm going to file a motion to exclude the crime scene photos as inflammatory. The DA'll still get some in.'

'Can we exclude evidence found at the house?'

'She called nine-one-one, invited them in, consented to a search. Even if she hadn't, it wasn't her house. And it was a crime scene, so that room was open to a search. But I'll still file a motion to suppress.'

'What about the tox report? Did they have probable cause to draw her blood?'

'Probably not. I'll file a motion to exclude that, too.'

There was an awkward moment of silence, then Scott said, 'She's not an addict.'

Scott gazed at Rebecca on the beach with the girls. She seemed like a girl herself, skipping through the surf, as if she were not soon to stand trial for murder.

'Has the possibility of life in prison registered yet?' Karen said.

Scott gestured down at the beach. 'One day she's acting happy, talking about us getting back together . . . the next day she's on suicide watch. I don't get her.'

'It's the cocaine,' Bobby said.

'What cocaine?'

'Scotty, I represented users. I know the symptoms. Cycles of depression and euphoria, that's a cocaine user. She's using.'

Scott shook his head. 'She only used it a few times with Trey. She'd never use it around Boo. No way.'

'Way.' Bobby pointed to the beach. 'Go down there and do a blood draw, I guarantee a tox screen would come back positive for cocaine.'

'Where would she get it from? And how would she pay for it?'

'Scotty, you staying objective? About her?'

Think like a lawyer, not like a man.

233

'I found a polygraph guy,' Karen said. 'On Bolivar Peninsula, retired FBI. Is she willing to do it?'

Scott nodded.

'Are you worried?'

'She's not.'

'It's the cocaine,' Bobby said.

'Crack dealers,' Pajamae said, 'they killed this man down in the projects one day. Just walked up and shot him dead, right in front of everyone.'

'Shit,' Boo said. 'I mean, damn. I mean, wow.'

Scott had come upstairs to say goodnight to the girls. 'Fear. They wanted to scare you.'

'Well, Mr Fenney, it worked.'

'Why'd they kill the man?' Boo asked.

'He owed them money.'

'Why didn't the dealers just hire a lawyer and sue him?'

'Boo, folks in the projects don't sue each other. Lawsuits are for white folks who don't have guns.'

Boo nodded, as if Pajamae's statement made perfect sense.

'Nothing exciting like that ever happens in Highland Park. It's so boring.'

'What do folks in Highland Park do for excitement?'

'Shop at Neiman Marcus mostly.'

'Ain't no Neiman or Marcus in South Dallas.'

'So what did you do for excitement down in the projects?'

'Walk outside.'

Boo nodded then turned to Scott. 'I saw something on TV this morning about Mother's boyfriend.'

'Boo, I told you, when something about the case comes on, change the channel. There's a lot of stuff you don't need to know yet.'

'Stuff like her boyfriend used drugs?'

'Yes, stuff like that.'

She hesitated, and Scott knew what her next question would be. She had to ask.

234

'Did mother use drugs, too?'

Before Rebecca had left them, whenever Boo had asked Scott tough questions like that, he had always answered like a lawyer: he had fudged the truth. But when he became her only parent, he had started answering her like a father instead. And so he answered her now. He lied.

'No.'

An eleven-year-old girl did not need to know that truth about her mother.

'Good.' She seemed relieved. 'So, if Mother doesn't go to that prison, is she coming home with us?'

'Do you want her back?'

'Did you come down here to get her back?'

'I came down here to defend your mother so she doesn't spend the rest of her life in prison for a crime she didn't commit.'

'But you want to understand why she left us?'

'Yes.'

'Because you blame yourself?'

'Yes.'

'Which is why you won't ask Ms Dawson out?'

'Yes.'

Boo nodded. 'I don't understand her either. Mother is a complicated person. But you two wouldn't get married again unless we all decide?'

'No. Never. We're a family. And a family makes decisions together.'

'Good. Oh, A. Scott, there was a segment this morning about statins. I really think you should be on one. You're thirty-eight now.'

'Boo, I know thirty-eight sounds really old to you, but it's not. I'm still a young man. I'm not going to die on you.' He put a hand on each of their shoulders. 'On either of you.'

'You'd better not,' Boo said.

Scott kissed them goodnight then went into his bedroom, which shared a bathroom with Carlos and Louis's bedroom. They were downstairs watching TV, so he undressed and showered. He was still naked when he opened the door to his bedroom and saw Rebecca standing there. She too was naked. Incredibly naked. They stared at each other.

'You look good, Scott.'

So did she.

'Let's finish what we started on the beach,' she said. 'For Father's Day.'

He wanted her. But he resisted. Because he had to think like a lawyer and not lust like a man. Because she needed him as her lawyer more than he needed her as his lover. Because she couldn't be a bad influence and a good mother.

'We can't.'

He turned, walked back into the bathroom, and shut the door, but he did think, *That's an odd place for a tattoo.*

Chapter 28

'It's official. Medical Examiner ruled it a homicide.'

The next morning, Galveston County Criminal District Attorney Rex Truitt handed the final autopsy report on Trey Rawlins across his desk to Scott. He passed it to Bobby. The Assistant DA sat in the corner like a kid in timeout.

'No change to the cause of death,' the DA said. 'Sharp force injury. The knife killed Trey, not the cocaine.'

'Who told Renée about the cocaine?'

'Detective Wilson denied it, but lots of people saw that tox report.'

'It's not right, Rex, for someone in your office—'

'I don't know it's coming from my office, Scott.'

'It's coming from someone in law enforcement, and that's not right, leaking evidence to the press. That's depriving my client of a fair trial. Find your leak, Rex, and plug it, or I'm filing for a change of venue.'

'That won't make Shelby happy.'

'Keeping her happy isn't my job.'

Bobby, always mindful of Scott's blood pressure, diverted the conversation.

'Rex, what about the fingerprints?'

The DA had said the fingerprint results were back. He read from another report. 'None of the prints you gave us matched the unidentified prints at the crime scene. But your "TM" – comes up Teresa Daniels in the system – she was arrested for solicitation five years ago, in Nevada.'

'Figures.'

'The item marked "NM", Nicholas Madden in the system, he was arrested for DUI ten years ago, deferred adjudication.'

'Not surprised.'

'And one of the five "CW" prints belongs to a Hector Garrido, fugitive from Mexico, wanted for murder. That's why I called you soon as I got this report. Where'd you get his prints?'

'He's working on the judge's house, down the street from Trey's house.'

The DA nodded. 'We'll pick him up this morning.'

'Can you hold off till five?'

'Why?'

'Those Zetas might've killed Trey.'

'I thought Pete Puckett killed him? Or the caddie?'

'I think Pete did, but the Zetas had a good motive, too.'

The DA hesitated before asking the question he did not want to ask.

'And what motive was that?'

'Trey owed Benito five hundred thousand dollars.'

The news knocked the DA back in his chair. 'Hank said you got in to see Benito. He tell you that?'

Scott nodded. 'Trey bought a lot of cocaine from him.'

The DA's shoulders slumped. 'When the tox screen came back, I figured him for recreational use, but five hundred grand – that's vocational.' He blew out a breath. 'It's like when A-Rod fessed up to steroids. I couldn't believe it. He always seemed so righteous, love of the game and all. I guess we want to believe someone's above all this crap.' He shook his head. 'But why didn't the Feds pick up Trey on their surveillance of Benito's place? It's twenty-four/seven.'

'Because he never went there. Benito delivered the cocaine

238

to Trey's house, every week. Said Trey gave him a key to the garage, he put it in the dumb waiter.'

'Why the debt? Trey was rich.'

'Trey disputed some deliveries, accused Benito of cheating him. Benito said he made the deliveries.'

'Rex,' the Assistant DA said, 'we can probably keep Trey's drug use out at trial, unless they can show a direct connection to his death.'

'Unlikely it'll be suppressed, Ted, but that's not the point. Trey owed half a million bucks to a Mexican cartel, and that's a goddamned death wish.'

'And a motive for murder,' Scott said.

'Except her prints are on the murder weapon.'

'The Zetas are professionals. They wouldn't have left prints.'

'True. So what's that got to do with those construction workers?'

'They might've stolen the cocaine. Carlos is working down there, to find out.'

'A man on the inside. Good thinking. Okay, we'll wait till five to pick up Hector, take that long to get the arrest warrant anyway. Tell your man to hightail it out of there before then, the cops are gonna round up everyone with brown skin till they figure out which one's Hector. I can't have a wanted murderer running around the Island.'

'Boo wants me to teach her to surf, boss.'

'You want to take my eleven-year-old daughter out half a mile into the Gulf of Mexico on a surfboard?'

'Uhh . . . I guess not.' Carlos pointed down the street. 'Here they come.'

In the Jetta parked at Trey's house, Scott and Carlos had a front-row seat as six Galveston Police Department cruisers arrived with lights flashing at the judge's house down the street and police bailed out with their guns drawn at the Mexican workers sitting on the porch drinking beer. One worker bolted and slid down the dune to the beach and ran to the water as if to escape via the Gulf of Mexico. The cops captured him at surf's edge.

'That's Hector,' Carlos said. 'He's mean.'

'Mean enough to kill Trey?'

'And Miss Fenney . . . only he didn't. Kill Miss Fenney. But they took the cocaine. Saw Benito stopping by once a week in that silver sports car, figured out what he was doing.'

'They know Benito?'

'Everyone on the Island knows Benito, except law-abiding folks.'

'So how'd they get into the garage?'

'Jimmied the lock. Found the dope in the little elevator.'

'What'd they do with it?'

'Used some, sold some.'

'Why didn't they rob the place?'

'Figured Trey would beef up security, if they stole other stuff. They wanted the cocaine more than they wanted his cars or his woman.' Carlos shrugged. 'That's what they said. They knew the party had ended when Trey died.'

They watched the shirtless, handcuffed workers being loaded into a police van.

'Guess that's the end of the show,' Scott said. He started the engine.

'Oh, boss, there's something else about the blonde girl and the big man they saw that day.'

Scott couldn't have sent Carlos with photos of Pete and Billie Jean Puckett – that would have blown his cover. But Scott was sure the big man was Pete and the blonde girl was Billie Jean. They had been in Trey Rawlins' house the day he was murdered. Once Scott got their prints, he would know for sure. And so would the DA.

'What?'

'What they said happened. Said right after lunch, the blonde girl drives up in a black Mustang, goes inside, they don't see her for maybe four hours. Then a cab drives up and the big man gets out. This was after five 'cause they were already drinking beer. The big man, he don't go in the front door like the girl, he goes around back. Maybe fifteen minutes later, he comes out the front

240

door dragging the girl by her arm, puts her in the Mustang, and they drive off. She was crying.'

'How could they tell she was crying from that far away?'

'Binoculars.'

'They had binoculars? What for? To watch the seagulls?'

'Uh…no, boss. To watch the red-haired woman go out on the back deck . . . naked. Said she had a tattoo.'

Chapter 29

Two days later, Scott flew to San Antonio, rented a car, and drove to the La Cantera Golf Club on the north side of town where the San Antonio Open was being played. He found Nick Madden talking on his cell phone and watching Pete Puckett putt on the ninth green. When Nick ended the call, he had a big grin on his face.

'Never thought I'd be so happy to hear someone say "erectile dysfunction". They want Pete to endorse for them.' He gestured at the green. 'Twenty years, he couldn't win a fucking putt-putt tournament, then he wins the US Open. I'm getting a dozen endorsement offers a day.'

'He suffers from ED?'

'He does?'

'Why would he endorse that stuff if he doesn't?'

Nick gave Scott a dumbfounded look. 'Money. You watch golf on TV – what are the commercials for? Drugs to make your dick harder, your prostate smaller, your hair darker, and your golf ball go farther. How to get it up, keep it up, look younger, and hit it longer – that's the WM squared fantasy, Scott, and sponsors pay big bucks to anyone who can help them tap into it. Old fart like Pete whips the young studs out here to win the Open, he's the perfect pitchman for that stuff: "Guys, if I can win the US Open, you can win the babe. All you gotta do is color your hair and swallow this pill."' He paused. 'I guess you want his prints?'

Scott nodded. 'And Billie Jean's. What kind of car does she drive?'

'Black Mustang. Why?'

'A blonde girl in a black Mustang was seen at Trey's house the day he was killed.'

'Shit.'

'And a big man came and dragged her out of the house.'

'Double shit.'

'That's why I need their prints. I need to know.'

'I'll help you.'

'Why?'

'Because I need to know, too. I'm working these endorsement deals, last thing I need is him involved in Trey's murder. Sponsors get nervous when criminal stuff's involved, unless it's an NBA player, then it's just part of the deal. Sooner you mark Pete off the list, sooner I can close these deals and make some money.' He paused. 'Did you mark me off the list?'

Scott nodded. 'Did you know Trey used cocaine?'

Nick didn't react for a moment. Then he exhaled and nodded.

'I told him snorting coke, he'd never win the Open. But he said he had it under control. Famous last words, right?'

'I thought the tour was drug testing now?'

'They are.'

'How'd he pass?'

'He didn't. I did.' Nick shrugged. 'I peed for him. He kept a clean sample in his locker. They tell him it's his turn to pee, he'd sneak it into the john, pour it into the cup. It ain't exactly San Quentin out here.'

'Did you know he owed his dealer half a million dollars?'

'*Half a million?* Shit. No, I didn't know. Why?'

'He thought the dealer cheated him.'

'Jesus, he was in deeper than I thought. You think the dealer killed him?'

'Maybe the Zetas.'

Nick nodded. 'They executed some people in Houston. I wouldn't want those bastards after me.'

'Why didn't you get him into rehab?'

'He didn't want to go. Besides, he goes into rehab, the whole world knows about it the next day – and his endorsements dry up. WM squared don't like dopers, Scott.'

'You just sat back and watched him go downhill so you wouldn't lose your commissions?'

'Scott, I couldn't make him go straight. But I sent him to a sports psychologist.'

'Who?'

'Dr Tim. Timothy O'Brien. He works with a lot of athletes, helps them keep their heads on straight when the world's telling them they're gods. Usually doesn't work.'

'He wasn't exactly the Trey Rawlins you sold, was he?'

'Scott, we sell what people want. They want that All-American, golden boy image. They want their heroes. They need them. The public doesn't want reality, hell, they can get depressed enough watching the evening news. Last thing the public wants is the truth.'

'Well, Nick, they're going to learn the truth about Trey Rawlins at trial.'

'When?'

'Twenty-six days.'

'Not much time to find the killer.'

They found Billie Jean Puckett sitting in a tree.

'Hi, Billie Jean,' Nick said.

He had startled her. She almost dropped the red snow cone she was eating with her fingers. She stared down at them and said, 'What do you want?'

'Come on down, kiddo.'

'No.'

'He just wants to talk to you.'

'No.'

244

'Billie Jean,' Scott said, 'did you go to the Florida tournament with your dad?'

'No. I stayed in Austin.'

'But you didn't stay in Austin, did you? You drove to Galveston. You were in Trey's house the day he died, weren't you?'

'No.'

'You drive a black Mustang.'

'No, I don't.'

'He knows you do,' Nick said.

'So?'

'So witnesses saw a blonde girl in a black Mustang at Trey's house that day,' Scott said.

'No one's gonna believe a bunch of Mexicans.'

'I didn't say they were Mexican.'

'Oh. Still, wasn't me.'

'Will you give me your fingerprints?'

'What for?'

'So he can cross you off the list,' Nick said.

'What list?'

'The list of suspects, people who might've killed Trey.'

'I didn't kill Trey.'

'I know that, honey. But he doesn't.'

'I'm not coming down.'

'Well,' Scott said, 'we're not going anywhere until you do.'

He leaned against the tree and whistled a tune.

From ten feet above: 'You can't carry a tune in a bucket.'

'Thank you. How long were you and Trey involved?'

'A few weeks . . . I said I don't want to talk.'

Scott started whistling again.

'I'm gonna tell my daddy and he's gonna beat you up.'

'Did he beat up Trey?'

Nothing.

'Did he kill Trey?'

More nothing.

'I've got all day, Billie Jean.'

245

'I gotta pee.'

'If I let you down, will you talk to me?'

'If you don't let me down, I'm gonna pee on your head.'

Scott looked up at her. 'Please don't run.'

She sighed. 'I won't.' She held the snow cone down to Scott. 'Hold this.'

He took her snow cone while Nick reached up to help her climb down. Her hands were red with the juice, which was now running down Scott's hands. He held the snow cone out to her.

'Here.'

In a quick movement, she punched the bottom of his hand, sending the red snow cone splashing onto his shirt. Then she ran.

'She's running again!' Nick said.

Scott dropped the snow cone, and they ran after her. They chased her across fairways and around greens, through crowds and tents and between concession stands . . . she was fast . . . and she was again heading to the ladies' locker room. And they couldn't catch her. She hit the thick glass door with both hands up high, pushed it open, turned and gave them a little red-handed wave, then disappeared from sight. Scott put his hands on his knees and tried to catch his breath. He ran five miles every morning on the beach and this teenage girl had run him into the dirt.

'You really think Pete might've killed him?' Nick said. 'He's got a bad temper, but sticking a knife in Trey?'

An older woman gave Scott a look as she stepped past him to the door, grabbed the handle, and pushed the door open. The door shut behind her, and as it did, the sunlight caught the glass – and Scott stood straight at what he saw: two red handprints.

'Don't let anyone touch that glass,' he said to Nick.

He jogged over to the concession tent and bought paper towels, a bottled water, and two strips of clear packing tape – the tape wasn't technically for sale; Scott had to pay $50 for a half roll. He wiped his hands on the towels, drank the water, and went back to the ladies' locker room door where Nick stood guard. Scott overlapped long tape strips across the glass to form one large piece of tape and smoothed the tape. Then he peeled the tape off the glass in one clean stroke. He held the tape up to the sunlight.

He had Billie Jean Puckett's fingerprints.

After securing the tape in a baggie in the rental car, Scott returned to the eighteenth hole where Nick was waiting. They watched as Pete Puckett putted out to complete his round. When he walked off the eighteenth green he stuck a cigar in his mouth just as cameras and reporters mobbed him.

'That's what winning the US Open does for you,' Nick said. 'Two weeks ago, he couldn't buy an interview.'

'There's Goose.'

They caught up with the caddie, who was lighting a cigar and who wasn't excited to see Scott.

'Go away.'

'Goose, I talked to Tess, Lacy, and Riley.'

Goose chuckled.

'Are there any others I should know about?'

'You want them in alphabetical or chronological order?' He chuckled again. 'I was with a couple gals before I got married, he was with a couple gals before lunch. Hell, I felt more like a pimp than a caddie. We'd be walking down the fairway, in the hunt for a win, and he'd spot a gal standing outside the ropes, tell me to get her number. One tournament, he screwed a two-piece in a corporate hospitality tent during a rain delay. Most guys pack protein bars in the bag – he packed condoms.' Goose shook his head. 'Trey cut a wide swath through the tour wives. You'd think he'd've been happy with the groupies and your wife.'

'We also know about Trey and Billie Jean. Did Pete kill him?'

'I don't know. But I sure as hell would've, if she was my daughter.' Goose spit. 'She's just a goddamned kid.'

'Why was he like that? Trey?'

Goose inhaled on the cigar then blew out a cloud of smoke.

'Back when I started out here the big stars – Palmer, Nicklaus, Trevino – they gave back more than they took and they didn't always take the best for themselves. Young guys today, they figure they're entitled to the best and screw the world. They've got no sense of responsibility, just a sense of entitlement. Trey was one of those guys. He took what he wanted, whether it was a Bentley or another man's wife. But you already know that, don't you?'

Goose hefted the big bag onto his shoulder and trudged off. Scott stared after him. He did know that.

'Goose is something of a philosopher on tour . . . and an asshole.' Nick slapped Scott on the shoulder. 'Come on, Pete's freed up.'

Scott followed Nick over to Pete. He was smoking the cigar and signing autographs. Fans were pushing their caps, programs, balls, and breasts forward for him to sign. Scott tried to make friends this time.

'Congratulations on the Open, Pete.'

Pete continued signing autographs on autopilot. He didn't look up at Scott.

'What do you want, lawyer?'

Okay, forget friendship. Scott pulled Karen's compact case from his pants pocket. He opened it and held it out to Pete.

'I want your fingerprints on this mirror.'

'Why?'

'He wants to cross you off the list,' Nick said.

'What list?'

'List of suspects. People who might've killed Trey.'

'His wife killed Trey.'

'Will you take a polygraph?' Scott asked.

'Did she?'

'Not yet.'

'Let me know when she does.'

'Then give me your prints.'

'Come on, Pete,' Nick said. 'Cooperate so we can get on to the new endorsement deals. With that Open trophy, I can set you up for life – heck, you can buy more guns. We gotta move fast before the window of opportunity closes.'

Pete chewed on that and his cigar a moment, then said, 'No.'

Scott decided to push Pete. 'You were at Trey's house the day he was murdered. You went there to get Billie Jean. You found them having sex, didn't you? We have witnesses who saw her black Mustang there, and both of you.'

'A buncha goddamn—'

Pete caught himself. He wasn't going to make the same mistake Billie Jean had made. He turned and faced Scott straight on, as if he were about to hit him – and for a moment, Scott thought he might have pushed Pete too far. His jaws were clenched so tight Scott thought he might bite the cigar in half.

'I was in Florida . . . and you can go to hell.'

Pete Puckett pivoted and walked off.

'That went well.' Nick shook his head and sighed. 'He's never gonna get a network announcing job when he retires, not with that attitude. He makes Johnny Miller seem lovable.'

'I'm not leaving without his prints.'

Scott followed Pete to the clubhouse. Pete ducked into the players' lounge and went straight to the bar. Scott stood just outside the door. The bartender filled a shot glass with hard liquor and pushed it in front of Pete. He reached out for the glass but froze. He turned – Scott ducked out of sight – and gave the room a suspicious glance. Pete then turned back to the bar, picked up a napkin, wrapped it around the shot glass, and downed the liquor. He stood and went over to the far side of the lounge where a security guard manned a door with a sign that read 'Men's Locker Room'. The guard opened the door. Pete walked through, and the guard shut the door behind him.

'Pete's got a bad back.' Nick had come up behind Scott. 'After every round, he needs a massage.'

'I need his prints.'

'Come on.' Nick led the way over to the security guard. He flashed his credentials and pointed a thumb at Scott. 'He's with me.'

The guard opened the door, and they walked down a flight of stairs and into a locker room. Pudgy white golfers in various stages of undress ambled past. Nick grimaced at the sight and whispered, 'I'm getting nauseous.'

249

Nick climbed onto a chair and peeked over a row of lockers. He stepped down and again whispered, 'Pete's over there.'

They backed out of sight. A few minutes later, Pete walked away heading in the opposite direction with only a towel around his waist. Nick motioned to Scott to follow. They hurried around the corner and to an open locker.

'This is Pete's,' Nick said.

A locker door stood open with Pete Puckett's personal possessions in plain sight.

'Don't the players lock up their stuff?'

'Only in the NBA.' Nick grabbed a set of keys. 'Let's go.'

Scott followed Nick back upstairs and out the front door of the clubhouse to a massive black RV stationed at the back of the parking lot.

'Pete's home away from home, like the country music stars travel around in,' Nick said. 'A lot of the players are traveling in these now, at least the ones who can't afford their own jet.'

Nick knocked on the door, then used a key to gain entrance. They climbed up and stepped inside.

'Five-star hotel on wheels,' Nick said. 'Cost a million bucks.'

The RV had leather upholstery and wood-paneled walls, a big-screen TV, and a full kitchen with granite countertops. Nick was glancing around.

'What would have his prints on it?' He snapped his fingers. 'Guns.'

'He carries guns with him on tour?'

'Pete? Shit, he doesn't get the mail without a gun.'

They walked down a narrow hall past a bathroom and into a bedroom at the rear of the RV. Nick opened several closets then said, 'Told you.'

Fixed in a gun rack in the closet were four rifles and two pistols. Scott pulled out the tape and tore off a piece.

'What's his favorite?'

'The biggest.'

Scott reached for a rifle but stopped at the sound of a noise up front. Nick stepped to the bedroom door and peeked out. He came back fast.

'Shit! It's Billie Jean.'

They searched for a hiding place.

'Under the bed.'

They dropped to the floor and crawled under the bed. They were lying close enough that Scott could smell Nick's last beer on his breath. The bedspread hung down low enough to conceal them, but they still had a line of sight down the hall and into the kitchen at the front of the RV. Billie Jean went to the refrigerator and poured a glass of chocolate milk then turned the TV on and watched a soap opera.

'Shit,' Nick whispered, 'if she doesn't leave soon, Pete's gonna come back.'

'That'll be embarrassing.'

'And dangerous.'

Billie Jean drank the milk then turned off the TV and walked toward them – they froze – but she entered the bathroom and closed the door. They soon heard the shower running.

'Let's get outta here!' Nick whispered.

They crawled out from under the bed and tiptoed past the bathroom. Once in the kitchen, Scott whispered, 'I need his prints.'

Nick pointed. 'Whiskey.'

'No time to drink.'

'No – take the whiskey bottle. It's half empty, means Pete touched it.'

'Could be Billie Jean's prints.'

'She only drinks chocolate milk.'

Scott grabbed a paper towel and then the bottle, and they left quietly. They jogged across the parking lot to the Jetta. Nick stared at the car and laughed.

'You had a Ferrari and now you're driving this? Nice career move.'

'Yeah, it's worked out well.'

'Least you still got your sense of humor.'

'And my daughters.'

Nick nodded. 'Kids are nice . . . but I'd rather have a Ferrari.'

'Where can I find Dr Tim?'

★   ★   ★

251

'Scott, if every professional athlete were a well-adjusted, mature, happy individual, what would psychologists do for a living?'

Timothy O'Brien, sports psychologist, practiced out of an office in downtown Houston. Scott had flown back to Houston and driven downtown. Dr Tim had agreed to wait for him. Scott felt stupid addressing him as 'Dr Tim'.

'We've invested so much in sports today, and not just money. Our national psyche. Who we are. We need to be good at something, but it seems we're good for nothing these days – the economy, the wars, health care . . . so we invest our self-esteem in sports, emotionally and financially. How much did the new Dallas Cowboys stadium up there cost?'

'One-point-two billion,' Scott said.

'For a football stadium – our twenty-first century monuments.' Dr Tim waved a hand at the world outside the window. 'The icons of Houston are no longer oil wildcatters or heart surgeons or even astronauts – they're quarterbacks and point guards and pitchers. We idolize them but we demand perfection from them, at least on the field of play. We treat them special – until they fail us. Then we turn on them. You read the sports pages or listen to sport talk radio? It's vicious now. A player strikes out or fumbles or misses a shot and his team loses, the media and fans attack him personally, as if he's a bad person for failing. As if he betrayed their city, even their country. I've had athletes get death threats for losing a game. That's a lot of pressure on a young man, too much pressure for some. I've seen the psychological damage it does to them.'

'You're telling me rich athletes are victims of society?'

'We're all victims of society, Scott. You have children?'

'Two daughters. Eleven.'

'Twins?'

'In every way except biological.'

'They might become victims of society, too.'

'Not on my watch.'

Dr Tim smiled. He reminded Scott of the girls' pediatrician.

'Tell me about Trey,' Scott said.

252

'Scott, I'd like to help, but what I know about my patients is confidential.'

'There's no doctor-patient privilege in Texas, and your patient is dead. I'm defending the person charged with his murder. I can subpoena your records and you to testify at trial. I'm sure you'd like to avoid that. I just need some information, to help me find his killer.'

Dr Tim pondered the implications of being subpoenaed, then shrugged.

'He is dead. Okay. What do you want to know?'

'Did he ever tell you he was going to marry Rebecca?'

'He never even mentioned her.'

'Did he tell you he was afraid of anyone?'

'No. Why?'

'He started carrying a gun.'

Dr Tim nodded. 'All my football and basketball players carry guns. Part of the culture.'

'Why was he seeing you?'

'Same as most of my patients. Addiction.'

'I've never understood addiction.'

Dr Tim smiled. 'Representing your ex-wife who's accused of murdering the man she left you for – that strikes me as a bit addictive. You want to talk about it?'

'No. I want to talk about Trey. What addictions did he suffer from?'

'The correct question is, what addictions *didn't* he suffer from? See, Trey had an addictive personality. He didn't just enjoy golf, he was addicted to it. Same with alcohol, cocaine, sex—'

'*Sex?* He was addicted to sex?'

'It's not a joke, Scott, or just a Hollywood diagnosis. It's a real addiction. Sex addiction is often connected to a narcissistic personality disorder. I've treated many athletes suffering from both. They obsess about sex, view pornography compulsively, engage in risky sex, public sex, short-term sex with numerous partners whom they view only as objects – some have claimed over a hundred sexual conquests.'

'A hundred women in one man's life?'

'In one season.' Dr Tim shrugged. 'For them, Scott, sex is fulfilling a need other than the human sex drive. See, teenage boys view pornography to watch the female, but the narcissistic personality wants to watch himself.'

'Trey was a grown man.'

'Not really. He suffered deferred adolescence, a lot of pro athletes do. They have people who take care of their every need every day, from their first day of college to the last day of their pro careers, just like their parents did when they were children. So they don't have to grow up until after their careers are over, and for many, it's too late.' He sighed. 'I'm afraid Trey was the perfect storm: a handsome, rich, talented, narcissistic, sex-addicted pro athlete suffering from deferred adolescence manifested by multiple partners, obsession with pornography, sex tapes—'

Scott snapped forward in his chair.

'Sex tapes? What sex tapes?'

Chapter 30

'You find the leak?'

'Nope.'

The next morning, Scott dropped the baggies containing the tape strips with Billie Jean Puckett's fingerprints and the whiskey bottle with Pete Puckett's fingerprints on the district attorney's desk. The DA studied the whiskey bottle.

'Good stuff. I'll get Hank to run 'em.' He held out a document. 'Trey's phone bills came in, we ran the numbers. One name caught my eye – Gabe Petrocelli.'

'Who's he?'

'Local bookie. Straight line to Vegas.'

'The mob? In Galveston?'

'Mob's been here since Galveston was Sin City. How do you think the Maceo brothers got Sinatra to play the Balinese Room?'

'Trey was gambling?'

'He had Gabe's cell phone number, and Gabe had his. I don't figure them for double-dating.'

'You see Obama's finally gonna pardon Jack Johnson?'

Gabe Petrocelli tapped a thick finger on the sports section of the local newspaper spread across the table.

'Who's Jack Johnson and what did he do?' Scott said.

'Heavyweight champion of the world, nineteen-oh-eight through nineteen-fifteen. Born and raised right here on the Island.'

'That's not a crime.'

'He married a white woman.'

'I was married to a white woman.'

'He was black. First black champion, the Ali of his times, the most famous athlete in the world back then. Wore custom suits, drove fast cars, and married three white women, which didn't sit so well with white men back then. They convicted him under the Mann Act for transporting a woman across state lines for immoral purposes. You know that law is still on the books?'

'I do know that.'

'Stupid . . . the law, not you.'

'Thanks.'

'After he won the title, there were race riots all across the country. That "Great White Hope" business started because of Johnson, boxing folks trying to find a white fighter who could beat him. Boy, must've been big betting on those fights.' Gabe sighed. 'Not much betting on boxing these days, everyone's gone to cage fighting and football. Like Trey.'

Gabe Petrocelli had curly black hair, a barrel chest, and the hairiest arms Scott had ever seen on a man. He appeared to be in his late forties. He had grown up in the bookmaking business and had taken over the family franchise. His bar – 'Gabe's' – was located in a renovated Victorian-style building on Strand Avenue in the entertainment district near the harbor. The bar was not yet open for business that day, but Scott's business card had gained him an audience with Gabe. His two goons had required Louis to remain outside then patted Scott down for guns and wires. Scott and Gabe now sat in a booth in the back while his goons watched *The Sopranos* on the TV over the bar.

'They love that show,' Gabe said. He chuckled and sipped his espresso. 'Lawyer with a bodyguard. I like that. Shows some style.'

'I try.' Scott gestured around at the bar. 'Classy place.'

256

'Used to be a high–class whorehouse. All these old buildings on the Strand, they got history. And that's all Galveston's got left . . . history. Everyone wishing this piece of sand was still important, like it was before the Great Storm. Those were the glory days.'

'So you're a bookie?'

'Italians, we been running the bookmaking business on the Island since Prohibition. It ain't what it was back in the day, but it's a living.'

'Gabe, you ever been arrested?'

He nodded. 'Charges were dropped.'

His prints were in the system, so the prints at the house didn't belong to him.

'How long had you known Trey?'

'Since he was a boy. Not personally back then, I'm twenty years older than him, but everyone on the Island knew of him. Then I'd see him out at the club. Nice boy.'

'He liked to gamble?'

'Trey was addicted to the thrill. High stakes. We get a lot of athletes.'

'What'd he bet on?'

'Football, mostly. At least with me. But only a few hundred grand. The big debts, he ran those up at the casinos.'

'In Vegas?'

'Everywhere. Trey knew the exact driving distance from every tour event to the nearest Indian reservation.'

'Indian reservation?'

'Casinos. Congress gave the Indians free reign to operate casinos on their reservations – which are like sovereign nations – but they don't know shit about craps or blackjack, so the big casinos made deals with the tribes to operate them, split the profits. Hundreds of Indian casinos now, they take in twenty-six billion a year. Shit, every Indian in America's a goddamned millionaire now.' Gabe smiled. 'White man took their land, now they're taking the white man's money.'

'How much did Trey owe the casinos?'

257

'Fifteen million.'

'*Fifteen million?* How?'

'How not? Five-thousand-dollar slots, craps, blackjack – you name it, he lost at it.'

'Did the mob kill him?'

Gabe didn't blink. 'I don't think so.'

'Why not?'

'First, I would've heard about it. His death, that came as a big shock to me. And he was a good customer, he had the ability to repay, so the boys would've given him time to make good on what he owed. Plus interest, of course.'

'And the second reason?'

'If the mob had killed him, they wouldn't have stabbed him with a kitchen knife in his own bedroom where they might leave DNA or a print behind. They would've grabbed him, taken him out on a shrimp boat, and cut him up for shark bait. That didn't happen. Ergo, I don't figure we did it.'

'*Ergo?*'

Gabe shrugged. 'I watch *Law and Order* on TV.'

'Noncustodial mothers are more common now,' Boo said.

Karen and the girls were sitting under the umbrella at the table on the back deck.

'Meredith did a segment this morning about mothers who leave their children,' Boo said. 'I bet she's a really good mother. Meredith. You could tell she'd never leave her children. But two million mothers have. Mother's not the only one.'

'She's the only mother who left you,' Karen said, then she caught herself. 'I'm sorry, Boo. I shouldn't have said that.'

'That's okay. You've been like a mother to us. And you've always been honest with us.' Boo glanced at Pajamae, who nodded. 'Karen, will you be honest now?'

'Yes.'

'Do you think Mother murdered Trey?'

'No.'

'Do you think she'd be a good mother to me and Pajamae?'

258

Karen Douglas had first met Rebecca Fenney seventeen days before, so she could be objective about her as an accused murderer. But Karen was carrying a baby inside her; she could not be objective about Rebecca Fenney as a mother.

'No. She's neither a murderer nor a mother.'

Chapter 31

At the time of his death, Trey Rawlins was the fifth-ranked professional golfer in the world. In less than two years on tour, he had won four tournaments and $9 million in prize money. He had earned $11 million more in endorsements and $4 million more from corporate outings and appearance fees. After commissions, caddie fees, and taxes, he had $12 million in disposable income – and he had disposed of it. He had a beach house in Galveston, a condo in California, and a ski lodge in Colorado. He had a Bentley, a Hummer, a BMW racing bike, and a yacht. He had an expensive cocaine habit and a $500,000 debt to his dealer. And he had a $15-million debt to the mob.

'We were gonna cut him loose.'

Twenty-one days before trial, and Nick Madden was ready to confess.

'Why?'

'The bad Trey.'

'Explain.'

'There was the good Trey – the way he played golf, the commercials, the charity appearances, the chocolate milk . . . When he was good, he was very good. But when he was the bad Trey . . . He had a dark side. A lot of athletes do.'

'Why?'

Nick rubbed his face. He seemed genuinely upset even though Pete Puckett had won the San Antonio Open, the first back-to-back wins in his long career. Two and a half million dollars in winnings in two weeks. Scott was back in Nick's Houston office the Monday after the tournament.

'I don't know, Scott. I was reading a golf magazine, they had an interview with Trevino, asked him what his prized possession was. He said his Ford Mustang. They asked a young tour player the same thing. He said his hundred-foot yacht, but he was whining because Tiger's yacht is fifty feet longer. It ain't the ball and the big drivers that changed the golf tour, it's the players' attitudes. Same with all athletes now. Like Goose said, they think they're entitled. 'Course, you tell a kid every day he's special from the time he's ten 'cause he can play ball, time he's twenty he's gonna believe it, figure the rules don't apply to him, that he doesn't have to live like everyone else. One time Trey sat right there and said to me, "Nick, the only rules I follow are the Rules of Golf". What makes a guy think like that?'

He shook his head.

'Now you know the bad Trey – cocaine and porn, gals and gambling.'

'Hard to believe he could lose fifteen million gambling,' Scott said.

'You read Daly's book? He said he lost *fifty* million gambling, had to send his endorsement checks straight to the casinos.'

'So why were you dropping Trey? You were still making money off him.'

'There was more to it.'

'What?'

Nick picked up the remote and pointed it at the big TV on the wall. The screen flashed on to a menu. Nick scrolled down the menu then clicked.

'This.'

Trey Rawlins' image filled the screen. He was young, he was handsome, and he was putting.

'Eighteenth hole, Bay Classic in California, early March. He makes this putt, he wins the tournament and one million bucks. A fucking three-foot putt.'

Trey missed the putt.

'He didn't miss three-foot putts,' Nick said.

Nick clicked through to another tournament and another putt to win.

'Five weeks later. Miami Open. A two-foot putt to win.'

Trey missed the putt.

'Not even close,' Nick said.

'The drugs?'

'The mob.'

'The *mob*?'

'He was throwing tournaments.'

'You're kidding? People gamble on golf tournaments?'

Nick chuckled. 'Hell, yes, people gamble on golf tournaments. Big money. And when the difference between winning and losing comes down to one putt, it's an easy game to rig. How many times have you watched a tournament and seen a pro miss a short putt and think, how could he possibly have missed that? All you need is one player in your debt. A really good player, someone who's going to have one putt to win. Or lose.'

Nick turned up the tape. The announcer was saying that the pressure got to Trey Rawlins.

'The mob got to him.'

'To repay his debts?'

'That's what I figure.'

'But if he'd made the putt and won, he'd have made a million bucks, paid that to the mob.'

'Yeah, but by losing, he probably made the mob five, six million in bets.'

'Why wouldn't he have just played badly and missed the cut?'

'Doesn't work that way. For gamblers to make big money, they've got to win against long odds. But that means they've got to bet against the star winning, because in golf odds are the stars are gonna win every time. So the star has to be in the hunt at the

262

end, otherwise no one's putting up any money. I mean, would you ever bet against Tiger? Neither would the mob. But the next best thing would be someone like Trey, a player who could win but who owed a big debt. He misses a short putt, you can't prove anything. Could've been nerves, a ball mark on the green, a bad putt. It happens. But not to Trey. I knew it. And I knew if he was our client – my client – when the shit hit the fan – and shit like this always hits the fan – SSI – and *me* – we'd always be linked to the golfer who threw tournaments. WM squared don't like that shit, Scott.'

'So you were dropping him?'

Nick nodded. 'Drinking and drugs, that's just part of the job description for a pro athlete today. But throwing tournaments – that's prison time, even for Trey Rawlins. That's a criminal trial. That's SSI – and me – dragged into court, on TV, in the news-papers, and for all the wrong reasons.'

'Did you tell him?'

'They killed him first.'

'You think the mob killed him?'

Nick nodded.

'Why would they kill him if he was throwing tournaments so they could win their bets?'

Nick clicked through to another tournament. 'Atlanta Open. Back in May.'

On the screen, Trey was stalking the green and studying a putt.

'Sixty-three-foot putt for eagle on the eighteenth hole,' Nick said. 'He's down by one. He makes it, he wins. Misses and he's got a long putt back for birdie to tie.'

The ball sat at the back end on the high side of the green; the hole was at the front end on the low side. The announcer explained that the ball sat three feet higher than the hole, so the ball would be rolling fast down the slope. It would either go in or continue twenty feet past the hole. Trey crouched over the ball, placed his putter behind the ball, and made a smooth stroke. The ball rolled across the green, hit the big slope halfway across the green, then took a sharp turn down and picked up speed. It was rolling fast when it hit the back of the cup, bounced up, and fell in. The camera cut to Trey. He appeared shocked. Nick hit the remote to freeze the frame on Trey's face.

'That's not the face of a winner. That's the face of a loser.'

'What do you mean?'

'I think he was supposed to lose that tournament. When he started the final round leading by four, the betting was heavy on him – I checked. Which means the mob could bet against him and make big money if he lost. So they bet big on him to lose – but he didn't lose. He won. I figure that putt cost the mob maybe ten million, and he knew it. That's why he looks like he does.'

'How do you know this?'

'I don't. I think it. If I knew someone in the mob, I'd ask.'

'That's exactly what happened,' Gabe Petrocelli said after his goons had patted Scott down. 'But that putt cost the Vegas boys twenty million, not ten.' He shook his head. 'I was watching it on TV. Big breaker, no way he can make that putt. When that ball dropped and they showed Trey's face, I said, there's the face of a dead man.'

'So the mob did kill him?'

'I think your wife beat them to it.'

'My client.'

'Can't let her go, huh?' Gabe gave Scott a knowing nod. 'They get to you, don't they? It was like that with my first wife, she drove me fucking nuts every fucking day. So we split up and I started drinking 'cause I missed her.' He sighed. 'Don't be a drunk 'cause of a woman. Be a drunk over something important, like baseball.'

'The mob wanted him dead? Trey?'

'Yeah, they were severely pissed, no question about it.'

'But you had nothing to do with his death?'

He held up an open hand. 'On my mother's grave. Cops here, they know me, we grew up together. A lot of them bet with me. They know what I do and what I don't do. I book . . . I don't kill.'

'Will you take a polygraph?'

Gabe smiled. 'I don't do polygraphs either.'

'But how can you lose twenty million on a golf tournament?'

'Easy. Three Brits bet eighty grand each, won nineteen million on a long shot named John Daly to win the British Open in ninety-five. Scott, today, you can win or lose millions betting on anything, not just the stock market.'

'But if Trey were making so much money, why didn't he just pay off his debt?'

'Fifteen million at twenty-five percent interest, that's tough to repay.'

'The mob charges twenty-five percent interest?'

Gabe shrugged. 'Credit card companies charge thirty percent. Shit, twenty-five years ago, there were laws against that sort of thing. Banks couldn't charge more than ten percent interest. That's where we came in. Now, the sky's the limit. They took our loan-sharking business and made it legal. Same thing with gambling. Hell, ten years from now, there'll be a casino in every town in America. What's next? Drugs? Prostitution? Before long, you won't be able to make a dishonest living 'cause every vice is gonna be legal. We're expanding into Medicare fraud and your other white-collar criminal activities, but it's damn hard to compete with Wall Street.'

'So what was the repayment deal?'

'Trey would throw five tournaments. He'd win some, too, and the boys would up their ante slowly, so as not to attract any attention. First two tournaments went like clockwork, the boys made a killing and Trey reduced his debt by six million. But then he made that putt. A twenty-million-dollar putt.' Gabe shook his head. 'The boys got greedy, bet real big. Too big.'

'Trey would get to keep the money when he won?'

'Nope. Everything was divvied up. Trey got one-third.'

'One-third of everything? Including the mob's winnings?'

'Yep. More money than he would've made winning those tournaments, and tax-free, the best kind of money.'

'How do you know?'

'Because I made the payoff myself. At his house. Three million cash. Hundred-dollar bills.'

'Why would the mob pay him when he owed them?'

'They figured on this being a long-term investment.' He shrugged. 'Once you're in the mob, you're in the mob for life.'

'I wonder where that three million is now?'

Gabe shrugged again.

'Trey won the California Challenge a week before he was murdered. Didn't that make some money for the mob?'

'Not twenty million.'

'I take it you wouldn't care to testify at the trial?'

'No, I don't testify either.'

'I could subpoena you.'

'That would be a mistake. Look, Scott, I'm a nice guy, I run a clean business, I've tried to be helpful. But right here, this is where I talk. Not in a courtroom. Okay?'

'I could subpoena your bosses.'

'You could get yourself killed. Scott, defend your wife and get her off, I don't care. But don't go chasing after the boys in Vegas. Nothing good will come of that.'

'What do you know about the Zetas?'

'Animals. See, the mob never kills for the sake of killing. It's always a business decision. And we never kill women or children or innocent bystanders. We're civilized. They're not. They give crime a bad name.' Gabe nodded thoughtfully. 'So gambling wasn't Trey's only vice?'

'No.'

'You looking at Benito for his murder?'

Scott nodded. 'And you.'

Gabe smiled.

'You know Benito?'

'It's a small island. We keep tabs on our competitors for your discretionary entertainment dollars. Benito likes the horses.'

'He bets with you?'

'He utilizes my services. But I don't utilize his.'

'Smart.'

'Benito's not a killer.'

'The Zetas are.'

Gabe nodded, and Scott stood to leave. 'You said a lot of pro athletes gamble?'

'Yeah. From every sport. So?'

'So does the mob have other pros on the payroll, throwing football and baseball and basketball games?'

Gabe smiled. 'Trade secrets, Scott.'

Scott walked away. He was to the bar when Gabe called to him. 'Scott!'

Scott turned back. Gabe was pointing at the TV above the bar. Scott looked up and saw Renée Ramirez's face on the screen.

'Watch out for her, Scott. She's like a rattlesnake – pretty but deadly.'

'Who killed Trey Rawlins?' Bobby said. 'Pete Puckett, the Zetas, or the mob? Three prime suspects for one murder, each with a good motive.'

'You're forgetting Rebecca,' Scott said.

'No, I'm not.'

'She's the only one without a motive.'

'Why would Trey call Pete Puckett thirteen times the last week and three times on the day he died?' Karen said.

They were at the table on the back deck. Karen was reading down Trey's cell phone bills. The DA's office had run the calls and identified each caller.

'He didn't call Pete,' Scott said. 'He called Billie Jean.'

'The list says Pete Puckett.'

'Phone's registered in his name, but it's Billie Jean's phone. Family plan, like the girls want.'

'First call to her was on May fourteenth.'

'Three weeks before his death. That's when their affair started.'

'Last call was at twelve-ten P.M. that day, same day he was killed.' Karen tapped on her laptop keyboard. 'My notes say Billie Jean was in Austin that Thursday, and Pete was in Florida playing at the Atlantic Open tournament.'

'They both lied. They were here. Billie Jean drove down from Austin in her black Mustang. She was calling Trey to tell him she was here because he left the club just after noon. Trey lied to Rebecca about practicing at the country club all day while she was shopping in Houston. He was here with Billie Jean. Pete flew in from Florida, confronted them at the house.'

'If Pete was in Florida,' Bobby said, 'how'd he know Billie Jean was here?'

'I don't know. Karen, find out what flight Pete took that day.'

She nodded then said, 'Is Rebecca still willing to take a polygraph?'

'Yeah. I've asked everyone else involved to take one – Pete, Benito, Gabe – no one else wants to.'

'No one else is charged with murder,' Bobby said.

'I'll set it up,' Karen said.

'Anything else?'

'The endorsement contracts. I reviewed the big one with Golf-a-zon.com . . . golf company. He endorsed their products, they paid him millions. Ten million guaranteed over two years, another ten million in performance incentives. He stood to make twenty million under that contract.'

'But once they found out about his drugs and gambling, they would've terminated the contract.'

Karen shook her head. 'They couldn't. The contract is iron-clad.'

'There's always a way out of a contract.'

'Only one way out: "Article Twelve: Termination upon death of Athlete".'

'Trey's sponsor wanted out of his contract,' Nick said.

Scott had called him from the back deck. 'Why?'

'Trey showed up at their big party flying higher than a kite. Stumbling, couldn't speak a complete sentence, mauling their wives. Fucking fiasco. I had to drag him out of the place. They were pissed.'

'But they couldn't fire him?'

'Nope. They were stuck with him.'

'Unless he died.'

'And he did.'

'Did they terminate the contract?'

'I got an email five minutes after his death hit the news. They saved about ten million, twice that if he met his performance incentives.'

'That's a pretty good motive.'

'To kill Trey? Shit, Scott, take a number. The motive line is long with Trey Rawlins.'

'Why didn't you tell me this?'

'You didn't ask.'

'Damnit, Nick, this is a murder investigation. And we've got three weeks till Rebecca goes on trial. You need to tell me everything you know.'

'I have . . . now.'

'Where's the tour this week?'

'Austin. We're doing the Texas Waltz: Houston, San Antonio, Austin, and Dallas. I'll be there tomorrow.'

'I'll find you. I want to talk to his sponsor.'

Chapter 32

The next morning, Scott flew to Austin and took a cab to the tournament site at the Barton Creek Resort. He found Nick Madden by the first tee on his cell phone.

'Two hundred thousand? I'll take it. Monday, nine A.M., at the Highland Park Country Club. Pete'll be there.'

Nick disconnected.

'Another deal for Pete?' Scott said.

Nick nodded. 'Corporate outing. Tour goes from city to city, so local corporations set up outings for their special clients then get a tour player to join in – for a fee. Hundred, two hundred, three hundred grand for the big boys. Guy spends four hours playing golf and acting like he gives a shit, walks away with a nice paycheck.'

'That's a lot of money for a round of golf.'

Nick shrugged. 'Tax-deductible.'

'And you get twenty percent?'

'Before taxes.'

They went over to the merchandise tent and found Golf-a-zon's booth stocked with golf clubs, balls, gloves, shoes, apparel, and two sexy young women. A man who looked young enough to be pledging a fraternity stood and greeted Nick.

'Nick, you find me a replacement player yet?'

'How about Brett?'

The man rolled his eyes. 'Please. He looks like the guy in *Sling Blade*.'

'Vic?'

'He's an accountant with a five-iron.'

'Donnie Parker? He just won the Houston Classic.'

'Yeah, and he's married to a porn star. After Trey, I want a goddamn altar boy.'

Nick laughed. 'On the pro golf tour? Got a better chance of finding a virgin.'

'Not in this booth,' one of the girls said then she and the other girl giggled.

Nick turned to Scott. 'Scott, meet Brad Dickey, VP-Player Development, Golf-a-zon-dot-com. They want to be the Amazon of golf.'

Scott shook hands with Brad. 'Scott Fenney.'

Brad pulled his hand back as if Scott had poison ivy. 'Rebecca's husband?'

'Lawyer. I need to ask you some questions, Brad.'

'You'd better talk to the company lawyer.'

'Brad, you can talk to me now or you can talk to me on the witness stand at trial.'

Brad turned to Nick with pleading eyes. Nick shrugged.

'Better to talk now, Brad, so he can cross you off the list.'

'What list?'

'The suspect list.'

Brad considered his options then said, 'Come on back.'

They sat in the booth and listened to Brad's story. He traveled with the tour, keeping his players happy – 'like the two-pieces' – and recruiting players to endorse his company's products. They weren't Nike, but they had taken the same marketing approach: they bet everything on one up-and-coming player.

'You can have the greatest golf product ever invented, but if the country club guys don't see a star player hitting it, swinging it, or wearing it, they won't buy it. We thought Trey could be our Tiger. Didn't work out.'

271

'You wanted to cancel his contract?'

'Would you want a cokehead endorsing your products?'

'But your contract was guaranteed?'

'Yeah, Nick's a hard–ass agent.'

Nick's chest swelled up as if he'd just been nominated for a Nobel. To Scott, he said, 'I shopped Trey right after he won the first pro tournament he played in.' Back to Brad: 'But I didn't force you to give him guaranteed payments, incentives bonuses, stock options . . .'

'You didn't tell me he was a fucking doper either.'

'I didn't know.'

'Sure you didn't.'

'Why didn't you have a morals clause?' Scott asked.

Brad pointed at Nick. 'Because of him. But every contract we sign from now on damn sure will.'

Nick was shaking his head. 'I fight those damn clauses every day now. One pro athlete . . . okay, a hundred pro athletes get arrested for drugs, rape, possession of firearms, and other assorted felonies, all of a sudden every sponsor wants a morals clause. Shit, you start canceling endorsement contracts for every criminal conviction, you won't be in the pro football or basketball market for long.'

'We're in the pro golf market,' Brad said. 'We expect better behavior from our players.' He turned to Scott. 'We bet the company on Trey Rawlins.'

'His death saved your company?'

'And my job.' Brad shrugged. 'Sounds bad, but it's the truth. We dumped our entire marketing budget into that bastard, only to have him shit on us. Drinking, snorting cocaine, screwing everything that walked . . .'

'Gambling.'

'*Gambling?*' Brad turned to Nick. 'Another dirty secret, Nick?'

Nick shrugged innocently.

'Look,' Brad said, 'I'm not crying because Trey's dead, but we didn't have anything to do with it.'

'Will you take a polygraph?'

'Why should I?'

'So I don't subpoena you to testify at trial.'

'Hell, I'd rather testify.'

'I can arrange that. So you owed him ten million more under the contract, plus incentives . . . unless he died?'

'Yeah. So?'

'So maybe you terminated Trey in order to terminate his contract.'

'This is the pro golf tour, Scott, not the NFL. We don't carry guns.'

'He was stabbed to death.'

'Or knives. Sure, we wanted away from him, but so did the tour.'

'Why?'

'Like I said, this is pro golf. It's all about image. Tour knew that when he fell — not *if*, but *when* — he was gonna fall hard. And he could make the tour look bad. These are tough times in the golf business — sales are down, country clubs are closing, Democrats are blaming rich white guys for everything that's wrong in the world . . . After Tiger's sex scandal, all we needed was Trey Rawlins exposed as a doper.'

Or as a gambler throwing tournaments for the mob.

'From the hottest WAG on tour to a prison inmate, that's a long fall. I voted for her, by the way.'

Royce Ballard dressed like a golfer but sported the arrogance of a lawyer, and for good reason.

'I went to UT law school, worked in a Houston firm for ten years, got passed over for partnership, those bastards, so I hired on with the tour. VP, player relations.'

Nick had gotten Scott into the tour trailer to see Royce, who agreed to talk only after Scott had threatened him with a trial subpoena.

'What exactly does a VP of player relations do?'

'I keep them in line. Corporate sponsors don't want to read about our golfers in the legal section of the newspaper, only in the sports section. Hell, we got enough problems with our sponsors – GM and Chrysler in bankruptcy, that fucking Sir Allen . . . *Forbes* said he was worth two billion. Shit, who can you trust anymore?' He chuckled. 'You see he's bitching because his cell isn't air-conditioned? And his lawyer's bailing because he can't pay, then he got the shit beat out of him in jail? I love it, the bastard. But our sponsors are bailing because of this recession. If it weren't for TARP—'

'The government bailout fund?'

Royce nodded. 'Tour sponsors got a hundred billion, thank God. GM got fifty billion, so Buick can still sponsor two tournaments. But they're history after this year.'

'Taxpayers are funding the pro golf tour?' Scott said. 'So players can buy yachts and Bentleys?'

'Some guys like Lamborghinis.'

'The official car of the PGA ain't Ford or Chevy,' Nick said. 'It's Mercedes-Benz.'

Royce was giving Nick a skeptical eye. 'Sounding a little Obama-ish there, Nick.' Back to Scott: 'Anyway, we can't afford to lose sponsors because of our players screwing up. Sponsors take their money to another sport, we fold up the tour tent.'

'And Trey Rawlins was getting out of line?'

'Porn, Viagra, screwing other players' wives . . . that's all consenting adult shit. But cocaine and gambling, that's NBA shit and no way we're gonna let that happen.'

'You knew all that? That Trey was throwing tournaments?'

'*Throwing tournaments?* What the hell are you talking about? *Nick?*'

Nick feigned innocence. 'I don't know anything about that.'

Royce stared Nick down a long moment then said, 'We keep close tabs on our players.' Another glance at Nick. 'Maybe not close enough.'

'But you wanted Trey off the tour?'

'Hell, yes. We can't afford to have another train wreck like Daly on tour, passing out in a fucking Hooters parking lot. Jesus, the guy looks like a goddamn bouncer with a three-iron. He actually hit a tee shot in a pro-am off a beer can.'

'I thought that was funny,' Nick said.

'The pro golf tour isn't a goddamn sitcom, Nick! It's a business! We don't want our fans having fun, we want them spending money.' Royce calmed and shook his head. 'Problem was, Trey was real popular, and not just with the WAGs. When he played, gate receipts and TV ratings shot up. Great White Hope, I guess. We figured the drug testing would take care of him, but he passed every screen.'

Scott gave Nick a quick glance.

'I'm responsible for that, too,' Royce said. 'Our doping program.'

'Is there a drug problem on tour?'

'Nah. Golf is still a Jim Beam and Jack Daniels sport—'

'WM squared,' Nick said with pride. Royce rolled his eyes.

'—but we've had a few guys smoking dope in the Porta-Potties during a round. Of course, they find out it's damn hard to make a five-foot putt for par if you're flying higher than a fucking kite – as Trey found out at the Bay Classic and over in Miami.'

Scott gave Nick another glance.

'Program's mostly a PR tool. Sponsors are sick of reading about steroids and drugs in sports so we're the squeaky-clean alternative.'

'WM squared don't like dopers, Scott,' Nick said.

Royce shook his head. 'Jesus, Nick, give that WM squared shit a rest, will you? You're like a fucking dog with a bone.'

'I'm gonna trademark it, make some real money.'

Royce looked at Scott but nodded his head at Nick. 'An entrepreneur. Anyway, we instituted the widest range of testing in sports. Steroids, HgH – all the PEDs – Performance Enhancing Drugs – as well as narcotics, stimulants, beta-blockers . . .'

Nick laughed. 'Except you allow TUEs.'

'What's that?' Scott said.

'Therapeutic Use Exemptions. Means if you get a note from your doctor saying you need a beta-blocker, you can take it – and putt better. How many TUEs you grant so far, Royce?'

'That's confidential, Nick.'

'Confidential? Shit, Royce, walk through the locker room.'

'So Trey never tested positive?' Scott asked.

'Nope. But we knew he was cheating. Hell, we even staked out his house down in Galveston, tried to catch him with his pants down . . . so to speak.'

'You can go to a player's home and make him pee in a cup without a search warrant?'

Royce nodded. 'You gotta pee to play.'

'Why would the players put up with that? It's their tour.'

'No, it's not. It's our tour, and they need us. Without us, they'd be giving golf lessons to old ladies at the country club.'

Nick snorted. 'The players need lawyers like you?' To Scott: 'Tour's run by a buncha fucking lawyers now. You ever read the Rules of Golf? Like reading the tax code.'

Royce shrugged. 'World's run by lawyers. Don't like it, get a law degree.'

'You ever go to Tiger's home? Get him to pee in a cup?'

'You mean, did I quit my job?' Royce chuckled. 'Tiger's not *on* the tour, Scott, he *is* the tour. Or he was.' He sighed and shook his head. 'He drives his Caddy into a tree and fourteen girls fall out. We may never recover from that fucking fiasco.'

There was a moment of reverent silence for the Tiger Woods fiasco. Then Royce turned to Scott. 'Tiger's been our meal ticket for thirteen years – the tour, the networks, even the other players – prize money's increased two hundred million since he turned pro. He made golf cool. And popular. Without him, we're back to a bunch of fat white boys nobody wants to watch. We're desperate for another big star, insurance that there'll be a tour if Tiger strays off the course for good. Or we'll all be looking for a job.'

'And you thought Trey might be that guy?'

'We hoped so. He won his first tournament, just like Tiger. Fans responded to him – it's a star system, and he could've been a big star. But cocaine and gambling, he crossed the line. We've got to protect our public image.'

Nick laughed. 'Players don't give a shit what the public thinks, Royce. Twenty million people are out of work, they can't afford

276

health insurance, their homes are being foreclosed, but these guys out here are lunching on lobster in the clubhouse and bitching because Obama's raising their taxes so poor folks can have health care and—'

Royce was glaring at Nick. 'You voted for Obama, didn't you? I knew it! You're a goddamned closet Democrat, aren't you, Nick?'

'No. I'm not. I didn't. I swear.'

Royce pointed an accusing finger at Nick. 'Players find out you voted for Obama, you're fucking through as an agent!'

'I swear to God, Royce – I've never voted in my life!'

Royce gave the agent a look of disgust, then turned back to Scott. 'You see the NBA playoffs, that Denver player walking off the court giving the Dallas fans the finger? Our golfers don't do that. They know the tour is their golden goose, so they play the pro-ams, they do the charity appearances, they say all the right things in public – we give them media training so they don't say anything stupid – they play the game on and off the course. They keep their noses clean. Trey, he stuffed coke up his nose and pissed away his money in Vegas. We couldn't let one player kill the golden goose.'

'Sounds like a motive.'

'To kill him?' Royce laughed. 'Shit, I'd have to get in line out here.'

'He wasn't well liked?'

'Bit of an understatement. Everyone hated his guts . . . except the tour women, his dealer, his bookie . . . and your wife.'

'Ex-wife. What were you hoping for?'

Royce shrugged. 'Maybe a head-on with a semi on that racing bike.'

Scott shook his head. 'On TV, you said the tour was like a family.'

'Yeah, like my family. Dysfunctional, full of misfits and jealous siblings.'

'We stopped over in Vegas all the time,' Rebecca said. 'He gave me some chips, I played the slots. He never said anything about being in debt to the casinos.'

'He was fifteen million in debt.'

'*Fifteen million?* That's not possible.'

'It's true. He threw two tournaments to pay the mob back. He was supposed to throw a third but he made a long putt.'

'In Atlanta.'

Scott nodded. 'You ever see a lot of cash around the house?'

'Like a few thousand?'

'Like three million. Mob money.'

'No. Never. The police searched the whole house – you don't think they took it?'

Scott stared out at the sea from the back deck. He didn't know what to think or whom to believe. Perhaps a polygraph would help.

Chapter 33

Retired FBI Special Agent Gus Grimes stood knee-deep in the surf wielding a long fishing pole. He lived in an isolated beach bungalow beyond a line of sand dunes on the next island over, or actually an adjacent peninsula. Scott and Rebecca had taken the car ferry from the East End of the Island across the Ship Channel and driven onto Bolivar Peninsula, where Ike had wiped the earth clean.

They had parked and knocked on the front door. When no one answered, they walked around back and found Gus surf fishing. He saw them and walked out of the water and across the sand to the house. Gus wore baggy shorts, an 'I'd Rather be Fishing' T-shirt, beach shoes, and sunglasses. Reading glasses hung around his neck. Gus's gray hair was ragged and a bit long and stuck out from under a fishing cap. He smelled of the sea and looked more like a beach bum than a former FBI special agent.

'Sorry. Lost track of time.'

Scott made the introductions then said, 'Nice place. No nosy neighbors.'

'Three thousand homes on the peninsula before Ike, only a dozen survived. Not mine. Rebuilt as soon as I got my insurance money, so the fish didn't get cocky.'

Gus led them through the back door and into the bungalow. The decor was that of a fish-and-tackle shop.

'You know Hank Kowalski?' Scott said.

'Sure. Hank comes out here on weekends. We surf fish.'

'Do all FBI agents retire to Galveston?'

'Only the smart ones.'

Karen had briefed Gus on the phone about the case. Scott now pulled out a document and handed it to him. 'Confidentiality agreement.'

Gus nodded. 'I understand.'

He understood that Scott did not want a bad result released to the press or the DA's office. Gus signed the document without reading it, then handed it back to Scott.

'You work at home?' Scott asked.

'No need for an office. I do a half dozen polygraphs a month, just a little extra bait money. Just me and the fish now. My wife died three years ago, son lives in New York. Lawyer with a big firm. Hates it, but the money owns him.'

'Beautiful view,' Rebecca said.

She seemed completely calm and relaxed, unlike Scott. Gus noticed.

'Who's taking the polygraph, you or her?' He slapped Scott on the shoulder. 'Lawyers always worry more than their clients.' He turned to Rebecca. 'Okay, sit down and I'll explain how this works.'

He gestured her to a chair next to a table on which sat the polygraph machine.

'Just like a laptop,' Gus said. 'Those analog polygraphs you see on TV, the little needles flying over scrolling paper, they've been replaced by these digital versions.'

He picked up a blood pressure cuff connected to the machine. He wrapped the cuff around Rebecca's left arm.

'Like at the doctor's office. Measures your pulse and blood pressure. And these are called pneumographs.'

He wrapped rubber tubes around Rebecca's upper chest and stomach.

'They measure respiration. And these little gadgets measure how much your fingers sweat. Folks tend to sweat when they lie.'

Gus attached little diodes to two of Rebecca's fingers.

'So what this machine does, it measures anxiety. We compare your physiological changes – pulse, blood pressure, respiration, sweating – against a baseline to see if you get anxious when answering certain questions. Anxiety is an indication of deception. And that's all this drill can do – tell us whether a person is anxious. It's not really a lie detector. It can't tell us if you're lying, only if you're anxious. That's why the results aren't allowed as evidence in court. Okay?'

Rebecca smiled. 'Okay.'

Gus put his reading glasses on. 'Scott, I've got to ask you to leave us alone for the test. Doesn't work with spectators. It'll take about an hour.'

He walked Scott to the back door.

'She'll do fine.' He chuckled. 'Most folks, they're as nervous as a cat in a dog pound. But not her. I don't see any anxiety in her at all.'

Scott whispered to Gus: 'Ask her about cocaine use.'

Scott walked down the desolate beach. Gus's house was the only one in sight. It was like being on a deserted island. A hot island. Heat waves shimmered above the sun-baked sand. Scott could feel the heat through the soles of his deck shoes. Even the gulls didn't light on the dry sand; they stuck to the wet portion of the beach that the tide cooled with each pass. He thought of his life – his past and his future.

Two years ago, he had had what he considered a perfect life: partnership at Ford Stevens. $750,000 a year. Highland Park mansion. Ferrari. Miss SMU for his wife. Boo.

Then, that life was suddenly gone.

Now, two years later, he could have his old life back. Ford Fenney. $1 million a year. The corner office on the sixty-second floor. The dining, athletic, and country club memberships. Life, health, and dental insurance. 401(k) plan. Ferrari. Rebecca. Boo. Pajamae.

But did he want that life back? Could it ever be the same? Would it include Rebecca? Or would Boo visit her mother in the women's prison? The clock was ticking: nineteen days until trial, perhaps five more days until a verdict. Rebecca Fenney might be down to her last twenty-four days of freedom.

Scott decided to take another run at Melvyn Burke. He knew something. Something Terri Rawlins wanted hidden behind the attorney-client privilege. Scott pulled out his cell phone and dialed. When Melvyn answered, Scott said, 'Trey owed five hundred thousand dollars to Benito Estrada. You know who he is?'

It took a moment for Melvyn to answer. 'Yes.'

'And what he sells? And who he works for?'

'Yes. Why the debt? Trey made that much in a week.'

'Trey accused Benito of cheating him, refused to pay. You know what the consequences of not paying the cartel would be?'

'Yes. I know.'

'Trey also owed fifteen million to the mob.'

The line was silent for a moment. 'Who told you that?'

'Gabe Petrocelli. You know him, too?'

'I know of him.'

'He works for the mob.'

'I know.'

'Did you know about Trey's drug and gambling debts?'

'Does Rex know all this? The cartels, the mob?'

'He knows about the drug debt. I'm seeing him tomorrow about the mob debt.'

'Maybe he'll dismiss the charges.'

'Melvyn, if you know something, please tell me. Don't let an innocent person go to prison.'

'Attorney-client privilege, Scott.'

Scott ended the call when he saw Gus waving from the bungalow. He walked back up the beach. When he entered the bungalow, Gus said, 'Rebecca, why don't you take a walk now, let Scott and me talk?'

'Okay.'

She kicked off her sandals, and they watched her down to the surf.

'You get lonely out here, Gus?'

Gus smiled. 'With all these fish?' His smile soon faded. 'My work is done, Scott. I'll play out my life here on this sandbar.'

Scott had put off asking as long as he could. 'Well?'

'Inconclusive.'

'What does that mean? Was she lying?'

'We don't say "lying", Scott. We say "truthful" or "deceptive" or "inconclusive". Inconclusive means I don't know.'

'Why not?'

'Because her physiological responses weren't significant.'

'So she was telling the truth?'

'Possibly. From her demeanor, probably. She exhibited no nervousness or anxiety at all, so I'd lean toward truthful.'

'Even about the cocaine?'

'Yep. Said she used it a few times with Trey, not recently.'

'But possibly she was telling the truth and possibly she was lying?'

Gus nodded. 'Which adds up to inconclusive. Which is why I took early retirement from the Bureau.'

'What do you mean?'

'After Hanssen – the agent who sold secrets to the Russians – and then nine-eleven, the FBI and CIA and NSA, they all started seeing spies and terrorists behind every government desk. So they instituted wide-scale polygraph testing. Hell, they'd test every person in America if they could. They did test everyone at the Bureau. Anyone failed, they were fired on the spot. I kept telling the directors, that's not the proper use of the polygraph. Just too many false-positives to fire folks for one failed test. They want to say these things are ninety-five percent reliable, but that's just not the deal. None of this stuff – not even DNA – is foolproof, but we want a pill to make us skinny and a test to put the right people in prison. But the Bureau's more worried about bad press than bad guys, so they said shut up and test. I was ruining too many good folks' careers, so I quit.'

283

'Yeah, but the DA won't quit this case on inconclusive.'

Gus shook his head. 'Nope.'

Scott headed to the door but stopped. 'You didn't ask me.'

'Ask you what?'

'Why I'm defending my ex-wife?'

'Oh. Well, working at the FBI you learn pretty quick not to ask too many questions.'

'That's comforting.'

Consuela de la Rosa-Garcia hummed a Mexican ballad while she rocked little Maria. She was holding her *niña* under the umbrella on the back deck and watching the girls play on the beach below and Carlos and Louis trying to surf the waves. *Hombres locos.* But they made her laugh. She heard a car out front, and Señora Fenney soon appeared down below. She walked out to the girls.

Consuela had never liked Señora Fenney.

When the Fenneys had bought the mansion on Beverly Drive in Highland Park and she had become their maid, she knew that her life would be difficult under her new mistress. It had been. Then Immigration took Consuela away that terrible day, to Nuevo Laredo. But Señor Fenney had somehow rescued her and obtained her green card and brought her back to Highland Park, and when she returned, Señora Fenney was gone. The last two years without her had been good for Consuela. She was the only maid she knew in Highland Park with health insurance. Maria was not born with a Mexican midwife in East Dallas; she was delivered by a doctor in a hospital in North Dallas. Consuela liked her life now.

She hoped Señora Fenney would not return with them to Dallas.

Chapter 34

'You really gonna call all these witnesses?' the DA said.

'You gonna find your leak?'

The prosecution and defense had exchanged witness lists, as the law required. Scott gestured at the empty chair along the wall.

'Where's Tonto?'

The DA chuckled. 'I liked the Lone Ranger.' He pointed a thumb at the window. 'I put Ted on intake duty at the jail. Figure processing drunks over the Fourth of July weekend might give him some perspective. He went home to change, can't abide the thought of someone puking on his three-hundred-dollar shoes.'

The courthouse was quiet that Thursday, the day before the long holiday weekend. The DA scanned the defense's witness list.

'You really think someone on this list killed Trey?'

'Or they know who did.'

'Looks like the leader board at the Open – Pete Puckett, Donnie Parker . . .' The DA looked up from the list. 'Gabe Petrocelli? You're gonna call Gabe? Why?'

'Because the mob might've killed Trey.'

'I thought the Zetas killed him? Or Pete Puckett? Or the caddie? Look, Scott, just because he bet on football games with Gabe doesn't mean Trey—'

'He owed the mob fifteen million dollars. Gambling losses at casinos.'

Scott had dealt the DA another body blow to his image of Trey Rawlins. It took a moment for the DA to gather himself.

'You know this for a fact?'

'Gabe said so.'

'You talked to him? In person?'

'At his bar.'

'No one talks to us, but they spill their guts to you.'

'You guys are cops, I'm a curiosity, a lawyer defending his ex. Benito and Gabe got a kick out of that.'

'They would. But Gabe wouldn't lie about Trey owing money to the mob.'

'Trey threw two tournaments, to pay them back, in California and Miami, earlier this year. He intentionally missed short putts to win.'

'I was watching on TV both times. Couldn't believe he missed those. So if he paid them back, why'd they kill him?'

'Those two tournaments didn't cover his full debt. He was supposed to lose at Atlanta, too, but he made a long putt to win.'

'I saw that putt. One in a million.'

'Twenty million. Gabe said that's how much the mob lost on that putt.'

The DA sat quietly a moment, then stood. 'Slow around here today. Feel like taking a ride?'

They climbed into the DA's black four-wheel-drive pickup truck. The DA lit a cigar then steered out of the parking lot and east on Broadway Street, a wide six-lane avenue with a grassy esplanade separating the east- and west-bound traffic. The DA gestured to the north side at a stretch of vacant lots.

'Public housing used to be there, before Ike.'

'Senator Armstrong said he doesn't want to rebuild, wants the Island to be another Hamptons.'

The DA nodded. 'BOIs been longing for the glory days for a hundred years, back when they built the Broadway Beauties'

– he pointed out his window at the Victorian mansions that lined the boulevard – 'back in the late eighteen-hundreds. Used to be real pretty when the azaleas bloomed.'

Most of the mansions sat vacant and sad-looking, like homeless people sitting on the curb in downtown Dallas.

'Ike,' the DA said. 'Seawall held off the storm surge on the Gulf side, but the water went around the Island into the bay and flooded us from the north side – reverse storm surge. Water came up six feet right here, flooded those homes and killed all our trees. Salt water.' He waved a hand at the stumps in the esplanade. 'Used to drive under a canopy of oak trees. Had to cut down forty thousand dead trees, most of them were planted after the Great Storm. Only the palm trees survived.' The DA exhaled smoke. 'I love the Island. Hard to look at her like this.'

They turned south and drove to the seawall then turned east. The DA gestured out at the beach. 'Those six thousand folks that died in the Great Storm, they were cremated right there on the beach. You'd never forget that sight, would you?'

The DA drove to the east end, then turned north and pointed out his window. 'Federal courthouse. No judge now. Last one sexually harassed his staff, then lied about it to the FBI.'

'Obstruction of justice.'

'Got him three years in prison.' He now pointed out Scott's window. 'I was born right there. UTMB. The med school and charity hospital.'

They continued past the harbor where tall cruise ships were docked and entered the Galveston Yacht Club.

'Scott, if you're serious about calling Benito and Gabe, let me get Hank to serve your subpoenas, so you don't get yourself killed. Or someone else.'

'Thanks. I've got a PI in Dallas, he'll serve the players and their wives at the tournament up there next week.'

The DA parked the truck and cut the engine but didn't get out.

'Married women, teenage girls, porn, cocaine, gambling

– that's not the Trey Rawlins I knew. He called me Mr Truitt, like he was still in high school with my boy. Out at the club, he'd stop practicing and teach the kids. He was that kind of boy.'

'The good Trey.'

The DA nodded.

'But there was a bad Trey, too,' Scott said.

'I guess he did have a dark side. You wonder if all this was hardwired from birth or was it because of his folks dying when he was just a kid? What makes a young man with all that going for him drive his life off a cliff?'

'Dr Tim said he had an addictive personality.'

'Dr *Tim*?'

'His sports psychologist.'

'He was seeing a shrink?'

Scott nodded. 'Said he was addicted to sex.'

'I'd like to try that for a while before I die. 'Course, it'd probably kill me.'

They got out and walked to the marina entrance. The DA waved at the attendant then led Scott down a wood plank walkway fronting the slips where speedboats and sailboats and small fishing boats were docked. He stopped.

'This one's mine.'

It was a twenty-foot fishing boat with a bolted-down chair in the rear and a canopy over the center portion.

'Looks new,' Scott said.

'It is. Found my old one on Broadway, after Ike.'

'You catch that sailfish in this boat?'

'Nope. I hooked that baby off the Bahamas. Two more years, all I'm doing is golfing and fishing.'

'And taking Viagra.'

The DA smiled. 'And that.'

'The old man and the sea . . . with an ED prescription.'

'Hemingway might've been a happier man if he had had Viagra. I know I am.'

'Well, I'll still be trying to make a living practicing law in Dallas, so think of me when you're . . . fishing.'

The DA puffed on his cigar and said, 'At the arraignment, your wife said you were broke. That true?'

'Yep.'

'Hard for an honest lawyer to make a living these days.'

'I have options.'

'The federal bench?'

'Not likely. The senator owes some sort of debt to Judge Morgan.'

The DA inhaled his cigar then exhaled and said, 'His daughter is a cokehead. In and out of rehab. Shelby keeps it quiet, made some calls to the police chief. It's a small island, smaller since Ike. BOIs stick together.'

'I understand that debt.'

'Come on, I'll show you Trey's boat.'

Scott followed him down the walkway. The farther they went, the bigger the boats became. Near the end of the walkway, the DA stopped in front of a FOR SALE sign on a large silver-and-black boat.

'Fifty-six-foot Riva, they call it a sport yacht. Full living quarters, galley, the works. A five-star hotel that floats. Heard Trey paid two million. Melvyn's got it for sale for half a million, be lucky to get that. Bad economy to be selling a luxury boat.'

'It wasn't damaged by Ike?'

'Heard he took it down to Padre to ride out the storm. Come aboard.'

Scott stepped onto the boat and followed the DA up a set of stairs.

'Flybridge,' the DA said. 'You can pilot this boat from up here or downstairs in air conditioning.'

'What size crew do you need to operate this boat?'

'One.'

'One person can drive this boat?'

'Pilot the boat.' The DA gestured with his cigar. 'Check out the galley.'

They went down two flights of stairs into the living quarters filled with leather and wood. The bed was king-sized. The kitchen was stainless steel and sleek. The liquor cabinet was well-stocked.

'Care for a drink?' the DA asked.

'No, thanks.'

'Don't mind if I do.'

The DA found a glass, blew the dust out, then poured two fingers of whiskey. He held the glass up with a solemn expression.

'To Trey.'

The DA downed the drink and poured another.

'Rex, tell me about Melvyn Burke.'

They had finished the tour and were now sitting on leather seats in the upper salon as if they owned the boat. The DA smoked his cigar and sipped his whiskey.

'Melvyn is the dean of lawyers on the Island. Honorable to a fault.'

'He seems burdened by his past.'

'Aren't we all.'

'I'm representing my burden. What's his?'

The DA puffed on his cigar then pondered a moment. He came to a decision.

'Scott, I'm gonna tell you something about Melvyn in strict confidence. He's too good a man for this to get out.'

'Sure, Rex.'

'Melvyn is BOI and five years older than me. Went to Rice then UT law. Top of his class, could've hired on with the big Houston firms, made a career representing the Enrons of the world. Instead, he came back to the Island and set up a one-man shop, figured on being our Atticus Finch, if you can believe that.'

'Well . . .'

'Anyway, he had a good paying practice, but he took court appointments, for indigents. Judges appointed him because they knew poor folks would have a good lawyer. A great lawyer. Melvyn worked their cases just like his paying clients'.'

The DA blew out a cloud of smoke. He watched it hang in the air above his head then dissipate.

'Melvyn caught a death penalty case, teenage orphan boy, what we called a "retard" back then, "mentally challenged" today. Black boy. Melvyn took a liking to him, got the judge to release the boy into his custody pending trial. Took him home with him, came to love him like a son. Melvyn proved that boy innocent – I wasn't prosecuting then, but I was there – but the jury convicted him anyway, sentenced him to death. Melvyn appealed all the way to the state supreme court, but lost. No DNA testing back then. State executed the boy a year later.'

'A year? That's fast.'

'That was back in the sixties when the State of Texas was executing black men like the Taliban executes loose women.' The DA paused and puffed. 'Few years later, the real killer confessed on his death bed. The boy was innocent.'

'Damn.'

'That case haunts Melvyn to this day. Blames himself.'

'Why? It wasn't his fault.'

'Because that's what good men do. Just like it wasn't your fault your wife left you, but you blame yourself. So you figure you gotta defend her.'

'How'd you know?'

'Twenty-eight years in this job, you learn about folks . . . and I've been there. Wife leaving you, that's tough on a man. You wonder what's wrong with you, how you failed her. You blame yourself. You start thinking differently about yourself. You go to the bar luncheon or the grocery store, everyone smiles at you but you know they're thinking you couldn't make her happy in bed, you couldn't satisfy her, you—'

'Weren't man enough.'

The DA nodded. 'My first wife left me twenty-five years ago. I always wondered if I had only been a better husband, a better man, a better . . . something . . . whatever she needed, maybe she wouldn't have left me. Took me a while to figure out it wasn't about me. It was about her. Just like it wasn't about you, Scott . . . it was about your wife.'

The DA drank his whiskey.

'She left me for a Houston doctor with a mansion in River Oaks.'

'Did she have an affair with the doctor, before she left you?'

'Yep.'

'Mine, too. I never knew.'

'We never do.'

'Looking back, the signs were there, I just didn't see them.'

'Life is clear in the rearview mirror.'

'When she left, I felt like I'd been stomped on.'

The DA inhaled the cigar and exhaled smoke. 'Scott, if you live long enough, life will stomp the ever-living shit out of you. And having a woman you love stop loving you, that qualifies as a stompin'.'

'How'd you get over her?'

'I didn't.'

'But you remarried?'

The DA nodded. 'Five years later. Took that long to stop drinking.' He held up his glass. 'This ain't drinking. You drink?'

'Not liquor.'

'Don't start. At least not over a woman. You seeing a gal up in Dallas?'

'No.'

'Prospects?'

'Well, there is this fourth-grade teacher . . .'

'But you can't take that step?'

'Not yet.'

He nodded. 'You will. One day.'

They sat in silence for a time and pondered women and life. The DA finally tamped out his cigar and said, 'Scott, even the bad Trey didn't deserve an eight-inch blade stuck in his gut.'

'No, he didn't.'

'Some folks do. Three decades of prosecuting murderers and rapists and gangbangers, I know some people deserve to die. Benito, those Zetas – but the law doesn't allow us to make that decision outside a courtroom. We can't engage in private executions, not even here in Texas. So I'm still going to find justice for Trey. The good Trey and the bad Trey.'

'You should. But his justice isn't Rebecca. It's the mob . . . or maybe the Zetas . . . or maybe Pete Puckett. I'm not sure. But I am sure it's not her.'

'Why are her prints on the knife?'

'I don't know. But there's something else.'

'Not Lee Harvey Oswald?'

Scott smiled. 'The mob wanted Trey to be a long-term investment. So they paid him a cut of their winnings for those two thrown tournaments . . . in cash. Three million dollars. Hundred-dollar bills. Gabe made the payoff personally – at Trey's house. You can't take that kind of cash to the bank, they'd have to report it to the Feds. Which leaves under the bed or in a tin can buried on the beach.'

'No tin can. Old-timers walk the beach with metal detectors, still searching for Lafitte's treasure.'

'Then under his bed.'

'What are you saying, Scott?'

'You think the cops might've taken it? When they searched the house that day?'

The DA considered the smoke ring he had exhaled then said, 'I want to say no, but in a world where a governor is caught on tape trying to sell a Senate seat to the highest bidder, who knows? I'll have Hank check it out.'

'You trust him?'

'Hank Kowalski's got no use for money. All he needs to be happy is a fishing rod and bait.' The DA finished off his whiskey and stood. 'Oh, prints on the whiskey bottle match the set on the kitchen counter, but the prints from the tape don't match either of the other sets. And Hank said thanks.'

'For what?'

'The whiskey.'

'That proves Pete Puckett was in Trey's house the day he was murdered.'

'Figure because Trey was screwing his kid?'

'That's a good motive.'

'Would be for me. But I thought Pete was playing in Florida that day?'

293

'He DQ'd, flew home that afternoon. But not to Austin where he lives. Karen got his flight – he flew from Orlando into Houston Hobby, arrived at four. Which puts him at Trey's house by five.'

'In the kitchen.'

'Where that knife was.'

'That makes him a material witness.'

'Or a killer. He had the motive, the means, and the opportunity.'

'I always liked Pete. Everyone I know likes Pete.'

'His WM squared rating is eighty-eight percent.'

'WM what?'

Scott shook his head. 'The cartel and the mob, they had motives, too. And they're professionals. They wouldn't have left prints behind.'

'They wouldn't have left your wife behind either. Not alive.' The DA grunted. 'Seventeen days till trial, Scott. We could ask the judge for a continuance, give us some time to investigate Pete, the mob, the cartel.'

'You mean, suspects with motives?'

'Yeah, I mean that.'

'Rex, she's innocent. Dismiss the charges and find the killer.'

'I'd rather find the killer then dismiss the charges. Look, Scott, I still think she did it, but no motive, that bothers me.'

'It should.'

'Guess if I dismiss the charges, I could always indict her again – no statute of limitations on murder. 'Course, she might make a run for the border.'

'With what? She's broke, too.'

'Good point.'

'She took a polygraph yesterday.'

'You're probably not telling me this because she failed?'

'Inconclusive.'

'That's not the same as truthful.'

'It raises questions whether she's guilty.'

'But it doesn't answer them. Who did it? The polygraph.'

'Gus Grimes.'

'Gus is good. And conservative. He doesn't jump the gun, say someone's lying when they might not be. From him, inconclusive ain't bad. But—'

'But what?'

'As I recall, the house inventory listed prescription drugs, Prozac and beta-blockers.'

Scott nodded. 'In Trey's bathroom. So?'

'So some folks figure they can beat a polygraph by taking beta-blockers and anti-anxiety drugs right before the test.'

'Gus said it only tests anxiety levels.'

'Yep.'

'Rebecca didn't know Trey was taking that stuff.'

'I'm sure.'

Scott pulled out his cell phone and called Gus. He was surf fishing, but he answered.

'Gus, if Rebecca took a beta-blocker or an anti-anxiety drug before the polygraph, would that have affected the result?'

'Did she?'

'I don't know. I'm talking to the DA about it.'

'Well, it'd pretty much guarantee an inconclusive result. Artificially reduces the subject's respiration, which is what the machine measures – changes in respiration.'

'Thanks, Gus.'

'You bet. Say hi to Rex.'

Scott hung up and looked at the DA.

'Well?'

'Gus says hi.'

'About the test?'

'You're right.'

'Inconclusive means the case still comes down to her fingerprints on the murder weapon.' The DA sat quietly. 'Why were her prints on the knife?'

'I don't know.'

'Tell me why, Scott – get me past that before trial, and I'll drop the charges.'

★　★　★

295

'I saw Trey's boat today.'

'You went to the yacht club?'

Scott nodded. 'With the DA. Nice boat.'

'I could live on it. I loved to pilot it.'

'You can drive that big boat?'

'Sure. We'd take it down the coast to Padre Island, we did that right before Ike hit, so the boat didn't get damaged. I wanted to take it to Cancún.'

Scott picked up a sea shell and flung it into the surf. They were on the beach having another confidential attorney–client conversation.

'Pete Puckett was in the house that Thursday. The day Trey was killed.'

'When?'

'While you were in Houston.'

'He broke in?'

'No.'

'But Trey was at the club all day, practicing.'

'No, he wasn't. He left the club at noon, came home.'

'Why?'

'To meet Billie Jean. She was there, too. Pete's prints were on the kitchen counter, right next to the knife drawer. But your prints were on the knife. I need to know why.'

'I cut stuff with those knives all the time.'

The time had come to tell her the whole truth. Scott turned to her and took her by the shoulders.

'Rebecca – your prints weren't aligned on the knife like you were cutting something, with the blade pointing up. The prints prove that you were holding that knife with the blade pointing down . . . as if to stab something.'

'Or someone.'

'Do you remember ever using that knife that way?'

'No. Never.'

'Your prints prove you did. Sometime. For something.'

She shook her head. He released her shoulders.

'And wouldn't Rosie have washed the knives after you used them?'

296

'Sure. Or put them in the dishwasher. She came that day.'

'Did you use that knife that day? Or that night?'

'I don't think so. I ate lunch in Houston, we had dinner out. Scott, we were drinking a lot . . . and the cocaine . . . I don't remember much from that night.'

He looked at her.

'I'd remember if I killed him.'

Chapter 35

Fireworks exploded in the night sky over the Gulf of Mexico.

Two nights later, they were sitting in folding chairs lined up on the seawall for the Fourth of July celebration. Boo and her mother sat side by side at one end.

'You're a complicated woman,' Boo said.

Mother smiled. 'Is that a compliment?'

'It means we don't understand you.'

'Boo, a woman's life is a complicated life.'

'That's something else I'll understand when I'm older?'

'Yes.'

Boo watched the fireworks for a while then said, 'Mother, if you don't go to prison, do you want to come back to us?'

'Do you want me back?'

'We're at that age – we need a mother.'

'Yes, you do.'

'We . . . *we* need a mother.'

Louis and Pajamae sat at the other end. 'You decide yet?' he said.

'Decide what?'

'If Mr Fenney's gonna be your daddy.'

'I did something real bad, Louis.'

'What's that?'

'When I said prayers last night, I asked God to send Miz Fenney to that prison.'

'Why?'

'So Mr Fenney doesn't marry her.'

''Cause you figure if he does, there won't be no place for you?'

'Unh-huh.'

'Well, you ain't figuring right, girl. You Mr Fenney's daughter, so if he marries her again, you're part of a package deal, see? She gotta take it or leave it, the whole package. Ain't no picking and choosing.'

'You think?'

'I know.'

The night sky exploded in red and white sparkles.

'That was a nice one.'

'Real nice.'

Karen and Bobby sat in the middle. Bobby was trying out names on her.

'Sam?

'Ron?

'Cole?

'Clay?'

Karen groaned.

'Is it time?' Bobby asked.

'No. Junior just gave me a big kick to the ribs.'

'Let me feel.'

Bobby placed his palms on her belly.

Scott was happy for his old friend. He had finally found someone to share his life. Funny. After twenty-five years of Bobby Herrin envying Scott Fenney, Scott now envied Bobby.

Scott sat between Louis and Carlos, who was bouncing Maria on his lap and pointing at the fireworks. Consuela was knitting a little sweater for the baby. Louis leaned toward Scott.

'Mr Fenney, I'm thinking about going back to school, getting my high school diploma, maybe go to college. I like learning things.'

'That's good thinking.'

Louis now pointed past Scott. 'We got company.'

Down the seawall, three Latino men were walking toward them: Benito Estrada and his thugs. Scott stood and walked toward the men. Louis and Carlos were on his heels. Benito waved like a kid come to play.

'*Buenas noches*, Scott.'

'What brings you out, Benito?'

Benito waved a hand to the sky. 'The fireworks. I never miss the fireworks. The Island, she is beautiful at night, is she not?'

'Why'd you bring bodyguards for the fireworks?'

'Them? Oh, they come with the job, like Obama and the Secret Service.' Benito glanced over at the others. 'Your daughters?'

'Yes.'

'Cute kids. I hope to have children one day.'

'Might want to change your line of work first. Be hard to tell your kids not to use drugs if you're selling them.'

'Five more years, Scott, then I am retiring.'

'But will the cartel let you retire?'

His expression turned serious. 'That is the question.'

'You could quit now, leave the Island, start over somewhere, use your business skills in a more productive – and legal – way.'

'I will never leave. I was born on the Island, and I will die on the Island.' His eyes seemed to go away for a moment, then he said, 'Scott, may we talk privately?'

They stepped down the seawall then Benito stopped and said, 'Scott, this subpoena, it is a mistake.'

'Why?'

'Because the cartel is watching this closely. Do not bring them into it. Things could get ugly.'

'Is that a threat?'

'No. Just friendly advice. Like I told you, I do not do violence. But they do. They kill women, kids, dogs – they do not care. You bring them into this, you endanger your family.'

'I could send them home.'

'You cannot hide from the Zetas. They are here now, in America. And they are here to stay.'

How does a lawyer zealously represent his client pursuant to the rule of law when some people make their own rules?

'Do you deliver personally to Senator Armstrong's daughter?'

'You know about her?'

Scott nodded. 'And I know what happened to Trey's cocaine.'

'What?'

'Those construction workers down the street, they stole it.'

'You are sure?'

'They told Carlos.'

Benito gazed at the fireworks in the sky above them. 'He was my friend, and I did not trust him. I hope I did not get my friend killed.'

The next installment of 'Murder on the Beach' aired that night on the late news.

'*This is Renée Ramirez live from Galveston. Rebecca Fenney might have less than three weeks of freedom left – her murder trial starts in fifteen days – but she seemed unconcerned tonight as she enjoyed the fireworks on the seawall.*'

The picture cut to the Fenney family on the seawall.

'She taped us!' Rebecca said.

Scott, Rebecca, Bobby, and Karen were in the living room watching the TV.

Back to Renée Ramirez. '*And here she enjoyed something else. Or should I say, someone else.*'

The picture went to a shadowy night scene on the beach. Two people strolling along the surf. A bare-chested man and a woman in a white bikini. The woman stopped and kissed the man. Then she skipped down the beach and removed her bikini and ran into the water. The man followed her and embraced her and they . . .

'Oh, my God,' Rebecca said.

'Uh-oh,' Bobby said.

'That's not you and . . .' Karen said. 'Oh, boy.'

Renée Ramirez had secretly filmed them that night on the beach three weeks before. It was clearly Rebecca – her red hair glowed in the moonlight – but it was not clearly Scott. The tape ended, and the screen returned to Renée Ramirez.

'*This was only ten days after Trey's death, and Rebecca Fenney was acting like a college girl on spring break. But I'm sure she loved Trey.*'

A thought occurred to Scott.

'Rebecca, you said Renée did a profile of Trey . . . When?'

'A couple weeks before he . . .'

'Did you go with him to the studio?'

'No. I was shopping in Houston that day. But they didn't do the interview at the studio. They did it here.'

'Here where?'

'At the house.'

Scott stared down at his ex-wife.

'Renée Ramirez was in your house?'

Chapter 36

With Renée Ramirez sipping a Mimosa in the foreground and the whitecaps of the waves washing ashore in the background, it was a chamber of commerce portrait of Galveston Island.

She was a stunningly beautiful Latina in a stunningly short skirt. She had shiny brown hair and smooth tan skin but her eyes were as blue as the summer sky. Her voluptuous body strained against her snug low-cut white top. She wore a turquoise-and-silver necklace and silver coyote earrings and no wedding band. She was young, beautiful, and perched on a high stool with her long bare legs crossed as if daring Scott – or any man within eyeball range of her – not to stare.

He stared.

Scott had called her station and set up a meeting at the open-air pool bar at the Hotel Galvez on the seawall for that Monday morning. Renée had arrived first and ordered the Mimosa. Scott had arrived with his blood pressure pumping, ready to give her a piece of his mind for putting his daughters on television. She attempted to preempt his fatherly anger by appealing to his manly vanity, as if that would work.

'Those football tapes, you were quite the stud in college, Scott. You look like you could still play.'

'Oh, thanks, I—' He caught himself. Damn, it almost worked. 'Don't put my girls on TV again.'

'Freedom of the press. You and Rebecca are news, you were in a public place, and they happened to be there with you. So how about an on-air interview?'

'No.'

She pushed her lips out. 'Odd. Most lawyers are begging to be on TV.' She sipped her Mimosa. 'Anyway, I was completely within the law.'

'Just because you can doesn't mean you should.'

'Should you and Rebecca have been groping each other like horny teenagers on a public beach that night?' She grinned. 'That was you, wasn't it? What was that about, for old time's sake?' She shrugged. 'I guess she is your ex. Screwing her is one thing, but why are you defending her?'

Scott got suspicious. He glanced around the bar for a hidden camera. He saw nothing, but he accused her anyway.

'Are you secretly taping our conversation?'

'You mean, like with a wire?'

'Or a tape recorder.'

Renée slid off the stool and stepped so close to Scott he could breathe in her perfume.

'You want to pat me down?'

Yes. Desperately.

'Doesn't look like you're hiding anything. Your clothes are so tight I doubt you could get a finger in between.'

'You could try.'

She winked at him then climbed aboard – her stool – and assumed her legs-crossed-I-dare-you-not-to-look position.

'So why are you defending her?'

'She's the mother of my child.'

'But she cheated on you with the guy she killed!'

'She cheated with him, but she didn't kill him.'

'You just can't let her go.' She shook her beautiful head. 'Men. You know the best way to get over her? Cheat back.'

'But we're not married.'

'Doesn't matter. You need to get over her – it's a psychological thing. And it'll make you feel better.' She uncrossed her legs and swiveled toward him then licked her glossy lips and leaned in. 'And I happen to be free today.'

Leaning toward him like that, she exposed a significant portion of her full, soft breasts – which attracted Scott's male eyes. Gabe Petrocelli was right: she was as alluring and dangerous as a rattlesnake. Rattlers are pit vipers – they hunt warm-blooded prey; they swallow their victims whole; and they are conniving slithering beasts. They coil up and shake their rattles to attract your eye, to distract you, to disarm you, then – ZAP! – they strike at you with jaws wide and sink their fangs into your flesh and inject their venom. Scott tried not to stare at Renée's rattles.

'I'd be afraid of seeing a tape on the evening news.'

'I doubt you're that good.' She gave him another sexy wink. 'But I'll guarantee confidentiality.'

The man who had not been with a woman in almost two years wanted to say, 'Let's do it!' But the lawyer representing his ex-wife on a murder charge said, 'I doubt anything is confidential with you.'

She frowned and sat up, taking her rattles with her. The lawyer had spoiled a perfect human encounter, as lawyers are wont to do. But the man was comforted by the knowledge that he was years away from requiring a Viagra prescription.

'Why'd you air that tape just two weeks before the trial?'

'Sweeps week. Ratings. Sex sells, Scott. I'm hoping the networks will pick it up when the trial starts.'

'You're hoping Trey's murder advances your career?'

She rolled her blue eyes. 'Save the righteous indignation, Scott. I know lawyers. And I know a lawyer's only measure of success is money and the things money can buy. Why do you want to be a federal judge, to save the world? Or because it's a taxpayer-guaranteed lifetime salary? You're willing to have your career advanced by an asshole like Armstrong, but you're judging me?' She almost laughed. 'Lawyers are always so goddamned self-righteous, always ready to criticize everyone else's ambitions and denounce everyone else's desires – at eight hundred dollars an hour.' She shrugged. 'Besides, I didn't kill him.'

He shook his head.

'Look, Scott, I graduated with straight As in journalism, but the only job offer I got was as a weather girl – and only because of my looks. I put myself through UT modeling for local stores in Austin, could've signed with a New York agency but I wanted a serious profession, like journalism. Turns out I was still modeling. Five years standing in front of a green screen pointing out cold fronts and high-pressure systems. Now I'm thirty years old. My time to jump to the networks is running out fast. This body won't last forever. I've got to spend two hours a day in the gym to compete.'

'For men?'

'*Men?* No – for jobs. In TV, you get fat, you get fired. Women anyway. Men can be old and fat and on-air, but women – once you put on a few pounds and the face sags, you're history. And that goddamn HDTV highlights every flaw. This is my shot, Scott. Minorities are in right now. You watch the network morning shows? Looks like the goddamned General Assembly at the UN. The Hispanic population is exploding, so every morning show has a pretty Latina. I want to be the next one. I'm an educated, articulate, hot-looking Hispanic – I'm perfect for today's demographics. Wall Street's vying for our business and Washington for our votes – why do you think we finally got a Supreme Court justice? It's our time. It's my time.'

She drank her Mimosa.

'Scott, I'm sorry you're upset about your kids, but this is my moment, and I'm not going to let it pass me by. I just need something big to catch a network's eye.'

'Like a murder case?'

'I don't make the news. I just report it.'

'Who's your source at the courthouse?'

'That's confidential.'

'You're tainting potential jurors.'

'A lifetime on this island tainted them.'

306

'You're denying my client her right to a fair trial.'

'Take it up with Shelby.'

Renée sipped her drink. Scott eyed her manicured fingers wrapped around the damp glass.

'I'm filing for a change of venue this morning.'

'Good luck with that.'

'You don't think I can get the trial moved?'

'Not in our lifetime.'

'Why not?'

'Scott, the typical murder case on the Island, it's drug violence – black on black, brown on brown. Go to the trial, won't be anyone there except the victim's family, if them. Case gets two sentences in the Metro section, not even a mention on my station's evening news. Why? Because Anglos could care less if blacks and Latinos are killing each other. More the merrier, they think.'

She drank her Mimosa and shook her head.

'Hurricane Ike whitewashed the Island, destroyed every public housing complex, sent the blacks and Latinos fleeing to the mainland, which made a lot of Anglos giddy – like your buddy Armstrong. They think Ike did the Island a favor, that an all-white Island will attract more tourists and rich folks to buy beach houses. So they don't want to rebuild the public housing – the minorities are gone and they want them to stay gone. That's the way it is here, Scott. That's why I want to get the hell out of here. This case – a star pro golfer stabbed by his lover – this is front-page news, lead story on every Houston newscast, updates on the network morning shows. This murder case is my ticket off this fucking island.'

Renée finished her Mimosa then slid off her stool and slithered over to the exit. She had a nice slither. At the door she stopped and turned back to Scott – he thought to see if he were looking at her – but she said, 'And it's Shelby's ticket, too.'

Chapter 37

'I'm not losing this case because you can't keep your dick in your pants!'

It was a week later – one week before the trial – and Judge Shelby Morgan was pointing a long manicured finger at Scott. The prosecution and defense teams had crowded into the judge's chamber for the pretrial conference.

'It's not your case to win or lose, Judge. It's ours. Issue a gag order.'

'I can't do that. There's a little thing called the First Amendment.'

'Then move the trial to Austin or San Antonio, out of the range of the Houston TV stations – everyone down here has seen Renée's reports. My client can't get a fair trial in Galveston County.'

'He's right, Shelby,' the DA said. 'Between Renée and whoever the hell is leaking the evidence to her, we'll have a heck of a time seating a jury of twelve folks who haven't made up their minds about the case. Hell, a week in Austin won't be that bad. You can look up old friends from your UT days.'

The judge shook her head. 'Moving the case now, seven days before trial, that'd screw up the cable deal for sure. Motion for change of venue is denied.'

'What cable deal?' Scott said.

'Renée made a deal with cable TV, they're going to air the entire trial, start to finish.'

'You're going to let her televise the trial? Judge, didn't you watch O.J.'s trial? It was a farce, everyone playing to the cameras.'

The DA nodded. 'Shelby, that was a train wreck of a trial. TV cameras bring out the worst in everyone – jurors, witnesses, cops' – he glanced over at the Assistant DA – 'lawyers. You don't want to go there.'

The judge leaned back in her chair, obviously weighing the pros and cons of TV cameras in her courtroom. Right now, she stood first in line for the federal bench; a bad TV experience and she could fall from first to last. On the other hand, a masterful performance could send her straight to the federal appeals court, a short step away from the Supreme Court. She sat forward in her chair.

'Yes – I do want to go there.'

'But, Judge—'

'I've made my decision, Mr Fenney.'

She shuffled papers on her desk.

'Motion to suppress the fingerprint evidence is denied. Motion to suppress the toxicology report, denied. Motion to suppress all evidence found at the house due to lack of a search warrant, denied. Motion to limit the crime scene photos shown to the jury, denied.'

'Scott,' the DA said, 'I won't go overboard with those. But the jury has a right to see the victim I'm representing and the crime they're sitting in judgment on.'

'Any other motions?' the judge said.

'Yes, Your Honor,' Karen said. 'Motion to exclude the expert testimony of Dr Holbrooke, the prosecution's psychiatrist. Our client is charged with murder, not manslaughter, which requires that she "intentionally or knowingly" caused Trey Rawlins' death. If the doctor is going to testify that she didn't know what she was doing because of the cocaine and alcohol, then he's testifying that she had no intent.'

'Then you should want him to testify.'

'Your Honor,' the Assistant DA said, 'the doctor is not going to testify that she didn't know what she was doing, but that the cocaine may be why she can't remember doing it.'

'Your Honor,' Scott said, 'this is junk science. You can't allow that testimony in.'

'I can and I am. The Rules of Evidence say admission of expert testimony is at the sole discretion of the trial judge. You want to appeal my ruling, you've got to prove I abused my discretion. Which means unless I'm screwing the expert, you've got no chance on appeal.'

'I don't care if you're screwing the expert, Judge, just that you're screwing my client.'

She didn't appreciate that comment.

'Jury selection on Friday, nine A.M. We're done.'

'A TV trial,' Scott said to the DA on their way out of the courtroom, 'that's going to be a circus.'

'And we're gonna be the clowns.' The DA chuckled then turned to Karen, 'You know, Professor, Rex Herrin has a nice ring to it.'

'Rex Herrin? That does sound nice. I like that. Tell you what – I'll name my son Rex if you'll drop Holbrooke from your witness list.'

The DA smiled. 'You sure I can't convince you to move to the Island?' He then motioned Scott away from the others. He lowered his voice. 'Prints you gave me last week – I got the results back.'

'And?'

'Not in the system, but they match the prints on the headboard.'

'You're kidding?'

'Nope. Whose are they?'

'I can't tell you, Rex, not yet. But they don't belong to the killer. At least I don't think.'

The DA shrugged. 'It's your wife on trial.'

'Rex, I need a favor from Hank.'

'Sure. Tell him what you want.'

Scott's cell phone rang. He answered. It was Helen from Judge Buford's office.

'Hi, Helen, what's up?'

'Scott . . . the judge died.'

Chapter 38

'Justice is served one person at a time.'

The church pews in front of Scott were crowded with hundreds of state and federal judges from across the State of Texas. They had shown up en masse just as the police do when one of their own dies in the line of duty. Judge Sam Buford had died on the bench. His body lay in the casket in front of the podium where Scott now stood. Scott knew this day was coming, but he still was not prepared for it. He now struggled to read his notes through his tears.

'Sam Buford was a husband, a father, a grandfather, a brother, a friend, a lawyer, a judge . . . and my hero. I was fortunate to know him, and I hope you knew him, too. Sam Buford was a man worth knowing.

'Judge Buford taught me the most important lesson a lawyer can learn, the lesson a lawyer must learn to be a good lawyer: justice is not something you read about in law books. It's something you live. It is a lawyer's role in life. It was Sam Buford's life. He served justice one person at a time, every day of his life.'

Scott gestured at the casket.

'There lies a great man. Not a rich or a famous man, but a man who cared. A man who made our lives better. Fairer. The world knew Sam Buford was here.'

At the reception, Scott met Judge Buford's two children and five grandchildren. He shook hands with lawyers he hadn't seen in years. And he ran into Dan Ford.

'Jesus, Scotty, what the hell were you thinking? Representing Rebecca for murdering Trey?'

'She's innocent.'

'She's broke. You're working for free again.' Dan shook his head. 'Another lost cause, Scotty?'

Probably.

'Hard to believe,' Dan said. 'Two years ago, she was living in a Highland Park mansion . . . a week, ten days from now, she could be living in an eight-by-ten cell in the women's prison. Leaving you didn't work out so well for her. She really use cocaine?'

Scott nodded.

'You're lucky she left you.'

Dan gave him a fatherly pat on the shoulder, as if consoling a son who had lost a ball game. 'Heard Buford put you up as his replacement?'

Scott nodded again.

'One million versus one hundred sixty-nine thousand. Seems like a no-brainer for a lawyer.'

'Not this lawyer.'

'Think of your girls, Scotty, what's best for them.'

'Always.'

Dan looked around. 'Nice crowd. Last funeral I attended was Mack's, a year ago. I was his executor, took the statutory three percent fee – twenty-four million. Boy, that was a nice windfall for the firm.'

'Even prostate cancer has a silver lining, huh, Dan?'

'I worked for Mack for forty years. With Clark dead, his entire estate went to Jean. She was only married to him for eleven years – why should she get it all? Hell, she still took home over seven hundred million. That's not a bad take for eleven years. I hear the trial's going to be televised.'

313

'The judge wants to move up in the world.'

'Well, he—'

'She.'

'A female judge? Shit, that's bad luck. Well, she'd better be careful. Having everything you say in court broadcast on cable for the entire country to hear, that can come back and bite you in the butt.'

'Fortunately, I have a nice butt.'

Judge Morgan had walked up behind them. When Dan turned and took her in, his eyes lit up as if she were a billionaire looking for a lawyer.

'Dan,' Scott said, 'this is Judge Shelby Morgan. Judge, this is Dan Ford, senior partner at Ford Stevens.'

'Ford Fenney,' Dan said, 'if Scott will succumb to my charms . . . and money.'

'I didn't know you were coming up for the funeral, Judge,' Scott said.

'Wouldn't miss it. The legal event of the year. You want to share a cab to the airport?'

'I'll find you in half an hour.'

The judge walked away to Dan's admiring eye.

'That'd be a nice butt to bite.'

But Dan's mind soon returned to his two favorites subjects: law and money.

'Think about it, Scotty – Ford Fenney.'

'Dan, all I've thought about the last six weeks has been this murder trial.'

'Messy.'

'More than you can imagine.'

'Ex-wives are like that.'

'Bourbon on the rocks,' Judge Morgan said to the flight attendant. 'A double.'

'Bottled water,' Scott said.

He leaned back and loosened his tie. They had shared a cab to Dallas Love Field and now sat side by side on the six o'clock flight back to Houston. Most passengers were forgoing the flight attendant's offer of water, coffee, or orange juice in favor of something stronger. Including the judge.

'Funerals depress me,' she said.

The flight attendant returned with napkins and a water for Scott and a plastic cup filled with ice and two miniature bottles of bourbon for the judge.

'Thank God.'

She twisted the tops off both like an experienced pro and poured the liquor over the ice. She drank half down then inhaled and exhaled slowly. Her face flushed pink when the alcohol hit her system. It only made her more attractive.

'That was a nice eulogy, Scott. You knew him well?'

'I did.'

'And he wanted you to take his place?'

'He did.'

She finished off the drink and motioned to the flight attendant for a refill.

'Now politics are standing in your way.'

'I have options.'

'Ford Fenney. Name partner at one of the richest law firms in Texas – most lawyers would love to have that option.'

The flight attendant arrived with another cup of ice and two more miniature bottles of bourbon. The judge fixed her drink.

'You been to the FBI yet?' she said.

'What for?'

'Fingerprints, criminal background check.'

'No point. The job's yours.'

She held her hands up and spread her fingers. 'I've never been fingerprinted. When they fingerprinted your wife, did the ink ruin her nails?'

'Weren't you fingerprinted when you were elected state court judge?'

She shook her head. 'State court judges don't have to pass criminal background checks, just get elected. But I'll pass. I've never been arrested, not even in college.'

315

'You'd really move to Dallas to be a federal judge? Dallas is a lot bigger city than Galveston, we've got congestion and crime and—'

'Neiman Marcus. I love that store.'

'Then you'll love Dallas.'

'And the Cowboys. I tried out to be a Cowboy cheerleader, back in college. I was a cheerleader at UT, all four years.'

'You like football?'

'I like football players.' She gave him a look; she still had that coed twinkle in her eyes. 'Even ex-football players.'

'Once a cheerleader, always a cheerleader.'

'Like your wife.'

'Ex-wife.'

She shook her head. 'I still can't believe you're defending her. You must really love her.' She paused, and the twinkle faded from her eyes. 'I never had a man love me like that.'

'Maybe you never loved a man like that.'

'You think she ever loved you like that?'

The last two years, he had asked himself the same question. Often. He now felt the judge studying him. *She's the judge – think like a lawyer.*

'I think she's innocent.'

'I hope for your career's sake she is.' She downed her drink. 'Anyway, back to me. I didn't make the Cowboys cheerleader squad, so I went to law school. But five years in Dallas will pass fast, then I'll move to Washington and you can have my bench.'

'Five years?'

She nodded. 'I want to be US attorney general. I'm too young now, so I figure five years on the federal bench, a few high-profile cases, I'll be ready to move up.'

'A woman with a plan.'

'You know what they call a woman without a plan? . . . A wife.'

She downed the second drink and leaned her head back. 'All I need from a man is sex.' She cut her eyes to Scott. 'You interested in trying out for the position?'

Scott's face must have betrayed his thoughts. She chuckled.

'Don't be shocked, Scott. Sex is about recreation, not procreation. I'm a woman who knows what she wants and takes it.'

Her blue eyes were at half-mast. She was only two years older than Scott but she looked ten years younger. She appeared lean and fit in her business suit with the skirt hiked up mid-thigh. Every pore on her body oozed sensuality. She caught Scott looking at her and winked at him. First Renée, now the judge.

'Aren't there any eligible men on the Island?'

'None I want sweating over me.' She smiled. 'That was you on Renée's tape, wasn't it?'

'Tell her to stop those "Murder on the Beach" reports.'

'She wants a network job.'

'She may get more than she bargained for.'

'How so?'

'At the trial.'

'Oh. That should be fun, lots of TV exposure.'

'Those are bright lights.'

'Scott, I've been waiting all my life for my moment in the lights.'

She leaned into him and put her hand on his thigh. Her scent had a higher alcohol content than the bourbon she was drinking. Scott breathed her in.

'So, Scott, you considering my offer?'

It was an attractive offer, like Ford Fenney. But both offers had downsides.

'Judge, we're in the middle of a murder trial.'

'I promise not to talk about the case or Trey. In fact, I promise not to talk at all . . . unless you want me to.' She winked. 'You need some excitement in your life, Scott, I can tell. You need some fun. Man fun.' She patted his leg, and he felt the heat rise. 'You think about it while I go to the little girl's room.'

She moved all four empty bourbon bottles to Scott's tray table, secured her tray to the seat in front, and pushed herself up then stumbled down the aisle holding her glass aloft. Scott couldn't help but look after her; the skirt was snug around her bottom. It was a very nice bottom. Judge Shelby Morgan was an incredibly sexy woman. And no doubt sex with her would be fun. Man fun.

He was like those other lawyers at Ford Stevens now – his only fun was father fun. Watching Pajamae play basketball, going on field trips with her and Boo, having lunch with them once a week at school, playing on the beach this summer with them – that was good fun. Fatherly fun. But sometimes a man needed the other kind of fun, the kind of fun that involved a sexy woman like Shelby Morgan . . . or Rebecca Fenney . . . or Tess McBride . . . or –

Scott sat up straight in his seat.

Judge Morgan lived three houses down from Trey Rawlins. She had just referred to him as 'Trey'. Not as 'Mr Rawlins'. Not as 'the victim'. But as 'Trey'. As if she had known him. Personally.

Scott's eyes dropped to the empty bourbon bottles.

Chapter 39

Two days later, only three days before trial, Scott escorted his ex-wife into the courthouse for jury selection. They entered an elevator.

'Rebecca, unless Benito or Gabe or Pete confesses on the stand, the case is going to turn on your credibility.'

'So I'll testify?'

'You may have to. So we need a character witness, someone who can vouch for your honesty. Tess had an affair with Trey, and her husband's on the suspect list, so that rules her out. Who are your other friends?'

She was quiet on the ride up.

'It's hard to be friends with women who are competing for your man.' She sighed. 'Must be why my friends have always been men.'

The elevator doors opened, and they stepped out. They walked down the corridor and into the courtroom. Scott stopped at the prosecution table and handed a baggie containing the miniature bourbon bottles to the DA.

'More suspects?'

'Just one.'

The DA shrugged. 'I'll get Hank to run 'em.'

Scott stepped over to the defense table where Bobby and Karen were prepping for *voir dire*. Rebecca went to the restroom.

'Guys, we want baby boomers, upper income, college-educated jurors who won't judge Rebecca guilty just because she left me for Trey.'

'Scotty,' Bobby said, 'this ain't Highland Park. Our jurors are going to be high school educated, working class folks who look at Rebecca as a cheating bitch who left her husband and daughter for a rich golf pro.'

'Bobby, that's not admissible.'

'It's already been admitted – in the press. By Renée. Main thing is, everyone in Texas knows the Mexican cartels, so if they're old enough to have seen *The Godfather*, we'll be okay.'

'That's a movie.'

'Same as the History Channel for most people.'

The judge entered the courtroom and sat behind the bench. Scott's eyes met hers; she raised her eyebrows, as if to say, My offer is still on the table . . . or I will be.

'Bailiff,' she said, 'please escort the prospective jurors in.'

They turned their chairs around to face the spectator section where the potential jurors would sit. Scott sat between the two tables, next to the DA, who leaned in and said, 'What's your strategy when picking a jury?'

'Prayer.'

The DA chuckled. 'Mine is to make sure all the jurors are over thirty.'

'Why?'

'Because young people today, they got no sense of morality.'

Eight hours later, they had seated a jury of seven men and four women; nine whites, two Latinos, and one black; two had been educated past high school; all were above the age of thirty; one had been reading *Wicca & Witchcraft for Dummies*. Rebecca seemed shell-shocked, like the girls the day they had learned the mechanics of sex in health class. The only greater shock in an American citizen's life is learning how the criminal justice system really works.

'My God, Scott. My life is in their hands?'

'Scary, isn't it? That's why innocent defendants take plea bargains.'

She clutched his arm. 'Scott, please don't let them send me to prison.'

Rebecca Fenney might have less than a week of freedom left. She knew it.

'I'm innocent.'

'Rebecca, I know you're innocent. But I don't know how I'm going to prove it to that jury.'

She gestured at the DA. 'I thought he had to prove that I'm guilty?'

'That's the great American myth.'

She slumped in her chair. 'I'm going to die in prison.'

'No, you're not.'

The DA gestured to Scott. He stood and walked over.

'You figure out why her prints were on the knife?' the DA said.

'No.'

The DA squinted at nothing for a moment then sighed. 'See you Monday.'

'What would you be doing if you didn't have this job?' Carlos said.

They were again sitting on their surfboards, even farther offshore this time, their legs dangling in the murky warm water that was the Gulf of Mexico, gently swaying with each swell. It was nice.

'Time. I'd be doing time. Career path for an uneducated black man in the projects is prison.'

'You think Miss Fenney's going to prison?'

'Hard to say. But I'm going to college.'

'Is that why you read all those books?'

'I read books so I'm not ignorant all my life.'

'You're smart.'

'I'm street smart, but not book smart.'

321

'You know how to survive in the projects, you could write a book about that. Shit, Louis, they put you on one of those *Survivor-Jungle* shows, you'd kick their asses from here to Sunday. Projects make the jungle look like Disney World.'

'I'd like to go there one day.'

'The jungle?'

'Disney World. After college, maybe.'

'I thought about going to college once, I was watching a football game – all those hot college girls bouncing for the cameras. Hey, Louis, we could go to college together, live in one of those coed dorms. We could be roommates.'

'One summer is enough.'

Carlos turned his head real quick like. 'Is that a shark?'

Louis jumped and Carlos laughed.

'Just kidding, big man. I read in the paper that you got a lot better chance of drowning than getting eaten by a shark.'

'That supposed to make me feel better?'

'You think there are sharks out there?' Bobby said.

He shook his head then turned back to Scott and Karen. They were working trial strategy on the back deck that afternoon.

'Scotty, the DA's got no motive, no witnesses, no nothing – except her prints on the murder weapon. We explain that, they lose.'

'He said if we can explain why her prints are on the knife before Monday, he'll drop the charges.'

'You ask her?'

Scott nodded. 'She doesn't remember holding the knife that way.'

'You don't stab a steak.'

'The alcohol and cocaine, she can't remember much about that night.'

'Not good. Well, here's how I figure this is gonna play out. Rex will put on a very perfunctory case. The 911 operator, the cops first on the scene, the detectives, criminologists, ME, the lab tech to testify to her prints, and his expert. That's it. State rests.'

Then he'll wait to cross-examine Rebecca – see if we put her on the stand.'

'Then we call everyone who had a motive to kill Trey Rawlins and see if anyone breaks on the stand. Not the best trial strategy.'

'Only strategy we've got. And it worked before.'

'So it did.'

'Subpoenas were served,' Karen said. 'I got all fourteen returns of service.'

She tapped on her laptop then turned it so Bobby and Scott could see the screen, too. She had drawn a flow chart of the suspects and their motives and alibis.

'Looks like the organizational chart of a Fortune 500 company,' Scott said.

'More than a few folks wanted Trey Rawlins dead,' Bobby said.

'Let's go back through everyone with a motive,' Scott said. 'Make sure we didn't miss anything.'

'First couple, Tess and Brett McBride,' Karen said. 'Neither of their prints matches the unidentified sets at the crime scene, and they were confirmed at the Florida tournament at the time Trey was killed. Brett played Thursday afternoon and Friday morning, made the cut, and played on the weekend. He didn't leave Florida until Sunday night.'

'And they're still married, so he likely didn't know about Tess and Trey. Next.'

'Lacy Parker, our favorite porn star, and Donnie Parker, a moron.'

'Maybe he loves her for her mind,' Bobby said.

'Only if her mind's located between her legs.' Karen returned to her laptop. 'Their prints don't match, and Donnie was confirmed in San Diego that Thursday, saw a doctor for his rotator cuff.'

'Also still married. Next.'

'Riley and Vic Hager. Prints don't match. Missed the cut in Florida, flew home to Wisconsin Friday. Confirmed. Oh, and Riley hates Wisconsin.'

'Still married. Next.'

'Brad Dickey, Golf-a-zon-dot-com. Trey's sponsor. Great motive – if Trey died, they could terminate his endorsement contract and save ten million dollars. And they did just that. But he was at the Florida tournament all week, confirmed.'

'They could've hired a contract killer,' Bobby said.

'A corporate marketing guy hires an assassin to off their marquee athlete?' Scott said. 'Where would he find one? In the yellow pages? Brad's just a guy trying to sell some golf balls. Next.'

'Royce Ballard, tour VP. They didn't want Trey to hurt the tour's image, true, but killing him?'

'Royce is just a lawyer. Next.'

'The construction workers.'

'No way a bunch of stoned roofers get in and out clean,' Bobby said. 'No prints, no DNA, nothing taken.'

Scott nodded. 'They just wanted his cocaine. Next.'

'Now the interesting suspects. First, Clyde "Goose" Dalton, the caddie. A live one, no doubt about it. Trey fired and humiliated him then refused to pay him the hundred thousand he was owed. Good motive. And he had the opportunity. He flew from Florida to Austin that Thursday afternoon, arrived at five. Four hours to drive here, he could've been here at the time of death.'

'But his prints don't match those at the house, and Goose doesn't strike me as the type to sneak into Trey's house at night and stab him while he slept. He would've woken him up first, so Trey'd know it was him. Next.'

'Okay, the big three: the cartel, the mob, and the father. First up, Benito Estrada. Trey owed him five hundred thousand. He knew the layout of Trey's house because he had been there before. And he had access to professional killers, the Zetas. French doors open, no problem for ex-commandos to enter the house, go to the kitchen, grab the knife, and stab Trey. And they wouldn't have left prints.'

'But they wouldn't have left her alive either,' Bobby said. 'They don't bother framing people for their murders.'

'No, they don't,' Scott said. 'I don't think Benito killed Trey or ordered it, but the cartel might have. They're definitely prime suspects.'

'But other than grilling Benito, what can we do?'

Scott shook his head. 'Nothing.'

'Next up, the mob. Big-time motive, millions in gambling debts then he wins that tournament he was supposed to lose, cost them twenty million. Doesn't seem like they'd let that slide. And they're professionals, too.'

'They wanted to kill him, no question about it. The question is, did someone beat them to it, like Gabe said?'

'Someone like Pete Puckett?'

'Exactly like Pete Puckett.'

'Motive, means, and opportunity. Confirmed presence at the crime scene that day. Billie Jean, sex . . . all the ingredients for murder are there.'

'And he's a hunter, means he's killed living things and he knows how to handle a knife. You can't be faint of heart to field dress a full-grown deer. It's bloody. Karen, read your notes, what those construction workers saw that day.'

She tapped on her laptop then read: 'The blonde girl arrived about one in a black Mustang, went inside the house. About five, a yellow cab arrived, and the big man got out, went inside. That's probably when Pete put his prints on the kitchen counter, but that's not when Trey was murdered. The construction workers saw the big man and the blonde girl leave ten or fifteen minutes later. So Pete and Billie Jean left the house seven or eight hours before time of death. They would've been back in Austin when Trey was murdered.'

'If they drove back to Austin.'

Scott pulled out his cell phone and called the DA's office; he asked for Hank Kowalski.

'Hank, Scott Fenney. Where would a guy like Trey put a girl up on the Island?'

'Galvez.'

'Would you do me a favor?'

325

'Another one?'

'Call the Galvez, see if Pete Puckett stayed there the night of June fourth. They'll tell you.'

'I'll call you right back.'

He did.

'One room, one night. A suite.'

'Thanks.' Scott ended the call. To Bobby and Karen: 'Pete could've driven home to Austin that evening. Instead, they stayed overnight. Why? Maybe to finish something he'd started. Maybe he came back that night and killed Trey.'

'But would a father really kill a man just for having sex with his seventeen-year-old daughter?' Bobby said. 'Rape, maybe, but consensual sex? She's not a kid, and at seventeen, she's legal.'

'True, but Pete's pretty protective of her, and he's got a violent temper.'

'Fit of rage, I could see that, if he had killed Trey that afternoon when he caught them together. But coming back eight hours later, after he's calmed down?' Bobby shook his head. 'I like the cartel or the mob. They're professional killers. Pete's a professional golfer.'

'I agree,' Karen said.

'That's it, then,' Scott said.

'Okay,' Bobby said, 'let me see if I've got our trial strategy straight. We're going to call the golfer who just won the US Open and try to get him to confess to murdering Trey Rawlins because he was screwing his seventeen-year-old daughter. If that doesn't work, we're going to call the Island's biggest drug dealer and accuse him and his Mexican cartel employer of killing Trey. And if that doesn't work, we're going to call the local bookie and go after the mob. Is that about it?'

'That's about it.'

'Sounds good to me.'

'Except for one thing,' Karen said.

'What's that?'

'Rebecca's got to testify, tell the jury she didn't kill him . . . and explain why her prints were on the murder weapon.'

Scott's cell phone rang. He answered.

'Scott, it's Rex. Can you come over? Now.'

On the computer screen, the black-and-white video showed the front entrance to a building Scott recognized. The same two Latino thugs bookended the front doors under an awning. A dark Corvette pulled up at the curb and a dark-haired woman got out and walked to the entrance. The thugs did not block her way; instead, one thug held the door open for her. She gave him a little wave as she disappeared inside.

'Like I said, Feds got Benito's place under surveillance twenty-four/seven. Black and white tape, they didn't put the woman and the car together.'

'She said she didn't know Benito.'

'She knows him now.'

'You figure she bought cocaine from him?'

'He doesn't sell women's shoes.'

'She's broke. How'd she pay for it?'

The DA averted his eyes then fast-forwarded the video until Rebecca reappeared in the doorway. She got into the car and drove off. Scott gathered himself and stood, but the DA said, 'I've got more evidence to share.'

Scott saw on the DA's face that this wasn't going to be pleasant.

'My tech man, he's been poking around Trey's laptop, hacking through firewalls and whatever you call that security stuff, and he found some videos. Trey and women. Homemade porn.'

Dr Tim had said Trey had made sex tapes. The DA could not make eye contact with Scott.

'Rebecca?'

Still no eye contact.

'I'm sorry, Scott.'

Scott stood and walked to the door and grabbed the handle.

'Scott, it's evidence. I'm obliged to give you copies.'

'I don't want them.'

Scott Fenney was thinking like a man as he shut the door behind him.

Chapter 40

At first light, Scott dressed in running shorts and shoes and went downstairs. Boo was already watching a cable show called *I, Carly*.

'It's appropriate,' she said.

'I'll be back in an hour,' he said. 'We'll have breakfast.'

She turned her eyes up to the clock on the wall. 'Okay. See you back at exactly seven-thirty-seven.'

Scott went outside and down the deck stairs and then hit the sand. He headed west. He was alone on the beach and with his thoughts. Eleven years they had lived together, slept together, and had sex together, but he had never really known her. He knew now that he would never really know her. Expensive clothes and jewelry – he knew that Rebecca Fenney. But not the Rebecca Fenney who snorted cocaine and starred in sex tapes. Who was that woman?

He hadn't known his own wife.

And he didn't know his ex-wife.

That day the girls said she had left wearing her black wig and returned really happy, it hadn't been chocolate, shopping, or sex – it had been cocaine. She had gone to Benito's and bought cocaine. She had come home happy because she was high. Scott

328

had confronted her last night. She swore she had used cocaine because of the stress of the pending trail and that she had paid Benito with her jewelry. She swore she had not found the mob money. Just as she had sworn she did not know Benito Estrada and did not kill Trey Rawlins.

Scott did not mention the sex tapes. But Renée Ramirez had on the evening news.

'*Sex, drugs, and videotapes. Tonight, a "Murder on the Beach" update. I've learned that the trial will reveal many salacious details about the lives of Trey Rawlins and his lover, Rebecca Fenney, on trial for his murder, including sex tapes. I've also learned that her ex-husband*' – she gave her audience a sly grin – '*I mean, her lawyer, has subpoenaed several professional golfers to testify at trial, including Pete Puckett, the reigning US Open champion. You won't want to miss this. I will host the trial beginning Monday morning, from opening statements until the verdict is read.*'

Scott soon arrived at the white house rising from the beach. He stopped and stared up at the second-story deck that led into the master bedroom where Trey Rawlins had died. If she were capable of cocaine and sex tapes, was she capable of murder? Had she lied to him about that, too? Was Rebecca Fenney the Guilty Groupie?

Louis went downstairs to the kitchen. Consuela was just stirring with the baby, and Carlos was rustling up his regular breakfast of chocolate milk and Cheerios. Pajamae was watching cartoons. Everyone else was sleeping in. Boo was standing outside on the deck in her swimsuit. Louis slid the glass door open and stepped outside. The sea breeze brought the smell of the ocean to him. He liked breathing the sea air, living on the beach. Maybe one day he would. After college. He walked to the far railing where Boo stood. She was staring out at the sea and gripping the railing real tight with both hands like she was afraid she might fall over-board. She did not turn away from the sea, so he talked to the top of her head.

'What're you looking for, Boo?'

'A. Scott.'

'Mr Fenney out running?'

'What time is it, Louis?'

Louis looked at his watch. 'Quarter past eight. Something wrong?'

'He didn't come back. He said he'd be back in an hour.'

'What time did he leave?'

'Six-thirty-seven.'

'Maybe he's running slow 'cause it's Saturday.'

'Not A. Scott.'

'You want I should go look for him?'

'Yes, please.'

She now turned to him. Tears were rolling down her little face.

'Louis, I think he had a heart attack.'

'Which way did he run down the beach?'

'I don't know.'

Louis walked back toward the house and shouted, 'Carlos!'

Carlos came outside with a red plastic bowl of Cheerios floating in brown milk.

'Yeah, bro?'

'You got your phone?'

'Yep.'

Louis pointed east. 'You go looking down the beach that way.' Louis then pointed west. 'I'm going looking this way.'

'What are we looking for?'

'Mr Fenney.'

Carlos's face got sharp. He tossed the bowl over the railing and ran down the stairs. Louis was right behind him. Carlos cut left and Louis right. Boo had not budged from her place at the railing.

Louis Wright weighed three hundred thirty pounds, but he often surprised people by how fast he could run and for how long. When he was sixteen and weighed only two hundred, he had run track in high school. Two-twenties and four-forties. He could move it for a big boy.

Still, he had to slow down after a mile.

330

Another mile, he saw a big white house gleaming in the sun and down on the beach, the tide lapping over a clump of something. Looked like a big brown dog curled up on the sand like road kill . . . or maybe some kind of brown sack full of something . . . or maybe . . .

Mr Fenney. Oh, sweet Jesus. Mr Fenney did have a heart attack.

Louis ran full-out until he got to him. He pulled out his phone and hit the speed dial for Carlos. When he answered, Louis said, 'I found him. Come my way. And Carlos . . . run.'

Louis pushed the phone back into his pocket then dropped to his knees. Mr Fenney's skin felt wet and cold to the touch. A sand crab crawled across his back. Louis flicked the crab away, then rolled him over to see if he was still breathing but he saw . . . blood. *Shit. He didn't have no heart attack. He got beat up. Bad.* Louis leaned over and put his ear to Mr Fenney's bare chest. His heart was beating. Slowly. He was still alive.

Most people thought Louis was older because black men look older when they're young and younger when they're old. In fact, Louis Wright was only thirty years old. But he had already seen a lifetime of violent crime down in the projects of South Dallas. People shot pointblank with handguns and short-barreled shot-guns, stabbed with screwdrivers, ice picks, and knives of all sizes, makes, and models, beaten to death with baseball bats, tire irons, crowbars, bricks, and even a carburetor from a 357-cubic-inch Chevy engine. Mr Fenney's face was cut and bruised and bloody, but Louis could find no mortal wound. Someone had beaten him mercilessly, but with fists.

A tear dropped from Louis Wright's eye onto Mr Fenney's tanned skin.

He slipped his arms under Mr Fenney's body like a forklift and stood with this man in his arms. This man who had opened his arms and his Highland Park home to him, just as if Louis Wright's skin wasn't black and he wasn't from South Dallas. This man who had given him books and a second chance at life. This man who Louis loved like the father he never had. Carlos came running up.

331

'*Shit*. What happened?'

'Someone beat him bad.'

'Is he alive?'

'He is.'

'Here, Louis, I'll help you.'

'No. Run ahead and get the car ready.'

Carlos ran ahead to the house. Louis carried Mr Fenney, his arms and legs hanging limp and bouncing with each step Louis took. When the house came into sight, Boo was still standing at the railing. She spotted them, screamed a shrill 'A. Scott!' and came running.

'Did he have a heart attack? Is he dead?'

'He ain't dead and he didn't have a heart attack. Someone tried to kill him.'

Boo touched his bloody face and cried into his bloody hands. Mr Herrin and Miss Fenney and Pajamae now ran up to them.

'Jesus,' Mr Herrin said.

'Found him 'bout two miles down the beach, by the big white house.'

'Who did this to him?' Miss Fenney said.

'Folks that done this gonna pay,' Louis said.

'No, Louis,' Mr Herrin said. 'He wouldn't want that. Let's get him to the hospital.'

Scott's face hurt. He opened his eyes to blurry visions of Boo and Pajamae.

Boo touched his face gently and said, 'Oh, A. Scott – I thought you'd died on us.'

Pajamae stroked his hair and said, 'Whereas, Daddy.'

Scott wrapped his arms around his daughters and pulled them close. They put their heads on his chest. He blinked to clear his vision. He was in a hospital room. Which was good because he hurt like he had never hurt before, not even on a football field. And he remembered. They had beaten him on the beach.

'How'd I get here?'

Surrounding his bed were Bobby, Karen, Carlos, and Louis. The DA. Hank Kowalski. A uniformed cop at the door. Rebecca.

'Louis found you,' Bobby said.

Scott looked to Louis. 'Thank you, Louis.'

'Hell, Scott,' the DA said, 'if you wanted a continuance, all you had to do was ask. No need to go to all this trouble.'

Scott tried to smile but it hurt. 'I'll be there Monday morning.'

The DA stepped to the bed; he wasn't smiling now. 'Who did this, Scott?'

Scott shook his head. 'I was running the beach, stopped at Trey's house. I was standing there thinking, all of a sudden I got cold-cocked. Two, maybe three guys, hit me until I went down. Then I passed out.'

The DA nodded. 'Well, if this is the work of Benito or Gabe or their people, we're gonna find them and prosecute them, I promise you.'

Scott and the DA's eyes met, and they both knew it was an empty promise. Some people would never be brought to justice, not by the law.

'Doctor said they were pros,' the DA said. 'Didn't damage any internal organs. They weren't trying to kill you, just send a message.'

'They could've called.'

The DA smiled again. 'Least you still got a sense of humor. Easier to survive in this world with a sense of humor.'

'I prefer a nine-millimeter Glock,' Hank said.

The DA turned to leave but stopped and pointed a finger at Scott. 'Until this trial is over, you don't need to be alone.'

'He ain't gonna be,' Louis said.

From that moment until they left the Island seven days later, Louis Wright never let A. Scott Fenney out of his sight.

Chapter 41

Another media circus. Another mob outside a courthouse. Once again A. Scott Fenney found himself pushing his way through a crowd of cameras and reporters shoving microphones and shouting questions at his client –

'Rebecca, did you kill Trey Rawlins?'

'Why are your fingerprints on the murder weapon?'

'Did you love him?'

– only this time his client wasn't a heroin-addicted prostitute.

It was Monday morning, and satellite dishes rose high above the TV trucks that lined the street in front of the courthouse, gawkers crowded the sidewalk, and the general consensus among the locals was that the murder trial would provide a welcome boost to the Island economy. It wasn't booze, gambling, and prostitution like back in the Sin City days, but it'd do in a pinch.

When Scott had defended Pajamae's mother on a murder charge two years before, he had thought she was guilty – her fingerprints were on the murder weapon – only to learn during trial that she was in fact innocent. Now, defending Boo's mother on a murder charge, he thought she was innocent – even though her fingerprints were on the murder weapon. What if he learned during trial that she was in fact guilty?

334

He pulled Rebecca through the crowd and into the court-house. She looked beautiful but frightened. He had spent Sunday recuperating; she had spent the day pacing the beach like a strung-out addict. She swore she was not – addicted to cocaine or guilty of murder. She was terrified of being sent to prison. She was now holding his hand so tightly it felt numb.

At one end of the corridor outside the courtroom, the cable network had set up a broadcast booth like the ones towering above the greens at a golf tournament. Renée Ramirez was stationed in the booth; she wore headphones and faced an array of monitors. She noticed Scott and gestured at his face and mouthed, 'Ouch.'

Annoying as hell.

The other end of the corridor looked like a scene out of central casting: Pete and Billie Jean Puckett and Goose sat on a bench at the far end by themselves, an aging golf pro and the only two people he had left in the world . . . Tess McBride, Lacy Parker, and Riley Hager huddled along one wall chatting in hushed voices like sexy sorority sisters . . . Brett McBride, Donnie Parker, and Vic Hager had brought their putters and a few balls and were exchanging putting tips . . . Brad Dickey, Royce Ballard, and Nick Madden conducted business on cell phones and laptops . . . Benito Estrada and one of his thugs leaned against one wall . . . and Gabe Petrocelli and one of his goons leaned against the other. Gabe gave Scott a sympathetic shrug.

'Sorry, Scott. Orders from Vegas. They don't want me testifying. You okay?'

'I'm good.'

That was a lie. He felt awful. The swelling in his face had come down, but the rest of his body still hurt with every move-ment. Gabe's goons were more skilled at maiming a human body than linebackers. Louis took a step in their direction.

'No, Louis.'

The defense had subpoenaed them; the law required they wait outside the courtroom until called in to testify. Which did not please them. The others glared at Scott as he walked their gauntlet to the courtroom doors – except Tess McBride. She smiled and bounced over to him, looked at his face and said, 'What happened to you?'

'Accident.'

'When do I get to testify?'

'*Get* to testify? I thought you didn't want to?'

'That was before I found out it's on TV – all these cameras, everyone watching. It's like an audition.'

'An audition? Testifying at a murder trial?'

Rebecca stepped close and said, 'How could you, Tess? Cheat with Trey? We were friends – and you're married.'

'You cheated with Trey when you were married.'

'But he was with *me*.'

Tess gave her a lame shrug and went back to the other WAGs by the wall. Scott entered the courtroom followed by the defense team and the defendant. The girls had begged to come, but he had refused. There were some things they just didn't need to know at age eleven. He didn't allow them to see PG-13 movies; why would he allow them to see an X-rated trial? When the crime scene photos of Rebecca covered in blood would be shown on the big screen above the witness stand? When there would be testimony about alcohol and cocaine and sex on the beach? When Boo's mother might have a starring role in a sex video?

He had taken Pajamae to her mother's murder trial – he had to do everything he could for Shawanda – but he couldn't do that for Rebecca. Or to Boo. And that trial had not been televised; this one would be. The girls didn't need to be seen on national TV. So they were at the beach house with Consuela and Maria and uniformed police officers out front and back – and under strict instructions not to watch the trial on cable.

Judge Morgan wanted a meeting of counsel in chambers before she swore in the jury. She looked at Scott's face and recoiled.

'Shit. Are you okay, Scott?'

'Yeah. Thanks for asking.'

'Because I don't want to delay the trial – we'll lose our

336

broadcast slot. Renée said the cable channel's booked up the next two months. Next week they've got a serial murder trial up in Chicago.' She turned to the DA. 'Rex, what's this about sex tapes?'

'Not evidence, Shelby.'

'Renée said she asked you for copies and you refused. Why?'

'Because it's none of her goddamned business, that's why.'

'You know what those tapes would do for our ratings?'

'Shelby, I'm about to go out there and ask a jury to send a human being to prison for life, so frankly, I don't give a good goddamn about cable TV ratings.'

'She's filing a Freedom of Information request with the AG's office in Austin.'

'She can file it where the sun don't shine, all I care.' He stood. 'I'm gonna try a goddamned murder case.'

'Jesus, Rex, every murder trial, you get really grouchy.' She stood. 'Does my hair look okay?'

Judge Morgan didn't sit at the bench; she posed.

When the jurors entered the courtroom and sat in the jury box, their eyes immediately turned to Rebecca Fenney. They would sit in judgment of her life – not just her actions that night, but her entire life. That wasn't the way it was supposed to work, but that's the way it was. They were fascinated with her. And they would be shocked by her life.

The Assistant DA read the indictment into the record, and Rebecca Fenney pleaded not guilty in open court. Galveston County Criminal District Attorney Rex Truitt slowly stood from his chair. He wore a seersucker suit, a white shirt, a blue tie, and black reading glasses. He looked like Hemingway himself stepping forward to read from one of his books, and if Ernest didn't have the DA's voice, he should have.

He stepped over to the evidence table, picked up the murder weapon encased in plastic, walked to the jury box, and said, 'The evidence will show that when the police arrived at the crime scene at three-fifty-seven A.M. on the morning of Friday, June the fifth, they found Trey Rawlins dead, lying on his back in his bed, with this eight-inch butcher knife stuck in his chest, right here.'

He put the blade against his chest.

'The evidence will also show that the defendant's fingerprints – and only the defendant's fingerprints – were found on this knife. And that the defendant had not held the knife like this, as if to cut a steak, but like this, as if to stab.'

The DA held the knife with the blade pointing down.

'The evidence will further show that police found the defendant in the bedroom covered in Trey Rawlins' blood . . . that the defendant's bloody footprints and handprints and fingerprints were found on the bedroom floor, wall, and phone . . . that no third-party's bloody footprints or handprints or fingerprints were found in that bedroom or anywhere in that house . . . that the only plausible explanation is that the defendant, Rebecca Fenney, took this knife from a drawer in their kitchen, went into their bedroom where Trey Rawlins lay sleeping on their bed, and stabbed this knife into his chest, killing him. Murder is the taking of a human life without justification. There was no justification for what the defendant did to Trey Rawlins.'

The DA stared at the knife a long moment then placed it on the evidence table.

'Now, defense counsel will argue that the defendant had no motive to kill the victim, that she lost everything when he died. Which is true. So why did she kill Trey Rawlins? I don't know. I've been in this job for twenty-eight years now, trying criminal cases and trying to understand criminals: why do they do what they do? Unfortunately, I am no closer to understanding my fellow human beings today than I was when I started this job. If you want to know why she killed her lover, she will have to tell you. I cannot. All I can do is prove that she did in fact kill him. And I will.'

The district attorney returned to the prosecution table. Rex Truitt had done this before. He hadn't promised too much or too little, and he had left a lot to be revealed later. Things that would shock the jury, like cocaine and sex. And he set the jury up to expect Rebecca to testify.

'Mr Fenney,' the judge said, looking not at him but at the cameras.

Scott did not move because her words did not register in his mind. His thoughts were of 'innocent until proven guilty'. The state bears the burden to prove the defendant guilty. The defendant does not have to prove herself innocent. That's the law. But every defendant bears that burden. That's the reality of a murder trial.

Americans don't believe that innocent people go to prison in America. That's something that happens in other countries, like Russia and China and Mexico. Maybe it's ignorance, maybe it's denial, or maybe it's fear – that it's better to imprison a few innocent people than risk guilty people going free and committing more crimes. But innocent people do go to prison in America. Unless they can prove their innocence.

'Mr Fenney.'

Scott stood and walked over to the jury box. The television cameras sat on either side of the courtroom. Behind the cameras in the spectator section were reporters, print journalists from the major Texas newspapers and the wire services scribbling on tablets, and locals there for a macabre form of entertainment. Terri Rawlins sat in the front row behind the prosecution table; Melvyn Burke sat next to her. When their eyes met, Melvyn averted his gaze. Scott turned to the jurors.

'Ladies and gentlemen, my name is Scott Fenney. I represent the defendant, Rebecca Fenney. First, my face . . . I had an accident. Second, Rebecca' – he would refer to her by her first name in order to distance her from 'defendant' status – 'and I share the same last name because, as I'm sure you've read in the papers or heard on TV, she is my ex-wife.

'I have great respect and personal affinity for Mr Truitt, but he failed to mention a few other facts that the evidence will show, including that the murder weapon was part of a matched set of eight knives given to Trey Rawlins at a golf event more than a

339

year before, that those eight knives had been in their kitchen ever since, and that Rebecca had used all of those knives, including the murder weapon, on numerous occasions for a variety of kitchen purposes.

'That Rebecca was covered in Mr Rawlins' blood that night because she had been sleeping next to him in their bed when she woke to find him dead – how could she have killed him then slept in his blood? Who could do that? Who would?

'That Rebecca was at the crime scene when the police arrived because she called nine-one-one herself. Rebecca Fenney did not run from the scene of the crime. She summoned the police to the scene of the crime.

'That Trey Rawlins loved Rebecca, that he provided for her, that he gave her gifts of cash and jewelry and a Corvette, that he asked her to marry him the very night he was killed.

'That Rebecca had no motive to kill Trey Rawlins. She had a great life with Trey – first-class travel, five-star hotels and restaurants, spas and resorts, money, jewelry, clothes. Without Trey, she has nothing – no travel, no hotels and restaurants, no money, no home, no life insurance. Nothing except a red Corvette and jewelry.

'Why would she kill the man who gave her everything?

'She wouldn't. She didn't. Rebecca had no motive to kill Trey Rawlins. But the evidence will show that other people did have motives to kill Mr Rawlins, that other people wanted him dead – and that some of those people had killed before.

'So don't assume the district attorney has this case figured out. He doesn't. I don't. But you must. At the end of this trial, you must decide if the prosecution proved Rebecca Fenney guilty of murder beyond a reasonable doubt. That is your legal duty. But that's not the reality, is it? Because in your mind at this very moment is a single question: if she didn't kill Trey Rawlins, then who did?

'We'll answer that question.'

Chapter 42

The Assistant DA stood and called the first witness for the prosecution as if he were an actor on a stage. Perhaps he was. Perhaps they all were. In America, there was no bigger stage than a courtroom during a televised murder trial of a famous pro athlete, whether the victim was Trey Rawlins or the defendant was O.J. Simpson.

Ronda Jensen, mid-fifties, a career county employee, was the 911 operator who took Rebecca's emergency call that night. She authenticated the call then the Assistant DA played the tape for the jury. Bobby would cross-examine the prosecution's witnesses. He stood and asked only one question of this witness.

'Ms Jensen, who made that call to nine-one-one?'

'Rebecca Fenney.'

The first police officer on the scene that night testified next. Patrol Officer Art Crandall was only thirty and had never come closer to military service than his stint in the boy scouts, but he wore his Galveston Police Department uniform with the same bearing as if he were the Chairman of the Joint Chiefs of Staff testifying before Congress.

'Officer Crandall,' the Assistant DA said, 'did you respond to an emergency call to the West End at three-forty-eight A.M. on the morning of Friday, June fifth?'

'Yes, sir, I did.'

'Please tell the jury what you did when you arrived at the address.'

'I pulled up out front of the Rawlins house—'

'At what time?'

'Three-fifty-seven.'

'Did you see any other cars or people out front?'

'No, but Officer Guerrero arrived right after I did. We then proceeded along the east side of the residence down to the beach.'

'And why didn't you go to the front door?'

'Dispatch said to go around back, which sits right on the beach. We climbed the rear stairs to the back deck. The doors right there were open. I yelled "Police!" and we entered the residence.'

'Officer Crandall, would you please look at your computer screen?'

The Assistant DA nodded to a staffer manning a laptop at the prosecution table. A color photo showing the front of the Rawlins residence appeared on the big screen above the witness.

'Officer Crandall, is this the residence you arrived at that night?'

'Yes, sir, it is.'

'Does this next photo show the east side of the residence?'

'Yes, it does.'

'And these are the stairs to the back deck?'

'Yes, sir.'

'And the French doors?'

'Yes, sir.'

'All right. You entered through those doors. What did you find inside?'

'We made entry into a large, white bedroom. The lights were on. I observed the room and saw a woman holding a phone.'

'And was that woman Rebecca Fenney, the defendant?'

'Yes, sir.'

342

'Did you see anyone else?'

'No, sir, I did not – not anyone alive, anyway. Directly in front of me was the bed on which the victim was lying. He had a knife in his chest. Blood was everywhere.'

'What did you do then?'

'I remained in the bedroom with the woman while Officer Guerrero cleared the house.'

'Did Officer Guerrero find anyone else in the house?'

'No, sir. The house was clear.'

'Was the front door locked?'

'Yes, sir.'

'Then what did you do?'

'I told dispatch to send out the detectives, ME, crime scene.'

'Did you touch anything in the bedroom?'

'No, sir. I waited with the woman for the detectives to arrive.'

'How long was it before the detectives arrived?'

'Maybe thirty minutes.'

'And what was the defendant's appearance?'

'She was wearing a short white nightgown. It was bloody.'

'Did the defendant change her clothes or clean up prior to the detectives' arrival at the scene?'

'No, sir. I was with her the entire time.'

'No further questions, Your Honor.'

Bobby stood and cross-examined the police officer.

'Officer Crandall, when you entered the residence, did you have your weapon drawn?'

'Yes, sir, I did.'

'Why?'

'Dispatch said the perpetrator might still be in the house.'

'But you and Officer Guerrero determined that the perpetrator was not still in the house?'

The Assistant DA stood. 'Objection. Defense is mischaracterizing his testimony. The dispatcher had no knowledge of any perpetrator. The officers determined that no one else was in the house. That does not mean there was in fact a third-party perpetrator.'

Bobby turned his palms up, as if confused. 'The witness said perpetrator.'

But the judge wasn't buying what he was selling.

'Sustained. Rephrase, Mr Herrin.'

'You found no one else in the house?'

'No, sir.'

'But you found the French doors open?'

'Yes, sir.'

'So if someone else had been in the house before you arrived, he could have left through the open French doors?'

'Yes, sir.'

'And the beach there is dark, correct?'

'Yes, sir.'

'So he could have come down the back stairs just seconds before you arrived and hidden just down the beach and you wouldn't have been able to see him, correct?'

'Yes, sir.'

'Officer Crandall, you testified that Ms Fenney was on the phone when you arrived. To whom was she talking?'

'The nine-one-one operator.'

'How did Ms Fenney seem when she first saw you entering the bedroom?'

'Relieved.'

'Thank you, Officer Crandall.'

The judge recessed for lunch. Scott walked outside the courtroom and saw Renée Ramirez interviewing Officer Crandall.

'Gosh,' the cop said, 'I was so nervous. You think I did okay?'

Like a contestant awaiting the judges' scores on *Dancing with the Stars*.

After lunch, Galveston County Medical Examiner Sanjay Sanjeev took the stand. Dr Sanjeev appeared unaffected by the cameras; he wore a rumpled cotton suit, a blue shirt, and a black tie loosened at his neck. He was a board-certified pathologist, and he testified from his notes like an old med school professor teaching a class.

344

He had arrived at the crime scene at just after five A.M. on Friday, June 5th. The deceased was 'found dead'. He pronounced Trey Rawlins dead at five-fifteen. He observed the body on the bed and the knife in the body. His death investigator took photos of the body *in situ*. The body was then removed from the scene under his supervision at approximately eight A.M. without removal of the knife. The body was transported to the medical examiner's office where he conducted a complete autopsy later that morning. It was his medical opinion that Trey Rawlins had died from a sharp force injury to the chest, that is, a stab wound that severed his descending aorta resulting in a sudden and massive blood loss; that he was alive at the time he was stabbed; that time of death was between midnight and three A.M. on Friday, June 5th; that manner of death was homicide. The Assistant DA did not show the autopsy photos to the jury.

Karen handed the autopsy report to Bobby. He stood.

'Dr Sanjeev, you conducted a complete autopsy of Trey Rawlins' body, correct?'

'Yes. I performed an external examination, an internal examination, toxicology, and microscopics.'

'What did you find on your external examination?'

'The deceased was a well-nourished white male, well-developed musculature, seventy-two inches tall, one hundred eighty pounds, age-appropriate, blonde hair, no scars, no tattoos. The body was unclothed.'

'Did you find any evidence that Mr Rawlins had recently engaged in a physical confrontation? A fight?'

'Yes. There was bruising on his upper body indicating that he had been grabbed forcefully, there were scratch marks on his upper arms and shoulders, and his upper lip was swollen and blood vessels inside had been broken.'

'As if someone had recently hit him in the mouth?'

'Yes.'

'Dr Sanjeev, was sand recovered from the body of Trey Rawlins?'

'Yes, it was.'

'From what part of the body?'

'The backside. In his hair, on his back, in his buttocks.'

'Indicating that Mr Rawlins had lain in the sand recently and prior to his death?'

'Yes.'

'What did you do with the sand?'

'Bagged it, gave it to the criminologist. It's in the inventory.'

'Other than the bruises and abrasions on the body – and the knife embedded in the body, of course – were than any other remarkable findings?'

'Yes.'

'And what was that?'

'I found cocaine particles in the nostrils.'

'Indicating recent use?'

'Yes.'

'You then removed the knife from the body?'

'No. I first X-rayed the body in its entirety then clipped each fingernail and toenail.'

'Did you find anything?'

'No. I then examined the body with a forensic light, but that was of no value as the skin surface was saturated with his own blood. I took samples of the external blood and oral and rectal swabs and hair samples, head and pubic. I then took fingerprints and DNA samples.'

'Did you find anyone else's blood on the body?'

'No.'

'Did you then remove the knife?'

'Yes. The knife handle was first bagged then the blade retracted from the body. It was photographed and measured then placed in an evidence bag and delivered to the criminologist who was attending the autopsy. There had been no medical intervention.'

'Which means?'

'The deceased had not been administered medical treatment for the stab wound in an effort to save his life. So the wound was unaltered.'

'Would you please describe the wound?'

'The wound was located approximately nineteen centimeters above the navel and measured four centimeters in width and extended almost through the entirety of the body. It was a fatal wound.'

'Did you then conduct an internal examination?'

'Yes. I removed and examined and took tissue samples from all major organs and glands. I collected and examined the gastric contents and peripheral blood for a tox screen.'

'And did the screen come back with any positives?'

'Yes. For alcohol and cocaine. So I collected liver and kidney tissue for follow-up tests. The deceased's blood alcohol level was point-two-six and there was cocaine in his system, six hundred nanograms per milliliter.'

'Indicating that Mr Rawlins had drunk a significant amount of alcohol and ingested cocaine immediately prior to his death?'

'Yes.'

'Thank you, Dr Sanjeev.'

During a short recess, the DA stepped over to Scott and said, 'Sanjay, he's a bit dry. Someone dies in a house fire, he calls it a "thermal event".'

Outside, Renée was interviewing Dr Sanjeev.

After the recess, the county criminologist, Herman Deeks, thirty-five, took the stand. He looked nothing like the cool crime scene guys on *CSI Miami*. He looked more like the guy working behind the counter at the neighborhood video store. He had arrived directly from a murder scene in shirt sleeves. The judge gave him a hard look then said, 'Mr Deeks, is that blood on your shirt?'

'What?' Deeks checked his shirt. 'Oh, yeah. Nasty crime scene on the mainland, shotgun to the head. Blood splatter was pretty spectacular and—'

'Thank you.'

Deeks testified on direct about his collection of evidence from the crime scene and from the body at the autopsy. He collected fingerprints from the murder weapon; fingerprints, handprints,

347

and footprints in the bedroom, the outside deck, and elsewhere in the residence; blood samples from the victim and the defendant and from the scene; clothing worn by the defendant; bedding; sand from the bed and floor; sand and DNA from the defendant's underwear; hair from the victim, the defendant, and unidentified blonde hair from the victim's closet.

Bobby stood and asked, 'Mr Deeks, you were just at a murder scene?'

'Yes.'

'Did you wear latex gloves while processing the scene?'

'Yes.'

'Why?'

'So I didn't get blood on my hands.'

'And so you didn't leave your fingerprints on the evidence?'

'Yes.'

'And so you didn't disturb fingerprints already on the evidence?'

'Yes.'

'Did you wear latex gloves at the Rawlins crime scene?'

'Yes.'

'Mr Deeks, what did you do with the prints you collected?'

'Sent them to the DPS lab.'

'Were any prints found that did not belong to either the victim or the defendant?'

'Yes. I found prints that belonged to Rosie Gonzales and three sets of unidentified prints – one set on the island counter in the kitchen, another on the headboard of the bed in the master suite, and another on the mirror in the master closet.'

'Have you subsequently identified those prints?'

'I have not. I turned the file over to Hank Kowalski, the district attorney's investigator. I understand that he followed up on those prints.'

'Mr Deeks, you examined and photographed Ms Fenney that night, correct?'

'Yes.'

'Did you find any evidence that Ms Fenney had engaged in a recent physical struggle?'

348

'No.'

'Did you find any skin tissue under her fingernails?'

'No.'

'Did you find any bruises or abrasions on her knuckles indicating that she had recently hit someone?'

'No.'

'What was the form of the DNA collected from Ms Fenney's underwear?'

'Semen.'

'And to whom did that belong?'

'The victim. Trey Rawlins.'

'Indicating recent sexual intercourse?'

'Yes.'

'And was sand recovered from Ms Fenney's underwear?'

'Yes.'

'Which would indicate that the sexual intercourse occurred on the beach?'

'Yes.'

The Department of Public Safety lab in Austin sent technician Stephen Haynes to testify about the fingerprints on the murder weapon. He seemed more concerned about his *per diem* travel allowance than his testimony. Under the Assistant DA's questioning, he testified that Rebecca's right hand fingerprints were found on the handle of the knife and aligned with her thumb toward the end of the handle and not toward the blade, indicating that she had held the knife with the blade down as if to stab rather than with the blade up as if to cut. Bobby then questioned the witness.

'Mr Haynes, when were those fingerprints put on the knife?'

'When?'

'Yes, when. Were they put there on June fifth or May fifth or April fifth?'

'I can't say.'

'Why not?'

'I have no way of knowing that.'

'Why not?'

'Because those prints could have been put on that knife the day before or the year before.'

'You're saying that Ms Fenney could have handled that knife a year before the murder and never touched that knife again, and her prints might still be on that knife?'

'Yes. That's what I'm saying.'

'Mr Haynes, if I put on a latex glove and removed the murder weapon from the plastic bag and then grabbed the handle right now in this courtroom, would I leave my fingerprints on that knife?'

'No. The glove would prevent that.'

'Would I obliterate Ms Fenney's prints that are on the knife?'

'Not necessarily.'

'Okay. So, Mr Haynes, your testimony is in no way stating or implying to this jury that because only the defendant's fingerprints are on that knife that she is therefore the only person who could have stabbed the victim with that knife?'

'No, sir, I am not saying that.'

'Mr Haynes, would scrubbing a stainless steel countertop with Clorox and soap and Pine Sol remove fingerprints?'

'Most definitely.'

'Your Honor,' Karen said. 'Defense requests a recess.'

The judge looked from Bobby to Karen, who had a funny expression on her face.

'Ms Douglas, your co-counsel is conducting cross-examination. For what reason do you request a recess?'

'My water broke.'

An eight-pound-two-ounce boy was born to Robert Herrin and Karen Douglas-Herrin at 7:37 P.M. at the University of Texas Medical Branch hospital on Galveston Island, one of 2,500 babies born there in the first seven months of the year. UTMB was the charity hospital serving Galveston County.

'Scott Carlos Louis Herrin,' Bobby said.

He stuck a big cigar in Scott's open mouth.

'Wow, Bobby, I'm honored.'

'We're gonna call him Bud.'

'Oh.'

'Just kidding. You guys are like our brothers. What better names?'

'You're a father now.' Scott hugged his best friend. 'Start saving money.'

Aligned along the glass window like visitors at the zoo reptile exhibit were Scott and Bobby, Louis and Carlos, and Boo and Pajamae. The girls had their faces and hands plastered to the glass, *oohing* and *aahing* at the newborns.

'I don't like looking at them through the glass,' Boo said. 'I want to touch them.'

Rebecca stood along the opposite wall. Scott glanced at her, and she motioned him over. He went to her; she lowered her voice.

'Scott, if they send me to prison, don't bring Boo to visit. I don't want her to see me though a glass window like that. I don't want her to remember me that way.'

Chapter 43

The second day of trial started with Detective Chuck Wilson giving his best Clint Eastwood imitation for the cameras. Scott could picture him pointing a gun at a kid trespassing on his grass and growling through clenched teeth, 'Get off my lawn.' He was fifty years old, he had a flat-top haircut, he wore a suit for his court appearance, and he had already retained a literary agent, a fact Scott had learned from Sarge. Wilson was an experienced homicide detective. He had worked the grimy Galveston murders for twenty-two years; now he had finally caught a glitzy tabloid murder. He was determined to make the most of the opportunity. He would present the prosecution's theory of the crime. District Attorney Rex Truitt questioned his star witness.

'Detective Wilson, what time did you arrive at the crime scene?'

'Approximately four-thirty A.M. on Friday, June fifth.'

'And how did you enter the house?'

'Through the front door.'

'Who was present when you arrived?'

'Two patrol officers, the criminologist, and the defendant.'

'And where were they?'

'In the bedroom. The crime scene.'

'And what did you see when you entered the bedroom?'

'I observed the victim lying on the bed with a knife in his chest . . . the bed soaked in blood . . . bloody footprints on the floor leading to the French doors . . . blood stains on the white curtains and on the wall around the light switch . . . blood on the phone . . . and blood on the defendant's white nightgown and body.'

It was time for the crime scene photos.

'Detective Wilson, would you please look at your computer screen, and I direct the jury to the screen above the witness.'

Scott observed the jury when the first photo was displayed on the giant screen on the wall. He expected a noticeable reaction from the jurors – gasps, recoiling in horror, averted eyes, something – but he got nothing. They acted as if a color blow-up of a bloody crime scene was nothing out of the ordinary. And then he realized it wasn't. They viewed similarly graphic scenes every night on television. It was just like watching a cop show.

'Detective, does this photo accurately represent the bedroom as you observed it?'

'Yes, it does. This is a view of the bedroom from the door on the north side. The French doors you see are to the south. Through those doors is the outside deck. On the east side of the room is the bed. The victim is lying on the bed.'

'That is the way you found the victim, with the knife still in him?'

'Yes, it is.'

'And would you identify this photo?'

The next photo was shown on the screen, a close-up of the deceased. Still no reaction from the jurors. Did they even understand that this was real? That a human being had died?

'This is a shot of the bed and the victim. He was naked and bled out profusely. The bed is covered in his blood except where the defendant had been lying, as the blood flowed over and around her body.'

'And this photo.'

353

The big screen now showed a photo of Rebecca from that night. She was covered in blood.

'That is the defendant as she was found that night wearing a short white nightgown and an undergarment. Blood is on her nightgown and her hands and arms and legs and face. Her hair was matted with blood.'

'Is this the woman you saw that night?'

'Yes, it is.'

'And is that woman in this courtroom?'

'Yes, she is. She's the defendant.'

'Rebecca Fenney?'

'Yes, sir.'

The DA gave the jury time to fully absorb the image. They did. Scott had instructed Rebecca to keep her head up and to look straight ahead without expression. She did.

The DA led Detective Wilson through a dozen more crime scene photos then asked, 'Detective, did you ask the defendant what happened that night?'

'Yes, sir, I did. She said she woke up with a chill, went to shut the doors but stepped out onto the deck, realized she was wet, returned inside and turned the lights on, whereupon she saw the victim lying in blood on the bed with the knife in him.'

'Did the defendant say who killed the victim?'

'No, sir, she did not.'

'Did you ask her if she killed him?'

'Yes, sir, I did. She denied killing him.'

'Did you subsequently investigate this homicide?'

'Yes, sir, I did.'

'And did you find any evidence that a third party, that is, a person other than the defendant or the victim, had entered that bedroom that night?'

'No, sir.'

'And the only prints on the murder weapon were the defendant's?'

'Yes, sir.'

'What did that evidence lead you to do?'

354

'Arrest the defendant and refer the case to your office with a recommendation that the defendant be charged with the murder of Trey Rawlins.'

'Thank you, Detective.'

The judge called for a short recess. The DA came over to the defense table.

'Who are these people? Those jurors didn't even blink an eye at the photos.' He shook his head in apparent disbelief. 'I need to retire.'

Karen Douglas sat propped up in her hospital bed nursing her new baby boy and watching the murder trial on the TV and listening to Renée Ramirez's narration. She had her laptop up and running.

After the recess, Bobby cross-examined Detective Wilson.

'Detective, when did you arrest Ms Fenney?'

'Friday morning, about eight.'

'At the time of her arrest, did you have the results of the finger-print evidence on the murder weapon?'

'No.'

'Then what evidence did you have establishing probable cause to arrest her for the murder of Trey Rawlins?'

'She was present at the scene and she was covered in his blood.'

'How did you know it was his blood?'

'No one else was bleeding.'

'So that's all the evidence you had?'

'That was enough. Besides, we got the prints back Monday, it became a mute point.'

'Moot.'

'That's what I said. It became a mute point—'

'Your Honor.' The Assistant DA was on his feet. 'The US Supreme Court ruled that an illegal arrest does not invalidate a subsequent conviction.'

'We're aware of that ruling,' Bobby said, 'but there has been no conviction. And don't interrupt my cross-examination unless you have an objection.' Bobby turned back to the detective. 'So, you arrived at the crime scene, saw Ms Fenney covered in blood, and decided right then and there that she had committed the crime?'

'Pretty much.'

'Detective, after you arrested Ms Fenney, did you take her to the police station?'

'Yes.'

'And did you interrogate her there?'

'Yes. Until she called her lawyer, and he instructed us to stop.'

'Because the Constitution requires that you cease interrogation when counsel so instructs pursuant to an accused person's right to remain silent?'

'Yes.'

'I mean, you can't waterboard an American citizen, can you?'

'Unfortunately.' The detective smiled, but no one got the joke.

'Detective, when you investigate a homicide, is it your practice to develop a list of potential suspects?'

'Yes, it is.'

'And did you develop such a list in this case?'

'Yes, I did.'

'Who was on your list?'

'Rebecca Fenney.'

'Anyone else?'

'No.'

'Why not?'

'It was obvious that the defendant had stabbed the victim.'

'And why was that obvious?'

'No one else had made entry into the room and only her prints were on the knife.'

'The French doors leading to the back deck were open, correct?'

'Yes.'

'And the back deck was accessible via stairs down to the beach, correct?'

'Yes.'

'And no blood was recovered from those doors?'

'No.'

'Which means that those doors were not opened by Ms Fenney after she woke covered in the victim's blood?'

'Correct. She stated that they slept with those doors open.'

'And you believe that to be the fact that night?'

'Yes.'

'So a third party could have entered the house while they slept through those open doors?'

'Yes.'

Bobby picked up the murder weapon off the evidence table. 'And if I wore latex gloves and picked up this knife I would not leave my fingerprints on the knife, correct?'

'Yes.'

'But I would also not obliterate any fingerprints already on the knife, correct?'

'Yes.'

'So Ms Fenney could have put her prints on this knife some time before the murder but someone else could have worn latex gloves, grabbed the knife from the kitchen, and stabbed Mr Rawlins?'

The detective snorted. 'Could have? Sure. Anything could have happened.'

'But your investigation of this homicide began and ended with Ms Fenney?'

'Yes.'

'And why is that?'

'Because I deal in reality. The fact that someone could have done all that doesn't mean someone did.'

'Fair enough. But is it also fair to state that you never even considered the possibility that anyone other than Ms Fenney might have killed Mr Rawlins?'

'Yes, that's a fair statement.'

'Now, Detective, when investigating a homicide, after having a suspect or a list of suspects, do you attempt to determine the suspect's motive in committing the murder?'

357

'Yes.'

'What did you determine was Rebecca Fenney's motive to kill Trey Rawlins?'

'I could not determine her motive.'

'Well, do you think she killed him for money?'

'No.'

'Do you think she killed him in a fit of rage?'

'No.'

'Was there any evidence of a struggle?'

'No.'

'Do you think she killed him because of a love triangle?'

'Maybe.'

'But you have no evidence to tie Ms Fenney to a love triangle?'

'No.'

'So that night, Ms Fenney and Mr Rawlins drank alcohol, ate dinner, used cocaine, and had sex, correct?'

'Yes.'

'Is murder usually the next step?'

'I don't understand the question.'

'Alcohol, dinner, cocaine, sex . . . do those activities usually precede a murder?'

'I wouldn't know.'

'Have you ever had such a case?'

'No.'

'But despite all that, you still think she killed him?'

'Yes, I do.'

'Even though she called nine-one-one?'

'Yes.'

'Even though she could have wiped her prints off the murder weapon before calling the cops?'

'Yes.'

'She killed him then invited the police into her house – does that make sense to you?'

'Murder never makes sense to me.'

'Wouldn't one way to try to make sense of a murder be to investigate the victim's life?'

'I suppose.'

'I mean, since you couldn't determine any motive for Rebecca Fenney to kill Trey Rawlins, wouldn't you want to know what was happening in his life to see who might have had a motive to kill him?'

'She happened in his life.'

'Did you investigate Trey Rawlins' life?'

'No.'

'Why not?'

'I knew who killed him.'

'So you were not interested in learning other facts about the victim?'

'It wasn't necessary.'

'Detective, when you arrested Rebecca Fenney, were you aware that on the day Mr Rawlins was killed a man wanted for murder in Mexico was working at a house less than one hundred yards from the Rawlins residence?'

'No.'

'Were you aware that Mr Rawlins owed five hundred thousand dollars to his drug dealer, a man tied to a Mexican drug cartel known for brutal killings?'

'No.'

'Were you aware that Mr Rawlins owed a fifteen-million-dollar gambling debt to the mob in Las Vegas?'

'No.'

'Were you aware that Mr Rawlins was having an affair with the seventeen-year-old daughter of another pro golfer and only one week earlier that golfer had threatened to kill Mr Rawlins if he didn't stay away from her and that Mr Rawlins had in fact not stayed away from her?'

'No. But none of that would have mattered. Because only the defendant's fingerprints were on the knife.'

'But the DPS lab technician testified that she could have put her prints on that knife a year ago, that another person wearing latex gloves could have held that knife and stabbed the victim, that the fact that her prints are on the knife does not mean that only she could have stabbed the victim with that knife.'

'Then why were her prints aligned in a stabbing grip?'

'She could have – '

'Coulda, woulda, shoulda – the fact of the matter is that she stabbed the victim with that knife.'

'So the prosecution's entire case is predicated on Ms Fenney's fingerprints being on the murder weapon in a stabbing grip, is that correct, Detective?'

He appeared perturbed, but not as perturbed as the one black and two Latino jurors; they knew all about cops who assume guilt without investigation. The defense was making progress.

'Of course our case is predicated on her prints because her prints prove she held the murder weapon in a manner used to stab the victim and she was covered in his blood – that's about all we need, I think.'

'I think the jury will decide that, Detective. So you ignored all other evidence that might indicate someone else killed Trey Rawlins?'

'I didn't have any other evidence.'

'Because you didn't look.'

'Because she did it.'

'You really believe that Rebecca Fenney killed Trey Rawlins then went to sleep in his blood?'

'Yes.'

'Why? Why would she do that?'

The detective gave an honest answer. 'I don't know.'

'Detective, is it true that you have hired a literary agent?'

'Uh . . . yes.'

'To shop the book you're planning to write about this case?'

'Yes.'

'But your desire to profit from this case did not affect your professional judgment or actions when investigating this case?'

'No.'

'Did your agent say whether a book deal is more or less likely if Ms Fenney is acquitted or convicted?'

'No.'

'So you want the jury to convict Ms Fenney only because you believe she is in fact guilty?'

'Yes.'

'And not because of your desire to sell a book and make money?'

'No.'

'Okay. If you say so.'

Chapter 44

There's an old saying among trial lawyers: you can't pick your fact witnesses, but you can pick your expert witnesses.

Fact witnesses testify to facts – what they personally saw or heard. They identify the perpetrator or the murder weapon or the getaway car or what they saw at the crime scene. A prosecutor can't substitute better fact witnesses. They might be too young or too old or too nearsighted or too much of a jerk for the jury to appreciate, but he's stuck with what he's got. The DA was stuck with Ronda Jensen, Officer Art Crandall, and Detective Chuck Wilson as the state's fact witnesses.

But he wasn't stuck with his expert witnesses. Because expert witnesses offer their opinions. If a prosecutor doesn't like the first expert's opinion, he can find another one who will give a better opinion – an opinion that supports the prosecutor's version of the case. 'Hard' experts testify as to 'hard science': fingerprints, DNA, toxicology, cause of death, manner of death. The criminologist, the lab technician, and the medical examiner were the state's hard experts.

'Soft' experts testify as to the 'soft sciences', primarily psychology and psychiatry. They testify as to the defendant's mental state. The DA picked a psychiatrist, Dr Richard Holbrooke, as the state's soft expert witness. He had white hair and wore black reading glasses even when he wasn't reading. He wore a crisp shirt under a tailored sports coat. He was not nervous because he was a professional witness. He would testify for the prosecution or the defense, whichever side paid him more. That day he was a prosecution witness because the State of Texas had more money than Rebecca Fenney.

A bad fact witness can lose the case for a prosecutor, but a good expert witness can win the case. Consequently, there's another old saying among trial lawyers: bad science convicts more innocent people than bad witnesses.

Scott stood and tried to make the best of a bad witness. 'Objection. Once again, Your Honor, defense objects to the testimony of Dr Holbrooke as being junk science that will in no way assist the trier of fact – this jury of intelligent, thoughtful jurors – in their search for the truth, but is in fact merely an attempt to inject a Dr Phil moment into this trial.'

The DA had a slight smile on his face. The judge did not.

'And once again, Mr Fenney,' she said, speaking to the cameras, 'your objection is overruled. Whether Dr Holbrooke's testimony is relevant and admissible is my decision and I have made my decision.'

She seemed pleased with her speech. Scott sat. Bobby leaned in and whispered, 'What jurors are you talking about?'

The DA began his direct examination. 'Dr Holbrooke, have you reviewed the toxicology report on Rebecca Fenney?'

'Yes, I have.'

'And did she have alcohol and cocaine in her system the night of Trey Rawlins' murder?'

'Yes, she did.'

'How much?'

'Point-two-two alcohol and four hundred nanograms per milliliter of cocaine.'

'In layman's terms.'

'A lot.'

Bobby's laptop pinged. He read Karen's message then said, 'Objection. If he's an expert, he can do better than "a lot".'

'Overruled.'

'A whole lot, then,' the doctor said.

'Doctor, in his opening statement, Mr Fenney posed a question for the jury and Mr Herrin just posed the same question to Detective Wilson: how could a normal person such as Rebecca Fenney have killed Trey Rawlins then slept in his blood? That is indeed a perplexing question. Do you have an expert opinion that might help the jury answer that question?'

'Yes, I do. With that much alcohol and cocaine in her system, she could have stabbed him then passed out in his blood.'

'I see. Is it likely that she remembered much from that night?'

'No. That night is probably a complete black hole.'

'She could have stabbed Mr Rawlins and not remember?'

'Yes. She quite likely remembers very little from that night.'

'Thank you, Doctor. Pass the witness.'

Bobby stood. 'Dr Holbrooke, you're a professional witness, correct?'

'I'm a psychiatrist who testifies in court.'

'You get paid for testifying, correct?'

'Just as you get paid for representing your client.'

'Who's your client – the State of Texas or the truth?'

'I am here to offer my professional opinion.'

'For a fee. What percentage of your income is derived from testifying in court?'

'I'm not sure.'

'Best guess.'

'I can't guess.'

'Okay, how much did you earn last year from treating psychiatric patients?'

'Nothing.'

'Ah, now we're getting somewhere. Do you have any other sources of income, other than testifying in court?'

'No.'

'So one hundred percent of your income is earned by testifying?'

'Yes.'

'See, that wasn't so hard. How many times have you testified in a criminal trial?'

'I'm not sure.'

'More or less than a hundred times?'

'More.'

'And were you paid for each time?'

'Yes.'

'How much is the State of Texas paying you for your testimony today?'

'Including my review of the case files?'

'Your entire bill.'

'Ten thousand dollars.'

The DA stood and said, 'State calls Rosie Gonzales.'

Rosie was thirty-two, single, and a Mexican national with a green card. She spoke English; she took classes at the community college. She wanted to be a registered nurse. Since immigrating from Matamoras two years before, she had been a maid.

'Ms Gonzales, did you clean Trey Rawlins' house?' the DA asked.

'Yes, I did that.'

'How long?'

'Maybe, four hours.'

'No. When did you first start cleaning his house?'

'Oh. One year ago.'

'And how often did you clean the house?'

'Two days each week – Mondays and Thursdays.'

'And did you clean the house on Thursday, June the fourth of this year?'

'Yes, I did that.'

'What time did you arrive that day?'

'Maybe, eight.'

'In the morning?'

'Yes.'

'And what time did you leave?'

'Noon.'

'Was anyone else in the house while you were there that day?'

'Mr Rawlins, but he left at nine. And Ms Fenney, she left at ten.'

'And did you see them again that day?'

'No, I did not see them.'

'And what did you do that day?'

'Wash the clothes, vacuum, windows, dishes . . .'

'Let's talk about the dishes. When you arrived, were there dirty dishes to be washed?'

'Yes, in the sink, and the dishwasher.'

'Were there any dirty knives?'

'Yes.'

The DA stepped over and picked up the murder weapon. 'This knife?'

'No, not that knife.'

'Other knives from this set?'

'Yes, one.'

'And what did you do with that knife?'

'I washed it.'

'How?'

'With my hands.'

'Did you use a washrag and soap?'

'Yes, I did that.'

'Did you scrub the blade?'

'Yes.'

'Did you scrub the handle?'

'Yes.'

'Is that how you always cleaned the knives, by hand?'

'Yes, then I put them in the dishwasher.'

'You washed the knives first by hand and then in the dishwasher?'

'Yes, I do all the dishes that way.'

'You're very thorough.'

'Yes.'

'So, by the time you had finished with the knives, anything that might have been on them would have been washed off, such as stains or food or fingerprints—'

Scott stood. 'Objection. The witness is not qualified to testify as to fingerprints.'

'Sustained.'

But the DA had made his point to the jury.

'Ms Gonzales, after the dishwasher had finished running, what did you do with the dishes and utensils inside?'

'I dried them off and put them up.'

'Including the knife?'

'Yes.'

'And did you put that knife in the drawer with the other knives in that set?'

'Yes, I did that.'

The DA held up the murder weapon. 'At that time, was this knife in the drawer?'

'Yes, it was there.'

'Ms Gonzales, when you left at noon on Thursday, June the fourth, were there any dirty dishes, glasses, silverware, or knives anywhere in the Rawlins house?'

'No. I clean everything.'

Bobby had one question for Rosie: 'Ms Gonzales, did you ever hear Mr Rawlins and Ms Fenney arguing or fighting?'

'No. I did not hear that.'

The prosecution's final witness was Terri Rawlins. She was petite and pissed. Which was understandable: her brother had been brutally murdered. Since she was a prosecution witness, Scott could have had her banned from the courtroom until she testified. But he hadn't, because he wanted her to hear the truth about her brother – because Scott needed her to waive the attorney-client privilege. He needed to know what Melvyn Burke knew about Trey Rawlins.

'Ms Rawlins,' the Assistant DA said, 'you and Trey were twins?'

'Yes.'

'Were you close?'

'Very. We talked about everything.'

'He called you often?'

'Almost every day.'

'Do you miss your brother?'

'Every day.'

'He was your only living sibling?'

'Yes.'

'Did Trey ever mention to you that he was going to marry Rebecca Fenney?'

'No. Never.'

'Thank you.'

The jury seemed sympathetic toward Terri Rawlins, as well they should. So Scott whispered to Bobby, 'Be gentle.' Bobby nodded and stood.

'Ms Rawlins, I'm very sorry for your loss. I know you loved your brother, but I have to ask you some questions about him, okay?'

She nodded.

'Did Trey ever tell you about his affairs with wives of other pro golfers?'

She appeared flustered. 'No.'

'Did he ever tell you he was having an affair with a seventeen-year-old girl?'

Even more flustered. 'No.'

'Did he ever tell you that he used cocaine?'

'No.'

'Or that he owed five hundred thousand to his drug dealer?'

'No.'

'Or that he owed fifteen million to the mob?'

'No.'

'Well, Ms Rawlins, perhaps you and Trey didn't talk about everything.'

Chapter 45

'Bad time to stop smoking,' Bobby said.

The state rested its case, and the judge recessed for lunch. The DA would now wait to cross-examine the accused – if she took the stand. If she didn't testify, the jury would certainly convict her. If she did testify, she would open herself up to questions about cocaine and sex tapes, after which the jury would certainly convict her.

'She's got to take the stand, Scotty.'

Scott and Bobby needed food and fresh air to think and plot strategy, so they were having lunch on the seawall: shrimp poor-boy sandwiches and the sea breeze on the front deck facing the beach and the Gulf of Mexico.

'Rex did a good job with Holbrooke,' Scott said. 'Answered that question for the jury, how she could've slept in his blood.'

'Which is why she's got to testify.'

'And open herself up to questions about God knows what.'

'You don't think she's come clean with us?'

Scott shrugged. 'She's a pretty complicated woman.'

'That's a bit of an understatement.' Bobby bit into his poor-boy. 'Scotty, I looked at those sex tapes, to see if there were any surprises . . . you know, other than how many women Trey could have sex with at the same time.'

Scott had refused the tapes that day, but the DA had given them to Bobby, as the law required, so the DA could introduce them into evidence at trial.

'Bobby, she made those tapes just to make Trey happy. Dr Tim said he was a narcissist, he made those tapes to watch himself.'

'Weird.'

'Yeah. But Rebecca wasn't a porn star like Lacy Parker. This was private, consenting adult stuff.'

'You want Boo to see it?'

'No.' Scott watched the waves roll ashore. 'I'm sorry, Bobby.'

'For what?'

'For dragging you and Karen down here. Maybe it was a guilt trip.'

'Scotty, you had to come down here. And we wanted to come with you.'

'Why?'

'We came because we're your partners and you and me, we're brothers. You came because you've never gotten over Rebecca. If you didn't come down here and defend her and she ended up in prison, you'd never get over her. You'd blame yourself for that, too. You'd be taking Boo down to Huntsville every month to see her because you're that kind of guy. You'd be sentencing yourself and Boo to prison with her, you'd never be able to get on with your lives.'

Scott stared at the sea.

'You representing your ex-wife charged with murdering the man she left you for – there ain't another lawyer in the country who'd do that . . . at least not for free – but you're doing it 'cause that's who you are. So do it. You signed up to be her lawyer, so get your butt in the game and defend your client. She's innocent, now go in there and prove it. Put Pete and Benito and Gabe on the goddamned stand and get in their faces till they fess up. One of them killed Trey Rawlins. Now get off your ass and do your job. Like Pajamae says, Man up, Scotty!'

'You really think she's innocent?'

'Yes. I didn't before, but I do now. It's the Zetas or the mob or Pete, but it ain't her.'

'Thanks, Bobby.' Scott stood. 'Let's do it.'

'You gonna eat that?'

'What?'

'The rest of your poor-boy.'

Scott needed to build his case like a symphony to a crescendo – to the moment in the trial when the killer of Trey Rawlins would reveal himself to the world. So he started quietly.

'The defense calls Ricardo Renteria.'

A short Latino man wearing a black suit entered the courtroom and walked up to the witness stand as if escorting diners into the main dining room at Gaido's. He took the oath. He was the waiter who had served Rebecca and Trey the night of his death.

'They look very happy to me,' Ricardo said. 'Mr Trey, he drink very much, and Miss Rebecca, she drink too. They laugh and act like they are in love. When they leave, Miss Rebecca, she say Mr Trey asked her to marry him. She was very excited.'

'Where was Mr Rawlins when Ms Fenney told you that?'

'In the men's room.'

'Did they argue at any time during the evening?'

'No. But Mr Trey, he had the fat lip. He did not say why.'

'What time did they leave?'

'A little before ten.'

'No further questions.'

The DA asked only one question: 'Mr Renteria, did Trey Rawlins tell you that he had proposed marriage to Ms Fenney that night?'

'No. He did not do that.'

Now Scott would reveal Trey Rawlins' golf life. So he called Tess McBride. She walked up the center aisle wearing a skin-tight cleavage-revealing white blouse, a black miniskirt, and high heels. She looked like a high-class hooker or a Hollywood starlet. She took the oath then sat in the witness chair and assumed a pose for the cameras. She had cheated on her husband just as

371

Rebecca had cheated on him. But it wasn't his place to break up a marriage.

'Ms McBride, did you know Trey Rawlins?'

'Yes.'

'How?'

'He was a pro golfer on tour, like my husband. Brett McBride.'

'Do you know Rebecca Fenney?'

'Yes.'

'Were you friends with her?'

She glanced at Rebecca. 'Yes.'

'Did you and your husband socialize with Trey and Rebecca while on tour?'

'Yes.'

'Were you aware that Trey had affairs with other women on tour?'

'Yes.'

'Did you inform Rebecca of that fact?'

'No.'

'Why not?'

'It was none of my business.'

'Did Rebecca ever mention to you that she was aware of those affairs?'

'No.'

'Did she act in any manner that suggested she knew of Trey's affairs?'

'No.'

'Did Trey ever mention to you that he was going to leave Rebecca?'

'No.'

'No further questions.'

The DA stood and asked one question: 'Ms McBride, did Trey Rawlins ever tell you that he was going to marry Rebecca Fenney?'

'No.'

Tess McBride gave the cameras her best runway walk all the way out of the courtroom. Scott called Lacy Parker and Riley

Hager and asked them the same questions. They gave the same answers, except Lacy got in a mention of her new website where her movies could be purchased. The DA asked the same question to each of them and got the same answer. Scott then called Brett McBride.

'Mr McBride, did you know Trey Rawlins?'

'Yes.'

'And what was your opinion of him?'

'Not good.'

'Why?'

'I was pretty sure he was having an affair with my buddy's wife.'

'Do you think Rebecca Fenney was aware of that affair?'

'No.'

'Do you like Rebecca?'

'Yes.'

'Why?'

'She and my wife, they're like sisters. Neither of them were wild, like some of the other wives on tour. They're both good girls.'

Scott stared at Brett McBride. Not only did he look just like the guy in *Sling Blade*, he was just as dumb.

'Mr McBride, did you witness Pete Puckett throwing Trey Rawlins against the lockers in the locker room at the Challenge tournament earlier this year?'

'Yes, I did.'

'And did you hear Pete Puckett threaten to kill Trey Rawlins if he did not stay away from Billie Jean Puckett?'

'Yes, I did.'

'And that was one week before Trey was murdered?'

'Yes.'

'Thank you, Mr McBride.'

The DA stood. 'Mr McBride, did Trey Rawlins ever tell you that he was going to marry Rebecca Fenney?'

'No.'

Scott called Donnie Parker and Vic Hager. They dressed the

same, looked the same, and testified the same. They gave the same answers to Scott's questions and the DA's question. Neither had heard Trey express an intent to marry Rebecca.

Nick Madden took the stand.

'Mr Madden, what is your occupation?'

'I'm a sports agent with Sports Score International.' He turned slightly to the camera. 'SSI is the third largest sports agency in the world, but we try harder. We represent three hundred athletes in—'

'Mr Madden, what was your relationship to Trey Rawlins?'

'I was his agent.'

'And how long did you serve in such a role?'

'Almost two years.'

'Did you know Rebecca Fenney?'

'Yes.'

'Do you think Trey Rawlins loved her?'

'Yes, I do.'

'Were you aware of Trey's affairs with other tour women?'

'No, I was not.'

'Were you aware of his cocaine use?'

'Yes.'

'Were you aware that he owed money to his drug dealer?'

'No.'

'Were you aware of his gambling habit?'

'Yes.'

'Were you aware of his fifteen-million-dollar debt to Las Vegas casinos?'

'No.'

'Did you suspect he owed a gambling debt?'

'Yes.'

'And how did you think he was repaying that debt?'

'By throwing golf tournaments.'

'And what made you think that?'

'He missed short putts and lost two tournaments.'

'Do you suspect that the mob killed Trey Rawlins over that debt?'

'Yes.'

'But if he were repaying his debts, why would the mob kill him?'

'Because he made a long putt to win a tournament he was supposed to lose. I think it cost the mob millions.'

The DA asked the same question. 'Mr Madden, did Trey Rawlins ever tell you that he was going to marry Rebecca Fenney?'

'No, he did not.'

Brad Dickey, Vice President–Player Development for Golf-a-zon.com, testified that he had bet the company on Trey Rawlins only to discover that he used cocaine. The company wanted to terminate his contract, but legal counsel had advised that termination would subject the company to a breach of contract suit. Under the contract, the company owed Trey ten million dollars plus incentives. If word got out about Trey's drug use, the company would go bankrupt.

'Trey's death saved our company. But we didn't kill him.'

He, too, had never heard Trey express an intent to marry Rebecca.

Royce Ballard, the tour's VP–Player Relations, testified that the tour suspected Trey's drug abuse but could not suspend him because his drug tests came back negative. The tour brass wanted him off the pro golf tour, but he had no knowledge of the circumstances of Trey's death.

The judge adjourned for the day.

'My money's on the father,' Carlos said.

'Trey do my daughter,' Louis said, 'I might kill him, too.'

'You don't have a daughter.'

'If I did.'

'Hell, you had a daughter, boys be scared to come around her.'

'Good.'

An hour later, Carlos and Louis were sitting on their surfboards out in the Gulf. It was a nice way to end the day. Carlos waved to Boo and Pajamae on shore.

'You hear the boss might be a federal judge?'

'He'd be a good one. Treats folks fair.'

'What are you gonna do then?'

'I'm thinking professional surfer.'

'We are getting good at this, aren't we? But I don't expect anyone's gonna pay us to surf. What's your backup plan?'

'Whatever life brings me.'

'What do you mean?'

'I mean, Carlos, I don't worry about things like that 'cause I can't control things like that. It's like surfing. We don't create the wave and we can't control the wave. All we can do is ride the wave. We just trying to stay on top of the wave as long as we can and not get drowned by the wave. That's all life is – a big wave.'

Carlos considered the big man's words a moment then said, 'Louis, you're either the smartest man I've ever met or you don't know what the fuck you're talking about.'

Louis chuckled. 'I know there's a fine line between being one or the other.'

Carlos looked back and saw a nice wave building.

'Here comes a good one.'

But he saw something else. A big fucking fin sticking out of the water.

'Oh, shit, Louis! It's a shark!'

Louis shook his head. 'Don't start with me.'

'No, I'm not kidding this time! It's a real goddamned shark! And it's coming right at us! Paddle, Louis! Fast!'

'I ain't falling for it this time.'

Carlos dropped down and started paddling. Louis shrugged and followed. Carlos glanced back. The fin was almost to Louis.

'Faster, Louis!'

The wave came upon them, and they stood on their boards and rode that mother all the way to shore. Carlos crawled out of the water to dry sand and lay there on the beach. He had been sure the shark would eat them. He promised God he would never surf again.

'¡*Gracias a Dios!*'

He heard Boo's voice from above. 'Wow, Carlos, you're getting pretty good at that surfing.'

Scott was drinking a cold beer on the back deck and wondering why Carlos was hugging the sand when his cell phone rang. It was US Senator George Armstrong.

'Scott, if you put Benito Estrada on the witness stand, you will never be a federal judge in the State of Texas as long as I'm a US senator.'

'Senator, I know about your daughter . . . your debt to Judge Morgan.'

The senator's tone softened. 'She's only twenty-two, Scott. I've put her in rehab twice, she relapsed each time. I've kept it quiet. If Benito tells the world she's a cokehead—'

'It won't be good for your political career.'

'It won't be good for her. Scott, I'd give up my Senate seat today if I could get my daughter straight.'

Scott believed him.

'Why would Benito mention your daughter?'

'He knows she's his one-time "Get Out of Jail Free" card.'

'So why would he waste it over my ex-wife?'

'Because you put him on national TV and tell the world he's a dealer for a Mexican cartel, his employer is liable to use him for fish bait.'

Chapter 46

On the third day of trial, Scott Fenney stood and called Benito Estrada to the witness stand. Benito wore a white silk suit, crisp white shirt, and a white tie to court. He glowed under the fluorescent lights.

'Mr Estrada, I understand that you are a distributor of pharmaceutical products, is that correct?'

'Pharmaceutical products?' A little smile. 'Uh, yes, that is correct. I am a distributor of pharmaceutical products.'

The jurors smiled, too. They might possess only high school educations, but they weren't stupid.

'And did you have occasion to sell pharmaceutical products to Trey Rawlins?'

'Yes, I did have that occasion.'

'And did you allow Mr Rawlins to purchase your products on credit?'

'Yes, I did.'

'At the time of his death, how much did Mr Rawlins owe you for products he had purchased from you?'

'Five hundred thousand dollars.'

'And did he refuse to repay that sum?'

'Yes.'

'Why?'

'He disputed delivery.'

'He claimed he had not received the products?'

'That is correct.'

'But you did make delivery, did you not?'

'I did make delivery. To his residence.'

'And, subsequent to his death, did you learn that you were both correct?'

Benito sighed. 'Yes.'

'Why is that?'

'The products were stolen from his residence before he took possession.'

'Mr Estrada, what did you do about Mr Rawlins' outstanding debt?'

'I referred him to our collections department.'

'And where is your collections department located?'

'Nuevo Laredo.'

'Mexico. So yours is an international operation?'

'Yes, very much so.'

'And do you know if your collections department was able to secure payment of Mr Rawlins' outstanding debt?'

'I do not know.'

'Would you say that your collections department is aggressive in its collection efforts?'

'Aggressive? Yes. Very.'

'Nonpayment is not an option?'

'No, it is not.'

A common defense strategy is to preempt the prosecution. Rather than wait for the prosecution to present bad evidence about the defendant, a savvy defense lawyer will present it first, to lessen its impact on the jury. Of course, that strategy works only if the defendant has told the truth – at least to her lawyer.

'Mr Estrada, have you ever met the defendant?'

Benito looked to Rebecca and smiled. 'Yes, we have met.'

'Did she recently come to your place of business?'

'Yes.'

'And did she purchase pharmaceutical products from you?'

'Yes.'

'And did she pay for those products by giving you her jewelry?'

Benito frowned, and Scott knew the strategy had backfired.

'Jewelry? What jewelry?'

'Thank you, Mr Estrada. No further questions.'

The DA's head had been down during most of Benito's testimony. Scott now sat at the defense table, hoping the DA had missed the importance of Benito's last answer – but he knew Rex Truitt didn't miss anything.

The DA stood. 'Mr Estrada, do you know who killed Trey Rawlins?'

'No.'

'No further questions.'

The judge declared a short recess. After the courtroom had emptied, Scott turned to Rebecca. 'You said you paid Benito with your jewelry. He doesn't know anything about any jewelry. Rebecca, if Rex had followed up on that, he could've shown the jury we lied to them. We said you had no money. But you paid Benito in cash. You have that mob money, don't you?'

'No!'

Scott needed to calm down, he needed to find Benito, and he needed to use the men's room. So he stood and went out into the corridor. Gabe and his goon were leaning against the opposite wall. Renée sat in her booth; Scott walked over to her.

'Did you see Benito?'

She covered her microphone with her hand and whispered. 'He left. Fast.'

Scott continued down the hall to the men's room. He was standing at a urinal and thinking about Rebecca's latest lie when he zipped up and turned around and came face to face with Gabe's goon. And he realized that Louis hadn't followed him out of the courtroom.

'I guess I didn't make myself clear on the beach.' The goon grabbed Scott by his shirt. 'The Vegas boys don't want Gabe to testify.'

A toilet flushed.

A stall door swung open, and Louis's massive body filled the opening. He stepped out and loomed large over Gabe's goon – and blocked his path to the door. The goon released Scott's shirt.

'Sorry, Mr Fenney, nature called. Would you excuse us?'

Scott smiled at the goon and slipped past Louis and out the door. He walked back down the corridor to the courtroom. Gabe saw him and looked for his goon. But it was Louis walking down the corridor. Scott waited for him; they entered the court-room together.

'Louis, I didn't see the goon leave.'

'He left, Mr Fenney. Through the window.'

'But we're on the second floor.'

'Yes, sir, we sure are.'

'Mr Petrocelli, what line of business are you in?'

Gabe wore a plaid sports coat over a knit shirt. 'I own a bar on the Strand.'

'Do you make book?'

'I make martinis.'

'Did you know Trey Rawlins?'

'Yeah, I knew him.'

'Were you aware of a debt Mr Rawlins owed the Las Vegas casinos?'

'I heard of such a debt.'

'And did you hear that that debt was fifteen million dollars?'

'I heard that number.'

'And did you hear that Mr Rawlins made an arrangement to repay that debt by intentionally losing several professional golf tournaments thereby allowing his creditors to win their bets on those tournaments?'

'I heard that.'

'And did you hear—'

The DA stood. 'Objection. Your Honor, I'm not a stickler on legal technicalities, but every time Mr Fenney says "hear" and the witness says "heard" I think the witness' testimony might constitute hearsay, which would be inadmissible.'

'Your Honor,' Scott said, 'asking if the witness "heard" something is the same as asking if he "knew" something. It's just a more agreeable way for me to phrase the question, isn't that right, Mr Petrocelli?'

'Uh, yeah. That's right. It's more agreeable.'

The judge turned to the witness. 'Mr Petrocelli, do you have personal knowledge of these matters?'

'Personal knowledge?'

'Did you personally see the instruments evidencing Mr Rawlins' debt? Like a promissory note.'

Gabe smiled. 'Judge, there ain't no promissory notes.'

'So how did you learn of these debts?'

'I was told about them.'

'And now you're telling us what someone else told you?'

'Yeah. That's what I'm doing.'

'Well, that's the very definition of hearsay.'

Bobby's laptop pinged. He read: 'And, Your Honor, it is an exception to the hearsay rule if the declarant is unavailable to testify. Rule eight-zero-four.'

The Assistant DA jumped up and pointed at Bobby. 'Objection! He's cheating!'

'Cheating, Mr Newman?' The judge almost laughed. 'Mr Truitt already objected to the hearsay.'

'Yeah, but I'm objecting to Mr Herrin using messages from Ms Douglas. That's not fair.'

The judge turned to Bobby. 'Is she messaging you, Mr Herrin?'

'Uh, yes, Judge, she is.'

The DA turned to Bobby. 'Is it really an exception?'

Bobby shrugged. 'How would I know? I got a D in evidence. But Karen said it's an exception if the declarant is unavailable to testify due to death.'

'Who's dead?' the judge said.

'One of the Vegas boys testifies, he's dead,' Gabe said.

The DA had heard enough. 'Never mind, Your Honor. I

382

withdraw the objection. If Professor Douglas says it's an exception to the hearsay rule, then I'm sure it is.' He turned to his assistant. 'Sit down, Ted.'

'Very well. Continue, Mr Fenney.'

'Mr Petrocelli, did you hear that Mr Rawlins did in fact throw two golf tournaments earlier this year?'

'Yeah, I heard that.'

'And did you hear that his creditors gave him a cut of the profits, three million dollars in cash?'

'Yeah, I heard that, too.'

'And did you hear that Mr Rawlins was supposed to throw a third tournament but inadvertently sank a long putt to win?'

'I heard that, too.'

'And that that putt cost his creditors many millions of dollars, which did not make them happy?'

'Yeah.'

'Mr Petrocelli, did you hear who killed Trey Rawlins?'

'Uh, no, I didn't hear that.'

'Thank you.'

The DA had no questions for Gabe.

'Defense calls Clyde Dalton.'

The courtroom doors opened and Goose walked in. He was wearing slacks, a wrinkled shirt, and a clip-on tie. Scott had never before seen him without a golf cap on. His gray goatee needed trimming, and his gray hair was thin on top and pulled back in a ponytail. It wasn't a good look on a middle-aged man whose name wasn't Willie Nelson. Goose took the oath then sat.

'Mr Dalton,' Scott said, 'what is your nickname on the pro golf tour?'

'Goose.'

'Would it be more convenient for me to call you Goose?'

'Uh, yeah, that would be more convenient.'

Scott first took Goose through the facts of his employment with Trey as a caddie and the events surrounding the termination of that employment on a Mexican golf course during a tournament that Trey eventually won.

'And did Mr Rawlins owe you a caddie fee of one hundred thousand dollars?'

'Yeah, he did.'

'And did he pay you that fee?'

'No, he didn't.'

'Were you unhappy about that?'

'Uh, yeah, I was unhappy about that.'

'What was your opinion of Trey Rawlins?'

'My opinion was that he was a prick.' Goose caught himself and looked up at the judge. 'Can I say that?'

'You just did.'

'Maybe you should strike that remark from the record.'

'You've been watching too much TV. The jurors are over twelve, they've heard it before.'

'Goose, did you kill Trey?'

'No, I did not.'

'Were you aware of his cocaine habit?'

'I suspected. He'd be jumpy sometimes.'

'Were you aware of his gambling habit?'

'Yeah, I knew about that.'

'What about his gambling debt?'

'Nope.'

'Did you think he threw those two tournaments, when he missed the short putts?'

'Seemed a little strange 'cause he never missed short putts.'

'Did you ask him why?'

'Why what?'

'Why he missed those short putts.'

Goose chuckled. 'Uh, no, I didn't do that. You ask a golf pro why he missed a short putt to win a million bucks and you're liable to get a putter rammed up your . . . he wouldn't appreciate that question.'

'Do you now caddie for Pete Puckett?'

'Yep.'

'Where do you live?'

'Austin.'

'Where does Pete live?'

'On a ranch outside Austin.'

'Have you ever been to his ranch?'

'Yeah. He asked me out to go deer hunting.'

'So Pete knows how to use a gun?'

Goose nodded. 'Oh, yeah. Real good.'

'Did he shoot a deer the day you were out with him?'

'Yep. Big one.'

'What'd he do after he killed it?'

'Cut it up. He carries this big ol' Bowie knife looks like a god—'
He grimaced and glanced up at the judge. 'Looks like a sword.
He slit that deer from head to hoof, gutted it, hung it up—'

'He field-dressed the deer?'

'Uh, yeah. That's what he called it.'

'Bloody, isn't it?'

'Oh, it's awful.'

'So Pete's handy with a knife?'

'You could say that.'

'Would you say that?'

'Uh . . . he's handy with a knife?'

'Does Pete have a daughter?'

Goose nodded. 'Billie Jean.'

'How old is she?'

'Seventeen.'

'Did Pete know she was having a carnal relationship with Trey?'

'Nope. But he knew they were screwing.'

'How'd he feel about that?'

'He didn't feel so good about that.'

'Did he say anything to you about it?'

'Said Trey was a no-good mother—' Another sheepish glance
at the judge. 'Said he was a pervert.'

'Pete wasn't happy about the affair?'

'Nope.'

'Where were you on Thursday, June fourth?'

'Orlando. Caddying for Pete at the Atlantic Open.'

'Did you and Pete travel together to the tournament?'

Goose nodded. 'We flew from Austin that Monday.'

'Did Billie Jean go with you?'

'No, she stayed back in Austin.'

'Why?'

'Pete said she didn't feel so good.'

'So you arrived in Orlando on Monday, then what?'

'Played a practice round on Tuesday, pro-am on Wednesday.'

'And what was Pete's mood?'

'Foul. Something was bothering him, but he didn't want to talk about it.'

'What time did you and Pete tee off on Thursday?'

'Eight A.M.'

'What time did you finish the round?'

'About noon.'

'How'd Pete play?'

'Godawful. Shot an eighty-five. Couldn't focus.'

'Was that unusual for Pete?'

'Oh, yeah. Now, he don't shoot sixty-five, but he don't shoot eighty-five. He's a one-under, one-over kind of player. But he could always focus. Not that day.'

'Then what did you do?'

'Flew home to Austin.'

'After the first round of the tournament? Why?'

'Pete wrote down the wrong scores on two holes, signed his card. Automatic DQ. Disqualification.'

'Why'd he do that?'

'Like I said, he wasn't himself that day. He was real distracted.'

'By what?'

'Didn't say. But I think it was 'cause Billie Jean wasn't there. He was worried about her.'

'Did Pete fly with you back to Austin?'

'Nope. He took another flight.'

'So the last time you saw Pete in Orlando was when you left the tournament site for the airport?'

386

'Yep.'

'And when did you next see Pete?'

'Following Sunday. He picked me up at my house in his RV to drive down to Houston for the tournament there.'

'Goose, is Pete known on tour for his temper?'

'Oh, yeah.'

'Bad?'

'Terrible. If he could've controlled it, he could've won a dozen tournaments. But it'd get the best of him and he'd fling his club farther than most guys could hit an eight-iron. I'm telling you, you didn't want to be around Pete when he lost his . . .'

'What?'

'Uh, I think I said enough.'

'Goose, did Pete kill Trey Rawlins?'

'He didn't say nothing about that to me.'

'No further questions.'

The DA stood. 'Goose, in the two years you caddied for Trey Rawlins, did he ever tell you that he was going to marry Rebecca Fenney?'

'Nope.'

Hank Kowalski came over to the defense table during a short recess.

'Scott, you know anything about a guy diving out of the men's restroom here in the courthouse?'

'Uh . . . no. Sure don't. Is he okay?'

'EMTs took him to UTMB. He's broken up pretty good.'

'Fall from a second-story window, that'd do it.'

Hank smiled. 'I didn't say it was a second-floor restroom.'

Chapter 47

Billie Jean Puckett wore jeans and sneakers and a golf shirt. Her hair was blonde and pulled back in a ponytail. Unlike Goose's ponytail, hers looked very good on a beautiful seventeen-year-old girl. Her eyes were crystal blue and wet with tears.

'Miss Puckett,' Scott said, 'is it all right if I call you Billie Jean?'

'That's my name.'

'Billie Jean, how long had you been involved with Trey Rawlins before his death?'

'About three weeks.'

'Did you love him?'

'Yes.'

'Did Trey say he loved you?'

'Yes.'

'Did your father kill Trey?'

'No.'

'You're sure?'

'Yes.'

'Did you drive from Austin to Galveston on Thursday, June fourth?'

'No.'

'Billie Jean, we know you were there. We have witnesses who

388

can identify you and place you at Trey's residence that afternoon. We've also recovered your father's fingerprints off the kitchen counter at Trey's house, which proves he was in the house. You can tell the truth now, or I can prove you're lying and you can be charged with perjury. Which would you like to do?'

The tears were flowing now. Her narrow shoulders slumped. He felt sorry for this girl. But he had to question her.

'Yes.'

'Yes, you drove from Austin to Galveston that day?'

'Yes.'

'Why?'

'To see Trey.'

'And did you see Trey?'

'Yes.'

'Where?'

'At his beach house.'

'What time did you arrive?'

'About one.'

'Were you and Trey alone?'

'Yes.'

'Where was Rebecca Fenney?'

'Shopping in Houston. Trey gave her some money to get rid of her.'

'Did you and Trey have sex that day?'

'Yes.'

'Where?'

'In his bed.'

'After you had—'

'And in the shower.'

'After that, did—'

'And in his closet where there's a big mirror.'

Scott waited a few seconds. 'Anyplace else?'

'No, that was all.'

'Okay, after those sexual encounters, what happened?'

'My dad caught us.'

'Your father – Pete Puckett – caught you and Trey having sex?'

389

'Well, right after. We were coming out of the closet.'

'Your father was already in the house?'

'Unh-huh.'

'What did he do?'

'Cussed. Grabbed Trey, threw him against the wall. I thought he was gonna—'

'Kill him?'

'But I stopped him.'

'Was your father angry?'

'Yes.'

'Then what happened?'

'My dad told me to get dressed, then he took me away.'

'You left Trey's house with your father?'

'Yes.'

'In your black Mustang?'

'Yes.'

'What time was that?'

'Maybe, five, five-thirty.'

'And where did you and your father go?'

'To a hotel on the beach.'

'You and your father stayed overnight in Galveston?'

'Yes.'

'Why didn't you drive back to Austin?'

'My dad said we'd drive back in the morning,'

'And did you?'

'Unh-huh. We got up early and left.'

'Thursday night, did you and your father stay in the same hotel room?'

'He got a suite.'

'Did you go out that night?'

'No. We ordered room service.'

'Did your father leave the room that night?'

She didn't answer.

'Billie Jean, please answer.'

'I went to bed, but I heard him leave.'

'What time?'

'After midnight.'

'Did you hear him return?'

'No.'

Scott passed the witness. The DA stood.

'Miss Puckett, you knew Trey Rawlins was living with Rebecca Fenney?'

'Yes.'

'So you didn't have much future with Trey, did you?'

'He said he was going to leave her for me.'

'Really? And did he tell Rebecca?'

'He was going to tell her that night.'

'The night he was killed?'

'Yes.'

'Maybe he did. Thank you, Miss Puckett.'

Scott stood again. 'Miss Puckett, were you aware that Trey had had numerous affairs with other women on the golf tour?'

'I knew he had other girlfriends before me.'

'Do you think he might've told those women he loved them, too?'

'No. He only loved me.'

'I'm sure. Did you know that Trey asked Rebecca to marry him the night he was killed?'

'No, he didn't! He was going to leave her! He was going to marry me!'

'I'm sure he was.'

Scott gave the jury a look that said *what a sad young woman*.

'What's a five-letter word for a "gay World War Two bomber"?' Louis said.

'They had gays in the Army back then?' Carlos said.

'Enola,' Bobby said.

'Funny name for a guy.'

'They mean the plane, not the pilot. Enola Gay was the name of the plane that dropped the first atomic bomb on Hiroshima.'

'How do you spell that?' Louis said.

The girls had gone inside to clean up, and they were at the

table on the back deck after dinner – Scott, Bobby, Karen, Louis, and Carlos. But not Rebecca. Scott had tried to talk to her about her purchase of cocaine from Benito, but she was too upset after Billie Jean's testimony. She was now pacing the beach alone, as if she had only a few more such evenings left in her life.

Scott had stopped by Benito's office on the way home, but his thugs said he had already left for the day. Scott had then called Benito's number shown on the phone logs, but he did not answer. Benito had sold cocaine to Rebecca, and she had not paid him in jewelry. There was only one possible source of cash: the mob money.

'What's a four-letter word for "angry"?' Louis said.

'Pete,' Bobby said.

Chapter 48

Pete Puckett was pissed.

At nine on the fourth day of trial, he took the oath, sat in the witness chair, and glared at Scott. He didn't care about the cameras or the jury or the judge. He cared only about Scott. Pete looked as if he wanted to kill him – as if he could kill him.

'Mr Puckett, let's go back to Thursday, June fourth. That morning you played the first round of the Atlantic Open golf tournament in Orlando, Florida, correct?'

'Yes.'

His answer came through clenched teeth.

'You were accompanied by your caddie, Goose?'

'Yes.'

'Was your daughter, Billie Jean, there with you?'

'No.'

'Where was she?'

'In Austin.'

'You teed off at eight A.M. that Thursday?'

'Yes.'

'And finished about noon?'

'Yes.'

'But you signed an incorrect scorecard and were disqualified?'

393

'Yes.'

'Then you flew home to Austin?'

'You know I didn't.'

'You flew to Houston?'

'Yes.'

'Why?'

'To kill Trey Rawlins.'

The spectator section behind Scott erupted with excitement. The judge gaveled the audience into silence then stared at the witness. The jurors leaned forward as one. Scott stayed calm – their strategy was working. Pete Puckett was about to confess to killing Trey Rawlins.

'You killed Trey Rawlins?'

'No.'

'But you just said—'

'I said I went there to kill him. I didn't say I did.'

The entire courtroom deflated.

'Okay, let's back up. You flew to Houston, then took a cab to Trey's house in Galveston?'

'Yes.'

'With the intent to kill Trey Rawlins?'

'Yes.'

'Why that day?'

'My girl was there with him, at his house.'

'How'd you know?'

'I put a GPS tracker on her car.'

'You tracked your own daughter?'

'Wait'll your girls take up with a bad guy, you'll do it, too.'

'And you knew Billie Jean had taken up with Trey?'

'Yes.'

'In fact, you had confronted Trey a week earlier in the locker room at the Challenge tournament and threatened to kill him if he didn't stay away from her.'

'You know I did. Brett McBride's sitting outside, he was there.'

'But Trey didn't stay away from Billie Jean, did he?'

'No.'

'So you decided to kill him?'

'Yes.'

'You went to his house that day and found him with Billie Jean?'

Pete's stern exterior began to crack.

'Yes.'

'How did you enter the house?'

'Up the back stairs to the deck. The doors to the bedroom were open.'

'You caught him having sex with your daughter?'

Pete fought the tears.

'They were in the closet.'

'What'd you do?'

'I went into the kitchen.'

'To find a knife?'

'Yes.'

'Did you lean onto the island counter?'

'I don't know.'

'Your handprints were found there.'

'Then I did.'

'Did you get a knife?'

'No.'

'Why not?'

'Couldn't do it.'

'So what did you do?'

'Went back into the bedroom, they were coming out of the closet. I grabbed Trey and threw him against the wall.'

'What did Trey say?'

'Not much – I hit him in the mouth.'

'You would've killed him if Billie Jean hadn't intervened and stopped you?'

'Maybe.'

'But you wanted to kill Trey Rawlins?'

The tears broke loose now.

'Yes, goddamnit!'

'Just because he had sex with your seventeen-year-old daughter?'

'No!'

'Then why?'

'Because he gave her cocaine!'

Scott hadn't expected that. It threw him for a moment. And the jury. The judge. The DA. Everyone in the courtroom.

'Uh . . . Mr Puckett . . . Trey gave Billie Jean cocaine?'

Pete wiped his face on his sleeve. Several jurors were now crying. Pete Puckett was no longer a hard-ass; he was a broken-hearted father.

'What kind of man does that? What kind of man gives cocaine to a seventeen-year-old kid? Every time they were together, now she wants it all the time. What would you do if a grown man gave your girls cocaine?'

Kill him.

'My Billie Jean, she's a good kid, I'm trying to raise her right, but since her mama died, I don't know how to help her understand things . . . a girl needs a mama when she gets that age, a woman to talk to her about boys and what they'll say to get what they want . . . all I know is golfing and hunting . . . I've been lost since her mama died . . . we both have.'

He put his face in his hands and sobbed. The judge called a fifteen-minute recess.

Scott – and Louis – went to the restroom. Scott opened the door and came face to face with Pete Puckett. He had obviously just washed his face.

'I'm sorry, Pete.'

'Fuck you. You're a goddamn lawyer, don't give a shit about no one or nothing except getting your wife off.'

He stormed down the corridor.

When the trial resumed, Pete Puckett had gathered himself.

'Mr Puckett, you went to Trey's house that day to kill him?'

'Yes.'

396

'But you didn't?'

'No.'

'You dragged Billie Jean out of the house, didn't you?'

'Yes.'

'We know Trey was not killed until after midnight. We know you went to the Galvez with your daughter and checked into a suite. We know you were enraged and in town. We know you left the hotel after midnight. Did you return to Trey's house?'

'Yes.'

'To kill him?'

'Yes.'

'You put on gloves, didn't you?'

'No.'

'You went up the back stairs again, didn't you?'

'No.'

'You entered the bedroom and found Trey and Rebecca sleeping, passed out.'

'No.'

'You went back into the kitchen and you got a knife this time, a butcher knife.'

'No.'

'You went back into the bedroom and over to the bed.'

'No.'

'You stood over Trey.'

'No.'

'You raised the knife over Trey.'

'No.'

'And you stabbed the knife into Trey Rawlins' chest.'

'No!'

Pete cried again.

'I wanted to. God knows I wanted to kill him for what he did to my Billie Jean.'

'Did you?'

'No.'

'What did you do?'

'Sat outside in the car, trying to work up the courage. But I couldn't do it.'

'Why not?'

'Because I heard Dottie Lynn's voice. She told me, "Pete, don't do it. You'll go to prison. And Billie Jean will be all alone".'

Chapter 49

'That was unexpected,' Bobby said through a mouthful of fried shrimp.

The others had gone back to the house for lunch. Scott and Bobby had gone to the seawall. They were sitting at an outside table eating lunch. But Scott couldn't eat.

'Sad, ain't it?' Bobby said. 'Billie Jean.'

'She needed a mother.'

'I hope she can get clean.'

'I might've killed Trey myself, if he'd given cocaine to Boo or Pajamae.'

'I might've helped you.'

After the lunch break, Hank Kowalski stopped Scott again on his way into the courtroom.

'Hank, I didn't throw that guy out the bathroom window.'

'Never figured you did.' He cut his eyes toward Louis sitting in the spectator pews. 'And I know he's one of the goons who beat you up on the beach. Way I figure, all's well that ends well.'

Hank reached into his coat pocket and removed the baggie with the four miniature bourbon bottles from the plane.

'Got these prints back. They match the ones on Trey's mirror in the closet.'

'Shit.'

'So who do they belong to?'

'You don't want to know.' Scott tried to think it through. 'Hank, hold on to those bottles and hang around. I'm going to call you to testify next.'

Hank shrugged. 'I'll be here.'

Hank left, and Scott called Karen on his cell phone. She was breast-feeding little Scotty, but she answered.

'Karen, when you checked into the judge, did you find out where she was the night Trey was killed?'

'Santa Fe, speaking at a continuing legal education program. Didn't come back until Saturday.'

Judge Shelby Morgan was neither a witness nor a suspect. But she had been in Trey's closet. She had probably had sex with Trey. What was Scott supposed to do now? What was his ethical duty? He could bring that fact up and obtain an immediate mistrial. If he did, would the DA take Rebecca to trial again? If he did, would she get a fairer trial with another judge? Was Rebecca better off seeing this trial through? Was this her best shot at acquittal? Could Scott hold the judge's relationship with Trey in his pocket like an ace in the hole? If he did, was he risking his own law license? Or something more valuable, like his conscience?

Scott stood and said, 'Defense calls Hank Kowalski.'

Hank took the oath and sat.

'Mr Kowalski, after the police department referred this case to the district attorney's office, you were responsible for all the evidence?'

'Yes, sir, I was.'

'Mr Deeks, the criminologist, testified that he found three sets of unidentified prints in the Rawlins house – one on the kitchen counter, one on the headboard of the bed in the crime scene, and one on the full-length mirror in the victim's closet, is that correct?'

400

'Yes, sir.'

'And he testified that he handed those prints over to you?'

'Yes, sir.'

'And you subsequently determined that the set on the kitchen counter belonged to Pete Puckett?'

'Yes, sir.'

'And how did you do that?'

'You gave me a number of items bearing fingerprints of possible suspects. I ran all those prints, including an item with prints on it which you said were Mr Puckett's. I ran the prints and they matched those on the counter.'

'Did you subsequently determine to whom the set of prints on the headboard belong?'

'Yes, sir.'

'And how did you do that?'

'On a hunch, I obtained the subject's fingerprints and ran them. They matched.'

'And who was this subject?'

'Renée Ramirez.'

The courtroom audience gasped. It hadn't been Hank's hunch. After Scott's meeting with Renée at the Hotel Galvez pool bar, he had taken her Mimosa glass and given it to the DA for prints. Renée had interviewed Trey at his house only a few weeks before his death. She had given him more than a nice profile on the news.

'Renée Ramirez's fingerprints were found on the headboard of Trey Rawlins' bed?'

'Yes, sir.'

'Interesting.'

'I thought so.'

Unlike in federal court where the lawyers must stand at a podium to question witnesses, in state court counsel may stand next to the witness, if they so chose. Scott walked over and stood next to Hank but faced the judge.

'And what about the last set – the prints on the mirror in Trey's closet?'

'Yes, I've identified those as well.'

The judge's eyes came up.

'And to whom do they belong?'

'Well, Mr Fenney, you're gonna have to tell me that.'

'Why is that?'

'Because all I know is that the prints on the mirror match the prints on the bourbon bottles.'

The judge interrupted. 'Bourbon bottles? What bourbon bottles?'

Hank reached into his coat and removed the baggie with the miniature bourbon bottles. 'These bourbon bottles. Kind they give you on airplane flights.'

Hank handed them up to the judge. She looked closely at them, and when her face came up, Scott knew she had recognized them.

'Are these in evidence?'

'No, Your Honor, they're not. Not yet, anyway.'

'And what is the point of this testimony?'

'If I may, Your Honor, that will become evident.' Scott turned back to the witness. 'Mr Kowalski, where did you get those bottles?'

'From you.'

'And what did you do with them?'

'I had them checked for fingerprints. Which were found. I then ran the prints against the prints on the mirror. They matched. I then ran them through the FBI's fingerprint database. There was no match.'

'What does that mean?'

'Means that whoever these belong to has never been arrested and fingerprinted or otherwise had their fingerprints taken by law enforcement and put into the system.'

'On what occasions other than an arrest would someone have their fingerprints taken by law enforcement?'

'Oh, if you want to work with children, say in child care or as a coach, you have to have a criminal background check. If you want to be a cop or work for the Feds, you've got to.'

'Really? Most federal employees are fingerprinted?'

'The important positions.'

'Such as?'

'FBI, DEA, border patrol agents . . . White House personnel . . . persons nominated for federal judgeships, that sort of thing.'

'Mr Kowalski, what would happen if the person to whom the prints on those bourbon bottles belong was now fingerprinted by law enforcement?'

'Well, the prints would be put into the system and would be spit out as a match to these prints because they were involved in a murder case.'

'But no one would ever know the identity of that person unless that person were to be fingerprinted at some time in the future?'

'That's correct.'

Scott turned to the judge. Their gazes met for a long moment. Then he passed the witness. The DA gave Scott and the judge suspicious glances, but he knew better than to ask any questions.

The judge recessed the trial for the day. She seemed flustered when she stepped off the bench. Scott walked out of the courtroom and down the corridor. Renée Ramirez was not in her booth. She would not return to the trial. Trey Rawlins was her ticket off the Island after all.

Scott seldom slept well during a trial. That night was no exception. But there was a good reason for his restlessness that night: Rebecca would testify the next day.

He drifted off to sleep around one, but woke just before four. He thought he had heard a noise. He got up and checked on the girls then went downstairs. The sliding glass door leading out to the back deck was open. Rebecca was standing at the far railing, staring out to sea. Scott went to her.

'I couldn't sleep,' she said.

She was wearing a short nightgown tight against her body in the breeze and holding onto the railing as if afraid she might be blown off the deck.

'I had a nightmare – I was in prison.' She hesitated. 'Scott, if the jury acquits me, can the DA charge me with murder again?'

'No. It's called double jeopardy. Means the government can't try you twice for the same crime. But they can charge you with perjury if you testify and lie under oath.'

'Will I?'

'Lie?'

'Testify.'

'Only if you don't want to go to prison. Your prints on the knife, that alone is enough to get the case to the jury. They want to hear you explain why your prints are on the murder weapon, they want to hear you say, I didn't kill Trey. I loved him.'

'I did. Love him.'

She stared down at the waves, almost as if mesmerized. The moon offered the only light. All the color was washed out by the night. The world was painted only in shades of gray.

'I've lived my life in shades of gray,' she said.

Chapter 50

Experienced criminal defense lawyers will tell you that the last person they want testifying is the defendant because if the defendant is caught in a lie – any lie, no matter how small or how irrelevant to her guilt or innocence it might be – the jury will never believe another word she says. This was a lesson A. Scott Fenney would learn that day, the fifth day of trial in *The State of Texas vs. Rebecca Fenney*.

'The defense calls Rebecca Fenney.'

She wore low heels and a simple green dress. She looked more like a suburban housewife than the hottest WAG on tour. But she could not hide her beauty.

'Ms Fenney, did you kill Trey Rawlins?'

'No.'

'Did you love him?'

'Yes. Very much.'

'The night he was killed, did he take you out to dinner at Gaido's?'

'Yes.'

'Did he ask you to marry him?'

'Yes.'

'Did you accept his proposal?'

'Yes.'

'Did you and he have sex on the beach that night?'

'Yes.'

'Did you go to bed together?'

'Yes.'

'What do you next remember?'

'I woke up at three-forty-five in the morning and found him dead. I called nine-one-one. The police came.'

'Did you know Trey was having an affair with Billie Jean Puckett?'

'No.'

'Did Trey ever say he was leaving you for her or any other woman?'

'No.'

'He gave you money and jewelry?'

'Yes.'

'Before Trey's death, you lived in a beach house here in Galveston, an oceanfront condo in Malibu, and a ski lodge in Beaver Creek, you drove a Corvette, you stayed in five-star hotels, traveled first class, enjoyed spas . . .?'

'Yes.'

'Now you have nothing except the Corvette?'

'And the jewelry.'

'You have no money, no assets, no home, no life insurance?'

'No.'

'You had no motive to kill Trey Rawlins?'

'No.'

'And you did not kill him?'

'No, I did not.'

During a short recess, Scott noticed the DA and his assistant having an animated discussion in the corner of the courtroom. The DA's head was down, and his assistant was pleading. The DA finally nodded. When he returned to his table, his eyes met Scott's but not for long. And Scott knew. It was the sex tapes: the Assistant DA wanted to introduce the sex tapes, and he had won the argument.

The judge gaveled the courtroom to order, and the Assistant DA stood to cross-examine the defendant charged with stabbing a star athlete to death. This was his big TV moment, and he wanted to make the best of it. Rebecca had been calm and collected during the direct examination because Scott had rehearsed it with her a dozen times. But there was no effective rehearsal for cross-examination by a sneaky prosecuting son of a bitch, and the Assistant DA was just such a prosecutor. Rebecca Fenney was nervous, but not as nervous as her lawyer.

'Ms Fenney, let's talk about the jewelry Trey Rawlins gave you.'

The Assistant DA glanced at Scott and winked. And Scott knew that neither the DA nor his assistant had missed it. That was what they had argued about – not the sex tapes. They were going to show that Rebecca had lied – that she had paid Benito cash for the cocaine – that she had the $3 million the mob had paid Trey.

'Ms Fenney, during the course of your relationship with Mr Rawlins, did he give you gifts of jewelry and a Corvette?'

'Yes.'

'And cash that you used to buy more jewelry?'

'And clothes.'

'And was that Corvette in the garage of the house you shared with Mr Rawlins on the night of his death?'

'Yes.'

'Was the jewelry in the house that night?'

'Yes.'

'Subsequent to Mr Rawlins' death, his attorney surrendered possession of the Corvette to you?'

'Yes.'

'And all the jewelry Mr Rawlins had given you or that you had purchased with cash he had given you over the course of your relationship?'

'Yes.'

'When?'

'When what?'

'When did Mr Rawlins' attorney deliver possession of those items to you?'

'Well, I . . .'

'Does Friday June twelfth sound right for the Corvette?'

'Yes, I think that's right.'

'And Monday June fifteenth for the jewelry? Right here in this courtroom before your arraignment?'

'Yes.'

'Okay. Now, have you since sold any of that jewelry?'

'No.'

'Have you since sold the Corvette?'

'No.'

'So when you testified that you had no money, did you literally mean no money at all? As in zero? Not a single dollar?'

'Yes.'

'You have no money in a bank account, a shoe box, under your bed, or buried on the beach like Jean Lafitte's treasure? No money anywhere?'

'No.'

Scott felt sick. It was like watching a freight train bearing down on a compact car trying to cross the tracks too late and not being able to stop it.

'Ms Fenney, you were aware of Trey's affairs with other women?'

'No, I was not.'

'You knew he was going to leave you for Billie Jean Puckett?'

'No. He proposed to me that night.'

A little anger had seeped out.

'Where were you on the day of June the fourth?'

'In Houston. At the Galleria.'

'At what time?'

'I left the house at about ten and returned about six.'

'You were in Houston the entire day?'

'Yes.'

'Then you and Mr Rawlins went to Gaido's for dinner?'

'Yes.'

'At what time?'

'Seven.'

'And what time did you return to the house?'

'Ten.'

'What time did you go to bed?'

'About eleven.'

'And you woke at three-forty-five A.M. and found Mr Rawlins dead?'

'Yes.'

'But you heard nothing?'

'No.'

'Ms Fenney, did anyone else know that Trey proposed to you?'

'Ricardo, our waiter.'

'Because you told him?'

'Yes.'

'Did Trey tell anyone?'

'Not that I know of.'

'So it's just your word that he proposed to you?'

'Why would I lie?'

'Maybe because you killed him.'

'I didn't.'

The Assistant DA picked up the murder weapon.

'Then why are your fingerprints on the murder weapon?'

'It's a kitchen knife. I must've used it.'

'When?'

'Sometime. I don't know when. Maybe a year ago, like that state lab guy said.'

'Mr Haynes said you could have put your prints on this knife a year before, didn't he?'

'Yes, he did.'

'Except there's two problems with that scenario, aren't there?'

'What problems?'

'First, after you used this knife to cut something, perhaps a steak, what did you do with it?'

'I don't understand.'

'Well, did you cut a steak and then put the knife right back in the drawer?'

'No, I put it in the sink or the dishwasher.'

'For Rosie Gonzales to clean, correct?'

'Yes.'

'So your prints from a year before wouldn't still be on this knife, would they? They would have been washed off, wouldn't they?'

'I . . . I don't know.'

'That's all right, the jury knows. And second, Mr Haynes didn't know that Rosie Gonzales had cleaned the dishes that very day, did he?'

'I don't know.'

'Ms Fenney, you heard Rosie Gonzales's testimony, didn't you?'

'Yes.'

'You heard her testify that when she left at noon on June the fourth the entire knife set was clean and in the kitchen drawer, didn't you?'

'Yes.'

'Which means, Ms Fenney, that you did not put your finger-prints on this knife a year before or a month before or a week before − you put your fingerprints on this knife the same day Trey Rawlins was murdered with this knife, isn't that correct?'

'I don't know.'

'Sometime after Rosie Gonzales left at noon and before this knife was removed from Trey Rawlins' body, isn't that correct?'

'I don't know.'

'But you were gone all day, correct?'

'Yes.'

'You didn't return until six P.M.?'

'Yes.'

'So you had to put your prints on this knife between six P.M. and three-fifty-seven A.M. when Officers Crandall and Guerrero entered your house and found this knife stuck in Mr Rawlins' chest, isn't that correct?'

'I don't know . . . I guess . . .'

'You *guess*? Ms Fenney, did you use this knife that night?'

'I . . . maybe . . . I must have.'

'And what did you use this knife for?'

'I don't know. I swear.'

'Oh, don't swear, Ms Fenney. Just tell the truth.'

'I'm trying.'

'Telling the truth shouldn't be difficult.'

Scott stood. 'Objection. Badgering the witness.'

The judge stared at Scott. She had apparently realized over-night that he had actually saved her judicial career. She exhaled and ruled on his objection.

'Sustained.'

'Ms Fenney, you returned to the house at six P.M. You and Mr Rawlins then went out to eat at seven P.M., correct?'

'Yes.'

'So you didn't use this knife to cut a steak that night, did you?'

'No.'

'Did you use this knife for any purpose between six P.M. and seven P.M. that night?'

'No. I don't think so.'

'Okay. You and Mr Rawlins returned home from Gaido's about ten, correct?'

'Yes.'

'And went to bed about eleven?'

'Yes.'

'Did you use this knife between ten P.M. and eleven P.M. on June the fourth?'

'I don't remember.'

'You don't remember?'

'No.'

'You don't remember if you used this knife to cut anything that night?'

'No.'

'But we know you didn't use this knife to cut anything, Ms Fenney, because your fingerprints are not on this knife in the way you would hold it to cut something, are they?'

411

'I don't know.'

'You held this knife to stab, didn't you, Ms Fenney?'

'No!'

'Like this.'

The Assistant DA held the knife with the blade down, as if to stab. He stepped close to the witness.

'What did you stab with this knife, Ms Fenney?'

'Nothing!'

'You stabbed something, Ms Fenney. Between the hours of ten P.M. when you and Mr Rawlins were last seen at Gaido's and three-fifty-seven A.M. when the police arrived at your house, you used this knife to stab something, didn't you, Ms Fenney?'

'I don't know!'

She was crying now.

'You used this knife to stab Trey Rawlins, didn't you?'

'No!'

'You murdered Trey Rawlins, didn't you?'

'No!'

She turned to the jurors sitting just a few feet from her. 'He gave me everything . . . now I have nothing. Why would I kill him? I loved him!'

'I'm sure you did.'

The Assistant DA turned away and gave the jury a raised eyebrow – completely unethical courtroom conduct, but also very effective. He stepped over to the evidence table and replaced the murder weapon. When he spoke again, his voice was quiet.

'Ms Fenney, you were drunk that night, correct?'

She wiped her face. 'Yes.'

'And you were stoned on cocaine, correct?'

'Yes.'

'So you really don't remember much from that night, do you?'

'No, I don't. But I didn't kill him.'

'You used cocaine with Trey?'

'Yes.'

'And on your own?'

'Yes.'

'You know Benito Estrada?'

'Yes.'

'You purchased cocaine from him?'

'Yes.'

'When?'

'I don't remember.'

'Does Saturday June thirteenth sound right?'

'I don't know.'

'Well, we have you on tape visiting Benito's place of business on Market Street on that date. Did you purchase cocaine at that time?'

'Yes.'

'Well, let's see, Ms Fenney, you've testified that you have no assets except a red Corvette and some jewelry, is that correct?'

The train bore down on the car.

'Yes.'

'Did you give Benito your Corvette in exchange for the cocaine?'

'No.'

Closer now.

'Did you give him jewelry in exchange for the cocaine?'

'No.'

'You couldn't have because in fact you didn't receive that jewelry from Mr Rawlins' attorney until Monday June fifteenth, correct?'

'Yes.'

'And you have testified that you had zero dollars, correct?'

'Yes.'

'So you did not pay Benito with cash?'

'No.'

'And I'm betting he didn't take a check or a credit card?'

'No.'

'Well, Ms Fenney, exactly what did you pay Benito with?'

Rebecca's eyes dropped. She stared down and said nothing, as if hoping the Assistant DA would go away. He didn't.

'Ms Fenney, isn't it a fact that you are in possession of three million dollars in cash the mob paid Trey Rawlins for throwing two golf tournaments?'

'No.'

'And isn't it a fact that you used some of that money to pay Benito Estrada for cocaine?'

'No.'

'Well then, Ms Fenney, would you please tell the jury how you paid Benito Estrada for the cocaine? What did you give Benito Estrada in exchange for cocaine?'

The train now collided with the car – but it wasn't the collision Scott or the Assistant DA or anyone else in the courtroom had expected.

Rebecca Fenney looked up and said, 'I traded sex.'

Chapter 51

Scott knew now that it could never be the same. She could not be his wife or Boo's mother. He had wanted her back every day since she had left two years before. Every day he had woken wanting her. Every day he had run to forget her. Every day he had gone to bed missing her. Now he didn't want her back.

He didn't want her sleeping in a prison cot, but he didn't want her sleeping in his bed.

She had cheated on him, she had lied to him, she had used cocaine while living with him that summer. And with their daughter. Had she killed Trey Rawlins, too? Had she lied about everything? All the reasonable doubt they had created in the jurors' minds had been washed away like the West End homes during Ike with those three words: 'I traded sex.' With those three words, Rebecca had sentenced herself to prison — unless Scott could explain to the jury why her prints were on the murder weapon and aligned as if holding the knife to stab something. Or someone.

'A. Scott?'

'Yes, honey?'

'You lied to me about that, didn't you?'

'About what?'

'Mother using drugs.'

'You've been watching the trial on cable.'

'I had to.'

'Yes. I lied to you.'

'Why?'

'Because I didn't think you needed to know that about your mother.'

'I wish I didn't. There's a lot I wish I didn't know about Mother.'

'Me, too.'

'I've decided.'

'What?'

'About mother and us.'

'What have you decided?'

'I don't want her to come back to us.'

The sun doesn't set in July in Texas until after nine. They had eaten dinner in town. Boo wanted to talk, so Scott took her for a walk along the seawall while the others went back to the house. Except Louis. He came with them.

'I'll always love Mother, but I don't think she's right for us anymore. I like our family the way it is now.'

Scott put his arm around her little shoulder and pulled her close. They walked on a while then she said, 'Mother's testimony today – that wasn't good, was it?'

'No. It wasn't good.'

'Do you think the jury will send her to prison?'

'Yes, I think they will.'

'Do they have air-conditioning in prison?'

'No.'

'But it's hot in Texas.'

'Yes, it is.'

'She would sweat a lot.'

'Yes, she would.'

'I wouldn't want that.'

'Me neither.'

'I'll worry about her.'

'Boo, you're only eleven. You've got to stop worrying about everyone else – your mother, my health . . .'

'A. Scott, I'll always worry about you.'

He pulled her closer. They walked some more. The peacefulness of the seawall seemed so incongruous with the turmoil inside Scott's mind. His client – his ex-wife – the mother of his child – would be sentenced to life in prison.

'I've decided something else, too,' Boo said.

'What's that?'

'I don't want cable.'

They walked on in silence until they came to a fruit stand where an old Latino man was selling fresh watermelons, cantaloupes, apples, and oranges. He had a friendly face. 'I have cold melons, on ice,' the old man said. 'They are very fresh, just up from the valley.'

Texas' Rio Grande Valley produced the state's vegetables and melons. Scott pointed at a big watermelon.

'Three big slices.'

The old man leaned down behind his makeshift counter and lifted a huge green watermelon. He placed it on the white wax paper that covered the counter. He turned then came back with a large knife. He gripped the knife with the blade pointing downward, raised it about two feet above the belly of the melon, then stabbed the defenseless watermelon in its gut all the way to the hilt of the knife. He then dragged the knife down lengthwise, slicing the melon. He then removed the knife, flipped the melon around, and repeated the procedure down the other side. The melon fell open into equal halves, exposing the red pulp . . . just like the watermelon they had seen in the refrigerator at Rebecca's house on their tour of the crime scene.

Chapter 52

The judge had decided to finish the trial that Saturday – the cable network would be in Chicago on Monday, and she wanted a verdict live on national TV, much like the networks want a winner on Sundays at golf tournaments. So at nine the next morning, the sixth day of trial, Scott stood and said, 'State your name, please.'

'Raul Rodriguez.'

The Assistant DA stood. 'Objection. This witness was not on the list.'

But before the judge could rule, the DA said, 'State withdraws our objection.'

Scott turned back to the witness. 'Mr Rodriguez, have you ever met me?'

'No, I have not. But I did see you, yesterday.'

'Where?'

'At my produce stand on the seawall.'

'And what did I do?'

'You bought three slices of watermelon.'

'Well, Mr Rodriguez, my name is Scott Fenney and I'd like to buy another slice of watermelon.'

Mr Rodriguez smiled. 'I will be at my stand when I leave here.'

'I need it now.'

'But I do not have a watermelon.'

'I do.'

The doors opened, and Carlos pushed in a rolling cart on which was riding a large green watermelon. He placed the cart in front of the witness stand.

'Mr Rodriguez, would you please step down and cut a slice out of this watermelon for me?'

'I would need a knife.'

'I've got one right here for you.'

Which knife just happened to be identical to the murder weapon, a fact not lost on the jury. Mr Rodriguez stepped down from the stand and over to the cart. He took the knife, held it with the blade pointing down, and then stabbed the watermelon. He sliced it in half, then cut a slice out and handed it to Scott.

'Thank you, Mr Rodriguez.'

The DA had no questions for the witness. Scott recalled Rebecca to the stand and played the video Bobby had made of the kitchen and the refrigerator on their visit to the crime scene. He stopped the video with the image frozen on the watermelon.

'Ms Fenney, this watermelon was in your refrigerator at your house on the day that Trey Rawlins was killed, is that correct?'

'Yes.'

'When did you buy that watermelon?'

'I didn't. Trey did. It was there when I returned from Houston.'

'Did you cut this watermelon?'

'Yes, I did.'

'When did you cut it?'

'After we came back from Gaido's.'

'And how did you cut it?'

'The same way that Mr Rodriguez did.'

'Why?'

'Because that's how you cut a big watermelon. Every Texan knows that.'

The jurors did; they were nodding. Bobby nudged Scott and

gestured at his laptop. Karen had emailed a 'Yes!' Scott stepped over and picked up the murder weapon.

'You used this knife that same night to cut the watermelon that was in your refrigerator?'

'Yes, I did.'

'You stabbed that watermelon with this knife?'

'Yes.'

'Which would explain why your fingerprints are aligned in a stabbing grip rather than a cutting grip?'

'Yes.'

'Ms Fenney, you're on trial for murder because you stabbed a watermelon?'

'Apparently.'

'And what did you do with this knife after you cut the watermelon?'

'I put it in the sink.'

'Where the killer could have found it?'

'Yes.'

'No further questions.'

The Assistant DA stood. 'Ms Fenney, you used the murder weapon to cut a watermelon that night?'

'Yes.'

'But you still could have used the same knife to kill Trey Rawlins?'

'I didn't.'

'Why did you not recall before now that you had cut that watermelon with the murder weapon that night?'

'Because I was drunk and stoned on cocaine. I really don't remember much from that night.'

The defense rested, and the judge called a thirty-minute recess. Bobby leaned over and said, 'We win.'

'Not until the jury says we win.'

'Come on, Scotty, there's no way they come back from that.'

They came back.

★   ★   ★

420

When court reconvened after the recess, the Assistant DA walked over to the defense table with a stack of papers in his hands and a smile on his face.

'You just sent your wife to prison.'

'What are these?'

'The Facebook subpoena response. Messages between Trey and Billie Jean – and a motive for your wife to murder Trey. Thanks, Scott. We would've never thought to subpoena Billie Jean's Facebook account.'

The DA seemed almost regretful. He let his assistant recall Billie Jean Puckett to the stand on rebuttal. She authenticated her Facebook account.

'And did you communicate with Trey through your Facebook page?'

'Unh-huh.'

'Why?'

'He knew Rebecca read his emails.'

'He wanted to keep his plans with you secret from Rebecca?'

'He was waiting for the right time to tell her.'

'Miss Puckett, would you please read Trey's message dated Wednesday, June third of this year – the day before he was murdered.'

'Okay.' She read: '"Hi, baby. God, I miss you. Drive down tomorrow. I'll get rid of Rebecca, give her some money, send her shopping in Houston. Call me when you get in, I'll be at the golf course practicing. We'll meet at the house. I can't wait to touch you, be with you all the time. I'm going to tell Rebecca tomorrow night that it's over. I promise".'

'Trey Rawlins wrote that message to you?'

'Yes.'

'Based upon that message, do you think he really asked Rebecca Fenney to marry him the very next night?'

'No. He was going to marry me.'

'Thank you, Miss Puckett.'

Bobby tapped Scott's arm and pointed at a text from Karen on the laptop: *Shit! Scott, make her look like a love-struck teenager*

– *because she was!* Scott stood to cross-examine Billie Jean Puckett.

'Miss Puckett, had Trey been promising you that he'd break up with Rebecca?'

She nodded. 'For a few weeks, since we first got together.'

'You had only been with Trey for a few weeks?'

'Yes.'

'And he said he loved you?'

'Yes.'

'And promised to leave Rebecca for you?'

'Yes.'

'But he hadn't?'

'Not yet.'

'But he was going to?'

'Yes, he was.'

'You're sure?'

'He wouldn't lie to me.'

'I see you also posted nude photos of yourself. Why?'

'Trey asked me to. I'd do anything for him. I loved him.'

'Billie Jean, Trey was a liar, a drug addict, and gambler. He threw golf tournaments. He owed money to his drug dealer and to the mob. He lied to Rebecca. Why wouldn't he lie to you?'

'Because he loved me.'

'If he loved you, would he have had sex with Rebecca on the beach that same night, after he had sex with you three times that same afternoon?'

'No.'

'He did.'

'No!'

'Billie Jean, he used you.'

'He loved me.'

'I'm sure he did.'

They had explained Rebecca's prints on the murder weapon. But just as the Assistant DA had explained, the fact that she had used the knife to cut a watermelon that night didn't preclude her also using the same knife to kill Trey. It came down to her credibility. Trey's message and Billie Jean's testimony had hurt Rebecca's case. But Rebecca's own testimony had hurt her case even more: 'I traded sex.'

The jurors wouldn't forget that.

When in doubt, juries convict. Every lawyer knows that, and most defendants learn that. Scott knew it for sure when he looked at the jurors, and they averted their eyes. As if from a train wreck.

When Scott turned back, he saw Melvyn Burke sitting next to Terri Rawlins in the front row behind the prosecution table. Melvyn had attended every day of the trial. He had once been where Scott now was, wondering if a jury would acquit or convict an innocent person. He too had been looking in the jurors' eyes, and now his eyes turned to Scott. He had seen what Scott had seen, and he too knew the jury would vote to convict Rebecca Fenney. They regarded each other for a long moment. Then Melvyn took a noticeable breath and stood. Terri grabbed his arm and cried, 'No! She killed him!'

The commotion caught the judge's attention.

'Mr Burke, is there a problem?'

He pulled away from Terri and walked forward.

'Your Honor, I need a minute of the court's time. Outside the jury's presence.'

'This is highly unusual, Mr Burke.'

But Melvyn Burke had practiced law on the Island longer than the judge had been alive. He commanded respect. So the judge excused the jury and motioned Melvyn forward. The prosecution and defense teams followed.

'What is it, Melvyn?'

'This.'

Melvyn reached inside his coat and removed a folded-up document. He handed it to the judge. She unfolded the document, looked at it, then looked up at Melvyn.

'Last Will and Testament of Trey Rawlins?'

'Yes, Your Honor,' Melvyn said.

The judge glanced at the cameras then stood. 'In my chambers.'

They followed the judge through the door to her chambers. She was flipping through the pages of the will.

'It's not signed.'

'No, ma'am. Trey came into the office a month before he died. He instructed me to draft a will according to these terms. He said he'd sign it when he returned to town from the tour. He had an appointment the Monday after he was killed.'

The judge knew the section to turn to, and she did.

' "I, Trey Rawlins, devise and bequeath my entire estate to my wife, Rebecca Rawlins".'

She blew out a breath and handed the will to the DA. The district attorney stared at the document a long moment.

'Shit.'

'To say the least,' the judge said.

'Rebecca didn't lie,' Scott said. 'Trey did propose.'

The DA said nothing, so the Assistant DA jumped in. 'Judge, this is an unexecuted, unauthenticated—'

The judge addressed the DA. 'Rex, Melvyn just authenticated it and will with his testimony. You've contested Rebecca's testimony that Trey proposed to her and put on rebuttal testimony that he told Miss Puppy Love there that he was going to marry her instead. This rebuts your testimony. It's got to come in.'

'Your Honor—'

'Rex,' Scott said, 'you said you never wanted to send an innocent person to prison.'

'But—'

'It's not worth it, Rex,' Melvyn said. 'You won't enjoy retirement.'

'But, Your Honor—' the Assistant DA said.

'Jesus Christ, Rex,' the judge said, 'she's on trial for murder because she stabbed a fucking watermelon!'

Galveston County Criminal District Attorney Rex Truitt surrendered.

'Your Honor,' Melvyn said, 'there's something else.'

'Good God, Melvyn, what now?'

'Trey told me about his drug and gambling debts. Said he

had gotten involved with bad people. Said he was afraid. Said he bought guns. I told him to go to the police, but he said they couldn't protect him from those people. And if word got out, they'd kick him off the tour.'

'A loaded gun was found under his pillow,' Scott said.

'If he was so afraid,' the Assistant DA said, 'why the hell did he sleep with the French doors open?'

The judge turned to Melvyn. 'Why didn't you say something before now?'

'Attorney-client privilege, Your Honor.'

'Your client's dead.'

'The privilege doesn't die with the client, Your Honor. The personal representative may claim the privilege. She did. Miss Rawlins demanded that I keep the will secret.'

'So why are you violating her instructions now?'

'So an innocent person doesn't go to prison.'

Chapter 53

An innocent person did not go to prison. Trey Rawlins' unsigned Last Will and Testament was read into the record by his lawyer, Melvyn Burke, who testified that Trey had expressed his intent to marry Rebecca Fenney less than thirty days before his death. Twenty minutes after Scott and the DA had made their closing arguments and the judge had instructed the jury on the law of murder, the twelve jurors voted unanimously to acquit Rebecca Fenney of the murder of Trey Rawlins.

The next morning, the cars were packed for the trip back to Dallas. They all stood outside the beach house; the girls were getting in one last run through the surf.

'Thank you, Scott,' Rebecca said.

'Take care of yourself.' He pulled out $1,000 cash and held it out to her. 'I maxed out my last credit card.'

'No, Scott, I can't take that. You need it.'

'I have options.'

'I have jewelry.' She nodded past Scott. 'And you have company.'

The DA pulled up in his pickup wearing a fishing cap and smoking a cigar. He cut the engine and got out. Scott walked over; they shook hands and leaned against the truck.

'The old man and the sea,' Scott said.

'Yep. Me and Hank, we're heading over to Bolivar, surf fish with Gus. Drink whiskey, smoke cigars, eat red meat. Man stuff. You heading home?'

'Yep. Father stuff.'

'Good stuff.' The DA nodded toward the beach. 'Those your little gals?'

'Boo and Pajamae.'

'Cute kids.' He puffed on his cigar then gestured at Rebecca. 'She going back with you?'

'No.'

He nodded. 'Scott, when you get back to Dallas, call that fourth-grade teacher.'

'I think I will.'

'I enjoyed working the trial with you, Scott. Honest defense lawyer, nice change of pace.'

'Thanks, Rex. I've enjoyed knowing an honest prosecutor.'

The DA smiled. 'Two honest lawyers on the same case, what are the odds? I should've bought a lottery ticket.' He sucked on the cigar then exhaled a ring of smoke. 'Just so you know, I think the cartel killed Trey.'

'Why?'

'Benito Estrada was found dead this morning, in his bed, a knife in his chest. That's the sort of thing the Zetas would do. Send a message.'

'Damn.'

'The day he hired on with the cartel, he signed his own death warrant.'

They stared out to sea for a moment.

'Good thing you came down and defended her. Your wife. I came damn close to sending an innocent person to prison.' He puffed on his cigar. 'Scott, I really thought she did it. I wouldn't have prosecuted her if I didn't.'

'I know. You're a good man, Rex.'

'And you'll be a good judge. George – Senator Armstrong – called me this morning. Said Shelby withdrew her name for that federal judgeship.'

Scott nodded. He figured she would.

'I think I know why,' the DA said. 'Anyway, George said you're it. Said he'd be calling you. Congratulations.'

The DA stood straight and stuck a hand out to Scott. They shook again.

'I think justice was done, Scott.' He checked his watch. 'Speaking of which, I gotta go get Ted out of jail.'

'Your Assistant DA's in jail?'

'Yep.'

'What'd he do?'

'Nothing.'

'Why's he in jail?'

'I had him arrested last night.'

'Why?'

'Well, I saw this movie a long time ago, about a doctor who's a real jerk, doesn't treat his patients like human beings, until he becomes a patient himself, experiences the other side of the doctor-patient relationship. I figured it might help Ted to experience law enforcement from the other side – getting pulled over and hand-cuffed on the side of the road, hauled down to jail, strip searched, hosed down, sprayed for lice, spend a night in the drunk tank with a bunch of stinkin' bums puking their guts out . . . Might give him a little perspective – not everyone who gets arrested is guilty.' He chuckled. 'And it'll teach him not to leak evidence to the press.'

'Ted was the leak?'

'Yep. Pillow talk.'

'Ted and Renée?'

'Makes you kinda nauseous, don't it? That lucky little bastard.'

Scott laughed.

'That's how she knew Rebecca was out here, taped you two on the beach. Sorry.'

The DA got back into his truck and blew smoke out the open window.

'Oh, almost forgot. Hank checked out the cops and everyone else who worked the crime scene. They didn't take the three million – the mob money.'

'He's sure?'

The DA nodded. 'He threatened them with Gus – a poly-graph. Which got Wilson – the detective – to fess up to taking a couple of Trey's DVDs. Lacy Parker movies. I don't figure he'll be writing a book now.'

Scott waved at the endless sand. 'Maybe Trey buried that money out there somewhere.'

'Maybe. Maybe some old-timer with a metal detector will find it one day. Buried treasure. Not Lafitte's, but three million, that'd spend pretty good.'

He nodded at Scott then drove off. Before the black pickup was out of sight, Scott's cell phone rang. It was Senator Armstrong.

'Scott, you still want that judgeship?'

The politics and fingerprints had aligned for A. Scott Fenney, but did he want a federal judgeship that way? And to be appointed by a politician like Senator George Armstrong? The choice was clear: Judge Fenney or Ford Fenney. He made his choice for his girls . . . for the dissed of Dallas . . . for Sam Buford . . . and for himself.

'Yes, sir, I do.' Politics was putting him on the federal bench, but Judge A. Scott Fenney would be about serving justice – one person at a time.

'Good. Because you're it. Shelby dropped out. When you get back to Dallas, call the FBI office to get fingerprinted and your criminal background check done. They'll coordinate with my office. Your confirmation hearing will be in a few months in Washington, but it's just a formality for district judges. What I say goes. Welcome to the bench, Judge A. Scott Fenney.'

'Thank you, Senator.'

'Thank you, Scott. For my daughter.'

'Senator, may I ask you something?'

'Shoot.'

'Do federal judges get the same health care coverage as senators?'

'The best. A perk of political office.'

'Is there dental coverage?'

'Absolutely. And don't worry, only thing Democrats and Republicans agreed on when we did the national health care bill was to exempt ourselves. We're not gonna ration our own care.'

'Just the taxpayers'.'

'Exactly.'

Scott ended the call and thought, braces for Pajamae.

The girls were still on the beach. Rebecca stood alone, watching them. Scott walked over.

'Was he here about me?' Rebecca asked.

'The DA? No. You don't have to worry, Rebecca. The jury acquitted you – you're free. Like I said, the government can't try you twice for the same crime. But still, you might want to move, start over fresh somewhere else.'

She nodded. 'Maybe I will.'

Scott called the girls over then said to Rebecca, 'I'm going to be a judge.'

'Oh, Scott, that's wonderful.' She hugged him. 'You'll be a great judge.'

Scott took her hand and squeezed it around the cash. 'Take it. You can stay here till the end of the month, it's paid up. Good luck, Rebecca.'

'This time,' Rebecca said, 'you're leaving me.'

Scott nodded.

'You're finally over me. Now I wish you weren't.'

Tears came into her green eyes. Scott brushed her red hair off her face and kissed her on the forehead. He then wrapped his arms around this woman he had loved and wanted the last thirteen years of his life. He held her for the last time.

Boo Fenney walked over to her mother – the mother who had run off with a golf pro, used cocaine, traded sex for drugs, and been tried for murder – all before Boo's twelfth birthday. Her mother was guilty of a lot of things, but at least she was innocent of murdering her boyfriend. So she wasn't going to that prison.

But she wasn't going home with them either. How could she? Everyone in Highland Park would know everything her mother had done. How embarrassing would that be? How could Mother go on their field trips now? How many girls would tease her now? How many boys would Boo have to beat up? How many times would she have to tell the principal to 'Call my lawyer?'

It just wouldn't work.

They had a good family now, the three of them – an odd family in Highland Park, but a good family for them. They had a simple life, and Mother was a complicated woman. A mother Boo would never understand.

So while Boo would always love her mother, she did not want Rebecca Fenney to be her mother. Most kids don't get to choose their parents; they were stuck with what they got. But Boo had a choice, and she had made it. It wasn't an easy decision to say goodbye, but she knew it was best for both of them. For all of them.

She hugged her one last time and said, 'I love you, Mother.'

'I'll always love you, Boo.'

'I know.'

Boo got into the back seat of the Jetta with Pajamae and Maria. When they returned to Dallas, she would get A. Scott to ask Ms Dawson out. She and Pajamae were at that age, when girls needed a mother.

Scott Fenney had not failed Rebecca Fenney as a lawyer – or as a man.

'Goodbye, Rebecca. And good luck.'

'I'm a survivor. Don't worry about me. Just take care of Boo.'

'Always.'

Louis and Carlos drove off in the black Dodge Charger, followed by Bobby and Karen and the baby in the Prius. Scott got into the Jetta, started the engine, and drove slowly down the street, staring at Rebecca in the rearview. Boo waved at her through tears and the back window. Rebecca waved back. She was leaning against the red Corvette. The morning sun caught her red hair and she glowed. Scott wanted to remember her just that way. He knew he would never again see his wife.

Ex-wife.

431

Epilogue

The red Corvette convertible exited Interstate 10 and drove into Loretta, Louisiana, population one hundred sixty-one, give or take. This was bayou country, the backwater where people lived their entire lives without ever leaving Beauregard Parish. Where the residents were happy to be isolated from the outside world. Where modern conveniences were unknown. Where there's no cable TV because the few dozen mobile homes and half dozen single-family homes don't constitute a sizeable enough market for the cable companies to incur the expense of laying lines the one-hundred-twenty-seven miles from Lake Charles, the nearest big city. Where the information superhighway bypassed these people like the railroads bypassed two-bit cowtowns back in the 1800s.

In Loretta, Louisiana, the 'Net' is something you catch crawfish in.

The beautiful woman driving the red sports car wore dark sunglasses, a black funeral dress, black heels, black gloves, a black wig and a black scarf tied beneath her chin. The low-slung car kicked up a cloud of dust as she drove down Main Street past old black men sitting in folding chairs out front of shuttered store-fronts and spitting tobacco juice into Coca-Cola bottles; they perked up at the sight of a glamorous woman in their quiet town. She parked in front of the Loretta State Bank & Trust, the only banking institution in town. It was a family-owned bank that remained open only to provide jobs for the family, a small-town bank where a safe deposit box could be secured for a nominal fee with few questions asked. She got out with a large black satchel and walked inside through the front door past an old black security guard who tipped his hat to her.

'Afternoon, ma'am.'

She did not remove her sunglasses. She went directly to the vault entrance manned by another old black security guard and signed in. The guard craned his neck to read her entry through his bifocals then pushed himself out of his chair with great effort and said, 'This way, Miz Rawlins.' He led her into the vault.

'Box 8,' he said. 'One of the big ones.'

The guard found the box and inserted his master key and turned it. She inserted her box key and turned it. The lock released. The guard removed the oversized box and strained to heft it.

'Must've got gold bricks in here.'

He led her to a private room inside the secure confines of the vault. He placed the box on the table with a heavy thud then left her alone, shutting the door behind him. She removed her sunglasses and lifted the top of the box open. The inside was filled not with gold bricks but with neat stacks of $100 bills. Three million dollars. She was thirty-five years old, and she would never again be dependent on a man.

Two days later, Rebecca Fenney stood wearing sunglasses and a black bikini on the flybridge of her fifty-six-foot Riva Sport Yacht, one hand on the wheel, the other on the throttle opened wide, her red hair whipping in the wind, as the sleek craft cut through the waters of the Gulf of Mexico heading south to Cancún.

She loved this boat.

She glanced down at the photo attached to the dash, of her and Trey in happier times, in Hawaii earlier that year when she

433

was still the love of his life. In every woman's life, there's always another woman. First a prostitute in Dallas and now a teenager in Galveston. She sighed.

'You put me in your will then two weeks later you fall in love with Billie Jean Puckett?' She shook her head. 'My dearest Trey . . . did you really think I was going to let you leave me for a teenager?'

'Innocence is the absence of guilt,' the judge had instructed the jury. And the jury had found her innocent. Absent of guilt. And she was – entirely absent of guilt. She felt no guilt at all. Because a woman's life is not lived in a man's world of truth or lie, right or wrong, black or white; a woman's life is lived in shades of gray. Rebecca Fenney had simply done what she had to do to survive in a man's world, what any woman would have done. Sometimes a woman must take matters into her own hands.

Or a knife.